DESTINATION HOLY CROSS

BOOK 3

CRAIG DOMME

COPYRIGHT

DESTINATION HOLY CROSS © Craig Domme 2023

Editing: Ella Medler.

Book cover design and formatting: Paradox Book Covers & Formatting.

DEDICATION

To all my children and grandchildren.
To all the doctors and nurses who have taken care of me in the
last four years and the hundreds of people who support them at
San Juan Regional Hospital in Farmington and Presbyterian
Hospital in Albuquerque. Three doctors in particular: Dr. Burns
noted that severe back pain and swollen wrists were not part of a
Covid diagnosis, and it had to be something else. Dr. Bernard put
the stents in my heart with five minutes to spare, and Dr. Johnson
saved my right hand from sepsis. I am so grateful.

CONTENTS

INTRODUCTION

"Dizzy. DIZZY. TALK TO ME! I know you're there; answer me!" The captain was moderately frustrated with his companion. Dizzy was a magnificent being who existed in what he defined as his "three sense self," up and to the right of his host, the captain. Mr. Three Sense Self was invisible (simply because he hadn't packed the right suit), and it was a safe bet you've never met the likes of Dizzy. His real name is... never mind, you wouldn't believe me if I told you. Okay, I'll tell you but don't repeat it or tell anyone. Ready? Dzzitulatizebistauuugj FfffeekTTTraa Zzucobinnnlll.

See? I told you so!

Why do they call you Dizzy?

Are you God? No!

Throughout time and all the way back in time to just past the Adam and Eve point, it had always been the first question from the humanoids whenever they met the likes of Dizzy. Communication was complicated anytime the invisible routine was in effect, but in time the voice of Dizzy would prove to be very human. Dizzy's Universe had been watching from a distance, so to speak, seeing all the rescue goings-on in a desolate spot here on our Earth, namely the empty San Juan River Gorge in northern New Mexico where eventually the future Navajo Reservoir would exist.

There's a large historical marker about ten or twelve miles from Aztec that pinpoints where this happened, and why would anyone go through all the trouble of putting up a marker if it wasn't true? You talk about being out in the middle of nowhere; this historical marker is out a little further than that. In 1948, as the story goes, one year after the Roswell UFO crash and coverup, a tubular spacecraft, a flying submarine, crashed in Hart Canyon, and there were some terrified witnesses.

As the first of the first responders drew near that crash site, a sizeable disk-shaped vehicle slowly emerged from inside the vessel, hovered for fifteen seconds, and then burst away, flying over the eastern horizon on that same trajectory and disappearing. Unfortunately, it, too, crashed—with no witnesses this time—in a very remote corner of the San Juan River Gorge. From the moon, for example, one could see that crash site on Earth clear as a bell once Lieutenant Spaqu's wristband started sending out the rescue signal five years after their vehicle disappeared. The last contact with '*0*,' the name of the crashed vehicle, was not long after the initial disaster, where everyone except for the three saintly cadets and their lieutenant died. Initially, before the mothership bounced into the ground, they were headed for Phaethon's Library, only a short distance east-northeast, and would have been there in a few seconds, but like everywhere else lately, something went wrong, and they did the bounce. Devastating consequences with no apparent remedy.

There were obligations involved concerning Phaethon's Library site. That's why they were headed there in the first place, and sad as the bounce turned out to be, there was no point in canceling the purpose. They had come a long way, and people throw that term around a lot, 'came a long way,' but in truth, the three cadets, the triplet queens, had, in fact, come a long, long distance, through holes that mankind was unaware of, and currently incapable of believing in, much less all the rest. The obligations had to do with the hearts inside the cadets, meditations on Universal Numerics, twelve and three, essential and nurturing for their tri-mingled souls, long-term old-age survival-type stuff. Goes way, way back.

To the outside Universe, it was like they had instantly disintegrated, must have slid under a rock or something, because in every conceivable scenario, all kinds of investigations, the truth was they had simply vanished and left no trace of themselves. If 0 had been destroyed, blown to shreds, crashed, exploded, or anything of the sort, the machine (if you dare call it a machine) by its very nature could and would back up a micro-moment and broadcast all the information concerning its demise, and in so doing tell the Universe what happened. 0 still existed, because that had never happened, nor had the three cadet queens died, because they too had death beacons, as did Lieutenant Spaqu, who wore a typical life ring on his wrist. It took time for the news to penetrate to the top of the news cycle, but the Universe was devastated when it did. Finally, five years later, after putting out a galactic APB that went just about everywhere, a single "blue rescue beam" suddenly started transmitting from just off the corner of the library grounds, which told the inhabitants of the moon where to look. Immediately the beam was attributed to Lt. Spaqu, which meant Spaqu's remains had shed the wristband. Universally, that usually meant Spaqu was having a rough time somewhere. It was hard to believe that no one had ever looked there;

bureaucratic bullshit, no doubt. Unbelievable. Five years and no one ever looked there!

Okay, All Points Bulletin.

From the edges of the full moon, if one had the right equipment (and just about everybody did), you could see a human's face. The captain's face and his current best friend, Rahellio, could both be seen from the moon, retrieving Spaqu's Life Band and, in essence, saving the queens. That will get a man some attention. Those guys became Blue Planet rock stars, especially the captain, and they didn't even know they were. After the rescue was completed and the men were riding away for the last time, the previous seventy-seven hours of their lives were erased from their memories. During that seventy-seven hours of a forgotten time, Vincent Van Vedic, better known as 'Captain,' attained the status of "A Number 1 Human," completing the Dodecahedron of A Number 1 Humans, which most odds makers had decided would never be completed. Humans seemed to have more problems than most top-of-the-rung-type creatures everywhere else, and the entire species had been stuck on eleven #1s for so long that the Watchers were getting anxious and concerned. The captain being the twelfth A Number 1 Human in the last thirty-five thousand years didn't say much for the species, wasn't breaking any records by any stretch, and there seemed to be a lot of what everyone at the Watchers' parties agreed was that Neanderthal brain, that sorry-ass gene, that DNA link that appeared to be hiding in the Homo Sapiens. The Watchers had pretty much gotten rid of the Neanderthal look, the knuckle-dragging and grunting walking hairy-freak-type fellow. Back in the very early days, the Watchers and other Anunnaki-type folks toyed with their creation being hairless and naked, but that got nixed when ninety-eight percent of the test dummies froze to death the minute they stepped outside the cave.

Now, after what, four hundred thousand years, they once again had to mess with the formula until they decided on the naked idea with more emphasis on the brain and the thumb this time. Someone should have thought of the thumb thing a long time ago for the hairy one, and most of the design crew acknowledged it would have done better. Too late. Too bad, so sad.

It wasn't but maybe fifteen thousand years into the experiment when everything got out of sync, and just about everything froze solid. The climate engineers melted everything everywhere way too fast and drowned just about every single critter on the planet, and once again, they had to start over, and it's taken ten thousand years to get to this point. A lot of give and take.

The year is 1953, the late fall, and the universal coordinates for everyone's interest out there beyond close by are quite a bit longer than the eight digits the captain might have figured as his coordinates, along with longitude and latitude. The Milky Way alone is sometimes hard to find if you don't know exactly what you're looking for. Throughout the cosmos, everyone asked that same serious question during all this: "Why in the name of XXXLLLGGJJJXXX (the universally accepted name for God) were the queens there on this little blue Earth in the first place?" Truth be known, they were obligated by a directive from the *Gold Book* that demanded they stop at Phaethon's Library no matter what else was going on, and in a one in a trillion Zutacats, they crashed—more like bounced—and then slid under a rock ledge in the corner of the shrine.

The captain could still use some of his boating skills on land when it came to figuring out exactly where he was in the whole scheme of things, and from a special overlook not too far from his house, Captain Vincent Van Vedic discovered the "blue light," every night at sundown. Before the first viewing of the blue light, everything had been going to plan perfectly, one thing after another, starting as a daydream in one of the hell holes he found himself in back before, during, or after the Russian Revolution. He wasn't sure when it began, but he started building his dream horse ranch when he first fell in love with horses, which he did by age six. Now at the age of either sixty-five or fifty-five (there seemed to be a viable question as to which), and with just one horse on his horse ranch, only one thing seemed to matter. He grew obsessed with finding the source of the blue light, knowing the whole time he was being pushed that way, pulled from there as if he had been hog-nosed.

There exists a gentleman of considerable stature named Vincent Van Vedic, nicknamed 'Captain,' code-named 'The Gunslinger,' and proclaimed one of the twelve most significant human beings in the last thirty-five thousand years. Just recently, his name became synonymous with all of the other most famous characters in the known Universe, all because of his heroics. I know it sounds like a heavy load, but it is believable if you care to let yourself go. He culminated the Dodecahedron of Influential Homo Sapiens with his actions that weekend, an event that was televised universally and resulted in the Captain being acclaimed from one corner of said Universe to all the other corners, and most glorious of all is that he doesn't even know it. Dizzy and company erased seventy-seven hours of his memory because they had to, but he promised them, before they did that, that he would forever keep the secret, unlike Ezekiel. He knew why they were forced to abide by ancient rules, had it all explained at the time, and the logic was undeniable. Both he and Rahellio could not be allowed to remember their heroism, pure and simple; hard to swallow the reality of it all, the unknowing of it all, and the finality of the loss of those memories would haunt the rescuers unmercifully. Unbeknownst to the Captain or Rahellio, their names and heroics were plastered all over a memorial on one of the planets circling the middle star in the Belt of Orion.

The author of this book, *DESTINATION HOLY CROSS*, the third in the trilogy, is currently the oldest living male on the Aloysius John Domme branch of a vast healthy tree, 74 and counting, and there is no luckier historical fiction writer than me. Once again, no doubt in my mind, and I'll confess right here and now that for me to be struggling with this introduction is quite possibly a miracle, and I don't say that lightly. I will list my most recent miracles in a few paragraphs.

I started off the second book of this trilogy, *THE BELL ON THE BOW*, with a question at the top of page one. "What is a miracle? How do we explain those events that happen to us all the time, where all logic and reason seem to have been overruled and something is going on in front of our faces that we can only attribute to the actions of God? Every language on Earth has the word in its dictionary." That second book made it to publication in 2017, about a year after the first book, and primarily because I'm a procrastinator just like everyone else, I forced myself upon you with the need for a third book. Here's why it's so ironic that I'm writing the introduction to the third book that I ended two months ago.

This old man lives alone, I'm a widower, and for the most part, I'm doing okay. I enjoy writing and telling fantasies and historical fiction stories, and I've enjoyed the challenge of entertaining folks with my writings. Like all other authors, writers, and storytellers, I'm very humble and grateful to my editor Ella Medler, who makes this guy look good, and for the audience I may have. Everything considered, I've turned into a very loving old guy, even though some might say, "He doesn't look very loving."

There is a reality that I've been forced to acknowledge that causes me to understand precisely what it is I'm asking you to do next after this introduction. The book *DESTINATION HOLY CROSS* follows in the form of thirty-two chapters, and it's complicated to some extent, is moderately funny at times, and tips the scale at just shy of a couple hundred thousand words. In my humble opinion, the first two books set the stage for *DESTINATION HOLY CROSS*, but that's obvious.

This book will be one of eight hundred thousand published this year in the USA, falls under the category of Historical Fiction, and my very esteemed and well-educated brother gently explained as best he could that most folks don't have time for a fellow man's fantasy. He had asked me what I'd been doing lately, and that's when I mentioned I was almost finished with my third book. For quite a while that evening, and only because we had the time, this man who has a PhD in Catholic Theology explained to me—and for me—all the reasons my first two books never made it on the New York Times best-seller list. It's hard to keep plugging away, night after night, for years, paying all the expenses involved in the creation of the book and knowing the whole time it's not going to be read by hardly anyone. The best I can brag about is the truth that Ella Medler read it, edited it, and it gets an A+ for quality concerning all the most basic English Language requirements. I wish a reader I once knew could promise me that she'd read it this week, might even mark her copy with a few yellow stars for all sorts of reasons, close it up when she was done, and then tap on the pile of pages with a gentle drumroll of her fingers. One morning, she finished a thick paperback at the kitchen table and told me she thought I would like it. I asked her what it was about and when she looked up to tell me, she paused and said she couldn't remember.

Please bear with me, as I know very little about writing an introduction. I knew very little about writing a book too. One thing I did know was that there had to be a third book, because I knew I'd left my readership hanging. I apologize. After all this time, it's just like my wife said; I know you can't remember the whole story. It's been too long. Things happened in the last four years, miracles from my point of view that caused me to drag ass when it came to finishing the third book. But there was one thing for sure. I knew what the name of the book would be. *DESTINATION HOLY CROSS.*

MIRACLE NUMBER ONE. On the day after New Year's in 2019, in a white-out Northern New Mexico blizzard, one of the luckiest historical fiction writers from the class of '66 tried to poison his ignorant ass with a Di Giorno's frozen pizza. After turning myself inside out, I had one last call before lights out, and I doubt I would have lived till dawn, but my brother and sister-in-law live next door, and thankfully the in-laws answered the phone, found me five minutes later, and called 911. I felt like I was almost dead, soaking wet, with no shirt, all kinds of monitor stickies that were freezing when stuck to my half-dead torso, and then they wheeled me out of my front door into the blizzard. The ambulance got me to the hospital two miles away, at a snail's pace because of the storm, but they had everything they needed inside the machine to stabilize me, and all the problems aside, they saved the old boy. So they sent me home with no damage, where I continued with the creation of *DESTINATION HOLY CROSS.*

To say there was no plan is probably obvious, but I kept plugging away, and that, my friends, is the lesson. If all you do with my three books is stand them side by side on a shelf, *The Diamond Teardrop Illusion*, followed by *The Bell on the Bow*, and now *Destination Holy Cross*, I thank you for doing that. You must believe it's a miracle that I did that, that I finished the project before I died, just in case I'm dead and you're looking back. My hero, Vincent Van Vedic, never looked back, except once. The following remembrance explains that part of this story, and I want you to learn from my book without even reading it that if I could write three books, you can do similar things yourself. Whatever it is that you want to do, you can do it, and it ain't over till it's over. I knew I had to write the third book. I needed to get my hero Vincent Van Vedic where he belonged, and in so doing, I had to bend time. It's easy if you're careful. I take you to the furthest edges of the Universe, realistically, and in the entire cosmos, Vincent becomes a superstar, immortalizes himself, and completes the dodecahedron of the most sacred. Even though it's true, as part of the story, he doesn't even know it happened.

MIRACLE NUMBER TWO. In an effort to start off 2020 with a bang, I found myself on January 13th (we're back to that luckiest historical fiction writer issue once again) with a severe case of indigestion at four that afternoon. I was remodeling my old house, pretending to be a carpenter, a painter, a janitor, air conditioner repair man at the age of seventy-two, and I was positive a few Tums were all I needed. Wrong! I finished what I was doing, locked up the house, and drove rather rapidly to my new home, only four hundred yards away. I rushed in the back door and found the cabinet with the ancient bottle of Tums, which I recently checked for its expiration date—2012. My wife Susie bought them some time ago, and that, I'm sure, because she experienced indigestion all the time back then. I think they worked, and I'd ask her about it, but she's been gone for a dozen years. The first two didn't do anything for me, and by now, ten minutes into it, the pain was way past minor. So I figured my best and only hope was to go next door where my sister-in-law might be home, three hundred feet door to door. When I got there, she let me in. There were three babies downstairs sleeping, and in her typical joyful self, she found her favorite brother-in-law in a severe state of mess. Into the first minute, she could tell her guest was in deep trouble, and the luckiest historical fiction writer tells her there's a bad pain going down the insides of my arms. "Heart attack."

It was time for a few miracles there, one after another, until she brought the SUV to a screeching halt directly alongside the emergency room doors at my favorite hospital. She might have hit eighty at times along the two and a half miles, three stop lights, three stop signs, five minutes shop to shop maybe, and when we got there, she ran inside and left me strapped in, suffering a pain I can't describe. So—wisely, I thought—I decided to climb out and collapse on the sidewalk.

They rescued me off the walkway and loaded me into a wheelchair, pushing me past the fifteen people in the waiting room and into the Cardio Lab. I understand that there was a team all sitting there waiting for me. The doctor, Dr. Bernard, and a half dozen nurse specialists—and one of them actually knew who I was. The last thing I remember saying was directed at all the voices nearby. I couldn't see. I was just shy of gone, and I asked, "Can you do something about the pain?" A voice from above came back, "It's on its way." And just like that, in an instant, there was no more pain, and I lost consciousness for maybe thirty minutes. When I came to in the recovery area, a face was two feet in front of mine. He wore a mask, a blue skull cap, goggles, and gloves, and Saint Peter said to me, "Are you who I think you are?" Actually, this nurse was a friend of mine's son who recognized my name. I learned a number of things. Two stents had opened up two very seriously clogged arteries in my heart, two tiny things they put in place by going in at my right wrist, up my arm, and into my heart. The bandage was as weird a bandage as I've ever had. It had a window, and I could see it heal.

My right hand has taken a serious beating in my life, including being crushed by a large rock, been stabbed, snapped, and infected with sepsis, and during the sepsis time, I was lucky they didn't take my hand. It was close. There's a fifty-year-old half-inch-long scar on the inside of my right wrist, directly in between those two main ligaments that make your hand work. If you wanted to nail a man to a cross, you'd put your nail exactly where my scar is, and it's right alongside the similar tiny scar from where Dr. Bernard found the vein he needed. It allows me to tell a 'war story,' an example of how I often used the phrase when I was just talking about how challenging or exciting life might be. For instance, I have many 'war stories' from when I tended bar for four years, but this 'war story' is at least militarily grounded.

In the summer of 1970, the luckiest historical fiction writer from the class of '66 was trying to become a US Army Green Beret at Fort Bragg, North Carolina. If you don't mind, I'll brag a tad, because I graduated from the Green Beret School at Fort Bragg. Thank you. At that point in time, my college career had been interrupted by the "draft," but I had five college semesters to my credit, under the attack plan of getting a degree in English and journalism, and so in keeping with all that, I was keeping a journal the whole time I was in the army while attending the prestigious University of Pineland (a joke amongst the rank). My journal was kept in a waterproof plastic bag, fit like a glove in the big pockets of my field jacket or jungle fatigue pants pockets, with dimensions in the four-inch by six-inch range; it was a small six-ring binder for easy in and out of lined pages. My first MOS was O5B. I was a novice radio operator with a mountain of radio stuff to learn, and it was essential that I carried such a little black book, a thing I looked at off and on throughout my each and every day, and when everything was all said and done, the journal was six inches thick, front and back on many pages, and told a fantastic story that few other soldiers could tell.

To get the scar, I impaled myself on a dirty, filthy piece of rotten two by six that had an equally filthy and rusty old eight-inch nail waiting for my wrist just under the surface of the muddy water. I was climbing out of Lake James, probably during Phase Two, wearing a typical radio operator's backpack (i.e. very, very heavy). Once the four of us on my commo team were out of the water and up on dry land, this part of the exercise was over. We had found the camp and made it, and a real bed was definitely in our future. I pushed my hand into the mud bank one last time and came away from it as if a copperhead or a water moccasin had bitten me.

I felt like I was being electrocuted, and when I lifted that right hand up and out of the water, the board hung there. And I'm sure I made a fuss about it. The whole area was swarming with trainees and trainers, all kinds of Green Berets. I could not pull the board off my wrist, and I was taken to a medical tent that existed just for these kinds of occasions. The nail had gone in an inch or more and was nestled in between the tendons and ligaments, and there was no way I could have pulled it out alone. No way. My hand was practically paralyzed. Fortunately, I don't have a clear memory of all that happened, but the medics did whatever it was that they do in a situation like that, and me and my board parted company. I was given a tetanus shot, something for pain, and was in the process of lying back and getting over all this when the sky caved in. I began to have a reaction to tetanus. I don't know what it looked like to the staff and management, but it can be life-ending, they say, and it did happen to me again six years later—but whatever happened there in the medics' tent got me all sorts of attention. I was bandaged and drugged, and driven back to Bragg instead of having to walk. I woke up in the Training Group Commo Barracks a day or two later, and my hand didn't work. I couldn't hold a pen, couldn't write a letter, couldn't even dial the phone without being shocked to the max. Wham! I couldn't open a round doorknob, couldn't dump a forkful of food in my mouth, couldn't wipe my ass, couldn't bounce a Morse Code key, couldn't key a mic, and I was more or less halfway through what is traditionally called The Training Group. I was a radio operator, and bouncing Morse Code keys or keying microphones was what I was all about. Believe it or not, that damage slowly started to heal, but the action of a sharp army salute was sometimes akin to sticking one's middle finger in one's right eye and then squealing in the colonel's presence.

That year started off with Airborne School the whole first month of January at Fort Benning, Georgia (colder than a Billy goat's ass), and after getting the airborne wings, they bused us up to Bragg and the initial Green Beret challenge, a place called Camp McCall, right off the bat, for at least a month, and if a man survived that, we started phase one of three around April Fool's Day. The place is called The John F. Kennedy Center for Military Assistance, US Army Special Forces Training Group, and Special Warfare School. Don't hold me to that verbiage.

At this point in the game, I was unofficially a brick shithouse with a busted right paw, and this injury could very easily wash me out of the Training Group. To be honest, I do not know how I survived. We did a version of the daily dozen exercises that did us justice, many of which involved our hands, and to be even more honest, I base that opinion on the fact that I still can't throw a frisbee the way most people do. I hadn't thought of this in a long time. I should have gotten a medal, but instead, I kept it a secret and survived. There were many ways to exit the Training

Group, and injuries were often the cause. To add insult to injury, a former Green Beret trainee would likely end up in the 82nd Airborne Division. We called it the animal farm, it was just down the road, and they called us Girl Scouts. No respect.

From my hospital bed there in the Cardio Ward, January 16th, 2020, I watched a cheesy dude doctor on my TV—a spokesman for the World Health Organization, the guy with the black glasses, assured the world that the virus that was causing all the excitement was nothing to worry about. I didn't know what he was talking about so I went back to waiting to go home. A beautiful nurse came in and sat on the end of my bed. She had a thirty-three-page packet of discharge papers, a whole slew of short speeches about everything you can think of, and there at the very end, she looked me in the eyes and said, "You know, it doesn't work like this very often. You were down to your last five minutes, they said. Two stents with no complications, nothing else going on in the ER, and now you're going home after only three nights. There doesn't appear to be any damage. I want you to know how unusual that is."

Like everyone else on the planet, I was introduced to Covid. Like most old people, life changed for us, and we disappeared from each other and all the things we loved to do together. It was devastating for almost everyone, and even now, at the start of 2023, we're forgetting how desperate things were. Some of us fragile folks who have survived now question exactly what happened. *DESTINATION HOLY CROSS*, got a lot of my attention in 2020 because of my heart attack protocol and the Covid shutdown. Some chapters were written during my isolation, which might be evident; I don't know. You start seeing things, you begin imagining ridiculous stuff, and the next thing you know, it's real. Take Dizzy, for example. You're gonna like Dizzy when you finally get there.

MIRACLE NUMBER THREE. Having been a news hound for my entire life, I had to conclude that 2020 was the worst year I'd ever witnessed, and it appeared my beloved country had fallen into disrepair. *What are we going to do?* Christmas was just around the corner, the presidential election was an incredible mess, and other than a rather serious infection in my left forearm caused by a dog scratch, for the most part, I was off the heart attack protocol and not looking forward to the issues of the holidays. I think the world had decided to forget Thanksgiving, Christmas, and all the other holidays and wanted everyone to stay home and wear a mask. I, for one, didn't have any trouble with that. So did just about everyone I knew, and so on December 19th, 2020, I walked out to my wood pile, loaded two wheelbarrows full of fire logs, and brought them up to the porch. No big deal whatsoever. The next day my back hurt, and so did my right wrist; I appeared to be deadly sick and in considerable pain, so much so that my daughter took me to the ER at ten p.m. that night. Alexis's baby was two months old, and the hospital was in Covid lockdown, and after a few hours of me sitting there in a screened-off area on the edge of the ER, a rather brutal tattooed nurse took Alexis aside and told her what to do.

"Take grandpa home and nurse him as best you can. Follow the protocols on the list. It appears he may have Covid, and if that's the case, there will be quarantines, and you need to keep that in mind. The only way for him to be admitted to this hospital is if he arrives in an ambulance. You may use that wheelchair to get him to your car, park there in the handicapped spot, and please bring the wheelchair back when you're done. Take him home, and if his condition changes for the worse—his oxygen, pulse, and things you can monitor—if they go south, you call 911, and they will come and get him. It's the only way. As of a while back, the hospital has an absolutely no-visitors policy in strict effect, causing heartache on a level we've never experienced. Our staff has been hit very hard, to say nothing of the fact it's Christmas. Goodnight, good luck, and please don't bring him back here."

On my forty-second wedding anniversary, the 22nd, I had evolved into a mess of a 200-pound grandpa, the luckiest historical fiction writer from the class of '66. I was positive that I had pulled every single muscle in my back. Close to the spine, close to the shoulders, down by my kidneys, and everywhere else that might be considered a spot on my back. Not only that, it appeared to me that a brown recluse spider had bitten me at least once, maybe more, on the top of my right wrist. Where else? Just add it to the wrist list. Things to consider would include the notion that it was almost the dead of winter and spiders don't do all that well in winter, and besides all that, I've never seen a recluse in my entire life. So finally, I was forced to relent and considered rattlesnakes, vampires, and rabid bats.

Nonetheless, my wrist started to swell up and hurt me as badly as my back. I didn't know which one hurt the worst, and by late morning, I was a serious mess lying on the couch when I officially went south. Earlier, Alexis had to leave to take care of her baby, and without any other options, she asked my sister-in-law—who, as you now know, lives next door—to come over and keep an eye on me from a distance until my girls come up with a plan.

Everyone was afraid of each other but they all agreed that if my oxygen got below 90, someone should call 911, and that little gizmo they put on my finger showed Katie I was down to 84. She called the ambulance for the Di Giorno's pizza fiasco, and she drove me to the hospital while I had a heart attack. On her sister's forty-second wedding anniversary, she called 911 once again, and no one had any idea what was wrong with me. She told me to get ready, the ambulance was coming, and I think I said, "Good idea."

Sometimes in life, we get nothing but fastballs and curves. Some things are obvious, others are invisible, some make sense, and sometimes you simply lose consciousness and hopefully wake up someday. *DESTINATION HOLY CROSS* isn't even finished, but the luckiest historical fiction writer from the class of '66 is looking out the back doors of his ambulance, sees his neighbor and a friend standing on the sidewalk, gives a wave, and goes to sleep. I was basically going into what is commonly referred to as 'septic shock.' The infection in my arm had decided to kill me.

I don't know how one gets to be as old as I was and not know what sepsis is, but I managed, and I have a severe case of amnesia starting with that first ambulance ride until January 10th or so. When I was eyes-open conscious, I must have made it perfectly clear that the back and the hand were in big trouble, but I don't remember much. I was in and out of consciousness all through Christmas, and on that following Monday when I regained consciousness, my right hand was covered in a huge bandage. They had opened it up from the backside, scraped it clean, examined what was happening, and discovered the sepsis was everywhere. All I know is Doctor Johnson opened my wrist during the holiday season. He had absolutely no idea who I was. He knew nothing about me and how I used that hand in my life. Sepsis is such a monster that many folks don't survive the encounter; if they do, sometimes some of their vital parts and appendages don't continue to exist. At the time, my hand had died and didn't work doing anything. No writing, no twisting, no forking or spooning, brushing, or thumbing. The hand looked okay, but it didn't work, and then as the months passed by, slowly, the old body came back to life from having been to the brink and back once again.

Three times in three years, I found myself knocking on the door to my eternity, times when I knocked really hard, and I'm not kidding, but the gatekeeper wouldn't open the door. I didn't mind, but it was a very difficult walk during those times. Long nights and long days, isolated, no visitors, and not only that, after spending three nights in the Covid ward, room 409, they figured things out and moved me down to the second floor. I never got Covid. It was sepsis, a total curve ball to an industry that was learning how to fight a pandemic. Perhaps I had a few things to finish. My precious nine grandbabies all saw me in their first month of life, and my children call me all the time. There's only so much you can ask from life—another day, another week, another chance—and I'm here to champion the notion that if a person like me can do something like writing this book, a person like you can do something just as grand. Even grander, a grand slam in whatever game you like to play. Just go do it. It's never too late.

I went back to work on the story once my hand healed, and four or five months later, I made an appointment and insisted on being seen by the good Doctor Johnson. As for the reason for the visit, to show him the scar and thank him for not having amputated my hand. I sat in an examination room for who knows how long, and finally, the doctor came in with my HIP chart. He started off by saying he wasn't the surgeon who replaced my hip, with that being the most recent encounter I had with the place. I told him I wasn't there for that, and all I wanted to do was show him the scar and thank him. He very lightly examined the wrist up close, handed my hand back, and said, "So there's nothing wrong with your wrist? You made this appointment a week ago, waited to see me, and it seems your sole purpose is to show me my own work. I always do work like this. I do it like this every day. Bring me an autographed copy of your book, and I'll put it on my bookshelf. I doubt I'll ever read it, because I just don't have time. It's hard enough keeping up with the literature of my profession. Thank you for the beautiful acclaims and make good use of the hand for the rest of your life."

It took another year of dedication, one chapter after another, until Vincent couldn't go on any further. I wanted him to wake up and take another step, but he just couldn't do it. If you only do a chapter or two a week, I'm the lucky one, and being the realist that I am, I congratulate you for getting this far. I love you for that, man, or woman. Please have fun with my story.

CHAPTER ONE

THE MORNING AFTER

I n the predawn, Vincent woke staring into the underside of the massive cottonwood tree from his couch there, on the mid-deck. *Vanessa* and her trailer had miraculously stopped on a sandbar, with her starboard wheels only fifteen feet from the side of the fifty-year-old widowmaker, and only a few feet below the lowest of a hundred branches, some as big around as the wheel in the helm. The summer sun hadn't shown on the ground under this female tree in forever, the cotton seedlings still piled deep from when she'd bloomed two months before.

He had slept well, considering he had felt his heart beating like a machine gun at different times yesterday afternoon. He'd felt that feeling before, many times in his life, and lived through them all. Pleasant dreams, as usual, and he opened his eyes, gazing high up into the furthest branches those turkeys from yesterday apparently called home. They, too, were starting their day with that dog, Van Vedic, and the *Vanessa* blocking their usual way down, which was the same way they lumbered up into the tree in the first place, having roosted only moments before the *Vanessa* arrived. Things like this situation confused them to no end, and they began to discuss in turkey talk, forty birds or more—very loudly, the seaman might note—considering precisely what they should all do as a group. Keeping in mind that they were turkeys, after all, and touchy beyond belief.

Their plan would involve something they rarely participated in so early in the morning, which was launching themselves in groups from some of the highest branches in the tree, gliding up the ravine in the most glorious bird flight you could watch. Then, sporadically landing throughout the forest. Usually, they would work their way down, branch to branch, inside the tree until they would feel better, and then fly out. Within a few minutes, every bird was gone from the top of the tree except one beautiful male gobbler, who stayed up there all morning and watched Van Vedic till he and the dog walked away upriver at high noon. All his ladies and brothers returned at sundown that day and roosted where they always had, seemingly unafraid of the new attraction at the base of their favorite tree of all trees. That man and his dog were now watching them roost from far up above.

It was way past time to officially name the dog—not so much for the dog, as he seemed to answer to almost anything that sounded like food, but more for Van Vedic, to have something to say when he looked at it or needed it to do something. It sat there, three feet tall, near the foot of his bed, staring at him as if wondering what was taking so long for his master to move. His tail was swooshing the deck, his eyes were eager, and he seemed to need to piss in the worst way while refusing to piss on the patio. The captain slid on his boots and smiled at the mongrel; he needed to piss himself and wanted to stand on the ground, wanted to walk down to the river he could hear so clearly in the sunrise, and splash his face.

"So, what shall we call you? I'll think about it." The cur became excited when it realized its master was paying it attention. Up until that time, the dog had responded to a whistle that had half a dozen different pitches and pretty much thought that was his name.

Rested like he was, the captain examined his situation. Even though the lighting was much better and improving by the minute, his understanding of the consequences of the afternoon before were all now matters of fact. His *Vanessa* had survived and was now where she would be for good, for the distant foreseeable future, or at least until the water rose that high. He had the instant realization of where he was and how irreversible that situation was, and how it could have been so much worse but, in fact, it was actually better than the original plan. The captain imagined her being lifted off the trailer by the rising waters now that she was this close to the river many months, if not years, ahead of schedule. He kept muttering "Much better. Much better," throughout the morning, and it never failed to get No-Name's attention every time.

Van Vedic hadn't made many mistakes in his life that rivaled this one, and unless he told the world about it, no one would ever know he did. He could tell Rahellio that he changed his mind and did all this on purpose when he got to the last corner. There may have been plans and hopes to launch the boat from up by the cabin versus where he would actually begin *Vanessa*'s second life, but now that things were where they were, he was soothed to his core. "Much better!"

The voyage of the *Vanessa* was over, so when he got to the stern deck, he threw his three-prong anchor over the starboard corner, pulled it in tight, and lashed it to a cleat. It was a spiritual thing, something he had never failed to do when he berthed *Vanessa*, and even though it made no difference whatsoever, he did it just the same. It was a fishing-boat-captain thing.

Earlier, he had found himself down in the engine room, found himself standing on her keel while inspecting how everything had handled the rocky descent. All of the fuel containers, all the footlockers, all the toolboxes were precisely where they belonged, still strapped in place and, in some cases, safely hiding beautiful treasures, ingots of gold, and jars of diamonds. Every bench, every corner, every step, whether inside or out, was a waterproof locker—for food, for supplies. They were not called lockers for nothing and were always at least two layers deep.

While he stood there and calculated the consequences from the day before, Vincent could feel that keel under his boots, felt it touch his bones all the way up his body to the top of his head, a swirling sensation of completion, of belonging, of things being exactly where they should be. He reached up and grabbed the ceiling timbers, became the connection between all that up above and the keel down below, felt like he was holding Jude's cane again, and remembered that feeling from when he'd last held it in Rabat over ten years ago. The sensations that reverberated through his bones, his guts, his arms, and his legs were soothing and so fulfilling that when he stood like that, he felt like he could stand for hours. Just standing on that keel and holding up the roof, he closed his eyes and began to see things in another consciousness—the other one, where he'd been for so long, where the brightest lights blinded him, froze him in place; white lights, lights that made life stand still for years, but in his case not forever. He was forcing himself to remember a time that he existed in, was alive in, but had very little memory of. Ten years, the Coast Guard had said, and they could prove it. They had amazing pictures of before, during and after.

The captain saw in that bonding consciousness the idea that he was to be necessary once again. His being would be required soon for another difficult if not impossible task, and he would be shown the way. That emotion engulfed him, all at once, and demanded that he be ready to be essential again, like when he'd taken Jude to Gibraltar. This was just the beginning. Any time he stood atop *Vanessa*'s keel, he could feel her spirit; she seemed to be alive in another dimension. While he and Jude were crossing the Black Sea, even before the *Struma* incident, even before the pirates, he'd created *Vanessa*'s imaginary past in his mind and on paper. He'd continually discovered ideas of his fanciful *Vanessa* floating in paradise and would go what he called "writer-wild" until the thoughts were written down. Nothing mattered except getting those ideas on paper immediately—just a few words with a reminder of the dream, knowing it would always come back in detail and then some. He fabricated a water wonderland in the ancient past. She may have already floated in paradise, in ancient waters from long, long ago… if that was what Jude might have meant. She had a soul, and he knew it. Everything Jude ever said, he had managed to remember, and had written it all down as if his ears and pen were talking to a pilgrim who had been sent by God. Van Vedic was the protector, the reporter, the stenographer, the librarian, and most of all, the witness to his miracles. A time that came and went.

That keel had survived it all, had brought him to this tree, to this future launch site, and just like Jude had said, *Vanessa* would in truth outlive Van Vedic. Jude had guaranteed she'd float in paradise, again, someday. He'd told Van Vedic not to worry and just be happy to have been her captain for a time. He remembered that conversation from beginning to end—talking with Jude about dreams, about the cane, about *Vanessa*'s keel, about the future, and how those two items were intertwined, both made from the same material, perhaps from another world. The evolution of their creations in antiquity, the walkways and the waterways that had led them both to Pfeiffer and then had intricately wound together when Jude met Patton and they fished to Rabat. How miraculous. When Jude talked about his cane or spoke about the *Vanessa*, Vincent Van Vedic sometimes thought his passenger was a pilgrim from heaven and traveling through time.

The captain was more than aware of what the keel was or was not, but also that it was impenetrable. Even though he'd tried and tried as hard as he'd ever tried, he'd never left a scar on its visible surface. It was harder than rock, but wasn't rock. It didn't seem to make *Vanessa* heavier than any other boat her size. Jude had convinced him to simply leave the subject alone, appreciate it for what it was, and consider it his cane.

On that last night on the *Pilldersleeve*, Jude had reminded the captain how much he loved standing or sitting on *Vanessa*'s bow, touching the cane to a spot just back from the bow point, and that when he did, her keel and his cane became one. There were a dozen spots throughout *Vanessa*'s being that had that mark, where the cane would have stood by itself while he said Mass or fished or even took a piss. One particular mark the cane had left on the keel was absolutely dead center of the boat, the spot where Jude used to place the cane when he serviced the engine. The captain knew that keel, stem to stern, like the back of his hand, every inch he could see. And he also knew that the cane had made that mark for itself and the keel must have allowed it, because that was the one and only new indentation along that spine.

Van Vedic remembered that during his remodel of the front below deck back in Pfeiffer he had tried with all his might to drill into the keel but had failed miserably. He had tried to nail steel spikes but they bent every time, and he'd given up when nothing worked like it should have. He used the only holes that were provided, and it had turned out perfect in the end.

That last night in Rabat, Jude had assured the captain that his *Vanessa* would take care of herself and him as well. It was their last night together, lounging on *Vanessa*'s deck, who was securely balanced on the bow of the *Pilldersleeve*, high above the water and waiting for dawn. They were reminiscing about their journey, all the people they'd met, all their adventures, when out of the blue, Jude had guaranteed the captain that the keel on his boat was indestructible. It couldn't be sunk and had been designed as one of two unbreakable guides on the rudder of the Ark, the most critically overloaded boat of all times. Jude had looked at the captain, who was debating the feasibility of this truth in his mind, told him not to do that and just take it as fact; his forty-foot keel was Godly special. Why would anyone make up such a story? Well, the answer was they wouldn't. The real questions were, where had it come from, and where was the other one?

Vanessa's keel had been stored in a cave, balanced atop two boulders, miles from any sea, for a long time. The curators of the museum that owned it had no idea whatsoever as to what the forty-foot-long beam was intended to be, but the original discoverers imagined all kinds of possibilities, none of which spelled keel (they could only spell pole). They discovered that they couldn't cut it, drill into it, but they could transport it, and so they did. They took it to the local museum that had a spectacular ancient cave behind it, a cave so wide and deep that it could store the obelisk.

The oldest records Ms. Sophia knew of talked about a time when the beautiful piece of something had been placed in the cave out of reverence, primarily because of its length, and it became a famous attraction. The cave was part of a museum complex that featured unique and unusual artifacts from central Russia and beyond, especially the extra-large exhibits, and was visited by humans who didn't know what it was. It went on display for anyone to see. You could touch it, measure it, and give the curator any idea you might have about what it was, who'd made it, what it was made out of and what the holes were for. Just about every time someone had the answers, and after a few months on display, the curator told a tourist he'd already heard that bit of bullshashiska before, and no, it wasn't a dinosaur bone.

The beam featured an intricate pattern of holes, both sides of the center, each hole an exact depth and distance from the others. It was a long, arching rectangle that most people imagined standing straight up and down—some kind of a pole with holes. The only reason it was lying down was because it wouldn't be right to bury either end, and most folks only wanted to touch and measure it. It became an attraction and interested people for a while, but the amusement eventually wore off, and everything has a price...

Two aspiring boatbuilders, sons of boatbuilders, accidentally stumbled across the keel in the cave, now covered in dust and not even on the inventory of the museum's most special list; it was on the list of "long dusty things in the shelter." They planned to use it as the principal ceiling rafter in their new boat building shop since no one could find any other use for it, and the price was right. There was a lot of dust on the beam that hid so much, lots of bends in the roads for such a long wagonload, but they got it to their dock shop where their inspirations took hold and they shared an epiphany on how to build the perfect riverboat from simply laying their hands on its sides. Their fathers brought all their knowledge about boat building to the shop as well, and their ship became a family project that lasted for years, until all those men floated away in life. She was christened "the green-eyed queen of their sea," later re-named *Vanessa,* and was now hidden in a cottonwood forest on the other side of the world.

This new location would be no problem, the captain concluded after having thought about it for almost all night. Now, he would get *Vanessa* back on the water even sooner than he had previously planned. He should have known better than to think this wasn't the way it was supposed to be as he watched her disappear; this was what the Grand Omnipotent Designer had in mind. Vincent had logically planned to do everything concerning the *Vanessa* there on the plateau above, but the Designer evidently had other plans. Instead, *Vanessa* would wait on her useless trailer in the shade of an eighty-foot-tall, ancient cottonwood tree until the vast reservoir finally rose to float her again. She would be out on the water a year or two ahead of schedule.

There was a treasure on board that needed a new home, and dealing with that hiding place, with that future site, had Vincent's mind wandering and his eyes searching. He now owned two and a half thousand acres of some of the best hiding places on Earth, it seemed, including deep crevices high up on the canyon walls that all seemed to be gateways into who knew where and how far? He had to fathom approximately how high the water would rise up those cliff walls, gauge what that maximum depth would be, and think about hiding things from there on up. Many of the containers that had held parts of Basil's treasure were now empty, the ones that had been stored throughout the boat above and below deck when he'd left Russia so long ago. Everything under the bell would be a grand surprise. Below the pallet assembly for the bell was the sealed bow catch-tank, six by six by six, waterproof and never ever once used for holding fish.

9

Vincent flashed back to that Christmas time in 1941, on the banks of the Illava with Jude and Basil. Those days around New Year's when they loaded the *Vanessa* and sailed away, trying to beat the river freeze, with a boatload of treasure, supplies, a beautiful virgin marine diesel engine on a pallet, along with the Bell on the Bow. In so doing, they filled her catch bin with quite possibly the greatest treasure ever loaded on a forty-six-foot-long, white, Russian-made fishing boat, puttering into bull's-eye, the heart of what would later be named the Second World War.

Well over a hundred years before all that, in the 1820s, a man everyone piously nicknamed The Saint had found the lost treasure a German king had sent to Catherine the Great as a gift. His daughter had married her grandson at a wedding for the ages. The two sixteen-year-old children, eventual heirs to both the Russian and German thrones, had left her homeland, her kingdom in Germany, and were headed to Saint Petersburg, Russia, to live with Catherine the Great. They left Germany in a grand royal caravan in the spring of 1796, headed due east to Russia. It was hoped that Mother Nature would have her way with the young newlyweds. At the same time, they kept each other warm on the six-month journey, hopefully resulting in Catherine's first great-grandchild and possible heir to both empires being born in Russia.

Near the halfway point, three months into convoy living, it started to rain one afternoon as it had never rained in the history of Belarus. They were crossing a wide river valley, spread out alongside the river, when each wagon got stuck where they were, one after another. As nighttime settled in, the rain fell in torrents, filling the river valley to overflowing before the flash-flood wall of water buried the entire wagon train in a tsunami of debris at the speed of a racehorse. Every person, every animal, every wagon, and everything in them was lost in the deluge of 1796.

Among them was Catherine the Great's grandson, Prince Alexander, the handsome sixteen-year-old groom, and as of yet, unannounced secret heir apparent to the Russian throne. He, along with his wife Princess Marlane, first child and daughter of the King of Germany, plus every other person involved, all the soldiers, all the horses, all the dogs, and all the wagons. Everything was dead, buried, destroyed.

As for the yet unannounced secret heir apparent, only Catherine the Great knew any of this, as she had planned and schemed to bypass her own son and make his oldest son the heir to her throne. Parts of it came to pass, just like the prophecy had predicted, but there were so many hazards in the way, so many levels to her board.

Her grandson's new bride, also sixteen, was the First Princess of Germany. Still, neither his title nor hers or the plans and schemes of Catherine the Great could calm the anger in Mother Nature that summer in all of Poland, Belarus, western Russia, and eastern Slovakia. A storm time still unsurpassed even after a hundred and fifty years, still the benchmark of disaster, flatland-style. Every breathing soul, along with every single trace of the caravan, drowned quickly that night, and was then shredded in the floods. They were lost in the flatlands of Belarus, became river rubble somewhere, unidentifiable, unfindable for the most part, somewhere in a wilderness full of river valleys. They left only a hint of where they disappeared, wagon seat frames sticking up out of the sand, hooked to buried treasure and supply wagons, in the same valley where Catherine's dream had died.

The mystery concerning the loss bothered her so much that she lay down and died in her bath chamber that November, completely distraught over the bad news from her couriers and search parties. There was nothing her subjects could do for her. They didn't understand the depth of her chessboard, nor the bottom of her heartache. Even spookier was that Kaiser William Frederic of Germany died in his castle of a broken heart over the apparent loss of his Lilly Marlane on the exact same day Catherine died of a broken heart in hers. They must have agreed spiritually, somehow, that life needn't go on and then they both died on the same day over lost children a thousand miles apart. Proof? They had no proof. They only had the agony of never knowing what happened, waking up every day to the exact same question.

The old priest, The Saint, and his small congregation of monks, horses, and dogs, found the wagons in a sandy, dry riverbed and hauled the contents—including six king's treasure chests along with all sorts of other artifacts—over a thousand miles south to Pfeiffer, Russia. In the early 1800s, that struggling fledgling community had their log cabin church on the Illava, called it Saint Francis of Assisi Catholic Church, and had a population of believers. They watched The Saint and his caravan arrive one day, camped on the high side of Pfeiffer, changing life on that riverbank forever. Nothing would ever be the same again for those Volga German Catholic peasant people; The Saint had arrived.

Van Vedic didn't know exactly what was in those chests any more than he knew what he'd find in any of the other boxes, but he knew how much they weighed, more or less. The chests were laid side by side, three stacks high, with four smaller cases on top, and were sealed inside that converted catch bin. Finally, the bell had been lowered into position directly over three more handcrafted boxes that looked like a bell themselves when stacked together in the middle of the pallet. The bell flowed over them and landed on the catch bin lid, which amounted to almost a thousand pounds of weight on the secret chamber. Once in place, it had been chained down and had never moved an inch during the trip, not in the last eleven years, not even yesterday during the plummet.

Sitting there, shackled and embedded into the deck wood alongside the edge of the bell, sat the cross-shaped hammer, an upside-down T. Four inches thick on all legs, according to Basil, that hollow hammer was now full of melted gold and diamonds, weighing in at a hundred and seventeen pounds. He'd even named it "Hammer's Hammer" and then composed one of his masterpieces that caused the imaginary listener to think about diamonds and gold. With the cane pressed against his left cheek and his eyes closed sitting there in the candlelight, in the dead of winter, at thirty below zero, the Hammer's Hammer Overture bounced off the keyboard for no one to hear. He did, in fact, put it to paper, but that too may have been for naught.

The captain could remember Basil's face in the blink of an eye, could hear him laughing or bragging about those boxes he'd made, his pyramid of treasure. A creation that fit so perfectly in the center of the bell—Basil's first epiphany, he'd called them, brainstorms in the wintertime while trying to stay warm next to fires that never went out. Vincent Van Vedic and his new shipmate sat and listened to Basil talk about those days way back then because neither man had any choice; you just had to listen—it was an epiphany after all. After an epiphany was realized, it also resulted in one of his countless masterpieces at the piano. "Inside the Sound" was one such masterpiece, the result of hundreds of hours of cutting into the wood while making the three waterproof boxes and filling them with some of the most priceless artifacts from the basement.

When the snow was above St. Francis's knee in the dead of every winter, Basil and his cane would work for hours and hours with saws and hammers and drills, all the tools he found in one of the interior hallway rooms. In that workroom was everything he would ever need for his projects—a large chamber where Van Vedic had once put such things. Every load he'd delivered to Saint Francis would have a few special tools, someone's most cherished tool of all that had helped make a thousand tables, chairs, and furniture. Some had been used for a hundred years in the same family, the most beautiful wood-crafting tools ever made at the time by true artisans. No name, no date, no story. Just a saw, but unlike any saw you've ever seen or used. Hammers and hand drills, a fantastic selection of everything ever proved to be necessary for a woodshop.

It became one of Basil's many talents, and he gave all the credit for his final result to his cane that seemed to relish the workshop, and had actually pulled Basil that way at times, past the piano room, which wasn't an easy feat. His cane had a radiation zone that Father Basil most appreciated, which kept him warm in the dead of winter and breezy in the summer heat, within reason. At thirty below zero, above ground, for sometimes a month or more, he had no trouble working on his epiphanies with his cane in hand. Sometimes his two hands worked with the slats of wood and the clamps, the cane gently pressing into his chest and up across his shoulder, never in the way, guiding his touch and radiating a state of mind concerning the highs and lows of Mother Nature, also within reason. He learned that wood by its very nature demands to be used productively, touched, and molded with the understanding of whose wood it is and who grew that forest. Nothing that grows is worthless. Everything is part of the circle—but the communists can't see that reality, are asshole human beings, and that's all there is to it. The Ice Pick Assassin hunted them when they came out after the snow melted. Pocomaxa hibernated near the door, out of sight, while Basil lived at the piano, in the chapel, or in the woodshop.

For relaxation, for the sake of genius, he would retreat to the piano room and add to his musical story of what he was doing. He created notes on his piano that explained what gold was, what diamonds were, made one think of those things while listening and even played his masterpiece for Jude and Van Vedic the night before they left. The pianist was so overwhelmed with the story that Jude said that while he listened, his fingers were playing the keyboard in his mind on his imaginary piano, his eyes were closed but crying out the corners, and his lips were in a perfect sync with Jude's. Like the captain, he had the story memorized, and now Basil had put the words to music inside his mind. The sad truth was, no one would ever hear his most significant work except the two travelers, and neither would ever forget the sounds. Father Jude whistled it to perfection all the time, anytime he was thinking his motto, "Don't worry, be happy," and could put the moon to sleep in the darkness with that sound he made with only a slight pucker. Van Vedic had always loved the human whistle, had learned to use it in music, whistled while he thought of the words to a ballad, and could go from baritone to mockingbird with no problem at all. He was frequently his favorite musical entertainment, not shy or modest in the least.

"When was that? Nineteen forty-one, yes. Christmas in communist Russia, Pfeiffer on the Illava, saying goodbye to Basil and the St. Francis grotto."

Just like always, that Bell on the Bow reminded him of that promise he'd made to Basil, that he would get the bell to Kansas someday. It was the equinox. This required a particular note on his charts stand explaining how his boat was grounded, how the days got shorter and nights longer—fisherman logic. It was all downhill from here as far as the weather was concerned, with him realizing that he hadn't lived in wintertime in over ten years. He had, however, survived Russian winters all his life, had been to Tunguska, and to the Pacific Ocean, on the Siberian Railway in the winter, both of which had left lasting memories and volumes in his journal.

When Gomez and Rahellio had talked about the bad winters they had already lived through so far, Van Vedic waited and waited for the snow to get unbearably deep in the story, for it to get so cold you couldn't even move, but they never talked like that.

Forever and ever, if there would be one single memory Vincent Van Vedic would never forget, it would be that cattle train loaded with two thousand frozen bodies headed north, prisoners who were herded on alive and never made it to the morning. As the two trains slowly passed each other in the station, everyone on his train simply looked the other way, and no one saw him try to count the cars. That image of frozen white arms sticking out through the slats on the sides of the carriage, everyone's last supplication for life, and the price paid for ending up a prisoner. That was "Russian cold."

He had been sipping on his coffee, thinking on the far distant past, grateful for the morning and the possibilities ahead, when the silence and stillness were broken.

The bell began to gong, a sound he knew from his childhood, not loud like back then, standing under it, at the base of the steeple, he and his father, holding hands while memorizing a sound he would never forget. There was that sound again, only in grave tones, not an actual ring, more like a vibration, almost as if the bell was straining to be free from the chains, groaning the semi-silent bongs. He could feel it; the bell was talking to him. He interpreted the vibration as the bell pleading to be at least unshackled, not yoked down to the deck.

Even though he couldn't do it, couldn't crawl that far, Basil knew the grandfather clock in the far distant corner of the Great Room had to be wound up soon, or it would stop keeping track of time and, everything considered, that meant it might not ever get keyed again. There was just no way he could get there to wind those springs and then back to where he needed to lie down once again for the last time. For now and the foreseeable future, it still noted and chimed out the hour without fail, and to the best of Basil's knowledge, the second hand took care of that measurement quite accurately; that was all that was needed for everything to work. For the most part, "time" in its purest sense had seldom been a factor in his life, and ever since the fire, he measured it in sunrises and sunsets, in the lives of the four seasons, and primarily when he was wondering how deep and for how long the snow would last. He thought of the time it took to cross a river valley, the time a candle was allowed to live, how long it took if uninterrupted, and the time it took to die. That fabulous clock was more a piece of furniture, a decoration, something to look at, and never in the history of grandfather clocks was there ever one more ignored.

As he lay there in his bed, Basil needed nothing. He wasn't in pain anymore, and could still see the mirror on his dresser that managed to capture the light from the easter candle back in the chapel. He could hear the Diamond Teardrop waterfall, could listen to the chimes above the candle in the chapel, but there seemed to be a film over his eyes that he couldn't wipe away, and he knew he had to start the journey. It wasn't all that far to his final resting place, but it would take a great effort on his part as short a distance as it was, and he wished he had his cane, a wish he had wished over and over but only for that feeling one more time. He didn't want or need it back, just missed it and that feeling he once knew.

He saw a memory of himself inside Van Vedic's boat the day before he and Jude left, when he was touring and examining the engine compartment. He remembered touching his cane into the keel of the ship and being instantly transported into a realm he had never been in before. A state of mind and being where Pocomaxa couldn't move and didn't want to become a part of a bond between two entities from perhaps another world, another dimension, not of this globe, and felt able to be that bond between the two forever. He never had another sensation in life to rival that thirty-minute moment, not that he could recall, standing on *Vanessa*'s keel and holding the cane with both hands while it rested in a tiny notch that it had made for itself; dead center, halfway from end to end, perfect. Just a fleeting memory of a feeling he once felt because of the cane; he was guilty of still thinking about it here at the end. He gave the cane to Jude just before he and Van Vedic sailed away, but the cane was embedded in his backbone and kept him upright from thereon... except for now.

His bed had always been just shy of perfect, just the right length and just the correct width. Precisely the right height up off the floor, with ideally located shelves and platforms for reading lamps, candles, books, ashtrays, and cup holders. It was even better than some of the recliners he enjoyed here and there in the basement, and that was saying something. The route was understood, and all he had to do was slide his legs over the side and try to stand up; two days since he had done that. He hadn't any food except for the crackers, wasn't the least bit hungry, but he sipped a few ounces of water before he let go of the bedpost and reached for the door frame.

He leaned on the hallway wall, counted each step, and finally came upon the couch where Hammer had last rested so long ago. He sat down in the middle, steadied himself, and worked on his breath. That memory of Hammer had faded to some degree over time; twenty-five years ago, and now it was his turn. An arm's length away, the anointment items for the last rites still sat there, and before he reached out, he understood that they were necessary and his responsibility.

The purple sash hung around his neck, and the extreme unction was about to begin. There was no point in trying to read the book, as the film over his eyes had turned his world into a blur, but he remembered those pages from way back when, recited all the prayers in Latin, and spoke out loud his final confession. He then ordered his own penance and willingly said all five decades of the rosary in less than an hour as reparation.

"Through this holy anointing, may the Lord in his love and mercy help me with the grace of the Holy Spirit. May the Lord who frees me from sin save me and raise me up."

The bottle of holy oil had the lid screwed on too tight, which caused him to strain as he worried he was so weak that he might not get it off, but it broke free and allowed him to finish the anointing. He dabbed his eyes and his ears, his lips, and the backs of his own hands. His nails had turned blue—each one got a drop—and the veins in his arms were vivid, twice as high as he could ever recall. A drop or two on his blue toenails, his ankles, and his knees, and then he tasted the oil on his tongue to confirm that was what it was. He said more prayers until he couldn't remember any, and then it was time for his last Eucharist. He ceremoniously received the blessed sacrament that had been concentrated and placed in waiting back one hundred years before, just in case the anointed were still living at the time of the anointing. It was difficult to swallow through a parched mouth, and he felt the host work its way down to his soul, with the Eucharist being his final meal. He was ready.

On October 14th, 1853, the day the Saint had been entombed,

a holy priest had been anointed on this exact couch, and here it was, one hundred years later to the very day, happening again. The beautiful historic anointment box had never been used before the Saint was anointed, became treasured, and sat on the end of the couch from that time on, just waiting.

Only a month before, Basil had had the premonition. He knew it was time, and while he still could, he had prepared everything in advance. He got it all ready—six new thick wicks two by eighteen inches, standing in tripods by the door, waiting for a flame that would burn them to their bitter end. It would take days for the candles to expire, one at a time, all around the same time, which is the way of candles. There would be no one left to blow them out; no one would know when they expired, and when they did, it would be dark beyond dark.

On the other side of this foyer, that fourth door stood open and was pressed against the inside wall. A dozen steps at most, and he would be in that doorway, with nothing to lean on until he found that frame. Basil knew he could do it, knew he could get that far and he could rest before he started lighting the candles. Once that was done, once the candles were glowing, he would only have a few more steps until he could lie back down once again and forever.

His calves were pressed against the side of the couch when he started to stand; he was on his feet, steady, no swirling, and in the ever-worsening blur of his vision, he stepped forward towards that distant door frame. He used his candle, which he could see reasonably well, to light all the candles that were just inside the crypt, and when they were glowing, he set his own on a marble step and turned to the end. He wasn't sure he was breathing; in his mind he saw an hourglass filled with gold dust that was almost exhausted.

He laid his hand on the corner of the marble tomb. When he

found the middle, he stumbled into the three-step platform that climbed up the side and would take all of the strength he had left. The hourglass was almost empty when he put his foot on that first step, then the other, until he was off the ground. He balanced both feet on that third step and rose up till his arms were far above his head, and then whispered to Jesus.

"My Jesus, I am yours forever."

Basil lowered his hands till he touched the wooden walls of his open casket inside the marble sarcophagus with its eight-inch thick cap plate leaning against the Saint's tomb. His mentor, his inspiration, Father Carl Hammer, was on the other side of the Saint, safe and secure, as he had been for the last twenty-five years. His blanket was tucked against the inside wall, and all he had to do was climb over that ledge and lay himself down. Once he was centered, he covered his feet and legs, lay back, and brought the blanket up to his neck. With his very last ounce of strength, his very last breath, his last action of life, he reached up and pulled down on the lid of his coffin. In that previous blink of life, he folded his hands over his heart in the darkness, exhaled one last time, and entered eternity.

In a far distant land, thousands and thousands of miles away, halfway around the world, the bell from Saint Francis of Assisi began to vibrate where it was hiding in a river valley, being unshackled from the *Vanessa* at that very moment, the boat with her ancient keel that Basil had remembered. Vincent Van Vedic was standing close by on the deck of his ship and felt the vibration, the muffled gongs. He threw his arms around and hugged the bell like a lover would until it stopped; it took almost an hour but it finally did.

As those candles burned their way to the bottom. They all arrived there in the same hour, and one by one, they died. Their trail of smoke eventually petered out when that red coal in the wick disappeared. Finally, the last one died, and the light was gone. In that pitch-black darkness, the five-hundred-pound capstone to Basil's crypt slowly descended over his coffin, slower than the hour hand on a clock, until it was sealed forever, quietly, as if God had his finger on the corner and didn't want to finish the task. The easter candle burned for many, many months, until it too expired, and in the end, the only thing that didn't fade was the sound of the Diamond Teardrop waterfall. There was no way in and no way out. Everything was sealed in place, and in fact, the Saint, Father Carl Hammer, and Father Edward Basil would rest undisturbed until the second coming.

Vincent didn't realize at the time why the bell was doing that, why it was saying hello, why it got his attention, but he marked the moment as one of those he would never forget and started the unshackling procedures. The incident would go down in his book as a miracle. While the captain was directly alongside the bell and undoing a series of bolts, he pressed his shoulder to the iron, then both his hands and his right ear. It might have been an hour or so before he stood back up and finished the job he had started. His body was tingling. His fingerprints were etched into the metal, even his palms and thumbs. His handprints had changed the surface where he touched it. He could now see clear impressions even though there hadn't been any pressure, and most astounding of all, he could see the imprints of his ears. When he touched the bell a second time, he left no mark, but now there was a new sound in his mind that didn't bother him in the slightest. He had closed his eyes, pressed his ear to the top of its collar, and frozen in place. Clear as can be, he could hear Basil playing the piano like he was standing in the hallway just outside the music room. He'd listened to that work before—only once, with Jude on that last night in the basement—and even though he could whistle the tune, he had always wished he could have heard Basil do it one more time. When the symphony was over inside the bell, he raised his face, changed ears, and heard it again from the other side. Basil's most magnificent work of art. While it lasted almost an hour, never once did Van Vedic ask himself why. Somehow, some way, he and only he could hear this transmission through this symbol right through the center of the Earth. A musical masterpiece sent by Basil. It was one way to start the morning, have one of those miracle things bounce into one's consciousness, but he was getting used to it once again.

As he looked into the undercarriage of all the large branches that fanned out above, he could see in his mind that heavy-duty pulley assembly he had bought from the yard superintendent hanging from that fourteen-inch diameter branch about fifteen feet above the bell collar. He couldn't have made a better lift tower up by the cabin if he tried. He'd always imagined lifting the bell straight up with heavy-duty pulleys, then pulling the trailer and boat out from under it and finally setting it down in the back of the deuce. That had been the old plan, but this plan would work as far as lifting the bell off the pyramid, off the catch cover lid, off the greatest treasure ever floated on a fishing boat. So far, he hadn't figured out a way to get the bell anywhere except up and down a bit, and might have to wait for the water, but it was still only the first day.

It was time for breakfast, more coffee, time to thank God for his mercy, and then sit back and enjoy the morning. Everything he would need was scattered here and there inside *Vanessa*, and when he decided to dig a pit and build a fire, cook his favorite morning rancheros plus hash, he remembered that he had left his firepit shovel up there by her grave.

When that long afternoon was over, after Rahellio and his son went home, already a month ago now, he sat there by her cross, staring out over the valley at their first sunset together. It was memorable, setting behind the Chuskas through a thin veil of clouds a hundred miles to the west in a spectacular typical New Mexico display that turned the world orange. As he prepared to say goodnight, reminded her of his love way back then, and walked away, he'd spoken the words out loud, along with a promise that they would do it often. The view was utterly spectacular. The commitment included that he'd read her the book he was writing, sit there by her stones, weather permitting, that he'd try to write every day until he was done, and she would be the first to hear the written story of the voyage from Pfeiffer to Pfeiffer. With that grim task faithfully completed, he'd made a few more promises to the woman, and he was ready for bed. As he walked away at the time, he decided that he'd never use that shovel again for anything else, and left it propped securely against the sagebrush bush. He would buy a new one in Aztec someday soon.

He thought about how he would get the No-Name off the boat, thought about carrying him under an arm, but decided he would try to coax the dog to the rail and then just grab him. Van Vedic clamored over the stern and down to the ground, left the dog standing with his front paws on the railing, smiling eager eyes and waiting for a command. The captain looked at the dog and patted both his hands on his chest, and before he knew what to do next, the ninety-pound light-brown blur lurched over the side and right into his arms.

They both took a piss, and headed for the stream for a drink of water from the perfect-sized small mountain river thirty feet across, full of delicious trout that ate feathers tied to a hook. There were times while he sat along the bustling water near small waterfalls, and without fail, he would remember the Diamond Teardrop waterfall in the basement of St. Francis, a sound he would never forget. Above all the others, he would never forget that one. The river was easy to cross, not all that deep in the fall, but it did have a more stern side he hadn't seen in the time he'd been there. He filled the water jug, whistled for what's his name, and headed back up into the ravine for coffee, breakfast, and then quiet time as the captain of the *Vanessa* made his plan for the future.

After securing *Vanessa*, which didn't take much, he took half a dozen pictures and wrote a three-page history of the last forty-eight hours. He started a needs list for winter, covered her pilothouse with canvas, and inspected everything a time or two. Around noon they were off, down to the river, and would walk the bank for a mile or so back upstream until he came to the campground where he had parked the trailer, where he pitched that huge army tent that Rahellio and his son often slept in. Everyone liked it so much he'd left it up.

He re-discovered precisely why they had stopped the road where they did a long time ago. A series of massive boulders blocked their way along the riverbank. There was a thick forest of scrub oak that started up against the sheer rock cliffs of the canyon wall and came out to the edge of the boulders twenty feet away. If that long, deep forest weren't there, the semblance of a road could have proceeded along the bank of the river, way past where *Vanessa* sat hidden under that widowmaker almost a mile downstream. From those unmovable rock slabs downriver, the way became a seldom-used fisherman's footpath that was following a game trail. Rahellio and his son would be assigned to clear out the scrub oak, and it wouldn't be long till that fisherman's footpath saw its first deuce-and-a-half.

CHAPTER TWO

A BLUE BEAM INTO HEAVEN

THE AUTUMN EQUINOX, SEPT 22ND, 1953

His hike up the switchbacks to the big green deuce took over an hour with frequent breaks, and sure enough, the truck hadn't gone anywhere. Down at the *Vanessa* in the early morning light of day, Vincent realized he had only two choices: either climb back out the same way he had practically fallen down in, or walk back upstream to his first campground and then do the switchbacks on foot. One choice was approximately ten times as long as the other, and ten times more comfortable and possible, while the other was ten times straight up and not one bit necessary on his aging body.

When he got to the truck, he coiled up the winch cable, stared down into the ravine that had gobbled up his *Vanessa*, and saw that already some of the bushes and trees were trying to stand upright. Even in the afternoon heat, he was filled with the joy of knowing that everything that should have survived did, and *Vanessa* was now invisible. That initial swath in front of his face on the last hairpin turn was almost unnoticeable. This disturbance in the vegetation started on the edge of the switchback corner and headed due down from there, maybe thirty yards. Then it was over, over a ledge, and he couldn't see any further than that from the edge of the road. Besides, Van Vedic was usually the only person in the front seat with his eyes wide open on the corners, coming or going, the first or the last, and Rahellio had no trouble walking down. That damaged area would heal itself in no time, literally by the day and night, disguising the evidence that Van Vedic had run out of patience and had gambled it all foolishly. Still, in the end, it turned out to be a far better hiding spot, launch site, and fishing cabin by the river, with the fishing being a daily successful R&R. Fishing the river was a joy he truly loved.

So was the hunting. Between the pheasants, the fish, the jackrabbits, and only one young buck deer so far, he had a different form of meat every day, his preparations, cooking, and eating taking up hours of his mornings and evenings.

One of his surprising new habits was hunting dove with his six guns, keeping an alternating left and right ritual, always trying to hit them in the head, and he had more fishing feathers than he would ever need. One night Rahellio cooked up a dozen trout and seven doves that he had personally watched the gunslinger kill in full, fast, low flight. He'd never seen anything like it in his life and instantly thought of his friends listening to that story. He struggled with knowing that he had seen something that he would have to tell his old friends about, probably the next time they all sat around a fire somewhere, him telling the story and them giving him that look.

"Como se thesesay 'bullshashiska' in Espanol?"

Rahellio could see himself talking to his brothers and sons, could see himself mimicking those images, the left, then the right. He was shouting, "*BOOOM, BOOOM*! He would pull out his guns, sometimes the left one and sometimes the other, fire at a dove blurring by and blow its little head off. It didn't matter which hand, and he very seldom missed."

He could see them all looking at him, eyebrows bobbing while searching for their guitars, ready to start singing a song, trying to change the subject before someone started laughing, which would piss off the mortician. You just don't piss off morticians; it's a rule, especially if he's telling the truth and there are dollar bills at stake. There had to be a way to make money off the non-believers who might be willing to bet big on the impossibility of it all, might bet *mucho grande* big! Most folks would need to see it for themselves. There had to be a way, and maybe he and Van Vedic could split the profits. A demonstration down by the river where the doves fly by all day long. Rahellio imagined bleachers full of spectators, paying customers watching Van Vedic perform his quick draw and blowing the heads off doves with 45 revolvers.

Rahellio would be shocked almost every time by the explosion from the captain's quickly drawn 45. Out of respect for the cook, the marksman started shouting, "Dove," before he fired. The mortician would watch him blow their heads off in flight, one time witnessing a demonstration where he blasted a pair gliding side by side using both his weapons. He liked them crispy, well done, burned a bit, and ate it like a squab— everything. Same with the fish. There were only so many acceptable ways to cook a big trout where the meat literally fell off the bones. Bones couldn't ever be the problem for the men or their dogs and were best burned in the fire.

One afternoon, when they didn't have time to fish, the captain ordered Rahellio to take the long-handled fishing net, stand near the rapids downstream, and wait for the fish to float by. The captain stood atop an enormous boulder ten feet above the river and blasted the heads off the fish while they swam by in the calmer water. Sure enough, the headless trout would float to the surface, usually staying close to the bank, within Rahellio's reach, but if they didn't, no one seemed to care—just one of those that got away.

It turned out that Rahellio actually loved the dove, and in his whole life, he'd only eaten a few shot-down birds. He generally feasted on the stupid ones that his wife trapped in their backyard. She, too, was ruthless with dove heads, and stuffed their feathers in pillows.

There were many reasons for not eating shot-down doves, including the price of ammunition, the talent involved in hitting those birds in flight, then finding it blown to smithereens and full of lead. Van Vedic's method was much better. He removed the head before it hit the ground without the explosion of feathers from a shotgun. Some were very hard to find if you weren't zeroed in on the bird to begin with.

Vincent started the machine and pretended to forget the dog, who had not forgotten him. It was standing in front of the truck and near the corner, ready to run up the hill till they popped out onto the plateau. Of course, the dog was a running fool, and they had played this game before going back to Gomez's one day and then all the way back. The truck finished the corner without the trailer and had no trouble with that last climb up to the top and a short drive to his casa. The road was improving with every trip he made. After cresting that last corner, it made a lazy turn back south till he arrived in his favorite deuce-and-a-half parking space, which guaranteed that the early morning sun would warm up the cab.

Actually, his favorite parking space was atop El Bruto Whetto, with no saddle, a large mouth bridle, and a whisper in its ear. No man had ever ridden him bareback, no man ever tried, but Van Vedic and the beast had a session one day where the animal was assured. The creature hated saddles because they were always so tight, made for smaller horses, and when Van Vedic did his measurements, he discovered a beast that matched him with plenty of XXL once again. Just like Brutus. He even had the same farts. Unfortunately, that hundred-dollar saddle that came with the horse was three sizes too small, with Van Vedic concluding that it was equivalent to him walking through life with his feet crammed inside a pair of size-fourteen double EE. Two beautiful modern-day large saddles were being made in Ignacio.

El Bruto was more than ready for the ride, nipped the captain on the shin bone as a warning gesture, and snorted at what's his name. Van Vedic had sat them both down, so to speak, and explained that they were to become friends. They were a team, a threesome, and there was no room for it to be any other way. He told El Bruto that it was okay for what's his name to be close, that he was not permitted to stomp the dog to death, and the dog was to never again piss on the horse's leg.

Van Vedic had seen it all; saw the dog piss on the horse's front shinbone, and saw the hoofs just barely miss that stupid dog's head. He was so low in the ditch the horse would have needed a chisel to get under him. He slammed the ground all around the dog but never hit him, only stopping when Van Vedic fired his right-hand cannon to capture their attention. El Bruto was talked to till he couldn't smell the piss anymore, and Stupid was named and scolded right then and there.

"Stupid Dog!"

Every time he saw the dog for the next three hours, he called it "stupid dog." Every time the dog got all excited, did his dog smile, and wagged his tail like crazy.

"Stupid Dog" it would be. "Stupid Dog" and a whistle.

The threesome headed for that far corner overlook a quarter-mile east from the cabin's backdoor, a place he had already enjoyed many times, where he'd stand and look out over the rocky San Juan River Valley. Vincent was positive he was the only human for miles, for miles and more miles, a miracle and precisely what he had wished for way back in Rabat. It would all turn blue in the next eight years, God willing, and the creek did rise. He hadn't spent much time looking straight down because he wasn't particularly fond of being really high and close to the edge, which was precisely what the position provided.

His fondness for the lookout was becoming an addiction. Every night at sundown without fail for a month now, at least. His horse willingly picked a spot behind the fire so it too would have a clear view of the canyon, and the dog was now trained to sit, stay, and lie down with a firm finger snap and a point.

"Two, sprawl, five." And the beast would instantly sit, lie down, and stay that way until it was released, basically waiting for elk chunks. Ancient Russian dog training disciplines that this dog accepted quickly, the understanding of rewards and firmness— simple, basic stuff. Once the captain was settled in at his corner overlook, once the fire was going, a coffee pot perking, the sun would eventually set for the day behind his back. He didn't care much about that because his gaze was always pulled to a specific area of rocks and smaller ravines in the very heart of what would someday be the lake. Hard to say precisely, but at least five miles north in the canyon towards Arboles, towards where Rahellio lived.

Perhaps he was developing a habit that he couldn't break, but anytime he visited the southeastern lookout point around sunset, which was now every day as of late, his vision focused on that blue beam.

It was a fact he was sure of, positive there was no hallucination involved, no personal eye problems that were causing him to see those blue lights after sunset. Perhaps it was magic, Mother Nature playing tricks on him, and she captured the last sunbeams of the day deep in that canyon and then radiated a blue light after sunset straight up. A waterfall or a small lake might cause it.

Earlier on this occasion, when the captain got close, when he could see over the escarpment, he could pick out that enormous cottonwood tree directly below this overlook that he knew was covering *Vanessa*. The turkeys were back, and he could see them scattered around the highest branches like brown splotches on a green carpet. None of the other trees had such a blight. It was hard to tell how high any particular bluff was above the river, but some of the trees in the cottonwood glens at the base of the cliffs had to be eighty feet tall, and the cliffs dwarfed them many times. Someday soon, it would all be underwater forever.

From that angle, over five hundred feet above the treetops that hid his *Vanessa*, a feeling of perfect harmony washed over him. She was down there, safe, protected, and for the time being, so was the Bell on the Bow, along with the treasure underneath.

. . .

Out of the corner of his eye, he caught a glimpse of Stupid Dog bearing into the fangs and claws of a three-hundred-pound mountain lion in full attack, but instead of choosing the dog, the cat swiped it away and lunged for the captain.

El Bruto screamed a warning. Van Vedic turned, drew both 45s, fired them twice, and blew the puma's neck to pieces. He blew down the barrels, put both smoking cannons back where they came from, and marveled at what was left of the cat. It was a male and old. It'd had tooth issues, was starving in its old age. It now appeared that Stupid might have run between the cat and his quarry, attacked, and distracted the predator at the very last moment... and paid for it hard. Three deep slashes across his back, from shoulder to shoulder, caused him to lie down and let his tongue fall out, but he wasn't dead. He might die, he was hurt so bad; time alone would tell.

The sunset was almost gone when Vincent picked up the dog and headed back to the fireplace, where he'd stitch him up like they do horses—hoping all the way that he wouldn't bleed out before he got it stopped. Stupid was almost gone there for a while, passed out during the branding and the stitching, missing it all for his own good, but never quit breathing. He was carefully tied to the table from his muzzle to his nuts, and the animal seemed to know that was for his own good too. The surgeon surmised that the wounds were deep. He never saw bone or large vessels shooting blood, which is always a bad sign, but there was still a lot of dog blood all over its body. For sure, the surgeon had seen much worse in other times and places. He'd seen damage on people that would have led one to believe the victim could never survive, but they frequently did, and ended up wondering why. It's always about the blood. We only have so much, and if it pours out, we close our eyes and die, no matter what we are, man or beast.

He brought it all to bear that night, opened up the army medic's backpack that came with the truck, and discovered he had everything he would ever need for such a surgery. His life experiences showed up at the table, along with everything he knew about battlefield medicine, the correct practices, his stitches precise and locked. Once the hero lost consciousness, the surgery took twenty minutes, and the dog lay there asleep for the time being, with over sixty stitches made out of fishing string holding his shoulders together. Iodine and vodka killed the germs while also helping to steady the surgeon's hands. The bandage was brilliant, could be checked for infection or smell, and looped through his front legs and neck. The dog wouldn't be on his running feet for a while, assuming he lived through the night and the next few days.

He would visit *Vanessa* on horseback instead of walking, and was constantly planning that as soon as possible, he would try to follow the San Juan upriver to where those blue lights seemed to come from.

The seaman figured it would take days to get to the general area, then he'd wait for sundown when he was closer, and he admitted there and then to himself that he needed help. Every year—four times a year, for that matter—the sky changes. This was in the solstice time. Maybe the lights were all an illusion, perhaps water reflecting in the river, but his eyes had never deceived him in the past, and he hadn't been drinking much. He had seen the glow many times now, and it began to be all that he thought about. El Bruto could take him there. No matter what happened to the dog, it would have a new name, because Stupid didn't work anymore. If he lived, he'd have three chevrons on the shoulder, scars forever from a mountain lion, so his name should be Sarge.

The following day was sad, as Sarge wasn't sitting by the side of his bed and panting. Instead, every morning, whether at the cabin or down in the glen in the tent, Sarge managed to be the first thing Van Vedic saw each day. He wasn't able to do anything just yet, but there he was, panting and drooling and making noises. He was kind of like a rooster without feathers, and once the beast was underway for the day, he would manage to mark everything that even looked like it might be the edge of his influence.

Van Vedic discovered that half the time, the dog was faking it. He'd act as if he had just left his mark, would claw the ground with all fours while huffing some sort of dog attitude, and when the captain checked to see how much piss was there, he found there wasn't any; Stupid was faking. He wasn't pretending this time. When Van Vedic awoke and glanced towards the fireplace, Sarge was sitting up, resting against the hearth, staring at the floor. His tail wagged a bit when he saw his master, and then he lay back down. He would be fine, not even limp, but from that time on, he walked differently on the trails; his hair seemed to stand up like a red mohawk at least half the time, because now he knew what that smell was and what kind of vicious animal made it.

Van Vedic knew that he had disappeared for ten years, both physically and mentally. He had gone somewhere, and so had the boat. He had been inside a hurricane when the lights went on, and that was all he remembered. The lights went on—bright lights. It seems to be a fact because the Coast Guard had pictures, and the dates confirmed it. Every so often, he could see a flash of a memory, could see eyes that were beautiful, indescribable, and mesmerizing; that was all they were—just eyes, looking at him, so soft.

When it came to the memory of things, of times gone by, people, words, faces, his mind was on a level that sometimes surprised him. He'd be writing one of the accounts of his life, caused by a significant turn in the road, one of those Y's at an intersection that turned him and headed him home, back to Pfeiffer, and he would clearly see all the details as if he were living it again. No doubt, part of the miracle that Thousanctus Zerbe had prayed for and bestowed on him was the talent to tell the story in writing—any aspect of the story of Jude. When he sat down to write, it was like a flood of words that had to be written, and it seemed to come from somewhere else—his third eye. Then when he reread it and looked for mistakes, it was as if he was standing there again, back in that time, reliving that moment. Thousanctus Zerbe had prayed to his God of Reply for just such a blessing on Van Vedic, explained to him who that God was, what he was good at, and best of all, that it was a God who didn't ask much from man. Sometimes just the nod of our memory that he existed was enough.

With all the things that he knew he had to do, gradually, Van Vedic's obsession of riding on El Bruto to the source of the lights had become his only thought. Why was there a blue glow, a blue beam shining straight up into space, in a pitch-black canyon on the dividing line between the mountains and the desert?

While out riding the brute along the most northern stretch of his property, he stumbled into an Indian hunting party. A long way off, four shirtless men rode in a procession with their heads down. The closer he got, the more they changed into boys.

Indians were a new subject for the Russian, although not a lot different from some of the people back where he came from, like those mountain people near Tunguska. His only encounters so far had been a few glimpses of their homes along the train tracks—round shelters they called hogans—quite a few turquoise jewelry peddlers in Aztec, and most importantly, the four teenage boys who were hunting rabbits from horseback just off the county road on the north end of his property.

He learned they were proud to be called Ute, not to be confused with Southern Utes. They had ridden up from Ignacio, spoke three languages at least, and carried 22 single-shot long rifles—along with being juniors and sophomores at Ignacio High. They had small packs full of extra ammo and whatever else was allowed, each had a knife on their hip, and some skimpy rolled-up tube of clothes. They seemed to be on some sort of a camping trip for part of the summer, and were camped on his land, hunting rabbits, when Van Vedic rode up on El Bruto with his hand-made brand spanking new saddle. The giant cowboy had smiled and made friends with the young men, learning their stories and what they were doing. Later that afternoon, he showed them how to hunt rabbits with 45 revolvers blazing away, using only his legs to guide his beast, looping up the center of an arroyo and shooting rabbits in the head, birds on the wing, and rattlesnakes wherever they coiled. At least one each of those desert jacks for everyone, three-pounders, tall and lean. Jackrabbits are not on many menus because they are fast on their feet, which limits them from ending up on a skewer. After twenty-four hours or so, the young braves were only slightly used to the bareback idea in their quest to mimic the way it once was, some sort of advanced Boy Scout Indian-style summer horseback ride.

Their first night in the foothills was painful, to say the least. Shirtless, pantless, sockless, not near enough loin, and worst of all, they had utterly failed to get a fire going before it got black all around them like inside their outdoor shitters. You could have heard a pin drop when that last match was struck, the one they had all talked about, and how the spirits had saved it for later. All four got very spiritual there, on the verge of total darkness, but not to worry. The last one, the very last half match, was discarded over there somewhere because it had broken in half early on in their efforts to light the fire and had been trashed. Thrown away because there were plenty more where it came from, and there was no need to use half a match. After breaking all of the quiet campfire rules ever made by the ancients and wasting about half of the minimal amount of sunlight they had left, and for a myriad of illogical teenage reasons, they had all decided that the youngest of the four should strike that last spirit-infused half match and get that fire going. It would work like the trading post guy had promised, just so long as the fire end never got wet. Soaring Eagle's third son struck the half match against a rock, and he held it into the dry grass kindling until it burned his fingers and he had to drop it. Things looked good for about ten seconds, and then it went out. *Poof,* no fire.

The whole camping trip idea was just one stage in a process of attaining the status of young braves in search of "The Order of the Arrowhead." These four young boy scout braves on ponies— which is an Indian word for a full-grown horse—including the headband, loincloth, and leather booties, were out and back from Ignacio for as long as they could stand it with very few provisions, maybe four nights and five days. They didn't have saddles or bridles, but they did have blankets. All four wished they had saddles and quite a few other amenities. At the tops of the hills, they would always look back while resting, could see the mountains around Ignacio, and then considered their trip back home, understanding how difficult the ride home would be with just a blankie under their bottoms and loincloths. They all knew their ponies would be hard to control on the way back. The horses would want to run once they realized they were heading home. That was why they had their heads down when Van Vedic first saw them. They were already out of water and matches and hadn't had much fun so far. Van Vedic saved the day.

Once everyone introduced themselves, shook hands, and agreed on whose land this meet-up happened to be, once that friendship was established, they sat in the shade of some willows and talked about water, dinner, and who was doing what. That was when the captain discovered these little boys were not one bit prepared to be alone in the desert. The giant white cowboy also found out the boys knew Spanish very well, and it was decided that all five would go on the hunt for rabbits with the captain at the lead on El Bruto Whetto. This was a new technique for the Utes. They usually walked along in a line fifty feet apart in a field where they thought there might be a couple of rabbits, horses safely tied to trees, sneaking up on the jackrabbits four on one. As everyone who has ever hunted rabbits knows, the only way to get one is to sneak and slither up on them, quietly, silently, cautiously. No sounds at all. Jackrabbits' ears are twelve inches long, sticking straight up all the time and attached to hind legs that can go from zero to gone in the blink of an eye. You get one shot, maybe two. That's the way most hunters approach the delicious desert jackrabbit, but not even close to the way Van Vedic hunted jacks. El Bruto Whetto began a gentle trot in the very middle of the sandy arroyo, with the gunslinger scouring both sides for the slightest trace of a meal. He needed at least five. In less than a full mile, the gunslinger killed four jacks, two on the left and two on the right, ten doves all over the place, and a pheasant, leaving all four scavengers somewhat starry-eyed at the barbeque.

Each one of the scouts had stopped at different times to retrieve the prey, grabbed the bird or rabbit, and then tried to catch up with the trotters. At the campsite, at the fire pit, the four boys ate all that meat like they hadn't eaten in over a week. They hadn't skinned that many rabbits ever, were covered with blood and feathers, and two had even vomited at the scrap pit hole for all the guts. They had initially planned to make their camp in a desolate niche between enormous boulders, trying to be clandestine, leaving no trace of themselves, with this particular site only a few hundred yards from the nearest spring water stream. The whole idea was to mimic a time in the ancient world, long before the Mexicans ever showed up, when an army of Navajo warriors searched for four Utes who knew full well that if they were captured, they would have surely been buried alive on the edge of a red ant hill with their mouths propped open. This legendary story was known by both tribes and celebrated on the same day, but it had two different endings, depending on whose party you were at. The occasion still manages to rile up the warriors of both tribes all these many years later.

Van Vedic listened to their stories and told the boys he would be camped where that water bubbled right up out of the ground on the other side of the ravine for only one night, and they were welcome to join him. So, as they were dying of thirst, they broke camp in less than five minutes and then spent the evening teaching the captain about the Utes and their history.

CHAPTER THREE

A HELL OF A WAY TO DIE

Jude walked into the room and was shocked by the casual atmosphere exhibited by the three doctors and two nurses, but he also knew this had been going on for more than a week already, coming up on ten days, and the prognosis was way south of weak. They were all sharing a gallon of fresh soup, one-hour-old delicious little biscuits, each had a glass of milk, and they were deliberately trying to eat and drink out of their patient's view. But, of course, the general had nothing of the sort, had nothing much to say, nothing to show except big eyes when he saw Colonel Jude slash back the curtain that let the clear light cover his chest and face. His ears worked, and so did his eyes, along with his nose, which detected the biscuits in much the same fashion that we recognize fart molecules when released into the air, with there being one other thing for sure. His brain was most assuredly aware of pain and discomfort, which the doctors could easily explain were caused by the more than three hundred stitches involved in sewing his scalp back on his skull. Their opinion was that his third and fourth vertebrae were a total wreck, causing the quadriplegia. They couldn't be sure as to whether his spinal cord was severed or not, and for that reason, they would hope and pray that the cord was only bruised. Time would tell. The doctors and nurses were incessant about discovering any sort of movement on any limb he had.

"Can you feel that? That? There? Anything?"

The answer was always no. Finally, in an effort to get him examined three times a day by someone other than the doctors with whom he was pretty much fed up, the staff was introduced to a professional tester—a stunningly beautiful young nurse who could arouse the dead by simply fulfilling all the routine tasks of a nurse in confined quarters. It was an effort to stimulate the man —in the end for naught—a very thoughtful gesture brought to the table by Bea herself. Bea knew her man appreciated the female side of life, and when she first learned that about him, she used it to capture him. The entire staff was greatly disappointed when the young lady's casual attention did nothing to arouse the general. Every technique known to those surgeons when it came to stimulation was liberally tested, with George knowing about it, and often times when he didn't.

Three prominent surgeons designed the contraption that attempted to slowly pull his head towards the top of the bed, micro-millimeters at a time. It could and would be adjusted hourly if necessary, and seemed to require an explanation every few hours to anyone else in the room. Each doctor would insist the whole time he examined the general that the apparatus they were torturing him with was essential to keeping his dying body alive. The general couldn't see the hooks in his face and his neck, couldn't move anything on his body from the neck down, and so logically concluded that his condition would have a tragic end.

He really didn't want to be saved. He lay there waiting out his time and was finished giving orders, almost finished with this life.

His circle of life had shrunk to six feet or less, and everything out past that got lost in the noise they tried to hold to a minimum. He was fumbling with consciousness when he found two faces staring and talking to him from less than two feet away, asking him questions.

"Can you hear us?"

They both moved around about a foot or so, and the other doctor chimed in, "How about now? Can you hear us now?"

The general rolled his eyes back towards the rear of his brain and then back up to the front again. His memory flashed back to Gibraltar, Thanksgiving 1942, to that overlook where someone else had asked him the same questions. Jude had asked him that only three years before.

He showed the doctors the driest white tongue inside a mouth anywhere. Bea was standing nearby and insisted that they moisten the dying man's mouth and tongue and to hell with their fear of him swallowing the liquid. He couldn't possibly talk with his mouth so dry, and he had a few things to say to Colonel Jude and herself that couldn't be said with a dry mouth.

When he'd heard the doctors talking about Jude, that the colonel was in the hospital area and requesting the interview, two of his life monitors started bouncing around on the report paper, and his heartbeat and pulse started scaring the nurses. Finally, he stuck his tongue out an inch and back in, which could have been interpreted a thousand different ways, and managed a garbled, "Thank you, Jesus!"

It was close to the general's time to die. The problem was he couldn't say much, couldn't write a speech, and damned if he knew why this had happened this way; it had been such a minor accident. One moment he was staring out the side window of his chauffeured Cadillac, sitting at a small intersection in the road, and the next, he was bleeding all over himself, but he couldn't move his body or touch his injury. An army deuce-and-a-half truck with three drunk soldiers in the cab had caused the crash, and in so doing, they managed to kill their vaulted general and sabotage his glory. The absurdity of all irony, and perhaps even predicted by the victim. How could such a glorified, war-winning general be lying in a bed, and instead of all those accolades, he was now best described as a total and complete quadriplegic with little to no hope for survival? Human beings in this state seldom survived.

That was all true, but the terrifying pitch-black hallucinations, the vivid memories of previous reincarnations were only beginning—perhaps every hour, it seemed—but the clock only had one hand. Every night he could look forward to a recall of another lifetime—the rolling hills and the strangest fields in Africa, just outside the back doors of this hospital, where he walked with all the big cats, lions, and jaguars coming over to lick the wound on his neck. Then, one night soon after he got to the hospital, in his horrified mind, he relived his last hours in another lifetime, lying on a battlefield in modern-day Denmark, only it was the year 1397AD. The final great battle of the Kalmar Union Times. It was late in the afternoon that day he'd died. He'd been killed. He was a general there too, but a defeated general, and they had cut him to pieces. Wild men on horseback had ravaged all his battle flags and then routed the entire auxiliary guards. Crazy people who ran him and his men down like dogs, huge men with red hair who ate dead horses raw. They were her honor guard. Their queen, a beast of a woman in battle, protected like no other, Queen Margrethe, set things right during those times for sure. That was how he'd died that time.

He would be reincarnated again, and again, and again and go through the whole life process, just like this time, with no guarantees on how it all would end or that he would even know this was a reincarnation. One thing was for sure; it was in his best interests to refrain from telling stories of having been in battles a couple thousand years ago. Even though he could relive specific battles with pinpoint accuracy, it was difficult for his subordinates to believe the legend.

Eventually, after all the introductions and small-time talk, all the others left the area and allowed Jude to come in and stand there at the side of the bed, appearing to show the top of his cane to the whole room as he did so. Their eyes met; when embracing a person with quadriplegia, for the most part, it's all in the eyes. Jude then laid the cane on top of the sheets, neck to toe, bent over, and reached around the patient, consuming him in a full hug, with the cane cushioning the priest from causing any harm. Finally, after a long time of being cheek to cheek, the priest stood erect, but he left the cane on top of the blankets and nestled the face of Jesus into the general's cheek instead. There was no need for a time limit on this visit, and at the time, there was no reason to think it would be the last—close to the last, perhaps, but not the last. So, in the quietest whispers ever whispered, Jude explained all sorts of things to his general. He cleared up all the questions the general had, the ones that had accumulated over the past week especially, maybe more, maybe less, but his questions remained the same and were exceedingly simple. How much longer? Is there any chance at all? Can I ask that all efforts cease? Is there a heaven for sure—answer me true, because I know I get to go there. Do I have to do it all again? All that conversation happened between them, separate from the rest of the room, even from Bea, and it lasted for the longest time.

The general lay there on his elaborate hospital bed, arms at his side, with a light sheet covering his naked body. Jude placed his cane on top of his general's frame, from his kneecaps to his ear lobes, pressed it in place, and it looked as if the general had intentionally pressed his cheek into the top of the cane. His eyes didn't close, but they relaxed from that constant glare he had existed in since he became aware of his lot in life. His were angry eyes, furious eyes, but there was nothing anyone could do to lessen the lesson his life was teaching the world. If one were to read between the lines, if one were to know all the stories, all the facts, and the depth of the fall from grace for slapping a coward, that someone would witness the reality of an exceptional human being who attained the rank of four stars in the United States Army and then, in the blink of an eye, that general would be reduced to a quadriplegic veteran... He slowly closed his eyes and could see what that tuna couldn't ever know; they were not allowed to see into the times after death, into forever, if there was such a place. There was no forever in the mind of a tuna.

As Bea watched the two men reconnect, she could easily remember how this priest had overwhelmed her husband from the first moments they met. According to him, everyone else felt the same when they came in contact with the holy soul. His letters became one-subject affairs, where he would talk about Jude for page after page until he would just write STOP and then drift off into jabber about who hated whom the most and what he wanted for the future. She would caution him about his anger, about his hatred for the Russians easily equaling his hatred for the Germans, and that from her point of view, all that had happened after the last shots were fired would more than likely have nothing to do with him. His verbal tirades concerning what he would like to do to Adolph, that long oration about severing the man's tongue, was funny the first time, but enough was enough. Her man was a super soldier, not a politician, and politicians had almost always ruled the world. His job had been to take the army to Hitler's doorstep and kill the man, shoot Hitler in the heart, press a US Army boot on his throat, make him spit out his tongue, and while he gagged for air, cut that lying flapper off his face.

When George wrote her and told her that Jude had caught up with the headquarters unit and walked up to the situation table one dreary morning on the way to Bastogne, he'd explained how just about everything changed from that moment on. Everyone in that planning barn had heard the story. Many had heard Jude tell it himself back in Morocco, and many were now storytellers themselves. They were, one and all, true believers, and everyone studied the "short timers' calendar" every day, which counted down the days to doomsday. It was rolled out and stood up in the corner of every situation room the general and his staff ever congregated in. Way back when the general first came ashore in Rabat, Morocco, after sailing on the *Vanessa* from Gibraltar, Patton had ordered his office staff to build the calendar based on the premise that Jude had said they had until the winter solstice in 1945 to defeat Hitler, or else. He wanted everyone in his command to know that number—the number of days they had left to defeat the Germans.

Not long before he died, he wrote in his diary that he, Blood and Guts General Patton, knew where the real credit belonged for the great military and tactical decisions during the build-up to the Battle of the Bulge. "It is noteworthy that all the operations, including plans for attack executed on the 22nd of December 1944, were done by personal conference or by telephone, and that the highly complicated road and supply movements were only made possible by the old and very experienced General Staff of the Third Army and the high discipline and devotion to duty of all the units involved." All during those long days and nights when he and Jude and all the others deciphered the messages the Germans were sending to each other thinking the whole time their messages were safe, they had watched the Germans move many different tank and infantry divisions into staging areas that only his staff seemed able to detect. People would see things on the table, mention the knowns, and the whole idea would blossom into battlefield genius, with many questions and problems. The issue would be understood by everyone concerned, and it would usually involve time or the lack thereof. It never failed, but Colonel Jude and Lieutenant Sprindis would drive off into the worst of it, straight towards the front, and not be back, till dawn or later. Sprindis would get them close to where they needed to be, where the question mark was on the map, and then they'd stop, park, and listen. Many times, the priest would get out and walk into the woods by himself with his cane in hand, disappear into the blizzards and the howling snow and cross through frontiers that were death traps. The lieutenant would fret and worry the entire time his colonel was missing, but he would be the first to know what Jude had found out as they discussed the results on the way back to Patton and the staff.

The German plan was discussed in great detail by a host of high-ranking senior personnel who were holed up in a beautiful cottage that particular night in early December. The weather was horrible but they had plenty of wine and wood for their fire. All six officers would be leaving in the morning for the different staging areas where their tanks were being collected. The briefings were over, and now everything was moving after dark. Extreme vehicle and radio silence, and no lights in an effort at total surprise. A certain percentage of the entire German western front was being discreetly pulled offline and repositioned— infantry, armor, and artillery. It was a last-ditch attempt to kill the allied invasion in its tracks and would become known as the Battle of the Bulge. These officers were confident the plan they were a part of could turn things around, because things didn't look good for the most part. They gave speeches to each other and shouted the brave rallying cries of their respective battalions and divisions, and discussed all the battle plans they had been obligated to memorize once things started rolling.

Sprindis was left by the jeep on the edge of a thick forest when Jude walked away, all dressed in white winter wear, with just his cane and no weapon. On the far side of a snow-covered field, the priest entered the German lines and walked past a Panzer tank that had sleeping "tankers" inside. About a mile or so behind the lines, he came up to the cottage porch and sat down in the snow under the living room window. He began to whisper questions to these officers, men who had been in tank warfare for many years now and who were well aware that they would probably die on the battlefield. The officers thought they were asking these questions themselves, causing them to rehearse their own personal orders that would activate vast numbers of men and machines, all acting in perfectly timed and coordinated efforts that would result in super killing efficiency. That was not to be, and when everything was settled, the surviving Germans retreated back inside their borders if they could. Patton's Third Army won many battles against the elements and the enemy and received great credit for being elite among the elite, with General Patton himself receiving fantastic accolades and being the mastermind behind it all.

After the Battle of the Bulge, and once the chase had begun in earnest, the allies converged on the German border from every direction there was, and in only five more months, the war in Europe would be over. May the 8th would be labeled VE Day—victory in Europe for the Western Allies. On the eastern side of any line that anyone drew in the sand was Joseph Stalin and his Soviet Russia. Reconstruction would begin immediately in some places, but not all.

Patton's journey was almost over, and throughout this visit with Jude, this encounter with the most remarkable man he had ever known, he could see his final resting place for this lifetime. All he had left to do was be satisfied in his own mind with the life he'd led, close his eyes, and it would be over. Yet, for over a week now, he kept opening his eyes from those trances he kept falling into, reliving in spurts all those battles he had found himself in and managed to live through.

The "wallflower" nurse was always a bit concerned. She was evidently timing the way the general opened or closed his eyes, a pretty methodical record of his consciousness. She had a column for just about every facial gesture the quadriplegic could manage and what time it happened. For the most part, General Patton didn't know she was there, but all of his whispered words and prayers were heard, and when he called for Bea at any hour of the day or night, he was heard by her or one of the others.

THE STORY OF PATTON'S ACCIDENT

Patton and Gay left Bad Nauheim at about 0900 hours on December 9th in Patton's 1939 Model 75 Cadillac driven by Pfc. Horace Woodring. A jeep driven by Technical Sergeant Joe Spruce followed, carrying the guns and a gun dog. At about 1145 hours, in the northeast suburbs of Mannheim, an oncoming two-and-a-half-ton US Army truck swung across the path of Patton's Cadillac in an attempt to turn into a quartermaster depot. Woodring was unable to stop in time, and the two vehicles collided at a 90-degree angle, with the right front bumper of the truck smashing the radiator and bumper of the Cadillac.

Neither driver was injured, and Gay received only slight bruises. Patton, on the other hand, although conscious, was bleeding profusely from head wounds received when he was thrown forward against the steel frame of the glass partition separating the front and rear seats, and then backward again into his seat. There were, of course, no seat belts in those days, and whereas Gay and Woodring, having seen the oncoming truck, had braced themselves for the impact, Patton, who had been looking out the side window, had not. He knew he was seriously injured and apparently murmured, "I think I'm paralyzed," and later, "This is a helluva way to die."

The ambulance, which eventually arrived at the scene with two medical officers, took Patton to the 130th Station Hospital in Heidelberg, 15 miles away, where he was admitted at 1245 hours. He was paralyzed from the neck down and suffering from severe traumatic shock; his pulse rate was 45, and he had a blood pressure reading of 86/60. With blood covering his face and scalp from cuts that had gone through to the bone, he was diagnosed as having "a fracture of the third cervical vertebra, with a posterior dislocation of the fourth cervical vertebra." Whether or not the spinal cord had been transected or merely traumatized remained a matter of conjecture.

Patton was put in a crude and excruciating form of traction that evening, and the US Army Surgeon General in Washington recommended that a British neurosurgeon, Brigadier Hugh Cairns, and an orthopedic surgeon be brought in to assist. A plane was sent to London to fetch them, and after they arrived on the morning of the 10th, they advised some changes that turned out to be equally painful. Fortunately, Patton's condition began to stabilize. After nine days of agony, traction was maintained, and the pain eased by encasing Patton's neck and shoulders in a special plaster jacket.

Beatrice and an American neurosurgeon, Colonel Geoffrey Spurling, flew in from the States on the 11th. Patton's medical records for that day read, "Prognosis for recovery increasingly grave." Spurling and the other doctors knew it was impossible to operate to relieve the pressure on his badly damaged spinal cord to eliminate the paralysis. Patton, too, seemed to have known that his injuries were irreversible, if not terminal. His first words to his wife were, "I'm afraid, Bea, this may be the last time we see each other."

After two hours of having Jude by his side, it was as if the general simply closed his eyes and left the room. He had done this before, and the times were increasing, with the last episode lasting for three hours and fifteen minutes before he opened his eyes again. With no one to whisper to, Jude also left the room and found Bea sitting by herself in a small nearby patient's room. He pulled up a chair so he could sit by her side, took her hands, and smiled that smile of his.

"Your husband tells me he told you our story while the two of you were together in Washington a few months ago. There is another story concerning the captain of the *Vanessa*, Captain Van Vedic. He, too, was a close friend of your husband. You would have liked him. But, unfortunately, they say he's disappeared at sea, took his boat out into an angry ocean near Puerto Rico, and hasn't been seen since."

"George only knew him a short time, but just like with you, Captain Van Vedic has left a lasting good impression on my husband. It had something to do with handguns and biceps, and because of that tuna fishing trip, that man of mine was never the same again. He touched your cane and saw his destiny."

"The Soviets have already closed off all the borders, and they wouldn't let him or I travel to the main gates of Theresienstadt. We promised each other to be there as soon as possible after it was liberated, but the police won't allow it. They may be having epidemics there, too. That's one of the reasons the Soviets are using it. Your husband was right; our army should have gone as far east as we could have."

"I know about this passion we all have to liberate the camps. So tragic, so slow, so horribly foul."

"I told him just now that I needed to be done with my contract, that I needed to go that way immediately, walk into the Russian zone, as the sunsets and I won't be back. All the surviving brothers are returning from their missions—instinctively in my case—because we made promises to each other to be there if we can. He had a few questions that only I could hear, and there was one that asked... about when, and he hoped it would be soon. I told him he would be set free while he sleeps, set free completely, and for him to strive to sleep. Hopefully, set free from all the repetitions, too, which will happen at dawn in the morning. You should be there when he goes to sleep tonight. Goodbye, Bea."

A few hours later Colonel Jude was driven from the hospital there at Heidelberg, down the road to the Czechoslovakian border. It took about an hour, and when his driver pulled up at the checkpoint where the diplomats crossed into the Russian-controlled zone, a priest got out of the car instead of a colonel. Jude was back to wearing his sandals, back to his cassock, back to a white-collared neck ring, and lightly leaning on his cane. It was the Winter Solstice, December 21st, 1945.

CHAPTER FOUR

HDLPA

When the captain first considered how he would get that bell off *Vanessa* and into his truck long before the water rose this high, everything considered, he was somewhat overwhelmed. At this point in the game, with that question mark having perplexed him from the moment he opened his eyes that first morning, he rationalized that his situation really wasn't that bad after all. He figured the big green deuce was so far up above and out of the picture he might as well consider using one of those Sikorsky flying contraption things he'd seen down at Corpus Christi back a few months before. Now that was something—an incredible hovering crane; a helicopter machine, they called it.

He and the admiral, his favorite Coast Guard captain, and some other folks were having dinner on a balcony at the Naval Officer's Club that overlooked the harbor when the evening's entertainment showed up that day.

"HOLY MOLY! WHAT THE HELL IS THAT?"

In the world of 1953, dining outside at the Officer's Club, this flying and hovering helicopter machine suddenly appeared. The screaming contraption was carrying a Sherman tank. It set the whole thing down for a few moments on the edge of the eighteenth fairway of the golf course, then picked up its payload and flew away with it. The captain had never heard of such a thing. The loud helicopter looked like anyone's worst nightmare as far as dragonflies were concerned. It was flown by two tiny humans sitting right behind where the dragonfly's eyes would have been. Nevertheless, the pilots were smiling, waving, and looked not one bit frightened.

Sitting directly in front of his face that first morning was the bell. Since approximately New Years' Day 1942, the bell had been there in that exact spot. The bell covered a precise mold of itself in three waterproof boxes filled with what Father Basil described as his 'favorites.' The priest had handcrafted the circular containers and filled them with heavy gold objects and a myriad of other treasures, diamonds, jewels, and gold coins. He did all that back in the winters of the early thirties, the result of what he called an epiphany. A hobby and obsession that kept him alive and warm, physically occupied with the projects while the world outside was buried in snow and frozen solid for months. Under the burned-down remnants of St. Francis Church in Pfeiffer, his underground basement was as good a place as any to spend the winter. For Pocomaxa, hunting season would start again when spring came back.

The captain knew more or less what everything weighed, the dimensions, and what it would take to lift the bell an inch. In this particular case, he had to lift it at least its own height off its pallet to get at everything underneath and covered by it. But here on the beautiful *Vanessa*, like it was, it sat approximately the perfect distance from a thick tree branch directly up above his outdoor bed. The lateral branch was healthy, fifteen inches in diameter and out a long way from the trunk, directly above the bell's collar. With all its branches, this incredible living platform shielded *Vanessa* from the sun while providing the perfect scaffold. He could tie a chain around it in a heartbeat and hang his heavy-duty lift pully assembly exactly where it belonged. He already had the item in the back of the deuce, an article he'd seen rusting in a boneyard pile at the train yard. He and the yard's maintenance superintendent walked away from their battles that day the victors, when Van Vedic saw the rusting HDLPA.

"Is that an HDLPA lying way back there in the corner of your boneyard?"

The yard's boss man, the superintendent, guide, and HMFIC, started stumbling backward, flailing circular arm orbits, couldn't find his balance, and fell on his ass a dozen feet away. He was so embarrassed he'd fallen right on his keester and his hat flew off —bounced off more like it. With other yard hands watching from different distances and angles, he put up both hands, refusing any assistance from the captain. He got to his feet, found his hat, walked closer to the taller man, brushed himself off on the backside, and smiled.

"Funny you would be interested in such a thing, my captain. The man who used to run this yard, the great Olaf, told me and only me that a man like you would come along someday and need an HDLPA. He ordered and begged for us to never, under any circumstances, throw that HDLPA away. Never give it to the junkyard guys, the scrap metal scavengers, but keep it and save it for someone who would need it. Someone who would see it off there in the shadow, see the hanging hook, and know it for what it was and what it could do. Someone who would understand that piece of rust. Oh my God Almighty, that appears to be you.

Praise Jesus. How extraordinary for me to be here today, to be of service to you, to have taken this walk. I was the only one there that day when Olaf said that; I remember he put it right where it is himself. He and me, we were friends; you'da liked him. I thought he was just being Olaf at the time, messen with me, in love with an ancient HDLPA, and I remember thinking at the time that I had succeeded in humoring the old cuss. He directed that I should give it to whoever asked for it first in the future. No need to trash it. Save it, leave it back there in the back, and pour some old used oil on it every now and then. That is now you! Oh my God, that is you! You ask me here at sunset if that's an HDLPA back there? I tell you, my long-awaited friend, that yes, it is, and not only that—it's free. Yes, it is!"

Van Vedic wasn't quite ready for that sort of an answer, but he had to accept when the 'super' offered it to him for free. Olaf was a legend in Aztec, and among many other things, his memory haunted the railyard and all the streets of the little town. His passing was a personal thing for almost every soul in the community, very hard to take, and now all these years later, they still felt his mark. The first thing that came to mind for the captain was the idea that the HDLPA was simply one of those things that continued to happen along the voyage, put there by design. So he tossed it in the back of the deuce to be used at a later date, he supposed. There was no doubt that lifting the bell up and off of the pallet it was sitting on was a relatively simple matter—get high above the bell and chain up an HDLPA; everybody knew that. The captain had every intention of taking care of that business somewhere down the road. He would probably put the bell in the back of his truck and take it to Kansas that way. The other option involved the train, and even then, he would still need to deliver the bell to the train station in Aztec.

When he chatted with the railyard hands about where the train went from Aztec, they told him everything they knew and fetched him a copy of the train schedules and freight charges. He was lured into the main office area with donuts and coffee while he was there to pay an offloading fee and quite a few other charges. The captain was cautious at the start as he didn't want to offend anyone. He understood that he had showed up that morning near dawn and completely overwhelmed the community, and that fact, all by itself, had cost people money. Two standard rail cars, flatbeds with a boat load of cargo, including the boat, of course, and the trailer to haul it on. Plus a two and a half ton army truck. In a brief speech in front of the whole trainyard staff and who knew who else, he thanked them all for their professional attitudes about everything they did. There were no accidents or injuries to the workers despite the size of the operation, because that sort of stuff didn't happen all that often anymore.

Two or three times during different phases of the unloading project, workers spoke about the big rolling yard cranes, the things they saw come through town when something crashed five years before. Those cranes would have made their work with *Vanessa* quite simple. There were so many rumors about why they were needed, crazy stuff that made no sense, but the army was there immediately and kept things very hush-hush. Even experienced workers hadn't ever seen some of those kinds of railroad rolling workstations and the huge cranes they brought into Aztec back in 1948. For over a month, the Heart Canyon area ten miles north was off limits, and they cancelled train service for a time. The rumors persisted that something might have crashed up there and the only ways in were blocked by County Sheriffs and Army MPs. The northern branch of the rail line had collapsed, so someone managed to have the US Army come in and fix everything. It was somewhat unbelievable, how these trains converged on the local vicinity and waited on the spurs outside of town. They'd built a mile-long sidetrack where trains could pass in the future, but it was a very strange sidetrack if there ever was one, and all during the construction and remodeling, there was a very rude military presence about everything. They would bus the workers into Aztec, where they could get some food and entertainment, but they weren't very friendly and really didn't say much. Just as suddenly as it had started, it ended, and one very early morning that work train passed through Aztec going the other way—three engines and fifteen passenger cars and flatbeds with cranes and track hoes, big stuff, along with three long shrouded and concealed flat beds full of something, but no one knew what it was. At the end of the month, it was over and the rumors began to fly.

Some very influential and prominent locals were hauling two tractor loads of building supplies to a housing project at the end of Heart Canyon that morning in '48, first day of the week for the ten-man crew who would be camping at the work site. Without much warning, a fuselage-type projectile glided over their heads, whistling through the wind, and low. It cleared the hilltop by only a few hundred feet and disappeared up the canyon. When the tractors got to the top of the hill maybe half an hour later, there, on the far distant edge of the massive dry riverbed, lay the tube, no fire, broken open in three places, with bodies lying about. With everyone staring and thinking on the best footpath across the arroyo, suddenly a flying saucer maybe forty feet in diameter lifted off from alongside the giant tube, rose up to a few hundred feet and disappeared in a blink of their eyes.

Van Vedic was fascinated with their stories and wondered about it all, because many of these people who were standing around and adding tidbits about the goings-on back then seemed totally logical and God-fearing folk. Most agreed that whatever the fuselage was, it probably belonged to the government, and people in New Mexico all knew the state was flush with military secret places. They'd invented those war-ending atomic bombs in Los Alamos and Albuquerque a hundred and fifty miles east of there. Three years out from the end of World War Two, many of the attitudes about national defense were still on everyone's mind.

It was fascinating stuff to listen to, and the captain asked questions that brought it all back to now and today. When they talked about the tracks crossing over the continental divide, it seemed there were times in the dead of winter when all of the passes were mostly closed. Especially for trucks and cars, those mountain roads disappeared, and oftentimes so did the train tracks. Every year, guaranteed for a little while—but the route was simple, and so was the package. The yard's boss man, the superintendent, had assured the captain the first time around that his people could have removed the bell and stored it indoors, just waiting for when the captain would plan his trip to Hays. He'd politely declined because he never let it out of his sight for long, but the man blurted out something else, at which Van Vedic asked him if he were hard of hearing.

"I will bring it back here to you if and when I'm ready to do the train, but some of the vets said they'd drive the deuce to Hays, Kansas, no sweat. It's a brand new truck and runs great, but I have my doubts. I think the train idea is the best."

"Captain, I myself have ridden the exact route you're planning from Aztec over the mountains to Walsenburg; it's a beautiful ride that way, and you'll have to change trains, but that's easy. Slow and steady up and over the pass and downhill from there. I went down the line from Hays another hundred more miles to Topeka where the Atchison Topeka and the Santa Fe railroad have many of their headquarters. We built the train engines there. I'd say you'll be in Hays within twenty-four hours of leaving here."

It was all good to know and would be good food for thought as he rolled out of town a few days later. He was absolutely thrilled with these new neighbors and might have seen practically every single one of them in his brief first visit.

CHAPTER FIVE

RESUPPLIES IN AZTEC

In early October, Van Vedic made his return trip to Aztec, Sarge riding shotgun, with no trailer in tow. The whole time, he was whistling the song of the Volga boatmen, and then he sang the chorus with his full-throat baritone, probably the first time Russian had ever been sung in New Mexico. Going downhill most of the time in such a beast of a truck was invigorating; it got him carried away on a few stretches, because he felt like he was at the helm of *Vanessa* and was riding the waves once again.

Hopefully, he'd have a shed full of supplies already collected by his gold-miner friend and an eager mercantile owner with his order pad ready. The supplies list was long—everything from shovels and rakes to nails and rope, every square inch of tarp that wasn't being used—and he planned on having a wonderful time in the quiet little town and was looking forward to the full-course dinners. A side street just off their main street was lined with beautiful cottonwood trees—a well-maintained gravel road—and a church of one denomination or another on every corner.

His favorite and oldest was Saint Joseph's Catholic on the very first corner. They did the Mass inside that catholic church just like they did it everywhere else he'd ever been, just like Jude would have done it, and they had been doing it there since the first settlers arrived a hundred years before.

He found a seat near the back for the Sunday Mass, and while praying, a memory of another Saint Joseph's Church on the other side of the world suddenly flooded his mind—the image of him and his father whipping the horses and running over the dogs that got in the way as they bounced across the bridge, going as fast as he had ever gone.

While all the priests and parishioners were loading the wagon on Saint Joseph's south side that morning, the first shots from the ridgeline slammed into the church's north side. The barbarians were shooting from a thousand yards away and were frustrated, blocked by the river that wouldn't let them get closer. There was still time to finish loading the wagon, but not much, and it wouldn't be long till the gypsy gang would surround the town and start the squeeze. They were insane and came from deep in the outback; primitive and savage people, including their women and children. The village people wouldn't leave; they just wouldn't move, didn't know where to go, but decided to fight to the very last man, his woman, and their children. The villagers' weapons were old, but there were lots of them, plenty of ammunition, and even though they were seldom used, except for hunting, they were deadly to a few hundred yards downrange.

More than likely, his were the only eyes in the church that had ever seen such a thing, his ears had heard that kind of screaming when he was just a boy, and he knew the people around him had never known such horror. It had been all around him from his earliest days and was still going on in Russia. When the priest ended his Mass by saying, "Peace be with you," the captain heard an echo in his ears. "Prepare for a great adventure, my son. Don't worry, be happy."

He covered his face with the prayer book and whispered into the binding, "I will, I don't, and I am."

The Animas River flows southerly out of the Durango area down a beautiful valley until it intersects with the San Juan River on Farmington's western edge. The train tracks follow the river for the most part, and irrigation ditches pull out water anytime the river bends, on both sides, wherever possible. Those ditches turned that entire valley into a never-ending apple orchard way past Farmington.

A bed and breakfast triplex had caught his eye the first time through, managed by a beautiful hostess who promised the man that they had a most unique cottage with a bed big enough for a man like him and a tub to match if he were interested in such things. He was highly interested.

The woman looked at the captain and said, "Everything seems to have been made for you!"

It was made for Melania, her mom, by her dad, Olaf, when there weren't any little Olafs, but everything changed in half a dozen years, so they moved on down the road into a warehouse they turned into their home. She said they served a breakfast he wouldn't forget, and they became good friends while she cut his hair and beard, called him handsome, and even did his nails, which were almost an adventure all by themselves.

Her name was Vannie, a nickname for the obvious, a shortened version of the most important name in Van Vedic's world of names. Her name might have been shortened, but Vannie wasn't. Not only was she a beautiful, full-figured woman, but she carried it on a six-foot-two frame, with long muscular arms, and only forty-nine healthy years old. The woman had a reputation in the community as a person one should be cautiously polite around, and most folks found her somewhat intimidating; they always had.

There were at least half a dozen stories that the community couldn't forget. Anytime they talked about her at the bridge tables or along the bar at the Hi-Way Saloon, those stories were told repeatedly by her adoring family and friends. Everyone had their favorite. Everyone had a 'best story' and loved it more so than all the others, which would be why they told it all the time. To hell with those sorehead sons-a-bitches and anything they didn't like; most folks didn't care what the soreheads were sore about.

She was born on Christmas Day, and no one could ignore or forget that fact for some reason; it was both Jesus's birthday and Vannie's. In town, the only drugstore actually ordered Christmas cards that said *Merry Christmas and Happy Birthday, Vannie*, sold out by Thanksgiving one year, and never made that mistake again. Many of the cards they sold ended up on Vannie's wall, inside the beauty parlor, because she was so grateful, and it was a tradition to do such things with such things.

She was a Christmas baby girl to the family, Olaf and Melania's gift to each other, their fifth. Her four older siblings started with a set of twins a year older, another brother two years older, and the earliest at three and a half years. All four were big baby boys who ate like horses before they were even five.

When Vanessa arrived that Christmas morning in 1904, with no problems whatsoever, she broke all her brothers' records for length, weight—and gender, in Melania's mind. On page five, those facts were also written down in the *Bible*, with two more daughters added later. Of course, she only broke those records by an inch and a pound or so, but Melania knew that her first perfect daughter had big bones like Olaf, like women back in the old world, the Viking queens. That unrecorded ancient history of her forefathers and Olaf's convinced Melania in her soul that Vanessa would have been one of the chosen ones if she had lived when that dynasty existed. From the beginning, everyone noticed she was the spitting image of her momma, only more prominent; bigger is a better word. As she grew into her teenage years, it became stunningly obvious.

When it came to voting for the most massive guy in the railroad yard, everyone would have voted for Olaf. A sizeable man, six foot five, two-fifty at least, and pleasant as could be. He loved driving the county road maintainer around the community, waving and smiling at every person he saw while doing it. They always waved back and would shout, "Hello, Olaf!" He became the *de facto* road maintenance engineer, worked with the residents on how they wanted their private roads maintained, and usually made them that way. Then they built the gas well north of Aztec and piped it down alongside the rail line, which changed everything when it came to heating Aztec.

That was Olaf's baby—maintaining the main gas line road, understanding the engineering logic the pipeliners used, gravity, where all the shut-off valves were located, the safety locks, and of course, the keys. The earliest settlers had dug the irrigation ditch, and the gas line fit alongside that easement with the road in the middle. They sent the gas line route through the upper edge of town, set locations for the distribution hubs—and for every ten fans, there was a doubter, people who were afraid of the new science. The city planners managed to think it through pretty well, but there were still frightened people, and the "sore heads" were not one bit happy. This was right up there with the idea of that lightbulb thing. "Pure genius," was one of the critiques in the paper for how it all turned out. A fifteen-mile-long gas pipeline that was far ahead of its time and brought a heating fuel to people in one specific valley that the rest of the rural world could hardly even imagine. Many things were on the verge of changing in the valley, and a new frontier was waiting to be invented, discovered, and created. Oil and natural gas were down there deep in the earth, coming up out of the ground by themselves in places, and certain men could feel it, smell it, taste it, and be able to kill, in some cases, for the mineral rights.

Olaf went from being a young part-time road maintainer to city maintenance supervisor and, finally, the mayor. Even then, he still drove the blade. The entire time he was doing all that, he was also the yard maintenance supervisor for the train yard and always made a nice paycheck when many other folks didn't. He told everyone he met, "I can shave the hair off a gnat's ass with a nine-foot steel blade!" It was a response to a question he forced you to ask him: Why would you do that? Because he always reached out his hand to everyone he met and said, "Hello. I'm Olaf. Do you know how close I can get?" Of course, everyone would always say, "No, Olaf, how close can you get?"

Believe it or not, that was how he walked around the town one week before the election, introducing himself to everyone who already knew him and had already heard the question at least a dozen times in their lives. He was running for mayor and swept the election, with almost one hundred percent of the men voting for him.

These five guys scattered throughout town were just regular a-holes, always had a bone to pick about something, and had pissed and moaned their way onto everyone's shit list of disliked neighbors.

No one knew why they lived there. These sorehead sons-a-bitches didn't like Olaf because of his name, didn't like the idea of a man turning a warehouse into his home, didn't like Olaf's boys and those crazy daughters of his always racing through the streets of Aztec on their horses. However, there was one thing about Olaf that the sore heads didn't mind, never mentioned it when they were bitchin' about something concerning Olaf, and that was the fact that he had brought Melania to Aztec.

All in all, that family overwhelmed their surroundings, built their apple orchards outside of town along the river, survived the First World War, the Roaring Twenties—an era which never actually happened in Aztec—and succeeded in raising seven kids into the Great Depression.

Anyone who thought that was easy hadn't ever tried it and might be considered insane or from another planet for even suggesting such a stupid thought. The truth was it did happen in tough times, there, along the Animas. In Aztec, everyone got fed year in and year out; everyone helped take care of each other, family or not. As a general rule, everybody survived. There were exceptions, but that's just Nature's way. The Great Depression was a whole different ball game from the Roaring Twenties, and it, in fact, did find Aztec. The Great Depression found almost everyone—not everyone, but almost everyone—and in those times, it was all about what you could do with what you had. Olaf and Melania held their own, and so did their kids.

Then all hell broke loose. World War Two might have started in 1939 when Germany invaded Austria and Czechoslovakia, the 'Sudetenland,' but that's debatable. In early March 1939, the German army crossed over that border with Czechoslovakia like the plague, and among other things, they emptied Saint Michael's Catholic University and Seminary. The Germans ordered all of Saint Michael's inhabitants out of their homes and told them to pack a small suitcase with their most treasured things. They then force-marched the whole bunch of clerics, priests, seminarians, nuns, monks, cooks—everyone there, young and old—down their rural country road to doomsday, down to the railyards in a small village at the bottom of the valley. All those people were force-marched, driven, shot, and beaten almost every inch of the way like garbage-pit dogs. Those who survived the death march were crammed into cattle cars waiting at a railway station a few miles from the seminary, then transported like pigs and cattle to the Theresienstadt Reeducation, Work, and Concentration Camp a hundred miles back along the border due west. The story of Jude began that day.

CHAPTER SIX

VANNIE

The Great Depression began when people started jumping out of windows on Wall Street in 1929. The premature end to the Roaring Twenties made the entire world miserable in a month or less. In Russia, the communists were almost finished burning down all the churches while reorganizing the peasants into a viable society called communism. The collapse of nearly everything took a while to work its way around the world, but it did, making the 1930s a decade to forget. Eventually, the conditions were perfect for the Second World War, which sent people in other directions and seemed to highlight the Great Depression. World War II introduced parts of the world to a time with little precedent.

The First World War, sometimes referred to as the war to end all wars, brought terrible death and destruction for all of central Europe and a great loss of life, but it ended in 1919 when the planet was treated to a plague that they called the Spanish Flu.

World War Two started twenty years later in '39, was an all-world event, and because of it, a hundred million people died while the world changed and rearranged itself. As all those tribulations swirled through their life and marriage, Olaf and Melania became embedded in Aztec's fabric, this small town in northern New Mexico, evolved into essential personalities of the place, and raised their babies until they all grew up.

When Vannie was nearing eighteen and had turned into a stunning senior in high school, a chip off the old blocks, she led the Tigers to their second straight state basketball title; two undefeated seasons, MVP trophies, along with a wall full of ribbons from local track meets. Vannie was a star, with no doubt about it, and it all came to a crescendo when it was agreed in council that there would be one more game for the community her senior year. Both the Boys' and Girls' State Championship banners would be hoisted to the rafters, side by side, at the same time, before the start of the game. It would be the biggest game in local basketball history, not a seat left in the house, and the very last 1922 game. Small-town America celebrating itself with a parade, a picnic, and a basketball game.

The boys and the girls had won the state championships for their size school and were playing an exhibition game of local talent—two state champions playing standard high school rules for boys in front of a standing-room-only throng. Proud, boisterous, exceptionally loud parents in their standard reserved seats, classmates, siblings, and friends, all screaming their heads off. The cheerleaders and the pep squad were confused, because all of their cheers were for a Tiger, and the court was full of Tigers. The fact of the matter was they loved to cheer and were almost in heaven an hour before tipoff. Parents who had a child on each team were torn by their emotions—whom to cheer for or against—and for most, it was a lot of fun, though deafening, with everyone in silent agreement on the probable outcome. The eleven girls were actually great for girls. They annihilated the boys' B team every year since Vannie was a freshman and slaughtered all the other girl teams in their classification. But all that aside, everyone knew from the start that the boys would win. They were big. Big Bob was six-four, two six-foot-twos, more blazing fast guards than necessary, but all agreed that they would be gentlemen for the entire game and not their usual aggressive selves out on the court.

The boys' coach had his team in conference during practice one afternoon and told them to sit down at center court and take a break. The gym was moderately private and a good time for both coaches to give their perspectives on the upcoming event. They always did this center-court huddle and talked about their next game, the rules, the game plan, and all sorts of subjects. There were unwritten rules in this particular case, because it was against the girls this time. The young men all sat around in a circle and listened to the speech about how they should treat girls. They knew the names of every girl on the other team; they had all grown up together, and some even had sisters over there.

Each and every young man on the varsity had been on the B team no less than two years before, three as recently as last year, and none could forget that. When they were all on the B team, the practice was not any fun at all because they had to play the girls' varsity. Sometimes three times a week, for an hour, for three years now, where Vannie was the center for the girls. Her two best friends were six-foot-tall forwards on either side, and they seemed to play like one huge, beautiful, muscular female with a ponytail. The boys never spoke about it publicly, didn't record those hours in their diaries, but had been known to cry in front of their parents because their practices were so stressful. It was difficult for their parents as well, who tried to explain to the boys' B-team coach that the girls were beating them up and making them cry. After fifteen minutes of pep talk, both coaches tried to lift their spirits and get them in the mood. Then, it was time for questions. Silence in the gym as the players traded glances; the pecking order was relatively simple and ended up with Big Bob taking his feet, two appendages that didn't get very far off the ground or propel him forward or backward very fast. He slowly rubbed his hands together, fanned through his teammates' humbled eyes, and asked only a short question of his coach.

"Coach. What about Vannie?"

Vannie seemed to be the only reason Big Bob wouldn't play ball on the outdoor court at the Boys' and Girls' Club. He would go watch, but he wouldn't play, refused to ever again be stuffed in public by a big girl. She was always there with her friends, and the females had overruled the rule that suggested girls couldn't play in the pick-up games. It was just like playing pool; anybody could play pool, so why not basketball? The winners stayed on the court, three on three, with Vannie's team consistently winning. Next, the boys made a rule that there couldn't be three girls on a pick-up team, then that a team could only win three times in a row, all sorts of new regulations, but they never took their balls and went home; it was plenty fun just watching her play and beating up on their friends.

The community prepared for the weekend extravaganza with Thanksgiving banners and newspaper stories, including a Thanksgiving parade, four carnival rides in the train yard, and then the basketball game in the newly remodeled gymnasium. The game was a sell-out, breaking records for almost everything that had a history, including a live radio broadcast.

Late in the fourth quarter, with the girls up by a dozen, Vannie stole the ball and raced to the other end for an uncontested attempt at a dunk—salt in the wounds, if successful, for certain things said before the game. Her fans, coaches, parents, and everyone who had ever watched her play the game had been begging her to try just once. Begged her, "Please, see if you can hold the ball that long and do something no one in that high school has ever done before," not even her brothers. Instead, she insisted on never missing a lay-up, loved the roll-over-the-rim type points, had stolen the ball ten times in every game she ever played in, had practiced this approach a thousand times, and it was frustrating for everyone to watch her always lay it up.

Everyone who studied her game from the bleachers could feel it, could count her steps and hoped beyond hope to someday see her vault off that floor like she did for a rebound, just once, for that elusive dunk that would live in infamy. Vannie shot free throws like an assassin and usually scored half her team's points with a gaggle of assists. Some of her fans knew she could do it, and in her soul, she knew she could too. It was now or never. There would never be another game like this, never a crowd again like the one she was hearing, and she wasn't afraid to fail in front of her father.

Olaf had told her he thought she could do it with her right hand if she could learn how to handle the ball when her standing vertical leap convinced him of that. In that gym that they practically lived in was a two-foot-wide board, twelve feet tall, a ruler in inches that tested such a thing; only the boys ever did it in public. One night after practice in Vannie's junior year, she and her father stood alongside that wall. He challenged her to do it three times to the best of her ability and mark the board with her chalked fingerprints. Afterward, while waiting for their horses, sitting on the steps to the gym, he took her hands and said she could touch the moon if she wanted. Her last effort had been two chalked fingertips fourteen inches down from the top, and now they both knew.

Her stride was perfect, the distance unobstructed; she saw the launch spot, the rim, that ritual she practiced in the driveway when absolutely no one else was around. In her heart, she knew that since she could do it in the dirt in the dark, she could do it on the wood for sure.

Unfortunately, the four bolts holding the rim to the backboard didn't know what was coming. She hit the spot with her right tennie, launched herself with all her might, raised that right arm with that ball balanced on her fingertips, and cleared the rim by a foot. She turned the ball over, pushed it through, ran out of room up there, and her right-hand fingers grabbed the edge of the rim in self-defense. The rule book called it hanging on the rim, which in this case resulted in the entire assembly bursting out of the backboard in an explosion of round steel, nuts, bolts, and cotton netting still holding the ball, lying in a mess on the floor.

The game was over, and she became an instant legend, was featured in a sports magazine article out of New York City and ended what was to be a traditional event that would never be held again.

Twelve years later, in 1934, she punched to death a man who was trying to rape her, only hitting him twice in the face. He died naked on the floor. Neighbors and tenants in the boarding house had heard her screams, raced to the sounds from every direction ahead of the police, and came upon the scene. One man was dead, and the other was cowering in a corner with a broken jaw. Two drunken fools, hobos headed north, who should have never got off the train.

In 1940, she enlisted in the navy as a nurse aid and came home as a survivor after being captured by the Japanese in the Philippines and held in a POW camp for eleven months. Upon returning and after recuperating, she came home to Aztec. She purchased all her family buildings, including the oldest motel in town, a restaurant, a package liquor store with a bar, and three side houses—one for herself and her dogs, one for a beauty salon, and a unique cottage for tall people.

There had been times in the woman's life when she never thought she'd see the streets of Aztec again, and the memory of that POW camp would prove to be the hallmark year of her life. Nothing she would ever do for the rest of her years would compare to that time, and few would hear her story, because she found it awfully hard to tell. Way too hard to relive such horror and terror, like a black blanket there in her memory. She could go around it back in time before her capture, but she had difficulty pulling back that shade from that window. Few in Aztec were such confidants that she would confide in them the details of her time in hell. Seldom—as in rarely—did she talk about that place and those times in any great detail, but everyone she knew was aware that she had been there and had lived through it.

She was almost fifty now, lived alone, and sometimes had trouble sleeping through the night. Those ropes around her neck and wrists had left marks on her mind she could never scrub off. She might not ever lie with a man again no matter what they offered, because she had been raped a thousand times and torn apart.

She was now shackled with the memory, the utter distress, the trauma, long after the fact, and no one really knew her pain. Her dogs would be terrified at night when she bolted awake, reaching out to stop something, screaming at the closet, and still bleeding from wounds you couldn't see.

One morning, a little before four, she started screaming from her bedroom, sound asleep, reliving one of her nightmares and waking a dozen patrons in the corner boarding house.

"STOP ... STOP ... NOOOOOO ... STOP. STOP."

The people gathered there on the corner, looking towards her cottage and wanting to do something, get closer and help her somehow, but her sister came out the front door and stood on the porch. She'd brought her fingers up to her lips, wiped away tears, and said to the witnesses, "My sister was having a nightmare, which happens less frequently these days, but that was all it was. Sorry to have woken you all. Please keep this to yourselves and keep her in your prayers."

Vannie's sister Janie had heard those screams before, ever since she'd come home some six years earlier. Like everything else, time was healing Vannie's wounds, and the nightmares came not all that often anymore, but back in those early days, it was her every-night horror. The place she revisited was filled with screams, pleadings to stop, and that long, long, agonizing *nooooooooooooo*. Over and over, *nooooooooooooo, nooooooooooo, noooooooo, nooooo, nooo, no.*

Janie managed the boarding house and frequently watched over her sister at night. She would quietly slip into her sister's room after she fell asleep, snuggle into a chair in the corner, wrap herself in a blanket, and stay there all night long. She would sit and watch and listen to the most beautiful woman she had ever known after their mother, a hero who went to some hellhole every night in her dreams.

When Vannie finally came home to Aztec after the extended hospital stay, after all the surgeries and the rehabilitation, after all the ceremonies, including the White House dinners, she slept every day for eighteen hours, a practice that went on for months. She rarely opened up to anyone, couldn't do it for her sake and theirs, but Janie was different—the first sister, one of a small group who had heard her personal recollections of a day in the life of Vannie, one day by the pole... one of the hundreds of days on the end of a rope.

Vannie gave her family and close friends the details concerning one of her days by the pole, knew precisely to the inch how long the rope was, and had been raped unconscious until they thought the creature was dead. Her sister had been sitting there listening, crying as usual at just the thought of what had happened to Vannie, when she fainted out of sight at her end of the table. One moment Janie was sitting there, crying, trying to imagine the scene being depicted, and the next, she was gone, disappeared into a heap under the table. As she was nurtured back to consciousness, she started to cry even harder and begged Vannie to never talk about it again. She didn't want to know any more of the details—no one would. When that woman realized what her older sister had been through, she went mute and couldn't speak if those thoughts crossed her mind. The agony from knowing those stories would doom her to tears for hours. So true! She simply couldn't talk to anyone about her anguish, and every time she tried to say anything, she cried aloud, "Nooo, nooo!"

Vannie finally relented to her family, who begged her to "Open up, please. Tell us what happened," and so she decided to tell them some of the details of her captivity. Still, she wasn't ready for what happened to her siblings, for some of their immediate reactions—the haunted eyes, the instant tears, and the fainting. Her brothers became furious.

On the fourth of July, the entire family gathered for a celebration—a cowboy barbeque—back behind the cottages, with the understanding that Vannie would talk about her captivity, clear up some of the falsehoods and just talk about it with her people. It was time. They had brought the magazines, had all the pictures, and said they were ready if she was ready to talk about 1944. All of her brothers and sisters brought their families, along with a few necessary friends and uncles, to the barbeque, and afterward, they sat around the two fire pits under a full moon, adults only, and listened to stories.

Her favorite uncle—who wasn't really her uncle; more like her father's best friend but a highly decorated, disabled, army veteran—started off the gathering by telling one of his many famous "war stories." He started his second five-minute story with the image of war-hardened infantry storming a beachhead and shouting at the forest, "WE'RE HERE FOR OUR NURSES!" Next, he told how men would shout out, "That's for the nurses," when a Jap bunker collapsed or one got blown to bits. At the time, he didn't know one of them was Vannie, only knew the story of what the Japs did to some USA nurses. His recovery had taken three years, and finally, in 1948, his wife had their first son.

He was the sort of storyteller who could get people's attention and keep it, wasn't afraid to talk out loud about the South Pacific, and wasn't one bit ready to forgive the Japs for what they did and the horrific ways they did it. He saw all the beaches, and stormed ashore on almost every island, including Okinawa, where he lost his portside eye, the ear behind it, his left hand, and earned the Silver Star. His chest was plastered with medals, and when he was the guest speaker at the VFW, there wouldn't be enough room in the place for all the guests.

Vannie's siblings learned that night how the Jap soldiers had raped her every day, nonstop, tied to a pole, and finally, the little men ran away when the army came over the hills behind their camp. The soldiers filmed the rescue, went in fighting hard, and killed the enemy who were fleeing into the foothills. Vannie was one of eight women who were all tied around the neck with a rope, naked, filthy, wounded, each one tethered to a pole in front of a grass hut and evidently left to die as the Japanese fled the invasion.

Explaining to her brothers and sisters and some friends her thoughts when the soldiers drew close, trying to put into words what she felt when she saw them taking her picture—which became one of the Pulitzer photos from the war—to say the least, was terribly hard to do. The magazines' pages were full of all the other pictures besides Vannie's. Many others were besides it, even more horrible in some cases, but that look in her eyes melted the whole world's heart.

"What was I thinking...? I thought that I was going to live, maybe, unless they were monsters. I was having a hard time seeing right then. They learned immediately that we were US Army nurses. Everyone was crying as they untied us... grown men crying hard. 'They're not monsters.' That's what I thought. That's what I instantly realized. These men weren't monsters."

Vannie was only getting started, beginning her story with a jungle sunrise, still early in her day, and being raped before she even had a cup of water. She was in a trance as she talked and found herself repeating almost verbatim the stories she told the doctors and nurses at the hospital, those evenings when all the ladies sat through counseling together. Each woman had been tied around the neck with one end of a fifteen-foot rope tied to a bamboo post, each had a long grass mat, they ate everything that was poured into their bowls, and each was raped throughout the day and night for half a year. They all had the same stories, shared the same experiences repeatedly, knew the same men, talked to each other in whispers whenever they could, and shared a spot in hell together.

The entire story would live in infamy as one of World War Two's great miracles—that all eight women were alive when rescued. All eight survived, were very fragile for the longest time through their recoveries, and then the heroes went home. Their annual reunion was becoming one of their most cherished personal experience and still a highly publicized public event. None of the ladies were interested in the publicity anymore, and hard as it was to do, they tried to have that day together without any of the rest of the world finding out. In their case, they were not trying to re-live a period of time; they were celebrating the miracle that they'd survived. Superwomen, in a sense, are survivors of a great trial that only they could fathom together.

The pictures of that scene were initially displayed to the public from one of the distant snapshots, with no names, just pictures of US nurses savaged by our enemy, raped, and then left to be eaten by the beasts of the jungle. It had a profound effect on the audience, and as time went on and the story developed, the pictures became more exact, more up close and personal, with names, and rank, and hometown.

In the most widespread of all the pictures, there was one where Vannie was on her knees, her right side pressed against the side of an eight-foot-tall six-inch-thick bamboo pole buried in the ground. She had her head pressed against the pole, her arms around it, with an ugly, tattered rope around her neck and shoulders. It looked like the creature in the picture was using the excess cord to keep herself warm. She stared at the camera with the eyes of a survivor, a war hero; a once-in-a-lifetime photograph for the cameraman, and a Pulitzer Prize moment. She was primarily unidentifiable at the time, but that changed. It immortalized the woman in the eyes of the world for a time as her face and story filled up many a page in many a magazine, but in the end, she still went home to Aztec and started her life all over. With that fame came a burning desire in her subconscious to disappear from that world she had stumbled into, take care of her properties, cut hair in her salon, or supervise and cook in the restaurant. That was all she wanted to do.

It was a place she went back to very begrudging every now and then in her sleep, in those nightmares. Janie was in her chair, pale and shaking, crying on the magazine page, the one showing her older sister tied to a pole in the jungle.

The amount of love from her sister's broken heart was reward enough for the pain Vannie had suffered, knowing that someone loved her so much. When that evening was over, she thought that maybe she wouldn't ever have to do that again, but in fact, she felt good about having done it, and so did everyone else, even Janie. Vannie's captivity and torture would be her cross to bear, true enough, but people needed to know her feelings; she had a story to tell and could get better at telling it if there was more to it, perhaps.

One question created during her recovery was why she was still alive, that last day she had been saved? So close to being thrown over the cliff, dead and looking every bit like she was, yet she wasn't. Twenty-four hours or less to live, one more night, and they found her right before she would have died. There had to be a reason. Why not become a storyteller? Go out and tell the world the story of Vannie; try not to let them forget.

It seemed she would grow old and live alone unless the right man came along who could understand. She'd know him when and if she ever met him, would see it by the look in his eyes.

One fine day, Vincent Van Vedic walked into the boarding house, looking for a place to call home for a few days. He was dropped off near the front steps of the tallest buildings in town—not counting church steeples—and was met at the door by a damsel named Janie.

"So, what can I do for you, my captain?"

She smiled a beauty from her side of the counter at the

biggest man she'd ever seen. Even bigger than her daddy. Not only did she know who he was, but she also knew that he had been guided her way by the mayor himself and was prewarned to be ready.

He was wearing the most giant pair of boots the family at Candy Leather and Boots had ever made. There were no pictures of such a creation in the how-to guide, except for the notion that barefoot measurements were most important; each foot separately, and then follow the instructions according to the upsize chart. Old man Candy handled this customer personally while his entire staff watched the measuring procedures from different angles in the store and saw once again how Jack 'Candyman' Candy took care of customers, which was why his business did so well. While they were doing an inventory of the captain's feet, he suggested that Candy take notes, because if the boots carried the load, Van Vedic would need two more pairs.

The same held true for his cowboy hat. When you put it all together and stood him upright, most folks down below didn't know how to keep their head if he was up close and personal.

"I need a larger than normal bed for a starter, prefer high headers on doorways, eight feet or so, more than normal, and must have a larger than normal bathtub. You got something like that?"

"Not down here on the first floor."

"Okay, young lady, how about the second or third floors?"

"I'm sorry, Captain, but you've outgrown our stairs." And she purred that smile again. "However, we have a unique two-bedroom cottage that was made just for you. It's a bit more expensive, just up the street a way. I'll take you there this very minute if you are interested."

"Big bed, high doorways, and a horse trough?"

She smiled and nodded a yes.

The boarding house and motel took up the entire corner at the end of Main Street, with a series of storefronts, a restaurant, and three separate dwellings. He was introduced to the hair, beard, and whatever salon for a reasonable price from the owner herself, and an excellent restaurant fifty steps away from his porch. Janie opened the unlocked door and showed her captain Olaf and Melania's original home. Nowadays, she often rented it to groups passing through, honeymooners, government lawyers, three or four folks at a time. It was immaculate, did indeed have high doorway frames, and the bathroom was perfect. It was more than he needed, and not only that, but it also had a fenced yard for the dog and a big enough parking space for the deuce.

He complained about his hair and beard during the tour, and Janie suggested he stop at Vannie's Hair Salon. He felt like a hooligan, needed that bath, needed his whole head area worked on, and after his haircut and shave, his barber handed him her mirror and asked what he thought of her work. The captain held the mirror at different angles, thinking that he hadn't seen the top of his head in years. He hardly ever looked at himself in mirrors, unless he was shaving, and liked himself, liked how he looked. For the most part, he had asked for the hair to be short and the beard to be gone, and he found them both all over the floor when their eyes met in the mirror. Hers were emerald green, and his were the ones she had been looking for, simple as that; it's in the eyes. That look seemed to bond them together in that instant.

For several days, they met each other regularly, talked about all sorts of things, and might have fallen in love. It was an incredible moment when the captain told her the story that Jude had told Patton, which tore the general's heart apart, and talked about a horror that was almost too terrible to believe. The captain asked for her permission to tell it, and told her he knew a story that might help her with her extended trauma; that it would hurt her soul badly to hear it but do her good. Still, usually, especially in the past, the story had helped people understand how and why that monster out there had found them—found her, and so many others. They were having coffee in his rental, her parents' house from once upon a time, and enjoying each other's company. He needed her to trust him. He was actually filling up Olaf's favorite chair, the one he'd sat in the very day he died, while Vannie sat on the floor by the fireplace, remembering her parents. She looked over at the storyteller, smiled the smile of the month, and told him he could tell her anything he wished.

Sure enough, the story of Jude brought her to tears, but within hours she opened the doors of her memory to a man who had been born to listen to her story. She told him all about her time in hell, a story that complemented Jude's, and about her personal Theresienstadt that broke the captain's heart. Then, she took his hands away from his face and looked into the eyes of a man of the world, a seemingly gentle giant who had killed almost a hundred men in his life—a truth she didn't know quite yet. Two pairs of eyes met that night, and the eyes in the man were round and mad, a look she had seen in good men's eyes before but never quite so close.

CHAPTER SEVEN

WELSEY BLACK

The deuce was made for a man his size, an attraction all by itself, and when Van Vedic rolled away, the green monster was heavily loaded with supplies for the winter and orders for more of this, that, and the other on different salesmen's desks. He spent a lot of money in a town that needed it, never quibbled about the price for things, nor the nickname the locals gave him, of Captain. A few of the merchants agreed to collate their orders and then deliver it all to Gomez's backyard.

The first time through, Vincent met a miner and his wife who worked a minimal gold mine part-time up above Silverton in Colorado, two people who seemed to know everything about packing horses into the high country, which was evidently a challenging way to make a dollar. They had what was commonly referred to as "gold fever," couldn't talk about anything else, and showed everyone the golf ball-size nugget they owned that they had found near their claim and where there were hundreds more, they hoped. They would spend the winter preparing for the spring and planned to ascend that mountain as soon as possible, a challenging and expensive way to spend every dollar one might have, which seemed to be where they were financially.

Van Vedic had seen that fever before, in the Urals back in the thirties. People go one hundred percent stupid over gold. For a brief period, the captain felt like he was their confessor—he and Vannie, his waitress, that is—but when they were finished with their dream, Van Vedic asked the couple to buy everything he could think of in that regard, only this time buy the best and buy it for a big man. His measurements were at the tailor's on Main Street, the money was in the bank, and his new accountant would need receipts and timesheets for all the items on the captain's list.

They had fulfilled their task and found everything they needed to complete Van Vedic's wish and needs list for a trail ride over Wolf Creek in the spring. It even included a new stud-sized saddle for El Bruto and a Winchester Model 80 with a high-powered scope, zeroed in at five hundred yards, and lifetime fishing and hunting licenses in both Colorado and New Mexico. When the New Mexico Fish and Game folks were confronted with the question of issuing a lifetime license for hunting and fishing, they didn't know how to handle it, but they took the five hundred dollars and issued the first one ever; so did Colorado.

What had started off as just friendly banter in Vannie's breakfast parlor turned the miners into supply clerks for the next few months. Both husband and wife now had an income, had the assignment to collect everything Van Vedic had ordered from all the stores, pay the bills, keep good records, and he'd be back in two months to get it all. They even rented a garage to put it in.

One afternoon, the captain found his favorite bench that looked out over the beautiful Animas River on the edge of town when a familiar face came up and told him to slide over a bit. He made more than enough room for the former sorehead who just sat there at first with an ear-to-ear smile. But he seemed different, was different, and needed the captain's ear.

"Captain."

"Welsey."

"You remember my name?"

"Yes, sir. Welsey Black."

"Captain, I have to apologize for how I behaved that day we met, the day that changed my life, so help me God. I looked up after the longest time, and you were gone. I have never cried like that in my life, never. Even the police stopped to see what was the matter with me, but I couldn't talk, and they took me home. I never cried like that, not even when my dog died. I can repeat everything you said to me just in case you forgot, every word you said, that story, the story of Jude. I have it memorized. Why?"

"Welsey, my friend, I think we were destined to meet on that bench a little while back..."

"AUGUST FIFTH, FOUR THIRTY-SEVEN IN THE AFTERNOON, 1953!"

The janitor, Mr. Black, had jumped to his feet, shouting the words out loud and seemingly holding some invisible round thing, like a watermelon, and he was looking at it, shaking it. Then he shyly sat back down.

"Something that's happened to me personally, I'd guess a thousand times. People like you I walked into during my travels, people I told the story to simply because we were together, and they and I were guided to that spot. I know all about the tears, seen many tears in my years, and it's good that you cried. A spirit guided General George S. Patton himself—I call Him God, The Grand Organizer Divine—to the edge of the Rock of Gibraltar in

1941, just to hear the story of Jude from Jude, and he cried and cried after he heard it. He was guided there, and Jude and I were guided there. When George heard that story from Jude himself, I saw it on the beach, saw it happen a few more times after that, and saw the general cry like a little girl every single time. That was Thanksgiving back in '41, and then he went and helped win and end the war. He led the way to prevent doomsday and told the story of Jude to his fellow senior officers and staff whenever it was appropriate. As for me, I will only note that I also cried every time I heard it until I started telling it and then started watching other people cry. I know exactly what you heard, and I know exactly why you cried. One good way to quit crying is to become a storyteller."

Black began to ramble, "I haven't walked down to this end of town in a long time, and I started feeling it about noon; I guess something was lifting me, making me walk this way, not my normal way, and lo and behold, guess what? Here you are, taking up the whole bench as usual, and I have thought of nothing but you and that story you told me since the day you did. Captain, I have it memorized, a fourteen-minute-and-twenty-eight-second story, a story I only heard once, and now I record it every day, and it never changes. I don't read it; I just say it, turn on the recorder, and it's always the same. That story I heard from you, and now, today, and just like yesterday, I don't know what to do with myself."

"It appears you're not a sorehead anymore."

"Good God, NO! I even went to the two signs out on the ends of town, you know the ones—'Welcome to Aztec. 1,953 friendly people and five old soreheads.' I tried to change the five to a four in the dark of night, but now it looks like a zero. So I confess to you about the vandalism, you and only you. Something had to be done, so I admit I did it. All I had was my old Boy Scout knife and a big stick. You understand why I did it? Please tell me you do."

"I do."

Van Vedic looked down at Welsey, who seemed anxious for direction; you could see it in his pleading eyes that he couldn't wait to hear more besides two words so Vincent teased him with a question.

"What would happen if you told this story you now know to the other four soreheads? You know who they are, don't you? Think you could do that? Think you could tell them the story, just like you speak it into a microphone hooked to a tape recorder machine? Tell each remaining sorehead the story as you know it. Go find them and see what happens, help them understand there's no point in not being happy in this life if possible, and help them stop worrying about it all. 'Don't worry, be happy,' that's what Jude always said. There is nothing wrong with zero soreheads, and then, who knows what's after that?"

With that last encounter satisfied, Captain Vincent Van Vedic begged a goodbye from Welsey and walked back to the restaurant, anticipating the huevos rancheros the way Vannie did it. He had the habit of recalling a fond memory from the boat trip any time he was walking, thinking along the way about those same kinds of encounters when he toured the Caribbean back in '42. Remembering all those previous Welseys who showed up on those islands, found those gazebos, those shelters, those picnic tables not far from where he had berthed the *Vanessa*, people who didn't know why they were there until Van Vedic told them the story. Then they became storytellers too, people who understood and spread the story of Jude, just like Welsey would end up doing with the revised version. The "Don't worry, be happy" version.

CHAPTER EIGHT

SEEING THE BLUE LIGHTS

It took Rahellio a mental minute to prepare for the trip after Van Vedic said it was a go, a man who usually had other things to do in the fall besides riding horseback into the San Juan River Canyon looking for the "blue lights." His mortician business was moderately successful primarily because no one else wanted to do it or knew how. Besides all that, he sang and played a tear-jerking Mexican guitar with the best of them and was usually readily available, start to finish, since that's the way death seems to demand it, and he knew it. There is only so much time for funeral services in the rural areas of the world, with Arboles, Colorado, being as rural as rural gets. A territory entertaining the angel of death flowing over the valley every so often and usually coming as either a big surprise that generally changes everything or as no surprise at all, which also causes changes. The ends seemed to come in threes, he felt, and he didn't get all the business or even wanted it, for that matter. He and the local priests had their records, when and what happened to their clients, and most importantly, what cemetery or family plot the body rested in, just in case anyone ever cared again in, say, twenty, fifty, or a hundred years.

While considering everything necessary for this venture, one of his many prayers was that no one would need him to take care of their body, dig that grave, and sing those songs anywhere near Arboles until after Thanksgiving, at least. There was a good reason why there weren't any horse trails down in the center of the canyon. It might take weeks to map and travel up and back from any ledge near Van Vedic's vantage point. The mortician hoped it was possible to get down near the river from a few spots up by Arboles, but it wasn't a tourist trap, seldom attracted anglers, and few folks did it twice. The guitar player fervently knew that none of his old fishing caballeros would ever again pick the place for anything after having bothered once.

"Why in the world would anyone want to go down inside there? I can't imagine being a wild river mapper, if there is such an occupation, and I hate big rocks!"

He explained all that to Van Vedic, repeatedly, about the stones, the rocks, boulders, the problems the horses would have, the caca campsites... Everything his life had taught him about this valley told him not to go there. He talked about the misery of camping and hiking around in it, fishing in it, chasing cows and sheep in it, that incredible raging torrent in the middle, the never-ending noise, and he belabored in Spanish how impossible this idea was. All of that was in the early evening and the fading light of day. Finally, when he was done with his explanation, he sat down.

The captain was as relaxed as he'd ever been, sitting by the firepit he had built for cooking slabs and watching the "blue light" from the very best eastern vantage point of them all. He became addicted to the sunset in reverse after only one hit. In hindsight, he sometimes wished that he had buried Vanessa on this lookout, but he had put her to rest where he did for an excellent reason, and she was content there in his mind. While the rest of the world was watching the sunset, Van Vedic had become passionate about viewing the blue light far up in the canyon, which came on in a dim blur just after sunset as things got dark. It didn't appear every night, which was always depressing for the stargazer, but when it did, it lasted for an hour sometimes, and there were times when the word blur would have never come to mind; it was more like parallel beams straight up into the heavens until it disappeared or struck a cloud.

El Bruto Whetto stood there behind the fire and focused his huge ears on some sound or vibration he heard that was obviously coming from that source, something men can't understand. Those huge eyes were bigger than usual, concentrated on the blue light, and didn't move much. He didn't even breathe right, with no fussing and snorting until the light faded away. El Bruto was a different horse from what he had been before. He had met the man few horses ever found, and carried the captain like a backpack.

So was Sergeant Stupid. He wasn't near as stupid anymore. He licked El Bruto's front right hoof and then stood in between the horse's front legs with his ears pointed up all during the show, turning his head from side to side the way dogs do when they're adjusting those ears. Every time he had ever gotten near the ton of El Bruto Whetto in the past, his ears went flat against his neck, and he would never take his eyes off that mountain of muscle, especially the front hoofs.

Both of the animals seemed to relish the idea that the day wasn't over just because the sun went down, and in their nature that only they understood, something caused them to consider the blue lights—and those lights did the same thing to the man, times a thousand. Van Vedic noted that they could see what he could see because he noted such things that captured their attention completely, something he had never seen animals do. Their responses seemed to come from their guts, made them un-distractable, caught their full attention and kept it the whole time. The previous week, Vincent described it in his log as a "blue beam straight up into the heavens," wrote it that way and then closed the book.

He felt like he had seen that beam before, like he had felt it, knew what that light would feel like, and somewhere in his subconsciousness, he saw himself from above floating in nothing but light, breathing all right, not hungry or thirsty or aging. Then that flashback was gone, after just a few long seconds, but feeling like a valid memory from a time when time stood still. He now believed and knew it to be true that he had been in such a time, and it hadn't hurt him so far in his life. So that was where he'd gone for ten years—a place where time stopped—and he was then released to continue with life with no explanation for any of it. His was a story that the world knew about, but he hoped the world was forgetting his fifteen minutes of fame times two; he wanted to be done with all that. In the recesses of his mind was the burning desire to remember everything that happened, from floating in the hurricane to seeing the Texas coast, from 1942 to 1953. The lost decade.

The blue lights were invisible through the binoculars, which was incredibly depressing, along with being utterly incomprehensible. Sometimes, to his naked eye, it appeared there were two and even three blue lines of light, strings of it side by side, but when he focused those binoculars on the subject area, he could never find them. There came that moment when he got so flustered trying to understand why they didn't work that he refused, refused, absolutely told his entire body not to participate and demanded that every limb and organ he controlled could not, would not, dare not, including his eyes and fingers, check to see or feel if the lens covers were on for the third time. Finally, in his controlled temper tantrum known only to his pets, with all the demands in place, he lifted the leather strap behind his neck to remove the spyglasses and only briefly, very briefly, glanced at the glass eyes he had always trusted. Sat them down on the ground beside himself, rested his chin on his knuckles, and stared at those blue lights miles away up the canyon floor.

He had requested for Rahellio to plan on spending a few nights at the cabin, as there was some work to be done, but that was just a ruse. There was always work to be done. Still, most of all, he wanted the mortician to see the goal twice—once in the light of day and imagining a fishing venture and then in the light of sunset, where he might see that image far up in the north canyon, after which he could give an opinion. The captain had discovered a gem of a human in Rahellio, a simple countryman, humble in front of God and talented like few others he had ever met.

Rahellio had a notion about life that coincided perfectly and logically with his profound thoughts about death, something only lifelong morticians can fully understand.

"When you're dead, you're dead and you don't even know it! Everyone you knew before you were dead now knows you're dead, but you don't, so don't worry about it. Everything seems to get born, and then it dies; everything except rocks."

In the pre-sunset afternoon, the consummate fisherman got Rahellio going by suggesting that he simply wanted to go fishing down in the canyon, fish the mighty San Juan in its heart, and be able to say he did that someday. Thanks to Ellis, the miner, he now had all the necessary equipment and wondered what

Rahellio thought their chances were of getting to a spot he pointed at the heart of the canyon, five or more miles upstream. He didn't need anything except their opinions—Rahellio's and his son's—and later their vows and promises to be silent about what they might see, with a fair estimate of what he thought their chances might be for getting from here to there. What would it take, how long would it take, and was it even possible?

It was a typical late afternoon glorious sunset on this northern New Mexico plateau when Rahellio, with his son in total agreement, told Van Vedic that they didn't believe it was possible to travel down that river gorge. That area he was pointing at that they could barely see was at least five miles away. That opinion was in the light of sunset, and when that event was said and done for another day, the two morticians turned around on their stumps, away from the sunset, and saw the blue lights for the first time. They now knew why their captain wanted them to be there that night. They could see the lights, see the goal, and now they wanted to get there too, with different reasons. Big eyes, like in white-round, they managed a "What's that," in unison, "Impossible," then they were speechless, and after not exactly a long time, Julio dove off the deep end.

Most adventurers who had any first-hand experience with either edge of the San Juan River in the center of the canyon, the future middle of the imaginary Navajo Lake, either got there on foot or chaotically floated down the torrent in a terrifying life— or maybe death—out-of-control river cruise while never actually seeing the shoreline. A harrowing, screaming, praying, praying some more, hanging on for dear life, eyes closed, crying, more screaming ordeal if there ever was one. It was a terrible waste of money, time… and sometimes life.

·   ·   ·

There was an eccentric river rafting group, an outside group. Weirdos who thought they had to float the San Juan River at least once a year or so in either a twenty-six-foot wooden boat that resembled a Viking War Wagon on shrunk, or their twelve-person rubber raft. Just about everyone preferred the raft, with all the leather oh-shit handles, ores that were tied in place, and the ability to be lashed to the seats of the World War Two standard navy life raft with tiedown ropes and safety belts. It was understood and highlighted in the flyer that it was a BYO situation when it came to flotation devices. BYOLP, a catchy extension of BYO, which meant "bring your own life preserver." Followed by a sub-caption, SWYTYW—"spend what you think you're worth." The group had a few extra preservers, mediums and larges, but those sizes only worked about half the time and had US Navy insignia from World War Two. They were so heavy only an idiot would conclude that they floated.

They chose their words carefully, explaining how their lives might not be fulfilled if they didn't try at least once, and in at least three cases, people died trying to make their lives complete. For most folks, if the adventurer survived the first trip down the San Juan with the High Priest in charge, that was usually enough of that for life. When it was all said and done, not a single first-timer had any intention of ever doing that again on purpose, at least not under that command. As a result, almost every time the rafting company scheduled an adventure, there were extra seats in the float because it was a small group; a half a dozen fanatics along with their supporters (non-rafters) gathered weak-minded cohorts by chanting loudly outside the Aztec City Council room.

"We will drown ourselves in the reservoir, drown ourselves in the reservoir, drown ourselves in the reservoir, yes we will," they shouted while standing on all the handcrafted chairs and benches in the lobby of the council chambers. That chorus went on and on from about 5:45 until 6:10, when the sheriff of San Juan County, two of his deputies, and the police chief entered the room. Then, finally, he interrupted the concert with his traffic whistle—dead silence.

"You people get off the mayor's furniture, or I'LL KILL YA, I promise! Get down, sit down, stay down, and shut the hell up!"

His eyes were bulging out of his face. He stuck his right hip out and up, exposing the revolver, stared at it for at least three seconds, blinked at least five times, and grumbled to his palms, first the left and then the right. He tried to smile, but his lips just wouldn't do it; it felt like his cheeks were in the way. Maybe the back molars were acting up? Once he was sure his face was working again, he lowered the volume and warned the visitors, "There is a hearing we have to have, and we will have no more of you folks' bulllllshieet. Is that understood? I don't believe I've ever met anyone who would stand on a handcrafted leather-covered lobby chair. Now I have. I've always felt that this lobby makes me feel at home, like in my living room."

The protesters had a hard time getting their customers to protest alongside them or even float the river twice, which limited their gatherings and just about everything else they did.

At this last of the well-publicized hearings on whether or not to build the dam, one of their previous daredevil customers, a self-avowed 'beatnik from Qtown' (short for Albuquerque) was waiting on the sidewalk into Aztec City Hall. He wasn't there to protest against the reservoir; he was there to scream at the rafters. He verbally attacked the High Priest of the rafting company as the rafters approached the new City and County Chambers. The latter was sometimes referred to as the rafting company owner. The shouting got the attention of the entire Aztec Police Department, all six of them, along with the sheriff and his deputies. Once again, the highest-paid policeman in San Juan

County found the source of the noise, and as he rounded the corner with his gun drawn, positive there was a murder going on, he found the beatnik's back, which surprised him.

"HEY, YOU! Generally, we just shoot people who shout obscenities on city property!"

There's a great deal missing from the description of what happened next, such as the close proximity of the sheriff's mouth to the beatnik's ear, the accurate measurement of the total surprise from the backside, and, lest we forget, the shrieking volume of the declaration. The beatnik appeared to be standing on a spring, jumping like a cat over the retaining wall and landing in a wild sagebrush garden. Finally, after holstering his weapon and snapping the buckle closed, the sheriff managed an upward curvature of the corners of his mouth that resembled a smile. He told the Albuquerque native the meeting was ready to start and he shouldn't be rolling around in the bushes.

Midway through the meeting, it was the beatnik's turn to make a statement, and so he jumped up, pointing like a madman and screaming at the Aztec City Council that the freak with the really long white beard and the really long white hair on the other side of the room should be charged with attempted murder. The sheriff was getting aroused by the noise.

"Lock him up! Lock him up! They tried to kill me. That demon said the first ride was half price and my dog could go along, but they would have to charge book price every year after that because I'd be back again and again, it was so exciting. He said the thirty-mile experience was similar to the conditions on the Animas in the spring. That's a bald-faced lie! It's like aaah, aaaah, ooaaah, like going over Niagara Falls for three hours, over and over. Like waterskiing behind *Miss Bardahl*. Lock him up! My precious poodle Princess had to be kept on a short leash tied to my leg from the minute we pushed off north of Arboles and then that freak started yelling at me to row harder and harder, faster, screamed at me the whole trip. Then, when the Piedra River merged with the San Juan, all hell broke loose, and it stayed that way till we got a few miles from Bloomfield. Oh, God, you should have been there! We were always going backward over waterfalls, hanging onto the straps for dear life until one of mine snapped and I lifted into the air, both legs above my head. Princess was tied to my left leg but she broke the chain, rose high up out of the raft, the toboggan of death, that floating coffin, until she ran out of leash in the rapids, and I never saw her again! Lock him up! I can't believe I'm alive! Lock him up."

The beatnik from Albuquerque managed to impress none of the council, none of the police, and seemed at least as weird as the High Priest owner of Wolf Creek Water Wafting World. When the project's protesters got into a shouting match with the beatnik, they were separated to opposite sides of the chamber. The beatnik spoke first and seemed to forget what he was talking about there, near the end; he said there was a meditation salon in Qtown called the Purple Turk that he frequented. It was there where he claimed he had been ordered by Mother Nature herself to come to Aztec, float the mighty San Juan for the experience and then write a poem about it for posterity. Worst of all, he couldn't imagine himself talking before the chamber like this and was so excited about being able to scream at the High Priest. And he forgot to bring a copy of his masterpiece. Due to time restraints, he said he would mail everyone a copy and wasn't using his time to sell stuff. Suddenly, the daytime County Court clerk, a horrific bitch named Henrietta, sprang to life and demanded that everyone in the room had to forget they had heard anything about the Purple Turk. It was a den of Satan on Central in that sinful city of Albuquerque. Right there in front of everyone, she scribbled three complete sentences over the logbook and blacked out the entry like the evening had never happened. Then she glared at the beatnik, the infamous Henrietta look, and when the chambers fell quiet, she said, "Too bad about your dog. Your time has expired. Too bad."

The mayor and most of the office staff shivered from head to toe, having felt that glare at many city meetings in the past where the horrific creature would explain an ordinance that prevented an improvement to something, and not only that, but she also even smelled terrible. According to the protocol, with everyone's good health and wellbeing in mind, after his emotional statement, the beatnik was encouraged to have a safe trip back to Albuquerque, be most careful on Highway 44, and they would be praying for him for the next six hours while thanking him for his contribution. Both of his City Police escorts said they heard most of what he had said, especially about following orders from Mother Nature, helped him find his car down by the irrigation ditch, and watched him drive away in the wrong direction. At the same time, they both pissed all over the bumper of the sheriff's car.

He made a U-turn at the dead end, passed back by the Courthouse windows, stopped his car in the street, and screamed at the top of his lungs, "LOCK HIM UP. LOCK HIM UP!" Then he climbed back in and went back home to Central Boulevard in Qtown. The High Priest sported a full white beard to his belly button that he tried to talk through, thick white eyebrows he strained to see through, thick white hair that hung to his belt, and understanding anything he said was almost impossible. It was hard to believe that he didn't have trouble eating or smoking, to say nothing of breathing. After the introduction, he placed his business cards on everyone's desks—a small white card with the Wolf Creek Water Wafting World logo and his phone number. He took the lectern, smashed the back of his hand against the microphone as a test that scared the devil out of everyone, and began his protest.

"Muy busmneess izza aaat snake! Whhee doount neeeuda fuvving yezafour. Whhee doountneeeuda fuvving dhhm."

He scanned the room and realized they weren't offended when he said fuvving twiffe in puhhbee, so he continued with his presentation. Much of it was best described as muffled, and then after almost ten fuvving minutes, he was finally done. While attempting to groom the mayhem just under his chin, one or more of his fingernails on his left hand must have gotten tangled up in there and required his other hand to get things loose. It didn't look right. Plus, he was mumbling.

It was brought to the council's attention that the man's business card had a misprint, that it wasn't wafting, it was rafting, but the High Priest yelled that it was waftin' and not wafting. His tongue seemed to be fighting for a way out, was tangled up in a nest of hairs on his lower right lip, with that being his last hurrah. He stopped on his way out and wrote a note to the council secretary, which he requested she read to the council.

"If nothing else, fix and maintain the road to the damn dam, damn it."

Note: It took a while, but Aztec finally built a paved road to the dam site in the early sixties because of many said suggestions. Aztec received the "All American City!" award because of that accomplishment.

According to Rahellio's records, there were three empty coffins in three different cemeteries, based on the apparent premise that if you fell out of the boat, you were definitely on your own and more than likely finished. Finished rafting, getting to the headwaters where the raft was waiting, finished with everything. It didn't matter how much you may have spent on the life jacket. Before any other clothing, a waterproof plastic bag with all pertinent information about the rafter was taped around the chest with this new-technology gray tape that not even God could cut. The High Priest used it all over the raft, especially on the oh-shit handles. The raging torrent's core was nothing but enormous boulders, massive granite trail blockers one after another, forever, it seemed, all along the edges and out in the middle of the widowmaker. Most rafters had their eyes closed through the rough stuff, never ever let go of the safety handles, and could not have cared less about their personal one.

For those witnesses who happened to have that first-hand knowledge and were sitting in on the hearings in Aztec back in the late forties and early fifties about whether or not to flood the whole thing, almost to a man and one woman, their only question was, "How soon can we get this done?" Everyone who had any of that first-hand knowledge barely filled in the first couple of rows, and almost all of them shared that distant look, the one you see in survivors who had stared death in the face and lived through it and still liked coffee. The list of those who fought the whole issue was small, to say the least, and those who thought the other way were a thousand to one until, finally, everyone was satisfied, and the project was begun.

In the light of sunset, the guitarist estimated that the trip up and back would take at least five days—maybe a week, maybe more, but more than likely they wouldn't get very far to start, especially on horses, and they couldn't do it without horses. He knew Van Vedic had walked the river down to where it merged with the Los Pinos, but still a long way from the future dam site.

The captain knew how difficult that had been with just a dog, especially trying to remember all those dozens of dead ends, those backtracks, even on foot and close to the river. The fishing was excellent, but the ones he caught looked like they had had a rough ride for the last so many miles and probably all their lives. Some seemed so sad that he thought they might be sick, but after rationally thinking it all through, he realized the tears and impact marks on their bodies were from the trout bouncing off rocks in that rampage they lived in. It did not affect their taste in the slightest, and sometimes, it only took three to make a meal. In those calm pools on the edge of the current, it was as if they couldn't wait to be caught and seemed to love feathered hooks that floated. That fishing trip didn't count as the real thing because he was pissed off the whole time about the dead ends, times when he was only twenty or thirty feet from the edge of the river but he couldn't get there. He'd have to turn around and backtrack, find a different way, and it damn sure wasn't easy. Three or four of those in a row will piss a man off but good!

With the sunset just an orange glow on the western horizon behind him, Rahellio stared up into that black canyon and could see the blue light. He wanted with all his might to go there just like the captain did, and so did his son, who almost instantly decided it was the Blessed Mother. In that blue light, the Mother of God was up there in that canyon, and he became highly religious in only a few minutes. He had always been faithful and prayed like a zealot, which sent him over the edge, so to speak, but hopefully not. The young one, who would be best described as rough around the edges, started saying the rosary out loud, real loud, real fast, even had his arms up in the air, and seemed to be upset that his father wouldn't participate. No one could have joined in as his sixty-second rosary sounded and looked like he had lost control of his lips.

"Hail Mary, Holy Mary, Hail Mary, Holy Mary, Hail Mary, Holy Mary..." Basically, one illegal Hail Mary a second with an occasional 'Our Father' (The Lord's Prayer) every ten seconds until he finished his rapid version. His mouth had gone dry, and he was searching for his canteen with both hands, trying to feel for it like a raccoon, without taking his eyes off the blue lights. He was dazed and confused and looked exhausted when it was over, while his father stared at him for a long minute and couldn't believe that his son had shouted the rosary into heaven. His boy appeared to be in la-la land and seemed ready to start walking right then and there, maybe over the cliff, which worried Rahellio and the captain both.

"Julio, sit down and take a drink," Rahellio ordered, and so the young man did, but he didn't look right or left of the blue light. His eyes were glazed. He was seeing a miracle, or so he thought, and no one could talk him out of that explanation. The light was dimming away in the darkness, and they all knew it, glowing for an hour at the most, and then it was gone.

The vision was over, and time for another answer from Rahellio. "Can we do it or not?" he was asked, and while he sat there debating the obvious, his son stood up and started the rosary again in a loud, piercing first soprano. Once the young man was into it, palms to the heavens, there was no point in telling him to stop since he was halfway finished in thirty seconds or less. The fear was that he'd start it again and again and again, so his father got involved.

"Son, sit down and shut up. Didn't your mother tell you that it's a mortal sin to shout the blessed rosary into a canyon just after sundown at the top of your lungs? Huh? What's the matter with you? Everybody knows we don't do that, and I want you to promise me you'll never do that again." The young man was still in a daze but did as he was scolded while his father concentrated his attention on the question.

"Captain, I just honestly can't tell without some recon. The going will be mostly on foot, walking the horses for the most part, dead ends everywhere. It will be mucho, mucho hard for anyone to get to where those lights might be. Much as I want to know myself, very badly, I want to say yes, we can, but maybe not. It's what? Five miles? Impassable, or at least very difficult? Sorry. Sorry. The only way to know for sure is to go there and give it a look."

Van Vedic stared into the fire for the present time while Rahellio kept an eye on his son, stirred the beans, added more wood, and waited for his employer to respond.

"I was thinking I could afford to pay the two of you, each, ten dollars an hour, twenty-four hours a day, just to try for maybe a week or two. What do you think about that?"

"ARE YOU TALKING TWENTY-FOUR SEVEN? We'll leave right now, go home and get our horses. We'll leave tonight for our casa and meet you in the cottonwood glen tomorrow afternoon. I'll bring the Mighty Raton and my hunting dog, FFFffffiittzzzsss. We shall see you tomorrow, my captain. Our lips are sealed."

"No, sir. I was hoping you could bring your horses along with Raton and that dog up here to this very spot. I want them at this fire before we leave. Did you bother to notice the way El Bruto and Sarge paid attention? They both know where we're going; Raton should too."

Two older men who had seen a lot in their lives, seen it all perhaps, and weren't easily fooled, stared out over the river valley and knew what they knew. There were unexplained blue lights far up in that canyon that only honest eyes could interpret and identify, and none of that could be done from long range.

They both knew they had to get near there, wait for sundown each night, and hope they were close, and in that campfire silence, they heard it—a rapid-fire whisper of something resembling heavy breathing over near the bushes. "Hail Mary, Holy Mary, Hail Mary, Holy Mary..."

"His mother prays the rosary at least three times a day! What can I say?"

He and his son would ride their best two trail horses, bring a spare packhorse and Raton, the most enormous, smartest, most mellow mule ever to haul a load, and Fitzz for short, their dog. This camping, fishing, searching trip would commence in a few days. Van Vedic was concerned about the boy, about his version of the Hail Mary, the whole rosary for that matter, so he took him aside, and they had a come-to-Jesus meeting. The captain explained that it very well might be the Blessed Mother, but they had to be sure and reminded him that he had made a vow before the sun went down that he would be silent about what he saw after the land went dark. So, he vowed it again, and he and the captain shook hands on it.

They left the river campground at noon on October 15th, Vincent Van Vedic's birthday, supposedly his sixty-fifth, but he had his doubts about his body being that old. He now believed without a doubt that he had gone down a drain hole in the ocean in a hurricane, went somewhere for ten years, and on July 27th, 1953, he popped back to life off the shores of Corpus Christi, Texas. There were pictures of him that saddened the world in 1942, proved where he was in the end, and there was no way out of the eye of Hurricane #9. That rebirth had happened only a few months ago or so, and now he was where he belonged. Vanessa was where she was supposed to be, and his boat, his other *Vanessa*, was where she would stay until the water rose. He had his land, a horse and a dog, and lots of new friends who didn't seem to know much about his last ten years, nor did they want to. One new friend in particular, whom the captain now knew better than all the others, and for the life of him he couldn't quit thinking about her. The Coast Guard had honored his wish, maintained their Roswell Mode concerning everything about him, and allowed him to tell those he wished where he came from.

CHAPTER NINE

THE MIGHTY RATON

Raton was a magnificent mule, fifteen hundred pounds of gentle, who carried his rack like it wasn't even there, and almost everything they needed was stacked on his back. All the supplies were new—the tents, the bags, and the camping equipment arranged and prepackaged by an old miner named Ellis, whom Van Vedic had met in Aztec and put in charge. He'd told William Ellis to get it all ready, gave him the money, and told him he'd be back in a couple of months. The captain tasked the miner with preparing all the equipment it would take for three men to climb to the top of Wolf Creek Pass in the summer on horseback, just for fun, all those things that are necessary to make it an enjoyable experience.

Van Vedic explained that it was one of those things he loved to do, could do it from his ranch, and wanted all the supplies at his casa just in case he decided to go soon. One of his inspirations for camping in the high country came from listening to Gomez and Rahellio talk about the elk-hunting trips on horseback, the campfires, the music, and each and every time before they finished the story, they would both erupt into some ballad they knew from some camping trip ten or twenty years before.

"I-YI-YI-YI," and in less than a few heartbeats, everyone at the fire would have their guitars up across their laps. They'd all be simultaneously on the same note in the same song, with Rahellio's son Julio the easiest of all to listen to. He was a tenor who could growl, yodel the high notes, and sweat out the passion in the Spanish ballads. He had confidence in himself when he played his guitar and smiled while singing. He was never embarrassed to be the lead male voice and loved the church music.

The seven rivers were at their lowest at this time of the year, except for the San Juan itself, which is always a raging torrent fifty yards wide and thunderous. The trio's hope was that the blue lights were on their side of the river, because there would be no way to cross over if they were not. They'd have to come at it from the other side, the lands they called the Rosa, where no one ever went. A rock-strewn desert that would fall into the category of totally worthless unless there was gold down below. It sure didn't look like there was. Just like everyone knew and feared, the boulders were everywhere, piled in massive heaps that had fallen off the sides of the canyon walls millions of years ago, with that river working its way through wherever it could. El Bruto, Sarge, and Raton tried to work as one, easing the way by merely walking; they wouldn't go forward if it was a dead end. Sarge and Fitz were like sniffing river guides, disappearing back and forth, left and right, and then Sarge would bark a "come follow me" suggestion. The animals were right, sometimes like they could see through the stone, smell through the sand, sense a route ahead, and try to lead which way to go. There were many dead ends.

There came a spot where the rocks were so close together that they had to take all the saddles off the horses and Raton's backpack rack, haul it all through by hand, and guide and coax the beasts through, their sides rubbing on the rocks. They didn't like it one little bit, and not only that, it proved to be a dead-end after a few hundred yards, and they had to backtrack out of there.

After traveling almost a mile down into the gorge at a snail's pace, they came up to a wall, and found a long, unusual clearing that started at the cliff face and meandered down to the river's edge a few hundred yards away. The horses couldn't go any further because of this long mountain of boulders that paralleled the clearing, a strange formation if there ever was one, so the men found a spot and made their camp for the night. Julio caught enough rainbows in only an hour to feed them all twice. As he walked up from the river, you could tell he was proud, hoisting his stringer of sixteen rainbows. While at the river, Julio prayed and meditated the entire time on what he had seen the previous night. He prayed the rosary with all due respect, slowly, while anticipating the sunset that was still a few hours away. He found a massive boulder on the edge of the fortification, with smaller ones around the sides that helped him climb and work his way up the side but no further. They could not find a Safeway anywhere; they even had one in Aztec, for crying out loud. It was as if these boulders had all been positioned to thwart a man's effort every time. He considered how dark it would be when he came to jumping back down, so he climbed it three times for good measure and knew the best way down so as not to break a leg.

The tourists felt like piss ants in a rock garden. If you wanted to see anything at all, you had to have a plan—climb a boulder in Julio's case, which did him no good at all. He wasn't much over twelve feet higher, with three huge boulders blocking his way, ten feet tall, pressed against each other and preventing further progress.

Their choice of arroyos that would hopefully allow them access to the area they estimated would be close to the source of the lights was damn near perfect. The sun went down, the cliff walls went black, and the stars came out. The river was loud, far off in the distance, with her noise always echoing off the sides of the cliff walls, but it was peaceful in a sense—just loud, harmless Earth talk. Their cooking fire was now a campfire, with tons of dried wood all over the place within easy reach, crushed into rock crevices when the river flooded this high. All three bedrolls were laid out on the sand. Two fancy new gas lanterns would light up the site but hadn't yet been lit, as the waiting was almost over and they prepared to find their spots. The animals were tied, hobbled, watered, and fed, with El Bruto acting like he was ready to go somewhere, snorting and farting and looking for trouble. Standing beside him, the Mighty Raton got agitated, started making sounds that Rahellio had never heard before, then took a piss that turned into a small stream and lasted for almost five minutes. Sarge acted rather weird for a dog, always looking off into the distance, at the top of the barricade, with his ears up, which would only be expected, except he never stopped.

All the beasts heard something simultaneously, something the men couldn't hear. It got their attention, lifted them into their full animal mode—big eyes and twitching ears, and concentrated their vision on the crest of the boulders.

Julio was high up on his chosen rock, but the captain and Rahellio chose a spot in front of the fire, and they all waited. It wasn't long till a light blue film split the darkness not far from where they were, on the other side of the barrier but not far. As the minutes wore on, the entire canyon was lit up in turquoise blue, with no shadows because the light was everywhere, and it didn't hurt their eyes.

Van Vedic was mesmerized, though with it enough to be calculating a distance, timing it, watching the others, and paying attention to the animals. He found pentacles on the barrier crest that he lined up with the light's main shaft. He planned to use them the next day to zero in on the source. He predicted they were less than half a mile away, much closer to the cliff walls than their campsite. It would be challenging to walk towards it in the dark while keeping an eye on the lights. Unfortunately, the wall of boulders prevented any further progress, and it was then that the lights began to dim out. They'd have to find a way to climb through this blockage tomorrow, in the light of day.

To know they were so close to the source of the lights kept the men awake long after they'd laid down, speaking only Spanish while discussing everything under the stars. They had all slept together many times before, camped by a fire while working on the switchback road or down in the cottonwood grove, so they didn't have to start at the beginning when it came to talking about the Milky Way. It hadn't been that hard of a day getting to this site, and the captain hoped they could get a mid-morning start on their search, as they were way ahead of schedule; they hadn't planned on it being this easy. He was seriously excited about the morning's hearty breakfast, knowing that Rahellio would make his fantastic huevos on an open fire, with a tall mug of coffee, just the right way to start the day. Then they would make a plan when they could see better.

Julio had been on the verge of some sort of Mother Mary insanity the entire ride so far, chanting, singing, doing his one-minute rosary at least every fifteen minutes, and showing his disdain when his traveling companions weren't enthusiastically on board with the Mother Mary vision idea. His father had warned him several times that prayer is good and should be kept private to oneself and one's God. Quietly. He told his son that he should hold back and ride by himself fifty feet behind if he insisted on singing the same song repeatedly. He could sing to Raton and Fitz. The cowboy was in love with the mother of God, was way past saved, and had the Sunday Mass choir book that he knew by heart in his back pocket.

"Ah ah vei, ah ah vei, ah ah vei Marieaaaaa, Ah-ah vei..." Van Vedic kind of liked it, chimed in a few times, and told the kid to teach him another choir song, something that the deep throats can sing. Anything but Ah-ah vei. After some discussion, his father asked him to sing the ballads of the *Nine Lives of Elfego Baca*. He did just that, straddled his guitar in place, played while he rode, and sang about a sheriff down on the Rio Grande who carried two sidearms, just like Van Vedic.

He'd heard it before, loved it then, and still remembered the chorus; he remembered the night not too long ago when eight men and two women were resting by the river with his *Vanessa* on her trailer as a backdrop.

They were bushed from the day's hard work on the switchbacks and enjoyed a fantastic trout dinner courtesy of the women, with all sorts of trimmings, including tequila, beer, and wine. This was not these people's first campfire; all relatives and friends, so they knew their spots and found them. The captain had some of the guitar players on his right, some on his left, with singers in the front when it all began. That night by the river was indeed one of the most memorable concerts he could remember in his whole life. He could not believe that Rahellio's woman could sing that story like that, sing it flawlessly, backed by three guitarists who didn't look like they could do her justice. But they did. It was as if they had brought their best performance mindset to the river that night. Enough practices, enough rehearsals, that night was the night, and Van Vedic was the audience. Unbeknownst to the men involved, many other eyes were paying close attention.

Van Vedic led the way, high in the saddle on El Bruto, with Sarge racing back and forth and chasing rabbits. He would disappear for a few minutes, then come running by the parade like his tail was on fire, stop, turn around and race back the other way; poor Fitz couldn't keep up. Three Stripes acted like he was in dog heaven.

Rahellio had a long lead dangling from Raton's bridal harness, but it wasn't necessary because the brown giant didn't have a single lousy gene in his body and followed on command. The undertaker had a funeral carriage for special occasions in the local vicinity only, a beautiful black hearse pulled by the Mighty Raton for as far as the deceased may have wished. Shop to shop. In the foothills of the Rockies, sometimes the chosen burial site was near the top of some hill, in a family plot that still had room for one more; sometimes, the cars couldn't make it.

Many of his fondest funerals were the ones he managed that included the carriage ride, and even though it cost a whole lot more, the mourners would remember the day for a long time. He may have promised his future passenger a narrated ride through the countryside and would talk and talk and talk as they buggied alongside the roads of choice. The rolling hills and countryside around Ignacio, Arboles, and that area made for a great ride into the sunset if you loved such things.

After the huevos, they decided on a plan that involved moderately dangerous rock climbing and no horses while trying to find a vantage point and see what was on the other side of the unexplainable, almost unnatural barricade. As they searched the wall for an opening, a safe way through, a way over, any way at all, the mortician became frustrated with many of the features of the megaliths, laughed at the cracks in the granite, and hoped that it hurt when it happened, discussed how unnecessarily hard they all were, worthless in every way, and in the way of everything except water. He had gravediggers' disdain for rocks, which is different from, say, a ditch digger's disdain or a shithouse hole digger's disdain; it's hard to say, because they all hate rocks almost equally. And don't forget roots; everyone hates roots. Finally, after four hours of trying to find a way, they reluctantly returned to the campsite and tried to develop a new plan, which included lunch.

Julio was in a state of complete religious frustration. None of his prayers had been answered, and he'd hoping beyond hope that he could have met the Blessed Mother by now. He was practically crying while he asked the rock hater who could have possibly put all those giant boulders all over each other like they were. It was very unnatural, and that was all he knew. Every effort they made was foiled by the rocks, almost as if they were baited into thinking there was a possibility here or there, but no, not once. They learned quickly not to forget the route they used to get to the dead ends.

The captain and Sarge had walked alone towards the cliff walls while the other two rested under a tree at the campsite. They were on an alluvial fan, and he climbed at a moderate angle the entire time, perhaps a couple hundred yards uphill, with a few rest stops, until he made it to the corner. On the side of a massive boulder, twenty feet tall and semi-square, a fifteen-foot tall figurine of a stickman wearing a helmet with two antennas coming off the top looked down and greeted him. There was no way around the corner rock, a beast of a boulder pressed against the sheer rock cliff face as if an artisan had laid it there on purpose. More petroglyphs on similar stones, some the size of a school bus, were attached to the cornerstone, creating an unnatural formation twenty feet tall at the lowest point. There was no way through it or over it, not without ropes and ladders, a boundary that ran for hundreds of yards from the edge of the cliff to the edge of the river. Now all these petroglyphs, everywhere up high, caused him to remember some of the literature he had read that talked about a sacred Indian ceremonial site, deep inside the future lake, with the issues delaying progress on the reservoir.

When he looked back to where Rahellio was resting, he had an epiphany, discovering and rationalizing in his mind why so few mega boulders were blocking his way up the hill to the cliff face and the cornerstone. It was hard to see that geographical reality walking up the long clearing, but it was apparent when he turned around. His commonsense reasoning concluded that many of the barricade stones had once been lying in the sand where he now stood. The ancient Indians had evidently picked up all those boulders and laid them on top of each other until they had a wall over twenty feet tall. There was something on the other side worth seeing, and this barricade protected whatever was making the blue lights. He was sure of that, positive. A man stands very small next to megalithic boulders in a millions-of-year-old river canyon, especially when he discovers the boulders blocking his way had been lifted into the air and then placed where they were on purpose. It was almost impossible to comprehend how someone could have done it. Indians might have done the carvings, but Indians didn't move these boulders, not even an inch.

The first question out of his mouth was, "Who or what could have done this?"

Most of the artwork started at no less than ten feet off the sand—many more carvings in the rocks nearby, with there being far too many to count. Then he noticed there were more, fifty feet above him, maybe even higher, all over the cliff face.

His second question was, "Who could have possibly done that?"

There were circles and stars, animals of all sorts, and humans with big heads. The exhibit continued north around the barricade, with every bit of it very hard to see. He began noticing other drawings on the barricade boulders that he had overlooked while searching for a pathway. This was old ancient Indian stuff like he saw when he toured the Aztec ruins. Images in rock from a long, long time ago, carved into granite with granite chunks by men who didn't have metal. He tried to imagine their campfires when people lived in these canyonlands a couple thousand years ago, maybe ten thousand; no one knew for sure.

There he stood, staring at ancient carvings with one question after another popping into his mind, seeing the obvious for what it was and noting the ones that made little sense. An antelope with an enormous horn on its nose, elephants, a perfect depiction of the Orion constellation, and a wide assortment of men wearing helmets surrounding their faces.

With this new understanding of what he was looking at and having concluded from the day's inspection that they wouldn't get any further than this point, he decided to leave. He wanted to leave, but he couldn't go. There was no reason for lollygagging around trying to find a way through if there wasn't one, and he asked himself why he was standing there in the first place instead of moving. It was almost impossible to explain, and you would have had to have been there to feel it, smell it, to hear it, like Van Vedic did, but he was now standing on destiny's doorstep once again and didn't know exactly how he got there. They needed supplies they didn't have, which were absolutely necessary, namely ropes and climbing equipment. With a hard ride, the three could make it back to Van Vedic's by sundown if they left right away, and be back in a day or two. In a faster than normal stride, which is saying something, he headed down the clearing towards his friends, but he didn't get far. He stopped and abruptly sat down, overwhelmed with dizziness that caused him to drop his arms to his sides while tilting his head back, staring straight up at the sky.

Above him, far above him, three spots of light in the firmament grabbed his attention, side by side in the crystal blue sky. Three tiny diamonds on the edge of being invisible didn't move the entire time he sat there, not up or down, left or right, and when he'd blink and refocus, they were still there. These were not airplanes, and he knew that; way too high, miles high, and far higher than even the TWA Constellation flew. He felt a wind breeze itself into his space from all directions, filling the area around him with ten times as much air as before. Sensed a presence nearby—nothing physical that he could touch or even see, but it was there. Still, he could feel it, similar to that feeling he felt when his Spivey sense flared, his instantaneous sixth sense, the spirit that had aroused his neck hairs all through his life, the cause of the goosebumps on his arms. It had become a fact of his life, a Spivey sensation he had learned to trust instantly after the first few times, and as a general rule, any time he felt it, people died in gunfights. Not this time; however, his Spivey sense was too late. Whatever this was, this entity now owned him and turned him off, making him neutral. It wrapped itself invisibly, instantly, from his toes to his temples, inside himself. He stared at the three diamonds and lost track of reality, lost track of time, yet appeared to be resting against a rock, and after who knew how long, a stereo voice stirred his mind.

"Come back alone to this cornerstone tonight near sunset.

Send the others away, back to where they came from. Tell them not to come back. Immediately! Thank you."

As he sat there, a tingling sensation started at his forehead, spread all around his skull, went through his holes and into his brain, out again, and down through his body. Whatever it was, it could purr like a cat, touched him in every spot of his being, inside and out, and then let him go, freed him from the top down, and then vanished.

The captain regained his normal sitting posture and rose to his feet. A voice had spoken to him from somewhere nearby, given specific instructions with a time frame, and thanked him for doing it. The voice rang a bell in his memory; he'd heard it before and was sure of that, no doubt in his mind. So he looked around for the source, looked up at the diamonds, and they were still there, just tiny diamonds in the sky, and his were the only eyes on Earth that could see them, or so he thought.

The Russian mariner had arrived at another crossroads in his life, felt that, down deep in his bones, he was more than ready for the challenge, and waited to be released from the energetic embrace he had been held in for twenty minutes. He felt as if he'd been wrapped in an invisible web—maybe only in his mind, but he couldn't move. His reemergence had started inside his brain, all around his pineal gland, spread out and down from there, over his shoulders, down his arms, and all the way to the toes. He felt like he was unwrapping inside, spreading out on a cellular level, even in his brain, and then discovered that the feeling wasn't new.

The captain remembered crossing the pilothouse threshold, stepping towards the console, his wheel, the key, in super slow motion, leaving the white light behind and unraveling from something that had captured him. This déjà vu moment of a feeling helped him understand the past, a time when he forgot to remember or was prevented from doing so. What he experienced as he regained consciousness that day might have happened so slowly his brain couldn't remember, but now he did; parts of it, anyhow. The white world let him go. That's what he called it now, the white world. That place he discovered in the hurricane, where he disappeared into whiteness and evidently stayed there for ten years or more.

What was happening to him now was caused by the diamonds; they got his attention on purpose, made him look in their direction, and then he was had. Once on his feet, his first steps down the hillside were a coming-out party, out of another dimension, out of a dream, being reborn with a new understanding of what he didn't know. What that was, that understanding, he knew he had no knowledge of it whatsoever. At least not yet. Life was messing with him again, and he knew that for sure.

His mind was instantly working on his future conversation with the mortician, and by the time he got to the campsite, there was a plan in his mind. He would send them back, and they would man the lookout point at the cabin every night until he returned, which was the end of the subject as far as he was concerned.

He walked past the horses, pulled on Raton's ear, rubbed his nose, and then he saw them. Rahellio and his son were lying flat on the ground on their bed rolls with their arms by their sides, eyes open, clearly alive, with their boot tips pointing straight up. He looked up into heaven, found the diamonds still there in the blue, and then focused back on his friends.

They were breathing for sure, round open eyeball sockets, but apparently semi-unconscious, no blood, no wounds, while lying perfectly straight, side by side, a few feet apart. Fitz sat straight like a dog does at their heads, eyes wide open too, looking at Van

Vedic as if he had a secret to share and would if he only knew how to speak. Sarge walked up cautiously, smelled Fitz's ass, and then sat beside him, smelled his ear and nose, and now knew all he needed to know.

The captain went down to his knees between the two and wondered what to do next, so he set his hands on both their closest knees and gently moved them back and forth while staring at their faces. Within moments, Rahellio re-focused his eyes on the captain, then Julio did too. They both lay there that way for the longest time, apparently regaining consciousness just like he had done. They were coming to, it seemed, and both had glanced a smile at Van Vedic a few times but then went back to staring straight up. He gave them all the time they needed, and when he looked up, the diamonds were still there. That had to be what they were looking at, no doubt in his mind, but so far, his companions weren't all the way back yet; they still seemed mesmerized, immobilized, and not wanting or able to talk.

Slowly the two men moved things—their fingers first. Both turned their shoulders and stretched their necks. It looked like they were mimicking each other, following a sequence, shedding an invisible film, something from the top down, like a mariposa from the cocoon. Then, finally, they sat up and continued investigating the campsite with their eyes, acting as if they had been somewhere and were far more than asleep at the time. Now they shared a memory they might not be able to explain, a father and son who may have discovered the secret of the Universe. They both touched their knees for a moment and then studied their hands, both sides, wiggled their boots side to side, and rose to their feet.

Pushizsnoz had backed away and watched their progress, and reality filled up their faces. They were back but different from before, something he could feel in them and himself, not the same somehow. It was uncomfortable to be standing there in silence, awkward, so the captain looked up at the diamonds and pointed at them.

"What do you think they are?" he asked in Spanish in a low voice. He kept pointing, and watched them both look up. Then, instantly, he realized they didn't see anything; they might have seen the diamonds before when they were lying down, but they didn't see them now, so he brought his finger down.

Rahellio looked again, saw nothing, and told the captain so.

"Were they birds; eagles, geese? I missed them. Julio, did you see them?"

There was so much information swirling in his mind that Vincent had to find the coffee pot and think about all this from that vantage point.

Julio said he didn't see anything in the heavens, but there was a very unusual look in his eyes when he came back to earth, like he was sick all of a sudden and getting ready to puke. While the captain poured his coffee, Rahellio watched his son place his hands on his hips and suddenly projectile vomit six feet in front of his face. It was yellow, thick, ugly stuff that exploded out of his face and staggered him. His eyes were pleading for mercy when the second attack arrived, forced him into a mild backbend, and then he whiplashed forward, spuing mush and lunch on top of the yellow shit. He was exhausted, so he sat down now, and from out of nowhere, from out of the clear blue sky, his father chimed in.

"Oh, no! Oh shit! Watch out! Tell your mother I loved her. Here it comes, I Yi Yi Yi," and he almost blew his lips off. The huevos rancheros had fermented a bit after all this time and were being converted into gas when the indigestion arrived. He, too, had a second round, which was almost as much as he could take, forced him to his knees right next to the tenor, and they looked for some solace from the gringo.

Not to be outdone, and with the gallery down there waiting, it became Van Vedic's turn to vomit. No joking around for the big fella; he felt it way past down deep and knew it was time. They had inspired him. Some invisible spirit had ventured inside all three of them, shined a light on their guts, stirred up their innards, and had to be expelled. He could feel that feeling, so he tilted his head back and glanced at the spot in the sky where the diamonds still stood. Plain as day, they twinkled, unmistakable— at least to him.

He laid it out on a big rock off to his left a couple of times, considered a third, but it wouldn't come; just some spittle. After resting like we all have to do, they passed around a water bag, over and over, washing out their mouths and filling up their bellies with clean water.

That voice returned and reiterated once again,

"Come alone to the cornerstone tonight near sunset. Send these men away. They are forgetting things as I speak and need to go now. You stay here. Your horse and your dog should stay. You will sleep here. Thank you."

The mortician was fully recovered in ten minutes or less and was pestering his son about how he felt; he wanted to know if he had hurt his neck on the second one and where in the hell had that yellow shit come from? The lad was still feeling the after-effects of blowing his guts out. He had immediate ambitions to be with his momma. He whispered into his father's ear that he didn't want the captain to think he was a baby, but he wanted to go home. He was tired of fishing, and since that was why they were here, he had caught enough and wanted to go home. His tummy hurt.

The captain had rekindled the fire really well, and was

talking about food poisoning or a flu bug or something that had gotten all three and put a severe damper on their excursion. But now that it was out of him, he felt pretty good.

"That was just about as sour a spit-up as I've done lately. I don't know where it came from, and I sure as hell hope it doesn't come back. How you fellas doing?"

Julio looked bad. His father looked terrible, and they had decided to ask the captain if they could leave. Unfortunately, their fishing trip was over. Rahellio pleaded that the young man's mother would be distraught if he didn't make the right decisions about all this and quickly, and as the captain well knew, she was very unpleasant when she was troubled. She sure could sing, but there was a downside. He reasoned they could be out of the gorge in a couple of hours if nothing slowed them down. Once they made it to the top of the plateau, instead of going to Van Vedic's cabin, they could turn right and go home, be on the backside of Arboles near dark.

"Captain, I need to get the boy home. You understand?"

"Of course I do. What about the lights tonight? I have to stay, my friend; you understand that? Tonight's the night!"

"Honestly, we won't need the lanterns for our trip home because of the moon. You can keep them both, and you can keep Raton if you wish, but I need to pack it up and head for home. She's no fun when she's mad."

"I'll help you pack the mule. Take him with you. Are you sure the boy is good for a long ride?"

When Rahellio winked at the lad, indicating they were cleared to leave, he started packing up things and getting it all over by the horses.

That had always been his part of the deal so far—the runner. He was taught how to listen to the men and learn how to do things from the bottom up. The young man knew that it could be painful to be told something twice, and for some bizarre reason, he sprang to life like there was nothing wrong, like he hadn't been responsible for the yellow shit. What had taken an hour to unload and spread around the campsite took about ten minutes to organize and get reloaded. All except for Van Vedic's personal equipment, both lanterns, and before the trio knew it, they were saying goodbye.

"Senor Captain, thank you. I hope the two lanterns will be enough light for you tonight. Good fishing. Goodbye."

They headed back the same way they came, following their tracks from the day before, and would make it to the plateau without all the mistakes this time, having marked their trail really well.

The captain was alone save for Sarge and the brute, staring up the clearing at the distant cliff face and his destination. Higher than he could accurately measure, he saw that the diamonds were still side by side, still where they'd been all afternoon, still there in his vision.

CHAPTER TEN

SPAQU

E l Bruto Whetto was free to roam the neighborhood, anywhere around the new campsite at the top of the clearing in the shadow of the cliff face, with no saddle or bridle. The stallion had a master who would whistle if he needed the creature, and it spent every waking moment hoping he could take that man for a ride.

Captain Vincent Van Vedic had arrived as ordered. It was close to sundown, and he was early. He built a simple camp as he didn't have to worry about the weather. He laid out his bag, his trusty horse blanket, built a fire, and started his percolator. Sarge was busy smelling everything, leaving his mark, and continually sniffing the air, coming to a complete stop in his tracks, then perk his ears and sniff at the same time.

"I THOUGHT I'D GET HERE EARLY… if that's OKAY!"

His dog came running up, thinking the volume was meant for him, tail bouncing like crazy with his dog excitement thing going full-blast. That kind of response caused the oversized human to not only give it a firm pat on the head but also a nice slab of elk jerky that would keep him busy for an hour or more.

"You crazy dog, that wasn't meant for you. Good boy! I was told they allowed pets, so that means you get to be a dog tonight. Maybe they'll talk to you and El Bruto besides me. No, I don't know who they are."

Sarge carried the piece of meat a few yards away, but he dropped it, and suddenly his lion mane stood up high while he stood staring at the top of all the boulders, sniffing the wind and focusing all his attention up there somewhere, fifty yards away. No barking, but his full-blown cautious side was wide awake like he'd seen a bear. That behavior is precisely why we have dogs in the first place, and when they talk to us, we need to pay attention, especially when their shoulder mane is triggered and they stop gnawing on a chunk of elk slab.

The saddle lay on the ground, waiting for Van Vedic to press his body against it, close by the fire, along with his guns in their holsters wrapped around each other, forming a pile of leather and steel a foot high. For Sarge to act this way meant there was something in the rocks, somewhere; if it were a puma or a big black bear, his only defense was ten feet away. Being deep in the canyon the way he was, with sheer rock cliffs five hundred feet high between him and the actual sunset, it was hard to know when that actually happened. He never carried a timepiece when fishing or hunting, but he knew it was six or better.

He straddled the saddle and picked up his guns with a stern eye all over the rocks. Without so much as a glance at the assembly, it swirled out in front of him, then behind, up against his waist, and was latched in front in the blink of an eye. Leather straps held the holsters' tips to his thighs, which he somehow attached simultaneously with both hands in a second. With both boots set, hands at the ready, he prepared for combat, when a forty-pound male skunk came walking straight at him. Fast walking, if you're familiar with a normal skunk waddle. They fear no man, deal with dogs in the rudest fashion, and love elk meat. Vincent had no choice in the matter, so he had to turn and run like a little girl, squealing at the beast to leave him alone. He knew from previous experiences that you never shoot a skunk near the campsite but he still shouted, "I'll SHOOT YOUR ASS, SKUNK. BACK OFF, BACK OFF."

He ended up at least fifty feet from the fire, stopped, took a stand, and watched the goings-on at his campsite. Never in all his memories of campsites had he ever been run off scared. Never. Sarge was an intelligent dog sometimes, and sometimes not. This probably wasn't his first encounter with a skunk, but he was overwhelmed and confused from the start. The man who owned the elk slabs had suddenly jumped up and started running from the site, shouting at the intruder. All eighty pounds of Sarge was rapidly filled with the notion and emotion that that stinking black and white menace wanted to eat him. He fled with the best of them, disappearing into a cluster of sagebrush and boulders. The skunk went for the elk slab like he knew what it was, detected from afar by that tiny little nose of his, and when he found it, he bit it, picked it up, and waddled away. Slowly, the captain regained control of the campfire. He yelled at the skunk to not return. "Hey, you stinking skunk, things will be different next time!"

Having no intention of killing the animal but wanting to get a message across, he fired four 45-caliber bullets into the area where that tail was waving. Besides the noise, the explosions of sand all around his little feet were probably enough to keep him away for good, but the echoes of echoes of explosions, over and over off the canyon walls, were a forbidding sound if there ever was one. In comparison to everything around him, the man was tiny, but his ability to make a big noise had been underlined to the umpteenth degree. He might have forgotten there for a moment that he wasn't alone, that there was a voice making requests, and that was why he was there. Skunks can force a person to forget things like that.

El Bruto had gone for a drink at the river, got it, came back up the clearing, found a sand spot close to his master, and waited like they do. Sarge, too, found his place by the saddle with a fresh slab to gnaw on while Van Vedic made a hot cup of coffee. He was staring up at the rock art in front of his face, at a carving of a ten-foot-tall human with a round helmet on its head and two antennae sticking out of it, square shoulders holding its belly, and with only three fingers on its hands.

"Please remove your weapons."

The gunslinger looked around in two complete half-circles, finding no one to talk to. He thought to himself that his Spivey sense was nowhere to be found. Nothing of the sort, and the captain diagnosed the sound from the voice as friendly, non-threatening, and seeming to mean no harm.

"I always carry my weapons. I will consider the options after I've met and seen you. I don't know who you are. Please be aware that I am exceptionally talented with them, and under certain circumstances these weapons seem to have a mind all their own. NO! I will not remove my weapons! There are bears, big mountain lions, bobcats, and snakes in this canyon. Do you have invisible weapons?"

His horse had his head up in the failing light, and his dog was at his heel, both watching and listening for noise, and must have detected something in their exchange.

As the sunlight faded into the moonlight, then into a blue light that filled up the corner and made things clear, Vincent watched both his animals lie down where they were and fall fast asleep while noting to himself in the most honest of ways that he had never ever seen that one before.

"I am a peaceful spirit, and you need not be afraid. Walk towards the opening."

In this new turquoise glow on practically everything, the towering rock formation still blocked Vincent's way as he got close, but then a rock cluster the size of a barndoor turned blue. It wasn't rock anymore but a passageway that led into a tunnel fifty yards long, right through the barricade to the other side.

"Proceed."

He boldly walked forward, entering an immediate and complete state of amazement at the tunnel itself, floor to ceiling and wall to wall. The rocks were huge, each a little different from its brothers but perfectly aligned and seamed with their neighbors, with no debris underfoot, twelve feet tall and twelve feet wide. Not at all your average solid rock tube fifty yards long. It was dimly lit in blue all the way through. More like turquoise, and with no light bulbs. Once inside, Vincent found a whole new world of ancient ruins. Under a rock overhang of staggering dimensions, the structures started up the cliff's side that stuck out at least a hundred feet and protected everything below from the weather. Almost all of the structure was made of gigantic rock squares and other odd shapes but then blended together like puzzle pieces, incredible stone works the likes of which he'd never seen. This place could last forever, he imagined.

"We need your help."

"I thought you'd never ask."

"Funny human." A long pause. "We need your help."

"You must know that I can help you, or you wouldn't have brought me here. I will be more than happy to help where I can. Do you have any vodka?"

"Funny human."

"No, seriously, I work for vodka. Do you speak Russian? How about green olives and vermouth?"

"Funny human. Of course we have those items, but the olives are black."

"You need not apologize; black olives matter. What can I do for you? Does this voice have a body? I can handle just about anything. Are you friendly?"

"Funny human. He can handle just about anything! Funny human, keep on walking."

This fifty-foot-tall fortress was no less than a hundred yards wide, probably as deep as it was tall, with every single window and doorway except for a few facing an arena. It looked like a two-story-tall solid rock motel looking down on the central patio and the arena beyond that, but Vincent could tell it hadn't been occupied in forever. After only a brief evaluation of everything so far—the structure itself, the walkways, a spectacular view across the river to the other side of the canyon a mile away—he was awed beyond wow. Everything around him was best described as big, really big, complex, and beautiful. Nothing but huge, fitted stones. Fitted stone walls, many fifteen-foot-tall doorways, beautiful stone walkways, and as he followed the path down around the front of the structure, he saw the small arena with a round, elevated stage in the middle, all lit up in blue light. He had found what he was looking for. The source of the blue light was the arena itself, and he saw that there was not a beam pointing into the sky, but more a beautiful blue dome that covered the site. The full autumn hunter's moon had risen and bathed the canyon in moonlight, so he continued around the walkway till he arrived at the center point, turned, and marveled at the creation.

A peaceful voice came from up there and off to the right somewhere, "Rest."

"Rest? Are you kidding? I just got here. I might have walked a few hundred yards so far, and you call for a rest? You tired of showing me the way?"

"Funny human. The authorities wrote the script for this, and it was their opinion that an old man like you would need a rest by now."

"They did? Well, ain't that thoughtful. I tell you what, JACK, this old man doesn't need a break. What else might the authorities have in store for me? And for that matter, what have they done for me lately?"

"Well, first of all, my name is not Jack, and not long ago, our time, Captain Vincent Van Vedic, they decided to rescue you from inside a hurricane. I know there are many questions in your mind about that time. Yes, please sit down and rest, and we will answer them for you in the near future. Funny human, are you still with me? How about we rest for a time right here? We'll talk more when you are rested."

Vincent decided it could do no harm.

An escape pod plan that didn't work all that well after the launch was grossly overloaded to begin with, but the occupants had grandiose plans to be rescued in either earth or moon orbit. The craft known as *0* took four of them up, another ten miles further east from the mother ship disaster there outside of Aztec, where the pilot, an inexperienced but not infected junior lieutenant, managed a soft crash landing in the San Juan River canyon, on a clearing a few hundred yards from the raging torrent in the spring of 1948. This landing site was ancient, a holy place where a young teacher became marooned once upon a time. The project took four hundred and forty-four years of his life, and then he went home, back during the ice or even before the ice. It was agreed by all concerned, including the commander, *0* itself, and the cadets, that it was mandatory to stop, no matter what else was going on, and pay their respects. It said to do so in the *Gold Book*! Lieutenant Spaqulatizexistaooogj EeekSSSraa Zzocobizzzzlll piloted the escape pod, an entity known as '*0*,' filled with enough supplies for two thousand earth days, full hibernation capabilities, a cloaking ability, basically a three-seater, with a fourth one added. The cadets had been quarantined immediately after the crash, placed inside *0* as a safety precaution, along with the lieutenant, who would become their pilot, assistant, and had an extensive list of other responsibilities. It had been an expedient reaction at the time by all concerned to find whoever was even remotely capable of piloting *0*, who was positively not sick. When they found him in a minute or less, he was pushed inside *0*, and the hatch was sealed. The occupants of *0* watched through their viewing ports as every last member of that beloved crew died within hours, and *0* was ordered to leave. That, too, was contained in the *Gold Book*.

NOTES

"The mother craft was said to be 99 feet (30m) in diameter, the most massive UFO to date. Scully named as his sources two men identified as Newton and Gebauer, who reportedly told him the incident had been covered up and "the military had taken the craft for secret research."[3][5][6]

"Scully wrote that the crashed UFO, along with other flying saucers captured by the government, came from Venus, and worked on "magnetic principles." According to Scully, the inhabitants stocked concentrated food wafers and "heavy water" for drinking purposes, and every dimension of the craft was "divisible by nine." Science writer Martin Gardner criticized

Scully's story as full of "wild imaginings" and "scientific howlers."[7] ("Dennett says the UFO crashed May 21, 1953, about eight miles northeast of the Kingman Airport and that government officials sent a team of 40 scientists to the crash site to investigate."

"The object was described as metallic, 30 feet wide and three and a half feet high, oval-shaped with portholes," he says. "Inside were two to four, four-foot-tall humanoids, deceased according to most sources, with large eyes and wearing metallic suits.")

THE BLUE LIGHTS...

In the legends and traditions of the Navajo Indians, there are hundreds, if not thousands, of sacred sites throughout their domain. Mountain tops and rivers, mesas and wildernesses, places where their ancient ancestors held traditional ceremonies to honor their Gods. All of their Gods came from the skies. In mid-October 1953, Vincent finds one of the most remote and spectacular sites of them all. To say he found it might not be correct; he found himself standing in front of a barricade he couldn't climb. Not needing to be exact, he measured these coordinates to be only a half dozen miles downriver from Arboles and right at ten miles north of his favorite lookout now that he was standing there. Some of his first guestimates were way off, but he didn't care. It involved horseback riding, camping, and fishing, some of his favorite things to do.

. . .

Van Vedic had been called to help, guided, pushed, or pulled; he could feel it but didn't know which. Felt like destiny was once again on his horizon.

In Earth time, his entire journey after his awakening had taken just over three months. In the crashed alien time, it had been a lot longer than that and had reached critical. The survivors would never be rescued, because no human being had been inside the boundaries of this place in almost ten thousand years. The *Gold Book* demanded that every effort be made to save these cadets. So, the authorities realized they had a problem concerning what was possible, what they needed, and what it would take, all the while attempting to interfere with humankind as little as possible. Erasing memories in humans had proved to be a challenge. They took an inventory of all their guests and found Vincent Van Vedic standing in the doorway of his fishing boat.

In essence, they released him from their grasp and guided his path to the crash site to help the survivors because he'd said in his journals that he wanted to own a horse ranch in New Mexico. It was all very, very complicated, with the bottom line being that there were no secrets in the Universe's pure reality. God's creatures all have destinies, and the *Gold Book* insists that the first order for all life is to not waste it.

The three golden submarines' flight commanders had no choice but to save him at the time, first of all because it said to do so in the *Gold Book*, and secondly because it was easy. The golden submarines rose up to the surface inside of hurricane #9, in the middle of the eye, just like they always did, not expecting to discover the *Vanessa* floating there too. It would have been their tidal wave that would have killed Van Vedic, not the hurricane. It was their responsibility to protect him, or the court would have found them guilty of murder, and so they simply scooped him up just before the wave arrived. They scanned all his journals, counted all his gold, read his mind, and found a practically flawless human that surprised them. They also learned the story of Jude.

This slightly damaged UFO on the San Juan River was the only escape ship from the mother vessel that crashed near AZTEC in 1948. It was not really a crash; more like a crashed takeoff on the edge of the San Juan River. The sand clearing was long, paralleled the barricade from up against the cliffs, all the way down to the river, and was virtually inaccessible on the west side of the gorge from either direction, Van Vedic's side of the river. The entire site was ancient to the start of the ice age, based at the bottom of a five hundred-foot sheer rock cliff face, and was bounded on each side by a rock fortress over twenty feet tall.

((*According to Scully, in March 1948, an unidentified aerial craft containing sixteen*
humanoid bodies were recovered by the military in New Mexico after making a
controlled landing in Hart Canyon 12 miles northeast of the city of Aztec.))

Three of the original four occupants were time-honored cadets, almost four feet tall, and still alive five years after the crash. They couldn't dig for the life of themselves, weren't injured, but they were totally incapable of venturing very far from their craft, an activity that had been the cause of their lieutenant's demise. They had hibernated three times already while waiting for their rescue, an event they wouldn't even know had happened if they were subdued at the time. They awoke and recovered each time—challenging stuff, going from just shy of dead for eighteen months to being brought back to life. The procedure took weeks, and they could barely help each other recover; they always seemed extremely sick and weak. Hibernating was never ever taken lightly because of the recovery issues, and nowhere in their history was a story of someone surviving four hibernations. The fourth one would have no end time, no wake-up time, but it would be entirely peaceful. It only added to their increasing despair when they awoke each time to discover they were still in this hopeless situation. They knew full well that even if a rescue sister ship found them, there would be nothing that they could do either. "WE DON'T DIG!" was in the *Gold Book*, and number four of the twelve commandments of life. The cadets' rules to live by. A fundamental law. "We Don't Dig!"

Lieutenant Spaqu was in his early two hundreds, two fifty maybe, and had been a star all along his way. Everything he had ever done had been an unprecedented success, except for the current state of affairs, and as time wore on, he blamed himself. There was no doubt that he was distraught over his inability to save his precious cadets. So he walked away from his craft one day, naked in the morning sun, except for his wrist band, with no helmet, and after a few dozen steps, he became exhausted and had to stop and rest in the shade of a huge rock. He should have considered his booties, because his feet were the first thing to fail. That shady spot was where he got bit by a snake that was twice as long as he was tall. An incredible beast that lay there in the sun and intentionally cut off Spaqu's only route of retreat if he had ever considered such a thing. It coiled in a pyramid that disguised its length and sat there looking like King Tutt's golden headgear, vibrating its tail in a monotonous monotone rattle until it uncoiled in a blink, launching itself forward like a spring.

Poor Lieutenant Spaqulatizexistaooogj EeekSSSraa Zzocobizzzzlll was dead before all three of his terrified cadets made it off the porch back inside their craft, squeaking in panic and thinking they were next on the menu. If they had accidentally scratched their skin in the slightest, they would more than likely be dead in three days, or so it said in the *Gold Book*, and that was why they were always highly cautious in that regard, but most of their caution went right out the window when the monster unraveled itself. It had exploded forward at Spaqu, opened its mouth as wide as the space between their middle finger and thumb, and that's saying something, exposing two long curved spikes that the monster sank deep in his forehead.

From their porthole windows, they watched in horror as the creature swallowed him headfirst, taking two Earth hours for his feet to finally disappear. After that time, it slithered away with Spaqu crammed into a round bulge right in the middle of the serpent. It barely made it to a shaded sandbar near a pile of rocks, stretched out its eight-foot-long, ten-inch thick tube, rested its head on nothing, and stared at the porthole windows. There was no way for anyone to know for sure, since it never closed its eyes, but the glutton went to sleep for twenty-eight hours of Earth time, one of the longest waits in the history of extraterrestrial visitors. Finally, they saw it leave when Spaqu's wrist band surged, broadcast its movement on their monitors, and they were able to follow the reptile for a tedious mile upriver.

They amassed more data on snakes that rattle than any other animal they'd ever studied so far. After three days, all movement appeared to stop, with the band searching the newly found sunlight for power; within hours, the lens had cleansed itself and sent a signal for retrieval that could only be deactivated inside *0*. It was all that was left of Spaqu—a long, dark trail with his wrist band half-buried in the snake shit. It was glued to the sand, might never be found, always and forever sending out that signal into shallow space because of its neutronic systic/non-aligned power bead.

"Human. HUMAN! CAPTAIN, HELLO! ANYBODY HOME IN THERE?"

"Yes. Yes, I'm here." Vincent opened his eyes, wiser but still processing all that he'd learned while resting. He understood them better now.

"Please do not be afraid in any way. You can help us, and we will not harm you. We live by the rules in the *Gold Book*."

"I do too."

"We know that; we've read your book, so to speak."

"I haven't written a book yet! Am I awake? Will I remember everything that happens? The last time we met, we were together for ten years. They can prove it to me with pictures, yet I seem to have misplaced all those memories. Ten years!"

"You carry a Christian *Bible* with you through life. Do you know the book well?"

"I have read it… with difficulty, can't chant chapter and verse, and don't abide by turning the other cheek—if that's what you need?"

"Do you remember reading about a man named Ezekiel?"

"Not that I recall. Is this going anywhere? I would like to know a few things. No, make that a thousand things… ten thousand. For example, do I ever get to see you? You got a name?"

"You can't pronounce it."

"You got a nickname? I can do funny names. I had many friends in Czechoslovakia and Ukraine, and many of those folks have strange names. Yarasheski. See there? So, what's your name?"

"You can't pronounce it."

"UNBELIEVABLE!"

"You can't pronounce it!"

"Okay, I can't pronounce it, but I can hear it from you. Tell me your name and I'll decide. This is ridiculous."

"Ready?   Dzzitulatizebistauuugj   FfffeekTTTraa Zzucobinnnlll."

"Once again."

"Dzzitulatizebistauuugj FfffeekTTTraa Zzucobinnnlll."

"YOU ARE SO RIGHT. All I got was the DDDzzzzz part at the beginning."

"Funny human."

"Tell you what, DDDzzzzz, let's get on with the task."

"We must discuss Ezekiel first, a brief story which must be told; it's in the *Gold Book*. Goes way, way back. Ezekiel was a prophet from the earliest of times who had an encounter with his God. He wrote about it, and it's there in the early verses of your *Bible*. He spoke of wheels within wheels, gave exact dimensions of a hallucination, and at the present time, today, the story sits there waiting to be discovered for what it is. A man with a similar last name to yours—Von Daniken, I believe—will write a book in less than twenty years and shatter human thinking. It's a written record of Ezekiel meeting us and riding with us. The *Gold Book* talks about intervention, exact rules and procedures. In Ezekiel's case, those rules were broken; he was allowed to investigate and record something he should never have been allowed to remember. So, to answer your question, no. No, you won't remember much of what happens, but you will not mind, and you will more than likely be satisfied emotionally inside your heart when you learn about what is happening here."

"What about me seeing my new friend Dizzy?"

"Not tonight. I am not capable of showing myself just yet. I'm not acclimated. I'm not from here, not even close. Not even from the moon. I'll need a suit even then. Someday soon, maybe. Make that a really big *maybe*. I have to show you something right now, and after you've seen our dilemma, I will entertain some of your questions. I want you to consider your questions carefully; it will matter to us what you ask us. I ask that you continue on around the arena, to the far distant corner by the cliff. I will be by your side in my three-sense self."

Van Vedic walked along quietly and said nothing as his mind raced around like a brand-new car. Off to his right was another stone wall, just like on the other side, that ran all the way down to the river. It was created out of massive stones that interlocked as if they had been poured in place; they were so perfectly formed that there were no spaces between the boulders straight up and down, twenty feet or more. He was stretching his neck and trying to see better what was up in front at the corner. It was silver, sitting there in the moonlight, round all over, and tilted slightly to its front if you can picture a plate. When he got there all by himself, he could see that the disk was trapped under a rock overhang that forced the vehicle down in the sand on the dark side, the half he couldn't see. It didn't seem to be all that thick, maybe six feet at the crown, which he could see, and probably thirty feet across the diameter. There didn't appear to be any damage to this side, but he couldn't know about the half that was under the rock. It looked more like it was wedged from this angle.

"Dizzy?"

"Right here, my friend."

"Who did this?"

"I need you to know that there are three cadets inside, still very much alive, and they've been here since your year 1948, five of your years. They have been dying slowly, very slowly, but with your help, they will hopefully be able to start their craft and lift off out of here under the control of *0*.

"Everyone agrees that our objective is to dig where necessary and hopefully pull the craft out from under the overhang. The pilot lost control as we were lifting off after visiting this sacred site, to answer your last question. He panicked here in the corner, bounced on the sand, and slid along until he wedged himself like this. This place is one of many arenas where the teachers were brought and taught. It has been here since the time when ice ruled the northern world and is listed in the *Gold Book* as Sacred Level FIVE. If we are ever visiting an area where such a site might be, we stop and pay homage to the early ones. There is no level six."

"How much does it weigh? Are they doing okay in there? The cadets? What do they need? Water, food, alfalfa, spinach?"

"Funny human. Consideration is good. Before I forget, we also need you to find our lieutenant's wristband. As far as the weight is concerned, I am afraid to admit that this is the hyper fluxoid model, which is partially why it's here. Heavier and faster, half a billion mactoids at least, the cadets' favorite, and sometimes too much to handle. May I introduce *0* to you?"

"No shit!"

"It's okay to shit anywhere you want, just like fishing on the river."

"So, you think the crew is at fault because they are young and reckless? Fun flying. That's good. How old are these guys?"

"Being careful is advised; they are cadets and have exceeded the eight hundred level. The pilot of the craft at the time is dead. Lieutenant Spaqulatizexistaooogj EeekSSSraa Zzocobizzzzlll. He was in his early two hundreds, two fifty maybe, but barely into the prime of his life. He went walking around the crash site here when he was mercilessly attacked and eaten by a monster snake eight feet long."

"No SHIT!"

"I already told you it's okay to shit anywhere you want, just like fishing. Nobody cares! Go shit wherever you want."

"Spaqu met a monster diamondback, and now he's rattlesnake shit."

"Which brings up the search mission we have for you. It should be easy. Lieutenant Spaqulatizexistaooogj EeekSSSraa Zzocobizzzzlll was wearing his wristband at the time. Approximately four days after he was swallowed, Spaqu's band quit moving and has been in the same spot ever since. It's what activates the blue light that you see at night, and we must find it. Only you can negotiate the rocks and find the location where that monster left Spaqu's band. It has a neutronic systic/non-aligned power bead, after all, and we can't leave it behind. We have sixty-digit GPS, in case you didn't know!"

"Holy shit."

"Do you need a container? So we can have it freeze-dried and preserved forever? I thought you humans shit the same way we do, and I must have overlooked seeing you squat. I'm confused as to the holy shit; where is it?"

"Dizzy, I have no idea what you're talking about, but that makes me wonder if a guy like you has to shit while you're invisible; I guess it's invisible too? That is not one of the questions that we were talking about earlier. No way; that was just thinking out loud. As far as snake shit is concerned, it would be best to look for it in the light of the day. Now, I asked you how much the thing weighs, and I believe you said, 'half a billion mactoids at least.' Was that supposed to be a joke?"

"Let me think… A thousand of your pounds, maybe a bit more."

"A bit more? It looks like a whole lot more. Do the boys inside know that I'm here?"

"Yes, but they are deathly afraid of your size. They've never been close to a human, only seen pictures. They watched you walk up and immediately activated all the porthole viewing slats' automatic closing sequence. So now they can't open them for a few hours."

"You keep using this collective pronoun, 'we,' and I'd like to know who else is on this party line. I'd like to check on the animals ASAP too. Maybe go get them and make camp here. I can't wait for the sun to give us a better view."

Instantly, if not faster, the corner was lit up in soft blue light, with higher intensity beams out of nowhere nearby, focusing on the craft and illuminating the darkest under-corners. The rescuer jogged forward and was about to lay both hands on the hull when the silence was shattered with a scalding, "NOOOO! DO NOT TOUCH *0*!"

In an instant, the larger-than-normal specimen was halted in his tracks and then released from that bond to a standing position.

"Well, that was damn near too late. What happens if I do? I get electrocuted, burned to a frazzle, incinerated? Damn! The safety procedures at this rescue site are weak, and with that being the last straw, there is a new sheriff in town. That would be me."

"I was working on that warning, but I thought you might say something about the lights first—but no, you take off like these Catuhhibevpppics around here. I'm not used to things I'm talking to moving that fast."

"THINGS! I'll have you know I am a lot of things but a thing I am not! The only thing around here that takes off fast are jack rabbits and—"

"Yes, yes, those Catuhhibevpppics. I try to explain to them

that they need to be more respectful, but it's hopeless. They're all the same wherever we go except for the ones on BBBrrgtttte Three, a horrible creation called Possszziiimo Catuhhibevpppics that have overwhelmed and ruined that planet. They are much bigger than your horse, absolutely good for nothing, have tiny brains, and eat meat. The Watchers are thinking about starting all over. You can't touch *0* because one of the crew activated the protection procedures. This model injects you with thousands of neurotoxic and hemotoxic spineetts, which would probably go right through your hands. You would be dead before the spineetts retracted back into the shell. They say it can kill a full-grown Knnbewwwfit on Bovvetttiiectodettn if they try to stomp on it. This machine is very defensive. It can be extremely friendly, too. Its name is *0*, and *0* doesn't like to be touched by strangers. *0* doesn't want or like being trapped under this ledge one little bit."

"I've seen enough! Let's go. I need a good night's sleep, and we'll get started after breakfast. I'm anxious to see your suit. Can you talk with the passengers?"

"Yes."

"Dizzy, my friend, I'm going to get you out from under this ledge, trust me. I'll find a way. Rest well tonight, and sleep. I can find my own way back."

"We've been asleep for the last eighteen months, just recently woke from the experience, and won't sleep again for months. We'll all be waiting for the rescue to begin."

This time through the blue tunnel, he studied it more closely than before. It was an incredible piece of work, and of that he was certain. One of his many talents in life was lifting freight boxes and accurately estimating their weight within a few pounds. It's critical in the boating world to understand freight, know where it goes, and balance the load. He could usually lift far more weight than average folk, and he liked to do it all through life and show off how strong he was in his largeness. He had done just that on the beach at the Rock of Gibraltar when he and Jude met General George S. Patton in 1942. He had carried four large beach stones down to the firepit for everyone to sit on. The general noted that his stone was well over the two-hundred-pound range, couldn't move it much after Van Vedic had dropped it, and thanked him very much; it was perfect.

Vincent marveled at the wall, trying to imagine how the builders managed these massive blocks, how they'd matched them up with seamless perfection, and where the light came from, as there were no fixtures anywhere. These stones were big —they were extreme, too heavy for men to manhandle; thousands and thousands of pounds, tons even.

Back at the camp, he lit a lantern, built a fire, and started talking to his pets. They were both standing and listening, looked fine, being their usual selves, and still unable to talk back. He had to assume they were none the worse for wear and may not even know they had been asleep. If Dizzy could do that to a horse and a dog, he could do it to anyone, and so Van Vedic knew that Dizzy was listening.

"Dizzy?"

"Captain."

"You have any shovels?"

"Funny human, we don't dig."

CHAPTER ELEVEN

ALWAYS BE WORTHY

When the sun topped the eastern canyon ridgeline, it lit up the gorge with all its boulders, cliffs, and sandbars; all the shadows disappeared, and the cottonwood groves, with their changing orange leaves, matched the brilliant yellow light from the sunrise. There was no way to ignore the never-ending raging San Juan; its echoes bounced off the cliffs like lions' roaring. Everything came alive, came out of the darkness as if the king of the world was coming. Very few places on Earth are more unsuitable for humans than this one, and Vincent imagined being on the bottom of the lake someday, looking up through all the water that would cover everything down below. He couldn't think of a single reason why not to flood it.

He made his breakfast and coffee, packed up the camp, which was simple, and piled it all by his saddle.

"Dizzy?"

"Mr. Van Vedic."

"You can call me Captain; everyone else does. Does this mean you are going to continue with the invisible routine?"

"Unfortunately, yes."

"I was hoping you would walk up, and we could shake hands."

"Captain, this world of yours is perilous for us. We are not immune to so much. Something as mundane as mold on bread will kill us in a matter of days. It's not a good idea for us to bleed. Flies land on you, take a shit, and fly away; it doesn't faze you in the least. Flies land on us, take a shit, and we're dead in a day. It's the infections. I brought the wrong suits, and it will be a while till the supplies arrive."

"A while?"

"Exactly a CCLYPPP^^^FVFVFVFV."

"English, Russian, Spanish, something like that, if you don't mind?"

"Exactly a month here on Earth."

"That's too bad! I mean, that's really too bad. You know the old saying, piss-poor planning equals piss-poor performance? Now, you said you were in the 'three-sense you.'"

"Yes, where I can see, speak, and hear. All the other senses are left with my body inside the quarantine. Doesn't bother me to be limited like this, and I hope it's manageable for you. However, some creatures find it difficult."

"Not so far. We should go look at the crash site. Shall I bring the critters?"

"Yes."

Once he had El Bruto ready, packed with the camp rolls and two saddlebags, it was a short walk to the entrance for the tunnel, and before he even thought about it, Sarge had raced up ahead and vanished into the opening. The captain led his horse casually as they got close when suddenly El Bruto aggressively pushed into the captain's back and nudged him really hard. After almost falling on his ass, Van Vedic turned and started to scold the beast. Whetto once again nosed into him twice and was ready to do it again. The animal told its owner that it needed to step it up a notch; believe it or not, Van Vedic got the message.

"Dizzy, did you see what that yellow mountain of muscle just did to me? That's what you get for owning a horse: disrespect! I buy all the food, clean up all the horse shit, buy him an extra-large saddle, and then what? I get bullied around! And he has the worst farts. I could go on."

"How long have you two been married? He and I were talking yesterday, and he mentioned that you go on and on and on about the dumbest shit."

Van Vedic became mysteriously quiet and was now at a quick step as they entered the tunnel, still lit up in turquoise, with a bright sunlit exit fifty yards straight ahead. Even more so in the day, he was spiritually overwhelmed as he walked through a creation that told him, without a doubt, his fellow man had not made this. Not the Indians from thousands of years ago, not the people in Arboles or Aztec—none of them had anything to do with it, and that realization would challenge everything a man might ever know. Truth is truth. Men did not make this tunnel! The echoes from Whetto's steel shoes striking the seamless solid-rock floor bounced off the walls in a symphony of movement and continued till they emerged. Once out in the open, the captain took the horse's reins and prepared to mount for the ride to the far-distant corner. Once he was settled in the saddle, he leaned forward and talked to the horse directly between its ears.

"So... I go on and on and on about dumb shit?"

"Captain, are you talking to your mate or me?"

"He is not my mate, and nooo, I wasn't talking to you."

El Bruto Whetto did a one-ton hop-skip, lifted his tail, and blew air out his ass for ten seconds, with the breezes blowing south to north at about the speed of a walking horse. If you could have painted it green, you would have seen the beast walking in a green cloud with his nose way up high and his lip twitching. Unfortunately, the captain had no choice in the matter, other than to frantically wave his hands in front of his face while gasping for air.

Finally, the air cleared and the captain worked their way around the arena and then up the clearing alongside the north barricade.

"Dizzy, can I touch it now?"

"Let's talk for a while. I understand that you think you're looking at a machine that has crashed. That much is true, but 0 is not an it. Please! 0 is listening to our conversation. 0 is patient. 0 is most appreciative. But 0 is not an it."

"Everything that I'm seeing, hearing, and planning to do will not be remembered?"

"No, sir, not by you."

"Does 0 feel pain?"

"Brilliant question! Brilliant. Very good. Yes and no."

"Is 0 in pain right now?"

"0 is in pain, but there's so much more to it. It has to do with the cadets and the fact that they are still alive inside. 0 was born to fly and can't; that's incredibly painful. Primarily, 0 is the mind over all this, and the *Gold Book* demands much from them and from 0, the result of a technology that your mind cannot even comprehend."

"You won't get any argument from me on that one. I would think 0 has thought of everything concerning this situation, and so have you. I need to know as best I can what that is. I need to know what you think. I have no tools—two thin saddle ropes are all I brought. I want to get close to 0, look under the ledge, and put my hands back there. It's a thing we humans need to do; I need to touch *0*."

"Not just yet. Let us explain what we think the situation is, and then you'll know. The *Gold Book* demands that the MMDJWHKABNAYRN, the combined knowledge of these three cadets' existence and their unfortunate predicament, does everything possible to save them. Combined knowledge involves a theatre you would find unfathomable. The cadets are too precious and cannot be allowed to die. That's why you and I are here.

"We now understand that this rock face above us caused *0* to lose track of a guide beam they all use and was unable to offset the lieutenant's mind control at such a slow speed, a one in a trillion possibility. When *0* hit the sand back here to our right, you can see how he slid from over there to here. There's a substantial amount of sand piled in front that flowed up against the bow, and the windows up there won't open. This rock ledge that is possibly pressing down on the top of *0* may be slightly unearthed by all this, but we don't know for sure. You need to investigate it, look for cracks, and test that area. *0* seems to think from the way his sensors explain things that every micron of his skin is no longer touching the Earth after the last five years, except on the belly pan plates. It's a protective measure *0* uses to repel particles wherever *0* goes. His skin can get very hot. *0* can vibrate at a high velocity just sitting in place, and is capable of disintegrating from the inside out. If the cadets were to die, *0* would self-destruct and basically return to dust. It's all being scored in the *Gold Book*. This scene here is part of an immeasurable disaster we have experienced lately on Earth. There have been many, many other crashes, and we're not sure why."

"There was a rumor in Aztec of a large UFO that landed a

dozen miles east of there in a place called Hart Canyon, and that the army showed up and hauled it all away before very many of the locals were able to see the machine. They said it was huge. The army built a special loading platform along the tracks ten miles north of town to load it in secret. Is that true?"

"Yes, and *0* came from that exact mothership. When it broke open on impact, a deadly virus was let on board, spreading rapidly through the ship and killing everyone. These three cadets were immediately put aboard *0* after the crash, along with Lieutenant Spaqu, and were never exposed to the virus. They quickly loaded up supplies, and *0* lifted off and came here to escape being captured alive at the scene and to also pay their respects to one of the oldest of the sacred sights on Earth. The back side of Goradelchabbeitz, where all our medical facilities and spaceport operations are headquartered, would have been their eventual goal. They have gone through the hibernation process three times now and then through the recovery protocol three times. We use the fourth hibernation to end our lives if that is the only option left. That's always been the destination for the orbital craft, that or the South Pole."

"Let's see. You said there's a place that started with a G and ended with a z, and—"

"Goradelchabbeitz! The moon. Sorry."

"Our moon? That moon? You also said the South Pole?"

"We have a city the size of New Mexico under the ice, with geoengineering and climate control, and a sheltered land full of forests and mountains. The purest air of anywhere, no disease of any kind, and flowing rivers of the purest water on this arm of BKPLMOKNAZZZZ."

"Who taught you guys how to talk?"

"Excuse me, the Milky Way. Besides the South Pole, we have several very extensive under-ocean bases. Those seem to be the most sought-after environments for the travelers, the teachers, and those who come from the depths. It's as sterile there as anywhere. This brings up a story you will probably want to hear. You prided yourself in being a storyteller, and many of us now enjoy hearing the story of the white fishing boat that was scooped out of the sea by *DDccccV*. That would have been you. It happened over ten years ago, Earth time."

"Well, of course I want to hear about it, but then again, I want to get to work doing whatever it is that *0* needs and you think we should do right here and now with no tools to get him free. So, since you won't be helping in any way, you can talk; I'll work and listen."

Vincent attempted to say *DDccccV* so he could ask what that was, but his tongue got twisted quickly.

"Can't wait, as a matter of fact, but first things first. I'm waiting for you to tell me what's the first thing."

"Funny human. *DDccccV* is an interstellar starship, and you were its favorite rescue for a period of time. *0* is confident he can be pulled out from under the capstone by horses—three or four. There must be harnesses involved, heavy-duty pull assemblies, and not just a saddle. He believes we need a channel along the open-air side a few feet deep. This will give the vibrated sand a place to go. We must not damage the very top of *0*, which is so far undamaged. Perhaps it's a flaw in the design, but the very top of *0* cannot be covered by a rock of this type for very long, and it's been very long. The sun needs to shine on the peak for a while in order for him to be back the way he was. It's like *0*'s been neutered, partially turned off, but fortunately, it's easily reversed in this situation. When that happens, *0* will leave."

"Done! I'm out of here."

"Wait, wait, wait. Some rules are involved. The *Gold Book* talks about this situation. What were you planning to do?"

"Well, I was planning to ride to Arboles and get Rahellio and Raton, two more horses, and every inch of horse harness we can find. Shovels, rakes, canvas, ropes, and other stuff; lots of stuff! Food—lots of food—and tequila. What are some of the rules?"

"Now that I have confided in you a sizeable amount of information about us, you can't be allowed to remember what you've seen and heard last night and today. You knew this. The way it usually works is that when you turn your back towards me and walk away for the last time, a certain percentage of your memory disappears. That does not mean you can't go get the stuff. I love the word *stuff*. For example, when you tell Rahellio you need all this stuff, he will ask you why. He and Julio both saw the diamonds in the sky, but now they don't remember that. They think they went on a stupid fishing adventure, got sick, and now have no memory of the blue lights. The same thing will happen to you as you ride away from here."

"No shit?"

"Not again!"

"What?"

"We must find a reason that convinces you that you need all the stuff. The same reason you use to persuade and pass Rahellio's test, his commonsense question—why?

"Now, imagine you have forgotten everything about all of this as you ride away. We can't make an exception for you—that was precisely what they did with Ezekiel. They made an exception, and today it is what it is. Our scholars estimate the discovery will be made in the next twenty years or less, and then it'll take another fifty years to be accepted as truth. His wheel within a wheel depicts exactly what he saw and what our machine was doing. It wasn't God whom Ezekiel met. It was us. Another gentle giant from the ancient past would be Enoch.

Maybe humanity will be ready by then. Maybe not. Your species has always been a never-ending big surprise."

Vincent scoured his memory for the story in the *Bible*. These creatures with the "likeness of man," from what he could recollect, take Ezekiel with them in their craft, bringing him to a "temple" on top of the highest mountain. During his flight there, Ezekiel mentions feeling God's hand on him, which could be interpreted as the force of gravity, or g-forces, felt when lifting off. He is taken to these beings' "temple," which is likely a staging area or city where they reside.

"You're asking if humanity will be ready to accept you folks as our Gods?"

"The *Gold Book* won't allow that. We are not Gods. Mankind was awarded our undivided attention back in 1935, maybe '36, when scientists worldwide started understanding the atom and then created a weapon ten years later. It was used to kill an enemy. We watched you do it. Humanity crossed a boundary line at that time and has entered a period that you must survive, a period described as The Test, and which not every planet survives. As a universal rule, all developed entities that discover the atom must go through this test. The odds are against you; mankind has much violence in its gene pool, and that is possibly our fault in the first place."

"What's a gene pool?"

"Never mind that. Currently, there are half a dozen of your countries that have nuclear weapons. If you survive that long, within a hundred years, there will not be any; it's a very slippery slope! Nuclear war must be avoided at all costs. Our understanding of the examples of other planets that failed the test shows the damage to a world of this size would take ten thousand years to recover from. We study this phenomenon in great detail. When the atom is discovered on any planet anywhere, we start what we call the Doomsday Clock, with midnight being doomsday; the day the planet destroys itself. From the time of that discovery, every year that passes moves the clock closer to doomsday. The opponents here on Earth are already building arsenals of systems, doing whatever it takes for whatever reasons, no matter the cost. It's *MAD*, an attitude that forces participants to guarantee their enemies of *mutually assured destruction*. The competing countries will spare no expense while building bombs so huge that nothing will survive. Your homeland, Russia, Captain Vincent Van Vedic, is a miserable place for sure and ruled by a madman; they are in the early stages of building a bomb so big it may grow out of control."

Vincent got a sudden mental flash of a Soviet weapon called the *Tsar Bomba,* which would unleash almost unbelievable energy—in the order of 57 megatons, or 57 million tons of TNT, more than 1,500 times that of the Hiroshima and Nagasaki bombs combined, and 10 times more powerful than all the munitions expended during World War Two.

"This attitude is guaranteed to continue until they become so angry that they attack each other in a fury or by accident. Many of the failed planets destroyed themselves by accident, a misunderstanding, the reactions of computers, or through wars started and ended in days that killed their atmospheres with poison and radiation.

"Unfortunately, our crashed vehicles have been used to enhance this ability by leapfrogging over technology that usually takes a genius to discover. It's called reverse engineering, and you Americans are very good at it so far, but you're not the only ones doing it. Mankind has a problem understanding its importance in this Universe, a problem it didn't have when it was developing. The ancient peoples often took us to be Gods, and try as we did at the time, we couldn't get them to stop.

"So, that's the issue. How do we get you to ride away, go gather everything you think we need, along with a good reason, and then come back here and save *O*?"

"Is there anything you can do? I'm surprised, Dizzy, that you guys can't help a little."

"If you knew what we had to do to get you to this location, you would never say such a thing. All that aside, we are very involved but unable to be physical about it at this time. Do you believe that Rahellio can see the blue lights from his back porch?"

"No!"

"Rules that idea out. It could be arranged that your dog Sarge has an accident, has fallen into a crevice, and you can save him with a significant effort by pulling a large boulder out of the way. Unfortunately, he has slid off the rock and is now wedged in the crevice, and you can't get him out by yourself."

"Sarge won't be hurt?"

"There are few guarantees in this Universe. The script I am following has you finding the dog howling in the rocks, the very ones that disappear at the tunnel entrance. You instantly understand the particulars. You decide that if this one huge boulder in front is moved, you can get at Sarge from below and push him up and out. It will be rather traumatic for you, forcing you to make an instant decision; you'll be on the horse immediately. When you've gone out of sight, the boulders will disappear and Sarge will be free. The dog being in distress will bring you back, and we can start again with Rahellio and the beasts. We won't need Julio. Afterward, we will help you and Rahellio forget what you do here, when it's all said and done."

"It sounds like you folks have this all figured out, which is always a good thing, and when I think back on my recent past—and I'm talking about my entire life—all the Y's in the roads that sent me back to Pfeiffer… Is it true that you've been directing my life since way back when my momma died?"

"The Watchers needed a man like you to find Jude and then escort and protect him from where you found him in Russia to Gibraltar. From an abandoned village named Pfeiffer, Russia, on the Illava, then onto the Don, and right into the heart of the Second World War. Your passenger was an act of intervention by the Watchers, and getting him to Patton was essential in their plan to hopefully stop the Germans from attaining all the materials for the atomic bomb. From inception to being a weapon. Ten years and it would have become a killer weapon used for evil—or for good. When the monster 'Hister' was seen by Nostradamus in 1550, give or take, it was a call to the Watchers to prevent what they saw in the future. Things could be done starting way back then that would come to fruition in 1942. The second of three 'anti-Christs' would be threatening the world with atomic annihilation by the end of 1945 unless he were stopped in time. The Earth has come a long way in the development of its primary intelligent creature, and even though the odds are usually fifty-fifty at this point in the evolution of any planet anywhere in the entire cosmos, according to the *Gold Book*, the Watchers can apply for and receive additional funding if they think they can avert the planet starting off on the wrong foot. The Watchers were heavily involved with Patton, with Jude, with Monty, and quite a few others you stumbled into on your voyage. Any more questions?"

"Not at the moment."

CHAPTER TWELVE

WHY DO THEY CALL YOU DIZZY?

FRIDAY MORNING, OCTOBER 16TH, 1953.

The captain was ready to leave, snug in the saddle and totally frustrated by this impenetrable, unscalable wall of boulders. This unexplainable obstacle blocked his way completely, from the edge of the cliff face to the river. He planned to mosey home, up onto the plateau, and couldn't for the life of himself understand why he had bothered with this crazy idea in the first place. He worried over the image of the group puke and the possibility that he had damaged his relationship with Rahellio forever. He must have vowed four or five times to refrain from having these wild-haired excursions. El Bruto Whetto was more than willing, snorting, farting, and ready to run for some strange reason, which was not even in the captain's plan. The only thing missing was that heroic dog, who lived underfoot most of the time but was currently nowhere to be seen. Out of whistle range, evidently.

Whetto heard him first, which popped his ears straight up, and he even turned and started walking back up to where they had camped. Then, after a few dozen yards, Van Vedic could hear it too—the howling of an animal in pain up near the cliff face. When they got there, he leaped off Whetto, hearing the anguished wail, and raced up to the scene. Sarge was deep down in a crevice, all four legs first with his nose fifth, and fortunately only in the second row of boulders from the bottom.

Van Vedic climbed over a slab of cliff-face rock that seemed to be standing just to be an obstacle. Weird, he thought, that a rock would land like that while the agonizing sound seemed to come from around the side, so he looked there first. He could see through the narrow space four dog paws, about six feet off the ground and six feet back. He could barely extend his arm through the seam, but the paw tips ended up just out of fingertip reach. All he wanted to do was touch his pooch. He straddled the V in the rocks, three feet wide at the top, ten feet down, with the brown cur pinched at the bottom.

"Hey, Sarge. Hey, buddy, you poor guy!"

On the end of his body, the hairy whip said hello, two or three swishes left and right, along with a long-pained whine that sounded like an echo.

There was absolutely nothing the man could do. If anything, it appeared the hound could be pushed up from the bottom, because there was a cavity directly under the animal. But, unfortunately, that singular slab of cliff face blocked the way, and while standing there in utter frustration, Vincent put his shoulder into it and tried to push it over. Five feet wide, two feet thick, and eight feet tall, the size of a sheet of plywood, only made out of yellow rock.

"Sorry, buddy, I just can't get to you. You slid into place, didn't you? I think I could pull that rock out of the way with

Raton and Whetto, but it will take the better part of the day to get there and back."

The dog wagged its tail again and seemed to nod his head up and down, trying to see his master high up over his shoulder. Vincent was trying to be a realist, had the life of a fellow creature in his hands, and considered ending this heartache with his 45, but that would tarnish the weapon forever. Or he could go to Arboles and get help.

"I'll be back, Sarge. Don't worry, I'll be back!"

He jumped to the ground and ran to the side of El Bruto, climbed the saddle, and landed in place. Then, as fast as possible, they followed Rahellio's tracks out of the gorge, up onto the plateau, but instead of turning south towards his homestead, he turned north toward Rahellio's ranch many miles away, not sure how many, and planned on getting there in three hours or less.

Once up on top, the going was easy—not near as many boulders, plenty of cactus and pinon trees—so the captain and his steed set a pace that the beast was comfortable with. Rahellio's tracks were still fresh, and the Mighty Raton's prints were twice as deep as the horses'. Whetto needed no prodding, no kicks to his side. He seemed to know where he was going—back to the place where he was born. His nose and eyes were focused on what he knew would be up ahead—the corrals he had called home for so long, his horse friends, the coons, and the cows.

Van Vedic found himself at the critter gate, a half a mile from Rahellio's back door, slightly before noon. Good time, he thought, and told El Bruto so. He closed the gate behind him as per the order on the sign and could hear the dogs had discovered him. They would arrive in a few minutes, barking and yapping at the visitor, going from ferocious to friends when they figured it out. Rahellio would sometimes bring them to the switchback projects; it never failed to make Sarge's day. Just a pack of river dogs who ran around and played all day.

The captain arrived at Rahellio's back porch in no time at all, with his wife waiting to see who it was. Suddenly she let out a scream, threw up her hands, and rattled the walls at the top of her lungs.

"RAHELLIO! RAHELLIO, THE CAPTAIN IS HERE. RAHELLIO!"

He could feel El Bruto Whetto was surprised, as he did that horse muscle-twinge thing you can feel if you're sitting on him. Then she smiled a very soft and coy look, so much so that it was hard to believe she could yell like that, and Vincent remembered how Rahellio very much respected and loved her, partly because of her temper. Not exactly a small woman, she had frequently come to the worksites and did incredible women's things like cooking and patching up injuries or clothes. She could swing an ax like a man and actually loved to shovel dirt, to say nothing of the fact that she loved Jesus like you wouldn't believe and had taught her son the rosary. Her hands came up near her face. She was praying, "Hail Mary, holy Mary, hail Mary holy Mary," super-fast in Spanish. It was over in a minute (the prayer), and that's when Rahellio showed up at the door with the most surprised look on his face.

"Captain, how are you? Are you still sick, hombre? What can I do for you? What's wrong? Can I get you a drink? You know my wife? Me and Julio are fine, with no side effects. Where's your dog?"

"SHUT UP!"

The horse twinged again.

"Yes, my sweet mariposa."

"My amigo, the dog has fallen into a crevice. He is wedged between a rock and a hard spot back where we were camped, and

I need your help to get him out. It happened this morning; I just came from there. I think we can rescue him, but it's going to take you and me doing some digging, and we have to harness up Raton and El Bruto, at least, to pull a large flat rock out of the way. Five by eight by two, but it's standing up. I think we can pull it over. I told Sarge I'd be right back."

"Okay, okay, okay. It's too bad Julio is off with his friends in Ignacio for a few days. We could have used him."

"That is too bad. He's a good boy but we won't need him. We need Raton and all the harness you've got, maybe both the pack horses and harnesses for them. Plenty of rope and chains. A couple of good shovels, water, and maybe some food? He's waiting, and I think if we hurry, we can get this done before sunset. It's a big rock but it's not that big. So, I have to try."

"Si, senor. I'll meet you around back."

In little to no time, Raton had all the gear they seldom used strapped to his back on the frame, three expensive leather harnesses, and the one he wore when he pulled the funeral coach. They saddled another stallion for Rahellio and brought one more for good measure. Quite a bit of barn rope, a half-inch-thick steel wire tow rope with hooks, two shovels, a pick, a picnic basket full of food and drinks, plenty of well water, a two-gallon bottle of cider, and in only an hour, they were ready to leave.

"Tell the Mrs. that it might take a couple of days and for her not to worry."

"You tell her! Tell her it might take a week. Tell her in English; it sounds better."

Just before they turned the horses to leave, the captain acknowledged her overflowing basket full of food, tipped his hat, and said, "This might take a few days, maybe… maybe not. I'll take good care of him."

"Take as long as you both need. Fill the trout bag full."

After all the traffic over the last few days, the pony trail was well-worn and visible, and even though the going was a little slower this trip, they still made good time. They started the descent into the gorge by four, and an hour later, they arrived at the boulder wall. Van Vedic was way ahead of Rahellio and got to the spot where Sarge should have been just shy of dead, but instead, he was lying in the shade, sound asleep.

"Well, if that don't beat all! Hey, you mangy cur, how did you get out of the rocks?"

The dog was absolutely none the worse for wear, with no blood anywhere, and his tail was in over-swish. When Rahellio rode up and could see how happy the captain was with this discovery, he grew a big smile all over his face and dropped Raton's reins. He was saddle sore and needed to stretch his legs. He soon found the firepit Van Vedic had used the night before. The captain walked over to where the dog had been pinched and climbed back up to where he straddled the crevice once again.

"Rahellio, this is where the dog was trapped, and this is the rock I planned to move. I do not know how that dog got out of this mess, but he did, and that's all that matters."

The rock-and-root hater came up to the edge of the barrier, examined the stone that the captain wanted to move, and he, too, could see how trying to pull it over would have solved the problem. But, now, the problem had been solved. When he stood alongside Van Vedic and tried to imagine the dog being stuck down there, he couldn't figure out how the dog would have got out either. The sides were too steep, too smooth, with nothing to reach for or stand on. The facts of the matter left both men confused, so they decided in unison that it was a miracle.

As the captain followed Rahellio working his way off the boulders and down to the sand, the mountain of rock suddenly began to rub against itself, screeching and sliding. Both men,

Sarge, and their horses stood in a group with all their eyes and ears focused on the rocks in front. It instantly turned into the tunnel again, with the turquoise glow on the ceiling, walls, and floor, the distant sunlit opening on the other end, and a neon walkway waiting to be crossed. The dog was the first one through. Everything the men and beasts had been forced to forget was relearned entirely in the blink of an eye, along with a few additions.

At that moment in time, Rahellio was trying to comprehend what he was looking at. He now remembered the blue lights shining into the sky and their original goal of finding the source. This must be it. Everything was exactly as it should be. Since the captain was already headed towards the tunnel, he mounted his stud and gathered Raton's reins, along with the extra packhorse's, who more than willingly followed along. There was no fear whatsoever from the animals, creatures who usually might not take to the blue tunnel idea all that much. Instead, they never flinched. The posse entered the arena area in the far southwest corner close to the cliff face. This was Rahellio's first vision of the shelter. Looking at it from its side, he realized it was a fantastic creation; he could not believe what he was seeing, had absolutely no idea, not the faintest conception, that such an ancient structure was pressed up and under the cliff face. No one he knew had ever walked in this part of the gorge.

"Captain, what is this place?"

"It might have been a university, a sacred ceremonial site; someone lived here a long time ago. I don't know for sure."

"Indians didn't do this. No bueno. No man could do this."

"That is true, my friend, but if everything goes as planned, it will end up under a few hundred feet of water someday. As you very well know, this site is right in the middle of it all. We are here for a different reason, however. Dizzy? Dizzy?"

A pleasant voice answered about eight inches from Rahellio's face, or so it sounded, causing him to swing his arms in front of his body and push back something invisible.

"So, this is the famous Rahellio?"

The famous Rahellio was frazzled to no end. He jumped off his horse and looked everywhere for the body that went with the voice. The captain watched him carefully and then started his explanation.

"Rahellio, the voice belongs to Dizzy, and he's our guide. He'll explain everything there is to know much better than me, and besides all that, all you need to know is that he doesn't dig. They have invited us to dig out a problem they have, and he'll tell you about it. Speaking just for me, I am honored to have been chosen to be a part of this. Truly honored, Dizzy."

"If the captain is, I is too. Hello."

From there, the two men worked their way down toward the theater's top and could look directly into the middle of the entire creation sitting there on their horses in absolute awe. All their animals were highly motivated for the same reason. These four studs were not intimidating each other but seemed ready for excitement, different from their sometimes casual selves, just excited about something. The truth of the matter was that they, too, were honored because of their understanding of what they had been told at the entrance to the tunnel. The voice of Dizzy had entered their brains, calmed their minds, and continued to soothe their spirits as they carried on being animals. Dizzy could talk with them, and they had never been spoken to before, not like that.

Dizzy was telling them all a story of how life was lived at this ancient spot, during the ice age at least forty thousand years before, maybe even much longer ago than that, acting almost like a tour guide on the Thames, whether he knew it or not.

"...The austerity of being self-taught, learned, practiced, for centuries, right here where we walked. Those graduates went on to live for thousands of years in sssLLLOCCCsss."

Rahellio had been getting used to the voice, kept petting the horse's ears and whispering encouragement. It wasn't too far after his exit from the tunnel that the questions started piling up one after another until he had to stop Van Vedic and get some answers. This side of the barrier wall was straight up and down, twenty feet high or more, and the most beautiful stonework anywhere on Earth. He damn sure wasn't an expert on stonework, but he'd laid a brick or two in his life, and these bricks were six or eight feet square. One was as big as his smokehouse, a perfectly flat face twenty feet tall, with smaller blocks to its side and no space at all between them. He even touched it, both hands simultaneously, up and down on a perfect seam line.

"Dizzy, may I speak?"

"Yes, please do."

"Why do they call you Dizzy?"

"Only the captain calls me Dizzy; he's a funny human."

"Go ahead, tell him your name." Van Vedic was giggling and bouncing in his saddle, but Whetto wasn't moving.

"Ready?"

"Yes."

"Dzzitulatizebistauuugj FfffeekTTTraa Zzucobinnnlll."

"I didn't get that."

"Dzzitulatizebistauuugj FfffeekTTTraa Zzucobinnnlll. Dzzitulatizebistauuugj FfffeekTTTraa Zzucobinnnlll."

"Once again, hombre."

"Dzzitulatizebistauuugj FfffeekTTTraa Zzucobinnnlll," Dizzy said with all sorts of inflection, vocal enhancements, and yodeling.

"Dizzy works for me too. Next question, Mr. Dizzy. Are you God?"

"NO!"

"You said these graduates from here went on to live for thousands of years. Where?"

"sssLLLOCCCsss, the fourth planet around the center star of what you call the Belt of Orion, in the center of the Orion constellation."

"NO CACA!"

"You too?"

"I don't know what to ask you next. So, you've come from the Belt of Orion? My wife uses the belt up above to say the first three Hail Marys of her rosary when she's praying at night. Those stars get her thinking 'rosary,' and off she goes. It's a prayer we say. I'm so anxious to hear more. Sorry for bugging you. Tell me anything about everything. She can say a rosary in fifty-four seconds and once prayed the rosary constantly for all of Holy Week. Constantly for a week, morning to night, for seven days. I may not be ready for this, but since you're not God, do you know who He might be?"

"I can answer questions like that one if you insist, but it's necessary to remember that soon you will not remember any of this, and that truth makes many questions pointless and moot."

As they rounded the point and headed up the other side, Rahellio was even more astounded by the wall to his right, and had been the whole time. It looked entirely different from the outside, where the dog had been trapped. That side was megalithic chaos. This side consisted of enormous, smooth, red and yellow boulders, seamed together like someone was playing with clay. Master artistry twenty feet tall.

He could see something over Van Vedic's shoulder far up ahead. It looked like an airplane had crashed. At that point,

Dizzy started telling him what it really was, what the plan was, and how he would be needed. Next, Dizzy reiterated once again the old news to the gravedigger that everything he learned now wouldn't be remembered, and why his memory must be erased. Lastly, he told him the stories of Ezekiel and Enoch as they walked up on *0*.

There were no objections at all from either man. They understood the pure logic of Dizzy's explanation.

Dizzy was repeating almost verbatim what he'd told Van Vedic earlier that morning, with some additions. When they brought their horses to a stop, the captain and Rahellio were totally up to speed on the planned excavation, what *0* felt was necessary, exactly where to dig and how deep. After claiming a campsite spot to call home, they unpacked Raton, grabbed their shovels, and outlined the long trench they planned to remove. Dizzy was soft-spoken, kind and soothing while asking Rahellio to mark a spot at the top of the silver circle four feet out from the craft. Then he dragged the tip from there to the tail, the other end, thirty feet away or so in a semi-circle. From bow to stern, if there are such points on a flying saucer, out from the visible round side while the other half lay hidden under the rock shelf. Dizzy was exact on his instructions, and Rahellio was as precise as possible with his shovel tip while trying to do what Dizzy wanted. This project resembled the holes farmers dug when burying old horses, and precision was never a part of it; simply draw a circle and get all the dirt out.

"Dizzy?"

"Rahellio."

"Have you ever dug a grave?"

"NO."

"The captain says you don't dig. Never have in your life? You've never dug in the dirt?"

"Not once, not anywhere, never. It's the motto of the Space Academy, 'We don't dig.' Here on the planet you call Earth that we call WWwWweebbbTmmuumm, there are places where things dig, like right here. Many of the creatures on this planet dig simply because they can and should. Some of you do it for fun. There are many reasons why creatures dig, and this is one of them. There are places where everything swims or floats, where life lives in the liquid, which I personally like. There's not a lot of digging in the liquid worlds. No one is very interested in digging where the worlds are places that are covered with ice; lots of those, but like at your South Pole, we live under the ice. There are places where we go that are covered in GGgvdd Eicccc liIIIoom, and we damn sure don't dig in that."

"Neither would I. No shit!"

"No shit? That's exactly what it is. Four planets in the OOOfrTTT SSppprRrR System are completely covered in what any human would describe as shit. It's like being sent to the Eastern Front in your Second World War, and worst of all, the *Gold Book* demands that any of us who are assigned to that sector must dig the GGgvdd Eicccc liIIIoom. After serving time there, they never do anything wrong again as long as they live, which is frequently for thousands of years."

"Okay, enough of that. Dizzy, now you understand I'm going to throw all the dirt from this line out here into this area as best I can? Try not to get in the way. I probably won't need any further instructions from you. Can we touch *0* now?"

"Gently. Announce yourself. There is absolutely no excuse for touching *0* accidentally, especially hard, like with a shovel tip. Please. You may not step up on the surface of *0*."

There was a touch of humor as Van Vedic watched his friend talk to a voice with no body, knowing from previous experiences that anytime Rahellio started to dig, it was accompanied by whistling and a lone hero's ballad in Spanish. Dizzy, *0*, and the cadets were about to hear the music he felt was appropriate, might be recorded, and they would all end up being better space travelers for it. By now, the captain was so familiar with some of the songs he'd first learned while working on the switchbacks that he'd blend in as an echo baritone at times, having fun with his part in the concert. Spiritual sounds while working hard, and Rahellio was very good at keeping himself satisfied with the music.

0 began to glow as if the ship's skin was a light bulb. There were rings around the outer edge of the spacecraft that were totally different from each other, on a level almost too small to measure, almost too thin to see, paralleling each other and all tilted towards the stern. Since they had been given permission, both the captain and Rahellio stepped forward and laid their hands on the surface of *0*, feeling him like they would anything they had ever felt before. We humans touch things, and in most cases that feeling never goes away; it's with us, inside us, for as long as we're an us. We flinch from heat and cold, love warm water, and when Rahellio looked at Van Vedic as they touched *0* together, he grew a giant grin all over his face. It would be impossible to explain the feeling—like having a gigantic strawberry shortcake. Van Vedic didn't know what to say, didn't want to let loose, and smiled like he was saying hello to the oldest friend he ever had. *0* taught them what it's like to say hello to new friends in his universal understanding of such things. While this hand-laying ceremony was going on, a group of slender windows opened a foot from the top of the machine, six identical beautiful eyeballs gazing through at their saviors. Both of the diggers nodded to all three pairs of eyes, with all those looks tallying a million words or more, those eyes of the cadets sharing that moment and begging for success.

Rahellio dug in right away and shoveled sand like a human digging machine. There was a rhythm to it; Rahellio's concert for six started with a melodic whistle, up and down the score, whistling while he worked. He'd been there a thousand times before, sometimes alone and getting ready to dig a man's grave. Standing above the first shovelful, he had always paused and asked Mother Nature to take this body back, ashes to ashes and dust to dust. Shovel in, slam the shoe, tilt it back and throw it through. It wasn't long until the ballad began. El Fego Baca's ballad without the guitar. An instrument had been packed when they left, but you can't play and shovel simultaneously.

The captain walked around the craft, up the sand embankment, and onto the overhang that had *0* trapped. It was solid rock, ten feet thick or more, jagged and extending out at least fifteen or twenty feet with half of *0* tucked underneath. He looked for any evidence of a crack or failure where the rock may have split because of the impact, but there didn't seem to be any. It had been almost five years now, so he doubled down on his inspection, speaking out loud so at least Rahellio could hear. Dizzy, *0*, and all three cadets listened to every word.

"This rock protrusion has no cracks anywhere; I don't see anything that shows it was affected by *0* sliding under it. Nothing! I think we're good to go."

Van Vedic followed the ledge across the top of *0*, describing what he was walking on, the color of the stones, the two monkey lizards along with a four-inch-wide horny toad that ran ahead, and how it descended into the soft sand where Rahellio was working. It immediately began to wiggle and vibrate until the entire little creature, save for its eyes, disappeared under the sand completely. This was the tiny creature that had inspired *0* to consider vibrating out from under the ledge. *0* understood instantly that the sand would need a place to go. Gravity would suck the sand towards the river. The gravedigger made good progress in the soft sand, with few rocks so far and no roots of any kind. He hated roots more than stones. It's a gravedigger thing.

Vincent climbed off the ledge and down alongside Rahellio and began to shovel in the same area. Both men knew this project would take a few hours, if not more. For some strange reason, the captain started humming the song of the Volga boatmen when he managed to get a tune in edgewise, which was one of his ballads that Rahellio knew and enjoyed joining in on. Besides that, both gravediggers and rowers share a tedium that some men know all their lives, and sing while they're doing their work. The next thing they knew, Dizzy was in the choir with a beautiful tenor voice, had brought several string instruments into the background from who knew where, and the two men dug into their digging mode. It was fun.

During one of the breaks, the captain talked into his coffee cup, "Dizzy, your voice is beautiful and the background strings were stunning, made us want to sing forever. But if I didn't know any better, I'd have to say you already knew that song."

"I wanted to join in when you and Jude were singing it, out on the great open waters there on the Don River in Russia. Remember? Plus, you sang it by yourself at night, crossing the Black Sea. For a while there, it was the only song everyone sang on the third switchback."

"No shit."

"Funny human!"

Very quietly, back near the end of *0*, a three-foot-wide section opened up and rose majestically, creating the exit portal, with a fancy little two-step shelf that came out of nowhere just below the rim line. It damn sure wasn't made for humans. Dizzy's voice interrupted the singing.

"The cadets are protected in film and would like to see you two humans. Unfortunately, they have only seen pictures. Please don't sneeze or cough in their direction. You may look inside *0* from his rim, but you may not enter."

With one six-foot-eight human on one side of the door and one a foot shorter on the other, the three cadets sat inside, looking out. Van Vedic could instantly tell that they were in lousy shape. He had no idea what a healthy cadet would look like, but these three representatives weren't it. These three fellas were dying, and he could see it in their eyes. Their heads were shaped like hearts, not as big as humans' but very large for the size of their upper bodies, large, beautiful, shiny black oval eyes, and holes where everything else was supposed to be. Things like ears, mouth, and nose were missing, and only the holes were left—especially their mouths, slightly more significant than the other holes but not by much. There was no hair on their heads, no mustache or eyebrows, just bald as could be. A shield obscured their bodies from the middle of their chests down, but their tiny, frail arms were folded on top of the guard, and they actually waved their hands with three long fingers and a thumb.

Dzzitulatizebistauuugj FfffeekTTTraa Zzucobinnnlll began the introductions with great respect in his voice, a rather long and tedious declaration of precisely who they were and where they had come from. Their distant forefathers had lived here at this site in the very distant past, and it was sacred beyond sacred. Dizzy said they hadn't moved much in the last five years and need to soon, but probably not here on WWwWweebbbTmmuumm. It was the very best medicine for them.

Van Vedic filled up the opening when he centered himself twenty feet out and climbed out of the trench he was working on.

He smiled, nodded his head up and down, and then saluted the cadets.

"My three amigos, we're going to get you out of here and on your way as soon as possible. My name is Vincent Van Vedic, and this is my compadre, Rahellio Candelaria. It is our great honor to be of assistance to you. Sorry you're having a bad visit to WWWblubber Earth, but I'm gonna fix that. We need to get back to work. Wonderful to meet you." He was trying to say WWwWweebbbTmmuumm, but the word would require him to wiggle his lips like Raton before a sneeze and gargle at the same time, using w's, b's, m's, and a t, so he missed the name by a smidge.

The afternoon wore on as the trench got deeper and longer, proving to be easy digging in the shadow of the cliff face. The saviors rested periodically, built a fire about fifty feet from the open passageway door, started a percolator, and set up camp. All three cadets could see the campsite and appeared marveled at the view. They watched the humans eat and drink, were fascinated by the horses, and smiled their tiny holes when Sarge nearly ran inside 0. A creature often defined by extraterrestrials as large vermin, the dog was almost ready to initiate his all-excited, glad-to-be-here jumping maneuver, which would have landed him inside 0. But, unfortunately for him, it was as if he had been frozen in action. His entire forward motion was stopped in an instant, and he fell over flat on his side, still in stride, with his eyes open wide and his tongue hanging out on his hide. The captain thought his dog was dead as it tumbled off the front edge of the step and landed flat on his back with all four paws sticking straight up. He tipped over and lay there for a moment, but then he stood up, shook himself head to toe, gently raised his head up out of the trench, and looked at the cadets sorrowfully.

Dizzy's voice split the airwaves, accompanied by an apparent

Orionian giggle, "No dogs! taduddalalicka taduddalalicka, lic lic lic."

The theory 0 had developed consisted of him vibrating at his core, just like the horny toad lizard, causing the sand underneath to shift and settle in the river's direction. Sand always wants to be at the bottom of the river, billions of grains vibrating to a lower level and trying to escape the relentless percussions. That was the plan. It was an exhaustive process for 0 and drained his being, which he seldom used this way—as in never. It was entirely physical instead of mental and challenging work. 0 realized during the horrifying crash that sand had been pushed towards the front as the ship slid under the ledge, lifting him a foot or more on the end. He was trapped and couldn't even be pulled out for fear of scraping the very top off his head. His entire consciousness and material being had to sink down and away from the ledge. Then perhaps he could be pulled out from under the danger.

The captain was shoveling hard under the edge of 0, near the portal. He'd throw fifty shovel loads from the right side and then fifty from the left, back and forth for thirty minutes, until he needed a break and a towel to wipe off the sweat. The same held true for the gravedigger, and he, too, looked like someone had poured a tub of water on him. Evidently, the cadets communicated with Dizzy and asked questions about what was happening and why the humans were melting. But, of course, they actually knew otherwise and were guilty of sharing a little Orionian humor with the voice. Dizzy counted shovelfuls of dirt, weighing them in the air, and calculated the distance thrown along with the spread factors after impact for no reason whatsoever. The two men had carved out a grave for a colossal banana, and when they were done, Dizzy asked them to put their hands on 0 once again. He had a gift as a thank you for their work so far. This hand ceremony was different, as *0* let his energy flow through their bodies for nine seconds and nine seconds only, filtered their blood, searched their bodies for problems, and partially cleansed them of future old age issues. The captain closed his eyes and could suddenly remember Jude's cane. He could remember having felt this feeling before and, at the time, he'd thought he never would again. But here it was. As they stood side by side admiring their creation, the two saviors weren't one bit tired all of a sudden. All the sweat had dried up, and it was like they had just woken up.

CHAPTER THIRTEEN

THE BAND

"Captain, we must find Spaqu's band. Now, before it's too late. Both of you, please. If you two humans could head for that corner, that's where we'll start. *0* is going to provide a safe container for the band. When you find the band, you must not touch it. It houses a neutronic systic/non-aligned power bead. Please do not touch it. *0* will provide a tool. We'll talk more about it on the way."

When he was done communicating, a long thin tube glided out the port opening and set down a small silver box near the steps, with a two-foot-long wand by its side. *0* retracted the line back into himself. The captain retrieved them both and looked them over really closely as he and Rahellio started their walk. The steps retracted without the slightest sound, the portal closed, and so did the windows. *0* changed color, went from silver to dark gray, and began vibrating. The ground all around felt different—a trembling in the small world, straight out and down from *0* and as far as the outer edges of their camp. Dizzy told them not to worry but to feel what they could and try to understand the power of *0*. Reluctantly, the duo walked away, and as they approached the barrier wall, it instantly formed a new tunnel, smaller than the one on the other side and seemingly designed with Van Vedic in mind, just the right height and the correct width, which was way past plenty for Rahellio.

The search was on, with the terrain riddled with boulders of every size there is creating an ideal country setting for a variety of cactus species and rattlesnakes, jack rabbits, lizards, and horny toads. Dizzy must have been following a map that ignored the size and complex problems the rocks created unless you were a snake. Right at the start, they had to detour their route three times, twenty or thirty yards left or right, trying to find a way through to get to where Dizzy wanted them to be. The killer snake's path was one hundred percent different from the one a man would take. These two men were more than capable of dealing with a monster diamondback; they actually had a bone to pick with the creature if he was still in the neighborhood. Men should never roam around in rattlesnake country with their heads in the clouds, and when you heard that rattle, you should try not to be stupid from there on out.

"When the snake attacked the lieutenant he was resting up closer to the cliff face, exhausted from his rather short excursion but perhaps unaware of the danger. He might have slept through the rattlesnake class at the academy, and then again, maybe not. His band will tell the Universe what he was thinking and how he felt at the time. It was over in an instant for him, and the snake slithered away. They cadets followed its progress on their scanners until the movement stopped and the band began to send out a rescue signal. It hasn't moved since. It will do that forever because of its neutronic systic/non-aligned power bead, unless and until it's put in a silver urn for protection. That's exactly what we shall do tonight."

It wasn't but a half-hour or so when Dizzy told them they were almost there. The band, he said, would resemble a humans' wedding ring; no way of knowing the color by now, but they were very close. "Stop." The men scoured the area, focusing on two boulders with a circular sand clearing in front, and there it was, partially buried and pointing straight up. Where a diamond should be was a glowing petite blue light, pointing at the sky.

With three warnings about touching it, Dizzy, who seemed to be somewhere up above him off his right shoulder, explained the retrieval procedure to Van Vedic. He was to situate the open silver box nearby, pick up the band with the wand, put it in the box, close the lid and use the wand to carry the box.

"Why are you above me? What's wrong with you floating down here with us? I know you're up there. If you tell me not to touch the band again, I'm gonna touch it. I'm going to grab it and swallow it, neutronic systic/non-aligned power bead and all. Don't say it. Doooon't say it."

"How's this," a voice inquired from about six inches in front of his face; kind of hard to tell exactly with the invisible issue going on.

"Too close."

"Vannie talked to you this close and you didn't mind. You talk to the horse this close. I'm just trying to find your happy zone."

"Ain't Vannie something else?"

"Yes, she is."

While Van Vedic was squatting down and finding a place for the box close to the band, Dizzy kept on talking.

"I have never seen a band that has gone into its rescue signal mode, and as you can see, the powers that be have demanded that every effort be made concerning all this. Were it not for this band and the fact that it was activated, the cadets and *0* would have had no chance. I wouldn't be a bit surprised to find out that Spaqu may have done all this on purpose and may have intentionally sacrificed himself so that his life band would be triggered. Now they do have a chance. Because of you two. Your reward will be great."

"Whoa there, cowboy. I don't need a reward. I've got everything I will ever need. Give it to somebody else. Rahellio's a different story, but I damn sure don't need a reward."

"Brilliant, brilliant. You know that old saying, 'It's way above my pay grade'? That is so true in this case. I am just a messenger. You won't remember any of this, so in a sense, it doesn't matter, but there is no doubt in my mind that you will be rewarded somehow. It's in the *Gold Book*."

"I keep forgetting we won't remember any of this. I keep forgetting that. Don't say it!"

The captain studied the silver receptacle one more time, analyzing how the wand would hold the band, how to close the lid, how to hook and carry the box, and now was ready to work. He knelt down close to the ring, set the container a few inches away, and slid the wand tip through. Gently, he placed the band in the box and noticed that the blue light went out, and instead of having to close it up, it did it by itself. The wand slid through a slot on the lid, and he picked it up and held it at half an arm's length, like holding a feather. He turned and followed Rahellio back to where they had come from, through the tunnel that then disappeared in a silent instant, gone. The men walked up to their campsite only to find a very unusual and frightening scene.

"Don't worry, the animals are fine; nothing wrong."

That was good news to the saviors because all four stallions were lying on their sides, all facing *0* just fifty feet away, with only one eye open, and so was Sarge, who had evidently been twisting his backbone into the sand. They all raised their heads as the humans arrived, looked around a bit but then lay back to feel the vibrations.

"*0* is now and has been moving sand. Can you feel it? He's almost done."

To the captain's complete amazement, as he walked up on *0* and where the port opening had been, the entire trench they had spent four hours digging was completely filled in and level. The banana was gone. All the dirt and sand that was excavated and thrown out, forming the banana in the first place, was also leveled out but not back into the hole; that sand was a different color and had spread itself away from *0* and towards the river. Gradually, the vibrations settled down until the men couldn't feel them any longer, the sand was warm, and when they stopped for sure, the animals all stood up and shook themselves.

The portal opened again, with the cadets staring out at Van Vedic. Rahellio got the fire going, put a pot of coffee on the edge of it, and the captain very respectfully set the silver box as close to the middle of the passageway as he could, set the wand down, bowed slightly, and stepped back. Once again, the retrieval tube came out from inside somewhere and picked up the box as if they were magnetized to each other, leaving the wand and retracting itself. All three cadets watched it once it was inside *0*, out of the captain's view. They turned their heads in that direction, staring at each other back and forth, and then the tube came out once again to gather up the wand. Spaqu was back. His recorder was safe. All his final feelings, thoughts, and sufferings were now instantly back inside the pilot's life memory system he was always so much a part of. His band would be immortalized in the Hall of Pilots in the Valley of Heroes on sssLLLOCCCsss.

Rahellio unpacked his guitar and began to play one of his

favorite songs at a funeral. Soft and easy to listen to no matter what you were. This was Spaqu's moment of remembrance, something both men discovered was happening as they watched the cadets. Suddenly Dizzy began to sing, sounding like ten thousand voices coming into their ears from every direction there is. Words, instruments, flashes of color, bursts of wind, and as all this commotion was going on, even *0* got involved. The ship began to glow and went through a gauntlet of the rainbow colors, a symphony of color flowing around his surface like thought waves. Mesmerizing for sure. The two humans were staggered by the ceremony, and when it was over, they were winded and had to sit.

"Wow!" Van Vedic said. "Wow!"

Dizzy was back to his old self and evidently proud of his performance.

"Thank you, Captain, don't mind if I say so myself. It sure is too bad you won't remember that ceremony. When Spaqu's life band gets home, he will live forever in the Valley. He has attained legendary acclaim throughout the Universe."

The coffee was good and black, plenty of wood for the fire as darkness settled in and the moon came up.

Dizzy spent the better part of his time telling cosmic war stories, but there were never any actual battles, no one ever died, and everything was always right in the end. Van Vedic couldn't understand why he called them war stories. One after another, fascinating stories about life on planets so far away time and travel were measured in lightyears. Finally, he explained what *0* had done while they were retrieving Spaqu's band and how he used a tremendous amount of his energy moving grains of sand out from under himself. How he treated the animals to a feeling they had never felt before, would feel a few more times, and which he was not sure could be erased from their memories. But that wouldn't matter.

"*0* calculates that his effort lowered the sand about a nnernnyernnndivvvv under his belly plates, with twelve nnernnyernnndivvvv being needed, at least, for him to be safely pulled out from under the ledge. The digging this time will be much easier, like shoveling dry rice. The same plan as before, and maybe three more times after that. *0* is unsure of his recovery time, but he thinks he can muster the same amount of energy again in three hours. If you gentlemen can have the trench cleaned out in the next three hours, *0* can do it again, and we'll see how close we are. If the trench were like a dozen or two dozen nnernnyernnndivvvv deeper, *0* thinks that would be much better."

Van Vedic was sitting on a nice rock near the fire pit, staring at *0* and listening to Dizzy. Then, finally, it was his turn to talk, and he remembered how Dizzy had warned him about asking stupid questions, but there was no way he could continue without getting some specifics.

"Dizzy, have you ever heard the word inch?"

"I couldn't bring it up in my vocabulary banks, but yes, inches and nnernnyernnndivvvv are pretty close to the same thing. We taught you that measurement about fifty thousand years ago, we being an all-encompassing concept of continuation. So I'll use inches from now on."

"An all-encompassing concept of continuation? Sounds a lot like a collective pronoun."

"Brilliant, brilliant."

Now, knowing what they were really talking about, the captain found his shovel and joined his compadre, shoveling out the rice. That was precisely what it felt like; lightweight sand that seemed buoyant, went almost as far as damp sand, and was practically effortless. In only an hour or so, maybe two, the banana was back, deeper by two feet, a little longer than before, and literally the length of a shovel handle under the body of 0.

They retreated to the fire and the treats that awaited them— jerky, smokes, drinks, horse smells, and leather. Dizzy invited them both to get ready for when 0 was recovered enough to start his vibrations again and that he was optimistic the new trench would fill in faster than on the first try.

"No offense intended when I called you cowboy; you have my full respect. It's a term I use now and then. Has anyone ever called you cowboy before?"

"I was a cowboy of sorts, spent time on WWrrrRRcoconnn during my plebe decade at the academy. That planet is somewhat similar to the moon up there, more immense, with lots of water, dry land, and ice on both poles. It's beautiful! The moon up there is a better duty station for us, primarily and especially because of the gravity issues, there being a lot less up there. The above-ground habitats up there on the dark side are remarkable, and of course, on the inside of the moon are cities that allow us to walk uninhibited, much more accessible than down here. The moon is hollow and has the most perfect living environment inside itself, so much so that many of the inhabitants don't ever want to leave. When the ancients made the moon and put it where it is, the Earth was still too hostile for living things, so the Watchers dragged the moon in place, which slowed it down, stabilized the Earth and made it livable. It was not easy to do; it took a billion or more of your years, and today we have what we have.

"That moon controls life on Earth more than anything else there is. The tides, your blood, the eclipses. Life couldn't live on Earth without Goradelchabbeitz! The moon."

"Captain, did you hear that? He said they made the moon. Did you hear that? Mr. Dizzy, will you say that again?"

"We made the moon."

"Did you hear that? He repeated it. Oh, boy."

"Goradelchabbeitz! Your moon. This type of counterbalance planet was common during the stabilization times for the Earth. Throughout this Milky Way, along with all the other Milky Ways, the Grand Designers placed Goradelchabbeitzes perfectly near blue or green planets, planets in the Goldilocks Zone, to stabilize their orbit, cool down the surface, and make green zone planets habitable in the far-distant future. Watchers are like never-ending Johnny Appleseed spreaders, Grand Designers who strive to make it possible for life to flourish in the cosmos. Mankind doesn't know this yet, but the number of suns, planets, and moons in this Milky Way of ours will astound you in the next fifty years. You will invent telescopes that can see all the way back to when the Universe began. It's inevitable. The moon is an engineering marvel, a goal of the rocketeers, an unnatural object that is still unexplainable even to us, who live there. Our *Gold Book* defines the Grand Designers as God's helpers, the Watchers. Our *Gold Book* defines God as undefinable."

About a quarter of a million miles away, Goradelchabbeitz shone down on them as *0* closed his portal and the ground began to shake. All the animals lay back down and even pressed their cheeks to the sand. The captain and Rahellio ended up sitting in the sand, touching the Earth, experiencing *0* in his essence. Physically speaking, the vibration was unlike any feeling the men had ever felt before. The rhythm soothed their joints, veins, and muscles inside their bodies, and if they held their teeth together, the feeling was euphoric.

From the captain's vantage point, he could see the sand flowing out from under *0*. Very slowly, all those grains of sand were moving towards the banana. While he stared at different specific areas along the underside of the saucer, he could see that the entire top layers of sand were flowing together, all at the same speed, in silence, towards the edge of the trench. Technological magic, incredible power, and it went on until the banana was full once again. Finally, *0* wound down after thirty minutes. The portal opened, the animals stood up, and Rahellio added wood to the fire, but most of all, the cadets appeared to be better; something was different about their eyes and arms. They might have been excited.

When the captain and Rahellio were finished digging the third time, the gravedigger noticed more space between the top of *0* and the shelf's underside. Before the vibrations, he couldn't see back there very far, but now he could. It was progress. Van Vedic agreed that was also the case on his end.

0 began to vibrate a third time, forcing wheelbarrows of sand to flow out and down into the banana, and for the longest time yet, all the mammals enjoyed their full-body sensations. Even Dizzy was treated to enchanting Orionian emotions from the experience—more mental than physical and a thousand times deeper, he said. An infrequent event in the cosmos for a messenger like him to be so entitled, and that honor was deeply appreciated. His resumé in the future would include this experience, and the recordings he would feed into the system would be enjoyed far and wide. It was all being viewed and recorded live from Goradelchabbeitz.

Like a few times before, the portal opened up, and a dim blue light created a glow, with the three cadets in their perpetual big-eye stare. They could see the fire, hear the music from Rahellio's guitar, and were very much still alive, with things looking better by the hour.

"*0* needs to rest. *0* needs the sunrise. You men need to rest, sleep well, and enjoy your fire. We shall start again in the morning. The cadets want to leave the portal door open all night and experience darkness. They will be safe, won't they?"

"Inside these walls, there is no doubt in my mind we will all be safe, especially them and O. The horses sometimes never sleep and make all kinds of noise if they're disturbed; Sarge is forever on guard, and so am I. So I'll go tell them myself not to worry about a thing."

The captain approached O and announced himself, smiled at his visitors through the portal, and promised them they would be safe.

"Don't worry, be happy," he said. "Darkness is frightening to some folks, but not me, and I would like to make you gentlemen an offer. If it's at all possible, I would love to carry you around outside and show you our world at night. I could do that if you can. It's going to get chilly tonight, so dress warmly. If not, don't worry; be happy about everything. That's what Jude always said."

He walked back to the fire, found his spot and ate half a dozen tamales smothered in a hot sauce dip that made him sneeze after the first bite. Big sneeze, big sneeze again, and a bigger re-sneeze. A Van Vedic sneeze is unusual, to say the least; first of all, there's a lot of body involved, there's a roar about it, plenty of volume, and sometimes the neighborhood is treated to three in a row. The cadets squealed their little squeaks in a panic until Dizzy explained what had happened, and then they explained what they wanted to do. All three wanted to be carried around the clearing, down to the river, into the sanctuary, for as long as possible. Could they ride on a horse? Could Rahellio carry them as well? Could he shoot his weapons off so they could hear that kind of a noise?

"Your wishes are our commands. Who's first?"

It took a while, involved the portal closing for some time, and when it opened again, all three cadets wore a clear glass helmet only slightly bigger than their heads, almost like a bubble, and solid gold-colored suits with cute as hell little booties and mittens. Their belts were technical things, pouches here and there, and little gizmos, but no forty-fives or anything close. Their small mouth holes sucked on a straw, their arms worked right and left, up and down, and they could walk, which was precisely what they did, out from inside *0* and onto the shell of *0*; all three stood there and stretched their bodies. But, again, it took some time, and included what appeared to be a dance involving swaying, bending, and lifting their arms in circles and squares. The big guy in the middle was almost four feet tall, skinny as a rail, had a pair of eyes you wouldn't believe, and his pie hole seemed more prominent than his friends'.

Goradelchabbeitz had risen completely brilliantly, smiling down, and the cadets discovered that they had cast their own shadows behind themselves. They'd know of such things as shadows but had never seen their own. Over eight hundred Earth years old, and not one had ever cast a moonlight shadow. So they turned around with their backs to Goradelchabbeitz and all the observation platforms up there that were watching and recording the goings-on live, with one of the most massive audiences ever to watch an interstellar broadcast.

"The rescue of *0*." It was a known fact that *0* had crashed under a rock ledge in a desert of cliffs and boulders on Earth, a site that had been observed the entire time from the moon because of a rescue signal beaming into the cosmos from that spot. Spaqu's wristband would have called for help for however long it took, usually broadcasting at sundown for the rest of eternity.

The cadets watched their own shadows, touched each other's shadows, squeaking in delight and getting back to life. They played, shaking hands and touching each other while watching their duplicates mimic every move they made. In this once-in-a-lifetime experience, the depth of personal emotion for the cadets was not appreciated to the fullest extent by the saviors, who had zero appreciation for intergalactic communication and knew nothing about the size of the viewing audience either. This sizeable constituent could watch this behavior for hours. After about fifteen minutes, which was actually not a recognizable period of time to cadets who can sometimes live for ten thousand years, Van Vedic announced that the horseback ride was ready to leave the corral. Almost instantly, complaints rained in on the broadcast station, because the audience thought they would break for commercials. Vincent started to consider the number of firsts this nighttime horseback ride would bring and was determined to make it so memorable these visitors would remember it for the next few thousand years, just a drop in the bucket for some of the folks involved.

Van Vedic's voice was broadcast to the furthest reaches of the Milky Way, with delayed broadcasts all throughout Andromeda and Orion. "Calm down, guys, calm down or you'll fall off the edge."

In many places throughout the cosmos, that was not exactly how cadets were spoken to, but Van Vedic was human after all, and humans had proved to be hard on Orionians in the past, especially when they came this big. From up and behind, Dizzy's voice entered Van Vedic's ears.

"Captain, these guys are ladies… sort of. They don't actually think that way, the way you do, and if they were to entertain such a notion, they would instinctively decide and conclude that female is far superior to the male based on their understanding of the Universe. It's one of the reasons they're so intrigued by both of you and your animals—all males."

"Gulp!"

"A real war story. In the SSSISEEEttNNNccc system, not long ago, an explosion of BLLLoooioiofker ate all the males of almost every advanced species on the planet. It didn't matter to the BLLLoooioiofker what species it was; it only ate the males. There were three highly developed groups, similar to you humans, and the females understood what was happening and tried to save their remaining males. They hid them away from the BLLLoooioiofker, attempted to replenish the population as fast as possible, but in many of the cases, the males died anyhow."

"No shit?"

"No caca?"

"Funny humans."

The horseback ride began with the captain lifting the big gal off the side of *0* and onto the lap of Rahellio. She was chirping, touching Rahellio's face, her eyes aglow, looking hard at everything around her. She felt the horse's ears and the top of his head, which he gently lifted backward to make it easier for her, something Rahellio knew this horse had never done before in its life. Dizzy asked her if she were comfortable and content, and both her mitten thumbs sprang to life straight up. The gravedigger was overwhelmed. He had her surrounded by his arms, had his face into the backside of her helmet, could see her skin, and he doubted that she weighed thirty pounds. She placed her hands on his forearms and nestled in; he could feel her fingers touching him, pressing gently into his skin, moving the hair on his arms.

El Bruto Whetto waited for the captain, twitching the muscles in his neck, waiting for the slowpoke to settle. Finally, they walked up to *0*, and the captain gently picked up one lady, set her on his left thigh, then the other on the other. The chirping was so much fun to listen to; all three chirping at each other, highs and lows, squeals and whistles, a super-fast communication. They seemed happy, didn't have a worry in the cosmos, and their heads were going left and right, up and down, and so were their arms. The entire Milky Way was watching, two hundred billion systems streaming the broadcast live throughout their inhabited zones. The excitement of the ordeal was reaching unparalleled emotion, except on DDDdUUuuUU8800, and everyone knew why that was the case. What a dump!

Whetto blubbered his lips and then let out his best horse whinny, the full-blown nostril noise, almost like he was laughing, held the notes as long as he could and started to walk toward the river. Rahellio's horse did nearly the exact same thing, and as the parade walked along, the girls began chirping again.

Dizzy was evidently following right by their sides, up about ten feet, talking with the cadets, squeaking like them, and assuring Van Vedic and Rahellio that the ladies were comfortable, overjoyed, and ecstatic. They wanted to see the insides of the sacred structure and walk right up the middle of the arena to the base of it all. Once again, he brought his musical talents to the moment, sounds the two men had never heard before and, unfortunately, would forget. Still, it was beautiful— Orionian horseback riding music, especially for the ladies. "For truthful reasons, we must exchange horseback for HIIIMWMWM TTT ICCEeeeAABs," he said, "a magnificent glowing beast with as many as fifty legs, bathed in soft white hair, as gentle as a breeze, which can cause the passenger to imagine they are riding on a cloud."

When they approached the top of the arena and stared at the ancient structure under the ledge, a gentle blue light lit up the entire network of doorways, windows, and rooms. Many different blue shades from so many places and patios, all of which had lights shining out onto the grounds. The light was pulsating, inviting. Dizzy directed El Bruto to meander forward slowly, because he was walking on hallowed ground, and gave the human version to the men. Everyone understood. For the most part, it was two levels high, with balconies here and there, two small bridges over walkways, and one spectacular centerpiece covered on all six sides in a foreign language, writings, and carvings like up on the cliff face. There were six large flat tables made of stone at its base for creatures much bigger than the captain.

The ladies were chirping at each other, sounding like echoes to the humans, and listening to Dizzy's explanation of this magnificent creation, an invisible entity that knew everything there was to know about life in this canyon fifty thousand years ago, if not longer, and then forward to this very day.

The captain cradled his ladies while they both squeaked out their joy. Rahellio paralleled his captain, and all three of their passengers held hands. The walkways were three horses wide, with flawless stonework, and these men had never seen anything like it before. Huge stones that fit together so snugly you couldn't see a crack, forming this massive fortification under a shelf at the base of a five-hundred-foot-tall cliff. Van Vedic counted two dozen or more separate and distinct large rooms as they strolled from one side to the other, then up a gentle ramp and through the top side rooms. Each room was a masterpiece, a solid rock place where a giant had lived and slept at one time before it went back to some other beings.

Dizzy was primarily talking to the cadets but had the humans informed way past up to speed, and so too were both horses and Sarge. He guided the tourists back to where they'd started from, walking along dry canals filled to overflowing by the Gods in ancient times. It was evident that water had flowed throughout the complex in the past.

After almost an hour, Dizzy told the captain that the noblewomen wanted to re-enter the largest center room, the one without a ceiling, and spend some quiet time reflecting on those who had departed from there. They wished to walk around for a while, talk to the ancients, and be alone with those memories in a triangular meditation. It was a cadet thing.

The perfect host and guide returned to the patio in front of the center room's doorway. He found a platform of stone that was perfect for his right knee rider to slide off and be standing by herself, waiting for the captain to return and lower her to the sidewalk like she was a damsel in distress. He turned El Bruto around and did the same with his left knee passenger, and so had Rahellio with his cadet. The captain dismounted and asked Rahellio to untie the blanket rolls from the saddles and take the animals back but let them watch. Dizzy had mentioned that the queens would need to sit during their meditations and that they had never done such a thing in such unkempt conditions, but their suits were impenetrable for the most part. This requiem they would relive dated back to the times when the ice melted, and that river down there was the reason why the ancients had to leave for a time. They built the wall to keep the water back, but there was so much ice melting at once it became too dangerous, so they went back to the moon for a time. For the most part, the Earth had gotten out of sync with the moon and damn near froze up, but they got it under control, and things warmed up a few degrees, which changed everything. Hopefully, it wouldn't ever happen again.

The best Vincent could come up with was kicking all the smaller rocks out of the way, laying down the blankets and even his coat, wherever they might want, which turned out to be more than enough. He lowered all three to the sidewalk in the gentlest manner imaginable and followed their progress into the room.

They were so tiny, forty-eight inches max with their helmets on, bathed in a turquoise light, with their big eyes gazing through the ceiling at the heart of the BKPLMOKNAZZZZ. They didn't stumble once, walked awfully slow for sure, but they hadn't moved much in the last five years, so slow was to be expected. Throughout the galaxy, the vast audience held their breath as the three cadets touched gloves, danced in a circle to their right, and then back to their left. Eventually, they carefully sat down on the filthy human things and began their ritual. To say the least, they were small, thin, and fragile, guarded by a massive human male, who left the room but then stood at the doorway, watching the cadets play ring around the rosy.

CHAPTER FOURTEEN

QUIET MEDITATION

"GGGdddyhyhjjjjj."

This word was spoken so close to his cheek that Van Vedic thought he sensed the breath of the voice on his face, kind of like his Spivey sense was triggered, and the gunslinger was totally unprepared for Dizzy's voice from out of nowhere. He freaked out in panic. Both 45s came out so fast, and each one went off in the direction of the moon, within inches of Dizzy's nothing.

"Whoooaaa there, cowboy, it's Dizzy. Please don't shoot them again. Please! I didn't mean to scare you."

"SCARE ME? 'GADIJ?' YOU SAID 'GADIJ' INTO MY CHEEK? Where are you?"

"GGGdddyhyhjjjjj. It means quiet meditation. My queens were in a state of GGGdddyhyhjjjjj. I thought you should know that's where they were."

There was one thing for sure. This would tarnish Dizzy's

resume. The captain put his cannons away, embarrassed by his horribly hasty actions. He wanted to get mad at somebody, but in fact, the bad guy was him. This mindset of rescuing the cadets and *0* might have overwhelmed him there for a bit, and his quickdraw proved him to be the kind of a human male you should never sneak up on. As the rescue was being planned and designed, there was plenty of talk among the Watchers about how dangerous and unpredictable humans could be.

Rahellio was standing about twenty feet away with his back to Van Vedic when he lost his footing (and who knows what else), the whites of his eyeballs huge as the echoes of those two shots rang off the canyon walls, many times, as loud as could be. When the captain turned towards where the cadets had been sitting, he found all three standing with really, really, really big eyes. They were blinking like super blinkers, Venetian blinds type blinkers, and two of them had lost their straws.

From the two best observation platforms on the moon, in ultra-universal slow-motion super tech, most of the BKPLMOKNAZZZZ—i.e. Milky Way—were *oooh*-ing, *awwwee*-ing, tweeting and chirping for joy at the time. The cadets were meditating on three and twelve on the dodecahedron. This single dodecahedron crystal would glow outward from inside the center room of the shrine, and by the end of the next day on Earth, they would be rescued by these two humans and four horses. This meditation ceremony had been made possible because of the kind and gentle humans, both of whom had become instant cosmic superstars and had no clue whatsoever that they were. They didn't know of their fame, and most intriguing of all was that they wouldn't remember any of their heroics—one of those intergalactic magic moments.

Instantly, the big human male had exploded and blasted two large hollow-tipped 45-caliber projectiles directly at the moon cameras, surrounded by brilliant fire halos, lots of smoke, and a thunderous noise, including echoes in the canyons. The two missiles never even got close. If the moon were the target, they fizzled out in no time, turned around, and went back where they came from. But the entire Milky Way went into what might be considered Defcon 9 for about thirty seconds.

"Soooo, what did you all think of that noise?"

Vincent couldn't think of anything else to say, thinking at the moment that he was the only soul who had heard GADIJ, but in fact Rahellio was the only creature who hadn't. Vincent Van Vedic had never felt so stupid in his entire life and stood there in his largeness, recovering from as big a blunder as he had ever blundered. Everything considered, he decided he was talking to Rahellio. He'd accidentally scared everyone half to death, but in truth, it was all Dizzy's fault. He might have been the one who slept through the class on scaring humans from the backside when visiting Earth in a sense-three mode; not even their dogs can smell a sense-three mode, and so have no idea an Orionian is in the air nearby. Everyone knows the human is a scary and dangerous beast sometimes, even the females, and frequently they carry weapons that can kill quickly. Some are reasonably good beings, but they all eat meat and do all sorts of disgusting things. Still have quite a way to go up the ladder, survive the test, evolve a lot, and then a lot more after that. The galactic definition of a human is rather extensive, but the bottom line is they are generally a little too smart for their own britches.

Because every minute detail of every second concerning every action by every party involved in the shooting event was now known, diagnosed instantly, and computed into the probability of violence towards the cadets at zero, the Defcon 9 was reduced to four. It was judged and juried to be one hundred percent all Dizzy's fault. The captain really didn't need to know anything about GGGdddyhyhjjjjj, and Dizzy should never again whisper such a thing to a human; nor should anyone else. Or they might end up digging in the OOOfrTTT SSppprRrR System.

The girls were done meditating for the time being, couldn't get back into the mood they were in before the cannons went off, and now, understanding what that incredible noise was, they were practically giddy. It was, without a doubt, the loudest sound any of the three had ever heard, and since it didn't hurt, they wanted to watch it happen again. All three came waddling up to the doorway, with two of them dragging a blanket, whistling and chirping to Dizzy. This was revolutionary behavior for cadets— touching filthy horse blankets, laughing out loud, so to squeak, having fun with each other and sharing it with everyone in the Universe. They felt and fell in love with life at the early age of eight hundred and seventeen point six nine two.

"They want you to do it again, please. They wish to see it happen."

Dizzy's voice was pretty close to being the same, but something was missing, and the captain could sense that Mr. Three Sense was embarrassed about having scared him like that.

"Don't fret about it, my dear friend. No harm was done to anyone. I insist that this apparent misjudgment on your part was caused by me, and only because we are such good friends did you think you could whisper 'GADIJ' so close and assume I wouldn't freak out. I was known as 'The Gunslinger' back in my younger days. I've killed many men in my time so far; usually, people die when my Spivey sense is triggered. GADIJ and Spivey sense are close to being one and the same. Maybe you can cough or something in the future, to warn me you're there. No offense intended, but I had forgotten you existed there for a bit. Tell these beautiful ladies I'd be more than happy to shoot my guns for their viewing pleasure."

That message got passed along quickly, and the next thing the captain knew, the big gal had one of his fingers, had one of Rahellio's, and the other two were out on the wings. They were all walking out into the middle of the arena, where the elevated circle grew out of the surrounding walkways. A rock-solid disk, seemingly warm to the touch, older than old, twenty-four inches tall, and twelve feet in diameter, right in the middle of everything. The entire complex revolved around this stage; this was where they did whatever it was that they did. They were breaking records for cadets with every step. Finally, they each found a soft spot on the rock surface, Rahellio stood nearby, and the ultimate gunslinger bowed to his audience.

"My queens, may I present Vincent Van Vedic, Captain of the *Vanessa*, the vessel saved by *DDccccV*, our interstellar starship."

The captain laid his coat on a rock and stretched his fingers. His left-side cannon was suddenly spinning on the middle one, up and down, left and right. Then the right-hand weapon was out there spinning, with the entire viewing audience falling into the numerical category of brazquadroellions; no way of knowing for sure. He holstered them both in the blink of an eye. Still, it was measured the right way because 'blink of an eye,' is one of the most racist comments there is. The system didn't know any other way and felt obligated to tell the brazellions who were wondering what that speed was and how it compared to ZZEWWWWwwERn or KkkkJeeemm, two of the fastest gunslingers ever.

Van Vedic walked up close to his audience and showed the gals the guns, took out the rolling cylinders, and then showed them all ten bullets. In very serious chirps, they all seemed concerned about the holes in the ends of the missiles, but Dizzy chirped in, explaining the expansion principle on impact, which got two whistles and an "eeeeee." Vincent put all the bullets back in their cradles but brought out two new cylinders with the magical number of twelve. The cadets had been meditating on twelve in relation to the entire Universe at the very moment when Van Vedic fired the first two shots. The irony of this understanding that twelve, no matter what, is twelve, and now with this human having twelve bullets to shoot, was not lost on most active minds, the universal dodecahedron of life, except there, on you-know-who and you-know-why—what a dump!

The captain asked Dizzy to explain to his audience what they might expect from his demonstration from the up close and personal point of view—the noise, the flash out the end of the barrel, the sound of those hollow points whistling by the ears, the standard stuff. The dodecahedron of hollow points.

"Funny human."

"Sorry. Hahahahhahhhabawa bwa hahah, hahaha." (Choke, slap a thigh.) "Bwa hahahah. Sorry."

"Funny human."

Somewhere out there, the prestigious Universal Defcon Council lowered their worry counter to two.

All three queens were giggling and gurgling with each other, moving their arms and staring at the sky.

Dizzy began tweeting information concerning the noise volume and then explained to the captain that their helmets protect the cadets automatically from noise, smoke, particulate, and things of that nature. They have been protected all their lives from real life, had never seen the night sky while standing under it, never felt the heat from the moon or cast a shadow in its wake, never ever met a creature like Van Vedic, and were in no hurry for the evening to end.

Rahellio had retrieved the saddle blankets and shaken them out like a cowboy normally did, popping both ends three times, times two, filling the calm air with a blast of hair, sand, and who knew what else. Then he laid them down end to end for the honored guests to sit on, where they willingly relocated themselves. There was enough leftover on both sides for them to cover their legs, which may or may not have made any difference, but they did it just the same; three peas in a pod. Word spread throughout the galaxies about the drama on Earth, about the three cadets who were being rescued, and the story was on all three channels in some places.

So the captain bowed to his guests, ventured off about six long strides, and started his routine, told Dizzy that he'd shoot out this, that, and the other stars up there and surround the moon with four 45-caliber bullet holes.

"Get ready," they heard, followed by a dramatic quick draw from both holsters, then three successive bursts of four slugs each, shooting out the Big Dipper, the North Star, then the moon, and finally the Pleiades. As he holstered the cannons, he knew in his heart that he had, in fact, hit all those targets, bull's eye, but he would be the only one who would know that—or so he thought. This demonstration was designed to make noise and fire, but after precise measurements from the moon's observers, each of the twelve targets' trajectories was sure and true at close range.

The decibel level was manageable, and when he turned to see his fans, they were all three standing, bouncing and touching their mitten tips together, over and over and over. This joyous display, which was being transmitted throughout space, was the first of its kind. Cadets had never been seen showing such emotion, not in public anyhow, and this was as public as anything that had ever happened. Well, that was somewhat debatable; there was the Dragon Star incident, the Ping Pong Ball Cluster disaster, and of course, who could forget the Bunter Hiden catastrophe?

Rahellio had retrieved both horses, rolled up and tied the blankets to the saddles with not near enough time for commercial breaks, and was ready for the ride down to the river. The complaints started overloading the broadcast system immediately, even though they never cut away; it was the thought that counted. Uncountable complainers knew the powers that be were thinking of going to a commercial break at the time. Everyone, universally, had seen that same damn pillow commercial so often that violence was considered a viable option against the producers and directors of NABPSSBCCBS UNIVERSAL, wherever they could be found.

The cadets were back to playing in the moonlight. They had found a platform they could use to mosey up a gradual incline and physically changed their own elevation. It was unheard of. Over two feet off the ground, to an elevated flat surface, a stage where they cast their shadows on a megalithic boulder while they waited for their rides. They had to use their hands for balance as they attempted the climb and ended up touching the Earth— another first; everything they did was a first. Like before, the captain lifted the taller cadet back up on the saddle in front of the gravedigger. She gently pinched his forearms, eeeeeing and chirping, touched the horse's forehead again, with the animal softly pawing the walkway, and lifting his head up and backward.

Van Vedic mounted El Bruto, picked his passengers up to each knee, and they all headed down to the top of the arena and then the river at the bottom of the clearing. It was a slow walk; Dizzy was singing and chirping, Rahellio was whistling, and the captain was soaking it all in. When they got to the raging torrent, the cadets suddenly went still and quiet, never having been so close to such a thing before, but Dizzy explained all the natural facts and assured the ladies it couldn't come and get them. They were anxious to walk in the sand, get close to the water's edge, and listen to and smell the place. The captain found the perfect boulder to set his ladies on, dismounted, and helped remove the one from Rahellio's care, then brought the other two down with them, holding hands and watching the raging San Juan. The moon was full and lighting up the gorge as if it were sunrise, the cameras were rolling on the moon, and the entire cosmos was treated to a saga of life on Earth at night. For the most part, very few creatures in the cosmos had any idea where this Earth place was; seriously, many were wondering what in the name of XXXLLLGGJJJXXX were they doing there in the first place?

With Dizzy talking in his ear, the captain was invited to walk along with the cadets as they discovered the beach. Their life suits were examining the environment as they lived in it, and there was nothing to fear so far. *0* was monitoring such things, recording everything, analyzing everything, and reporting a continuous readout to the moon.

"These cadets want you to know that they've successfully learned the three languages you speak, and you can use any of those to talk with them now. They hear you clearly and understand. But unfortunately, they can't speak back in the way humans do, and that's what I'm here for. They have names and would like for you to know that."

"Names? Of course they have names. I'm almost ready. I used to think I was good at names, but I've learned recently that I'm not. Yarasheski is no big deal compared to you folks. Do they know why I call you Dizzy? Ladies, do you know why I call him Dizzy?"

"They all said, 'No.'"

"What do they call you?"

"Dzzitulatizebistauuugj FfffeekTTTraa Zzucobinnnlll."

"They do not!"

"They do too! Besides, out there in the thick of it all, even though it is possible to mingle the species, the entities generally don't. It's a rule in the *Gold Book*. The cadets were never meant to speak at length to anyone or anything for their entire lives. Instead, they talk with their minds to each other. Part of my training was learning to be the voice of cadets. Dear captain, unfortunately, you can't know the depth of who they are, who I am, or what is unfolding, but I can assure you the powers that be, the Watchers, are most pleased. It's about time for an ancient absurdity to end, and these cadets are apparently doing just that. Anything you can do or think of to make this experience more exciting will surely go a long way in their favor. Did I say a long way? I meant a long, long way. There exists an understanding that goes all the way back."

"All the way back to what?"

"To fully understand the Universe, all of the species eventually come to a point where they accept the idea that XXXLLLGGJJJXXX caused an event that you humans will soon call the 'banger.' No, no, take that back. 'The Big Bang.' That's good, that's progress, but trust me, you have a long way to go. Humans still don't understand that it's the blood that matters; the package's appearance is of no concern. It's the brain and the heart and the blood."

"Back to the banger; who did that?"

"The word you use is God."

"God, the Father?"

"XXXLLLGGJJJXXX, GOD. I might add that you gentlemen are not made in his image or likeness, in any way, shape, or form."

The cadets had walked along the edge of the river, all the way to both corners and back, usually holding hands but sometimes all alone, holding their mittens out in front of themselves. The captain was always close by but not in the way and had no doubt they loved making figure eights or silently clapping their hands together, constantly chirping their curiosities and pointing at things. Dizzy was there with an answer every time, even explaining what the thing was that left the sixty-three round poops. Then, as the group was shuffling along, Dizzy began the introductions to the captain, finding it easy because they were lined up—one, two, and three.

"Captain, they have decided to make it easy for you—easy for me, primarily, because it will never make any difference, but you may refer to this cadet as number THREE, this cadet as number TWO, and this..."

"Let me guess... I guess this last cadet is number one."

"Wrong! THE TALL ONE!" The voice began to cackle, mimicking Van Vedic's laugh, with various inflections, almost haha for haha.

The cameras focused in on Van Vedic, watched his eyes roll back in his head, and the look on his face that said he'd been had. The galaxies were roaring.

Rahellio went about the business of gathering firewood and building a pit, had it going in no time at all, with the cadets listening to the voice tell them why the fire was necessary to the humans, primitive as it was. He laid out the blankets some fifteen feet from the fire and cleaned the area of small rocks and things that twist ankles, explaining the whole time to Dizzy the sanctity of the campfire, the do's and don'ts, the music, the way food tasted, all the things he knew about it. This one was supplying heat and light for the time being. Were it not for the moon, it would be very dark. Moreover, this canyon was only weeks away from the start of winter, a time that demanded a good fire or the humans froze.

"Rahellio, my new friend, that's precisely why they installed the blue lights."

The cadets just couldn't get enough of the river, and neither could the viewing audience. After two trips back and forth, side to side, the cadets came near the fire and studied it. It looked like they were mesmerized as they watched the hot ashes rise up through the heat and smoke and dim away. They never complained about the light wind or the temperature, and as Dizzy chirped out message after message, in unison, they all waved at the moon with both hands and blew kisses at it. That was a first for the cosmos.

From out of nowhere, Dizzy decided to offer a warning to the cadets, "Please don't touch the fire, my queens." As one might expect, they put their mittens on their belts and wagged their helmets side to side. Just because they'd never experienced fire before, it didn't mean they didn't know what it was.

As this fire died out, Rahellio took the stand and began a solo ballad that he had sung since he was a boy. He used his hands as if he were holding music wands, and ultimately captured the hearts of the cadets. He needed his guitar to sound better, but it was up by 0. Three, Two, and The Tall One were ready to leave, so the men gathered both horses and planned to proceed with their ritual.

Dizzy thanked them repeatedly, but they had a new plan; the cadets wanted to walk. This exercise they were getting was precisely what they needed. Their metabolism was unusual, because instead of getting weaker after strenuous exercise, they immediately became more robust, especially after hibernation; they were storing energy. So, they wished to walk ahead of the horses, hold the reins, and were excited about the uphill climb back to 0. It was precisely what the doctor ordered.

The Tall One took the reins from Rahellio and walked up

under her favorite horse's mouth, reached up and rubbed its nostrils and its lips. The horse lowered its head and came down till its eye was staring into The Tall One's eyes, even bigger than a horse's eye. Two and Three did the same thing with El Bruto Whetto, and as all this was going on, the most massive viewing audience in the history of eyes saw it live—or close enough. The ratings were off the charts, but the one major drawback, the one thing that no one seemed to be able to do anything about, was the pillow commercials. Fifty percent of the audience didn't even use pillows, sheets, or towels. None of that crap. As the complaints poured in, this dude named Mike interrupted the commercial and switched to mattress covers.

The Tall One, Two, and Three started up the clearing at a slow and steady pace, leading the horses with the captain on the left and Rahellio on the right. The weather was perfect for walking a few hundred yards uphill in the moonlight.

After not too long, the group spread out a bit, walking around boulders that lay in their way. Rahellio waited as The Tall One led his horse through a narrow spot, and her sisters guided El Bruto Whetto around the other side of the rock. The captain and the gravedigger followed last, when Dizzy's voice shattered the quiet.

"CAPTAIN! SNAKE! SNAKE!"

Van Vedic squeezed around the side of his horse and jumped in front of Two and Three, only to find, to his horror, a massive rattlesnake, more than twice as long as The Tall One was tall, and ready to strike. It stood coiled two feet off the sand, nestled in its four wraps below the head, with sixteen rattles for a tail, giving a warning that usually comes too late.

The Tall One was squealing, a sound that none of her sisters had ever heard before. Neither of them had ever squealed anything like it, and no one in the Milky Way had either. Her helmet blinders were closed down tight. Dizzy told her not to move, not to worry, because the captain was on his way. The entire known Universe was on pins and needles, the snake was in the air, and then 'The Captain of the Ship' drew his weapon and killed it dead. A substantial percentage of the audience had never seen such a thing, watched it over and over in slow motion later on, and were struggling with the idea that a lowly human being had saved a cadet.

Using only the right side 45, he instantly set his feet, pulled the weapon, and fired twice. One explosion after another hit the snake just behind the head and again about twelve inches down from there. It was dead in mid-flight, never closed its mouth, its two-inch-long fangs smiling in death. It lay there twitching on the ground at her feet. Every morsel of that entire sequence had been captured and shown to the whole of the Universe, with no commercial interruptions, no bobbing head analyzing everything —just raw life-and-death action on a tiny planet known by its inhabitants as the Earth.

Warning bulletins were sent out to the most massive audience in all of history that this was a live rescue, nothing had been staged, and it was all real. Much as the producers wanted to take a break, the actors on the ground did no such thing. They had to deal with the new reality, and as a result, the show went on. All of the players in this drama had been so scared from that audible squeal, a first for everyone concerned, including the horses and the watchdog, that everyone simply froze where they were—or were not, if you were Dizzy. Only Van Vedic could move, or more truthfully, he never quit moving. During the shooting, his momentum carried him forward until it appeared to the Universe that he was standing over his kill like a predator. When he was sure the beast was dead, he turned all his attention to The Tall One. She had not moved in the slightest, looked reasonably sound, and had gotten much thicker in the last two hours; her shoulders were different, like she had spread out, bulked up; hard to explain but noticeable.

He took her by the biceps and looked into her beautiful eyes as they opened, so big he could only look into one eye at a time, and asked her politely if she was okay. Did she want to ride on the horse the rest of the way, or could he carry her in his arms?

The queen stood there looking up at Van Vedic, even though he was down on his knees, took his face in her hands, and brought him close to her shield. She held him there for a minute or so. Her mouth was open, she was speaking with no volume, but Dizzy told the man all she said.

"She says thank you for saving her life, but no, she prefers to continue with the walk. She wants to bury the beast in the last banana hole you dig for *0*; it was only being a snake and will now become far more than just a snake. History will create something around all this."

"That's right, gonna be a big part of dinner."

"Funny human."

"No! Seriously. We eat these snakes. It's delicious meat, but we won't if it's now sacred or something. There will be plenty left for the hole. If it's okay. It might break Rahellio's heart and hurt mine something fierce, but we can eat stale old jerky like we planned."

"I don't eat snake unless I'm starving to death," came the almost inaudible comment from the gravedigger.

"Let me try to translate precisely what The Tall One's just said: 'Oh, for crying out loud! If he wants to eat a snake, he can eat a snake. He killed it, and everyone knows that humans kill to eat meat. We three would like to watch the ritual, the hunters at the campfire. Did he say stale old jerky? What becomes of those elk tenderloins that have almost thawed out?'"

The three queens gathered as a trio, holding mittens, with The Tall One in the middle, and off they went up the clearing to *0*. The captain led the brute just off their right side, and Rahellio gathered up the snake. When they reached *0*, the queens went inside but planned to return to see the campfire.

"Good shooting, my captain, but then again, I've seen you shoot dove on the fly. You killed the biggest rattlesnake I've ever seen, and I've seen lots of big snakes. This thing is a monster."

"That, I wouldn't know for sure, but I'm glad I made it around El Bruto as fast as I did. The monster had tilted his head back and started the strike, but I got off the shots with no time to spare."

Dizzy was filling them in on what the cadets were doing inside *0* as Rahellio popped the fire back to life and then cleaned up the site. The coffee was on. Two skewers of rattlesnake slab would replace two beautiful elk slabs, and alongside them simmered a pot of beans and a cider jug full of tequila.

"Rahellio, my friend, this rattlesnake is undoubtedly the biggest one on record, and there's a reason for that. This is, in fact, the creature that killed Spaqu. Many sophisticated tests have already been done on its metabolism, revealing the lieutenant's remnants in the beast's cellular structure. Spaqu was physically, chemically, and in every way possible, a perfect creation, intended to live long and prosper, like a Nimoy. He was never intended to be eaten. From a purely biological point of view, the benefits for the snake were incalculable, with all due respect to the hero. However, there is an issue with you gentlemen eating the snake. It's very technical. By eating the snake, you will ingest part of Spaqu like the beast did. He will become part of you. We won't be able to erase that from you when you leave."

"Hey, no problem. All of us snake eaters know that these big old crusty critters are hard to cook and end up a chewy lump of tough meat that's hard to swallow. The animal was over ten feet long, as big around as a man's leg, and probably twenty years old. We'll just bury him as he is. To be honest, these thawed-out elk slabs are just yummy."

Rahellio chimed in, "If that be true, that Spaqu became part of this creature, by burying the snake in the last hole we dig, it will mean there is a place in the Universe where his remains truly are."

"As you humans prepare your dinner, I would like you to know that how you feed yourselves is a curiosity to the cadets and me. They are so excited about sitting at this fire with you, so excited about the music, the horses nearby, the fire and smoke, and the list goes on and on. Even *0* is in attendance."

Goradelchabbeitz shone down on them, and so did the cameras, while hundreds of journalists worked their way to the surface and set up new telescope sites. It wasn't often that so many of the internal residents of the moon came to the surface to even look at the Earth, but with all the science available, they were able to pinpoint the exact spot on the planet, there along the San Juan River, where all of this was happening. It wouldn't last long. Who would have ever thought that something so exciting could be happening in this quadrant? The cadets would more than likely be brought to the moon once rescued if that was their wish. *0* could take them to almost anywhere if everything worked the way it once did—a big question as *0* lay there, not having budged in five years. Could *0* find the energy was a highly debated question.

It was time to have a campfire the way it was supposed to be, for the present moment. Where the campers had a nice stockpile of firewood, no wind, thank you, the full moon was lovely, and someone playing the Spanish guitar was the icing on the cake. It was soothing to the human, kept the demons away, and most of all, it calmed the soul; it really did, even if you weren't primitive.

Without a drum roll, the cadets were back in the opening, climbing down the steps with no problem, and the only addition to their appearance was that all three had a large button on their left booby. Real fancy stuff and shiny. As far as The Tall One was concerned, Vincent couldn't find her. They were all exactly the same height, their eyes were mesmerizing, the noises they made to each other were fascinating, musical, and they stole the men's breath away as they walked up to the fire.

Van Vedic had found three rocks he planned to use around the firepit. Thrones for his queens that could be moved left or right, dependent on the smoke. The two humans were doing something they had done thousands of times before in their lives, and for the most part, it was an enjoyable thing to do; however, the guests tonight were new to the traditions and obviously more than happy to be so. They needed nothing, it seemed, to make them more comfortable. That also held true for most of the audience up above.

"Dear queens, our plans for the rest of the evening are to heat up our meat, bring the beans to a boil, cook two tatters, and drink a bit of cider. The fire won't get much bigger than you see it now unless you want it to be; we can make it bigger. We throw dead wood into it and have plenty stored up for a long night. The purpose of this fire is to cook the meat and keep us all warm. Rahellio is a wonderful cook, and he sings exceptionally well, plays his guitar really well, and has turned out to be an excellent friend. I have no trouble singing along in the background. You're welcome to chirp in if you feel the urge. Seriously, this guy is good!"

"You are too kind, hombre."

Mr. Three Sense was up in that loft of his about ten feet or so above the captain's right shoulder; it was tough to tell because of the invisible thing going on, and without being rude, Van Vedic told Dizzy to get down near the ground or he was going to quit talking to him. He was getting a crick in his neck from looking up at nothing every time Dizzy said something.

"How's this?"

"Way too close!"

"I can make my voice sound like Vannie's."

"Okay."

"Funny human. The queens are curious to know more about Vannie. Can I tell them who she is?"

"Chirp away."

You would have thought an entire flock of chirpers had just landed at the campsite. It wouldn't stop, the aaaaaas and eeeees with low chirps and high chirps, giggling sounds, and periodically all three would turn their heads and look straight at the captain. All the cameras zoomed in on his face, and for a large number of the viewers, the captain was not so primordial anymore but more a highly compassionate beast. The campers started dinner and did things just like they usually did. The cadets were chatting with each other, with Dizzy all the time, asking questions about the horses and how they were tamed. Sometimes the captain answered and sometimes Rahellio, but the bottom line was it was a fun time for the Universe.

Sarge had been canine standoffish after his freezing moment and had learned a great lesson in life. As a result, he was now very respectful of the scent that came from inside *0* and from the cadets themselves. He always stood close by, anxious as all get-out to get close to the queens and lie there at their feet, but he needed a signal first and hadn't gotten it yet. So, he contented himself by sitting between El Bruto's front hooves and watching Rahellio feed the fire, pull off a pile of coals, and place the potatoes and meat on the grate. It smelled so good, which activated his non-stop begging routine, including slobbering and whining.

Three, Two, and The Tall One were not offended by any of the scents they encountered, not by the smoke so far, not by the smell of cooking raw meat and beans or the smell of tequila in the air. The men sipped it from tin cans with handles, making squeamish faces after a taste and hissing at the moon. It looked like it hurt them, but they did it every so often, so the cadets assumed it didn't hurt that bad.

The queens had watched all the goings-on and chirped out comments to each other and Dizzy. They watched the chef treat the fire with total respect. He would hold his arms out their entire length, show the fire his palms, and simply stand there and stare into the flames. He would talk to Van Vedic frequently, to the horses and the hound too, and it wasn't long till he hung his guitar from his neck strap and started to sing. Two short ones that involved the traditional thanksgiving prayer his wife insisted on before any meal, along with the Star-Spangled Banner in Spanish in memory of his son and his youngest brother and Gomez's son and his brother. Those young men had never come home from Bataan in the Philippines. They'd died on the death march or in a prisoner of war camp. They were all in the New Mexico National Guard when it was called up and sent to the Philippines before the war broke out. The gravedigger would tear up as he sang the anthem. Big salty blues would flow down his cheeks, and his voice never faltered or failed when he made the high notes. When the song was over, he set his instrument down because it was time to eat, and while the two humans prepared for their feast, Dizzy told the cadets about the war those men had been in and how it ended. The detonations of two atomic bombs. There was no such thing as war in their world, it never had been, and it

216

pained them greatly to know of that war and how it affected both these humans. The cadets were comfortable sitting ten feet from the fire, upwind of which there was little. They were looking at everything, and Dizzy told the boys about every subject they broached.

When they asked Dizzy about the future, he told the truth, told them he'd tell them when they would die but advised against asking that question because it usually ruined the evening, and for that reason, they didn't bother.

As far as dinner was concerned, both men had a large plate on their laps and tequila cups and coffee cups side by side down near their feet, with the three different entries filling up the disk. The slabs of elk were thick, hung over the edges of the plates at the start of the meal, and the ladies noticed there was actual blood still inside the chunks; they looked so red they were sure it was almost raw. Then, lo and behold, Van Vedic put half of his back on the fire and cooked it longer. Burned it, as a matter of choice, and nibbled on that chunk all night long. The baked tater was gone in four different encounters; that's what the observers called the forks full of bites—encounters. The total number of bites, each one's individual weight, and all the known nutritional benefits to the human were calculated in split seconds for the crowd out there who cared. There were sixty-one of those encounters, ten sips of black coffee and ten sips of one of Arboles' finest home brews. The *ooohs* and *aaahs* from his fans were deafening, his fame expanding by the hour, with his name getting close to being the most recognized name everywhere in the known Universe.

None of that was known to the rescuers, who were primarily concerned with how the queens handled things so far. He asked them in Spanish, English, and even Russian, but Dizzy said the best term he could find was that they were perfectly content.

"They want to walk around this area for a while, holding mittens occasionally. They wish to follow both you men and your dog and walk until their reservoirs are full. They are technically within a few of your Earth hours from being back to their 'prime' condition. They will achieve this accomplishment by merely walking around this clearing. It's been a while since they were 'prime,' been a long downhill glide from where they once were, but they can find that plateau here tonight. They are worried about the snakes."

Rahellio said he was astounded to see such a beast, he hadn't seen many snakes recently, and as a matter of fact, it was the first one since this trail ride started.

"This snake could eat a fawn, has never left this canyon, and spent its whole life waiting for today. It didn't rattle except at the very end, waiting for us to walk up. Senorita The Tall One, my queen, Captain Van Vedic saved your life. No doubt! It's a nice night for a walk, and there is no need to worry."

"The queens want to know if the dog can behave itself and sit by their sides like it does with the men."

Vincent called for Sarge, and here he came. He dangled his arm down by his side and showed the dog two fingers. He immediately ran around and stood by his side. From there, the two walked over to the cadets, where the captain had him sit once again.

"Captain, I need to communicate with your dog. No harm will come to him."

"Please do. If you get through to him, there are several things I want you to tell him for me. Don't hang up until you've talked with me, promise? Good luck."

Sarge was being an excited dog, looking at his master and the queens, when suddenly, he went standing up, dreamland, with his eyes fully open, his ears perked up and pointed, and his nostrils looked like flappers. Then, just as suddenly, he was back and mellow, politely walked up to each lady and set his nose on her lap. All they did was look at him and him at them. Each one touched the bridge of his snout, and after three times, he stood off a bit and waited with his tail going softly side to side instead of the exact opposite.

As the canine approached The Tall One, the Universe held its breath as another first was happening to the cadets. No creature like this one had ever been this close to a cadet, ever. NABPSSBCCBS UNIVERSAL was rocking the charts and had no intention whatsoever to interfere. When she touched the animal's nose, his eyes closed, and he was labeled a peaceful creature at heart, overly submissive, loyal, and protective. The relationship's diagnosis was that the dog would give its life in their defenses and treat them as priceless besides being calm. This phenomenon happened everywhere in the cosmos; "man's best friend" befriends the queens. It is, for sure, one of the oldest saying there is; every single green or blue planet has a best-friend agenda. Here on WWwWweebbbTmmuumm, it's a dog thing.

CHAPTER FIFTEEN

QUEENS HAVE NO TASTEBUDS

O was in a slow recovery state, primary operating mode, and would be so till dawn. Once the sun's rays struck the exposed side of his shield, all of his efforts to absorb that direct heat would settle the recharge and allow him to agitate the soil twice more. His self-diagnosis was all positive. There was space and light now where it had been pitch black before; his plan was working. The sand below his hull was fading towards the river because of WWwWweebbbTmmuumm's powerful gravity, but without the banana, it would have had nowhere to go. He anticipated filling the second to last banana by ten a.m. While he recovered from that, they could dig the final pit, lay out the serpent, and in the full exposure to starlight, this sun, O would use all his energy one last time to lower itself safely from under the overhang—unless there was a complication, like a large stone he couldn't move, but none of his deep-penetrating sensors saw anything like that for over nine feet below his being. The rescuers had found very few rocks while digging the first pits so far; *0* was sitting on a sandbar created during a flood ten thousand years ago.

Once that vision was realized, and the path out from under the rock was clear and safe, it would be time for the horses to pull *0* out into the open air under full exposure to this star. He would need one full Earth day even to consider liftoff. This very sophisticated checklist was adhered to in the most scrupulous detail, which was just *0* being *0*. His message to Dizzy came as all three cadets were ready for their walk in the moonlight. The captain and his first mate now knew the plan; it gave the upcoming events a timeline they could work with. Before the captain led the way for the cadets, he looked at *0* and asked Dizzy what sort of a harness did *0* suggest for his extraction.

"We're gonna have a hard time getting a good hold on this scooter; we sure don't want to break anything. But we've got some good ropes and good harnesses, have four mighty beasts of burden, and I thought you might give me a few clues?"

All along the outermost edge of *0*, where it was deemed most necessary and practical, large circles suddenly pushed through the hull from the inside and invited a rope or a chain to be attached somehow.

"Do you think any of those might come in handy?"

"Funny alien. I can't wait for the moment when we give it our first try. With those eye-bolts—I don't know what to call them… tie-downs?—Raton by himself might be all that we need. Very exciting!"

When the captain invited the queens to start their walk, Rahellio added some timber to the fire and then offered his hand for assistance, which two of the three accepted; unfortunately, he had no idea of their names, couldn't read their tags, and there was no way on Earth he could tell them apart. Even back at the start, he couldn't tell which one was the tallest. Their plans and desires were to roam around the crash site area, study the place, stay in motion as safely as possible, not worry, and be happy. That's what Van Vedic whispered to all three. "Don't worry, be happy." Now, with a tried and true bodyguard in a non-hostile environment, their anxiety levels were at an all-time low; they only wanted to walk around in the corner and meditate on Spaqu, twelve, and perhaps three.

Spaqu's heroism was now on a level seldom achieved in this Universe. The life band had recorded it all, been technically diagnosed by *0*, furthered up the line, and construction had already begun on his monument. His last thoughts, reasoning, motivation, bodily functions, and everything about him were recorded on his band, a part of his anatomy that recorded his entire life until he experienced instant death. All of that information was available to the pundits who wrote obituaries after the ring was removed from a deceased being, and not until. This one Universal *Gold Book* adaptation, the idea of a "Life Ring," changed the behavior of incalculable numbers of civilizations and caused the inhabitants to be extraordinary, influential, and noble from an early age because the band guaranteed and caused immortality. As all beings do, he grew into the bracelet, embracing the day when it wouldn't slide off and his real life would actually begin. There it hung from his wrist when he was so small and new, but in no time at all, it was there to stay.

The queens needed to expend energy. In immediate return, they acquired rebuilding power and renewed strength at phenomenal ratios until they were totally and finally back to their prime. The cadets were chirping; Dizzy was in the mix with everyone, including the dog, who had misplaced some of the information from a short while before about being too friendly and received a three-second wake-up call. He appeared to want to lick the cadets' face shields, which was a no-no.

The men were minding their business while the cadets were staring up the side of the cliff face, chirping to each other. Then they went in three different directions, the exact same number of steps, three, turned around, and regrouped. This ritual was repeated three times and served as an example of meditating on the number three.

Dizzy explained how he needed the men to use their imagination.

"Can you now see it, the circular nature of the structures, the arena, and the patio completing the circle from this upper corner? In the middle of it all, remember back there, the center room with no ceiling; that's a very significant chamber. This is where Phaethon lived after he angered his father. He was the one who built everything around us, a super being who could mold stone with his hands. Unfortunately, the dumbass was out of control half the time in his youth, and when he stole one of his father's favorite stars, his father shot him with a thunderbolt; had to kill him before he tore everything all to hell. That's what everyone thought, but it wasn't true.

"The young God survived the thunderbolt, held onto the only part left of his flaming chariot worth talking about, the right wheel, a blazing spinning disk that he managed to gain control of, and rode it down to the surface. The wheel found a resting place on the river's edge here in this canyon, settled into a sand bar, and started to cool down, with the bad boy, very much alive by the skin of his teeth, alone and fearful, standing nearby. It was later rolled to where it is now, at the bottom of the arena. It is believed that Phaethon lived for centuries here in the canyon until his father forgot what he did; the patriarch had many sons, lots of daughters, and lots and lots of wives. The great father of so many found it hard to keep track of those things that get in life's way, especially all the miscues his children were perpetually having. Phaethon caught a ride back home, supposedly walked into the dining hall, sat down at the table, and smiled at Helios. The old man smiled back, and all was forgiven. That's the story of this place. It looks like a keyhole from high in the sky, the chalice design with the base down by the river. Imagine seeing this spot from the eyes of the eagles, even higher than that.

"That era was a very long time ago. The ancient Sumerian explorers found this place after the truth emerged, and it became the home of one of the Anunnaki libraries, a name for a place that lasted for thousands of years. It became a sanctuary where knowledge was stored in sheets of silica and inside crystal spheres. They called themselves Watchers and Planners. In time, a long time, they eventually left. Only six of them remained, and they took every piece of evidence that proved they ever existed with them, except for the rocks and the structures. They went away in one night, took their identity with them, and left no trace of who and what they were. Their abandoned home with huge doorways suggests they were much larger than humans."

After an hour or so, the cadets were back near the fire, quieter than before and obviously pleased with their evening. Their body movements were much more fluid, their gait looked healthy and robust, and they moved their arms like ballerinas. You could see it in their eyes and hear it in the melody of tweets and chirps that kept them involved with each other. Sarge was near their feet, just sitting there and listening to every chirp he heard. Sometimes it was hard to tell who was doing the chirping, but all one had to do was look at Sarge, as he would be staring at the queen making the sound.

"After the ladies are rested, we could do that again if they wish."

"Captain, they returned to the fire because they thought you both needed a rest."

The two men continually messing with the campfire, poking it, throwing things into it while drinking coffee and tequila, and were constantly nibbling on something. From high above the canyon, the cameras watched the cadets and the dog as they watched the fire while the humans prepared to sleep. Of course, an audience the size of the Universe was put at ease when the larger-than-average human took off his guns and set them on his saddle. But, for the most part, the viewing audience couldn't get enough of every single detail, especially the 45s, Rahellio's guitar, and the dog.

With the ladies' permission, the gravedigger started a well-worn tradition for him. He was the guest artist, the entertainer, singing ballads and love songs and playing his guitar, which had become a refined passion in his life. He also played the background strings while the captain sang a few of his favorite Russian long-haul freight songs. Their reward was the joy their music brought to others. For another two hours, the concert played on, and when the maestro asked the ladies if they wanted to hike again before lights out, they all stood up and walked towards the cliff face, mitten to mitten, with their trusty canine directly in front. It was one question after another once again, as if the queens were storing information, asking many personal questions of both men while divulging little insight into who they were or where they had come from.

From out of nowhere, literally speaking, Dizzy had what he said was the last question for a while.

"*Cooouugh...* My queens are aware of your entire history, my captain, and have a joint wish. They know about the bell on the bow of your boat, how and why the *Vanessa* is nestled where she waits. They are most intrigued by how the *DDccccV* rescued you. How, at the time, things seemed impossible for you to be returned, but fate is the hunter, or so they say, and here you are today, saving these queens. In some circles, it's still the favorite suspense story in quite some time. They want to listen to you tell them the story you told so often, the story of Jude. They understand the primitive concepts of war, understand pain to some degree, and even though this goes against their very existence, below their nature, they want to feel what life was like in that most recent world war this planet's just survived."

"I will try my best to do it justice. Jude himself taught it to me."

"Taught it to you and to me. I was there."

"I keep forgetting that I won't remember any of this. I won't tell anybody anything, anytime, forever. I promise! I want you to remember that when I make a promise about something, you can be sure that I will honor my word. So, store this request in your archives, and reconsider the policy. I'm no Ezekiel, but in my opinion, I have a right to know what happens to me and my body. I figure you owe me that. I promise you once again."

"You'll be fine."

Vincent added some branches to the fire, breaking large dead driftwood with his heel while Rahellio laid out the audience's blankets. They all felt the warmth from the fire, and they, too, showed it their palms and stood there watching the flames up close, finding the spectacle of the fire, the ashes, the smoke, and the noise captivating, never having experienced it this up close and personal before. Once again, they sat down on their bottoms, stretched out their legs, and wiggled their booties with their new guard dog a foot in front of their toes. None of this went unnoticed out there in the zodiac of constellations.

The captain stood a few paces out from the ladies, upwind from the smoke and near the fire; Rahellio sat nearby. He remembered this same scene in the shadow of the Rock of Gibraltar, 1942, that November sunset when Jude told General George S. Patton his story. This was the man who would lead the Allies, the heavy brigades of infantry, into the heart of Germany to save the world and beat the deadline by six months. The captain and Lieutenant Sprindis were sitting on the sidelines, tending the fire as Jude brought his best performance to the scene. When he was through, the general cried uninterrupted, like a lad, sobbing at times, infuriated at other moments, threatening and very angry in the end. Like everyone before and everyone that followed, it took twenty to thirty minutes or so until he finally came around and recovered from the deluge of death.

For some reason, the captain felt like this was his Patton moment. From way back in time, when he first started telling the story on the *Pilldersleeve* to just recently in Aztec, his audience would cry every time, continuously wept, and suffered immensely. In memory of all that, Van Vedic would also bring his best performance to this fire, and the cadets would witness the last time he would ever tell the original story of Jude. It again crossed his mind that he'd never remember any of this, but fortunately and unbeknownst to him, the rest of the Universe would have it on file forever.

From deep inside his soul, he began the story exactly the same way Jude did, the same way he had done hundreds and hundreds of times himself, starting with the last days of St. Michael's Seminary and that march down the mountain into human insanity. The orator was gliding along with one heartbreak after another, human misery on a scale that made it barely worth living, causing his listeners to smell it, feel the cold, starvation, and what it's like to die from thirst. He told about Theresienstadt, the *Struma*, what Tucumcari was, and the rest of the trip until they met Patton.

He had been talking directly to the cadets, ignoring their gestures to stop, back up, rest; it was hard to tell what the mittens meant. Because of the lighting and some other factors, he hadn't noticed that their helmets had fogged up to some extent, and there were about two inches of water from their necks up, locked in, and, more importantly, an inch below the small black dot they called a mouth. Fortunately, the story was over, and from here on out, in most of the previous cases, the crying stops eventually, and the staring begins. Dizzy was mumbling gigantic words that meant something to someone somewhere, and then a long *wheezzzzze*.

"Captain, the cadets need your immediate assistance. On the back of their helmets is a blue button that must be pressed now, and it is hoped the fluid will drain out correctly. Please be careful and vocal as you do this."

Those tiny ear holes on the sides of the heads heard the tragic story of Jude through their helmets with no problem, and as their incredible brains absorbed the horror of it all, their brilliant and enormous eyes began to overflow. Their teardrops were directly proportional with their eyes' size, falling and filling up their helmets and starting to drown them. *0* was overwhelmed but helpless, and the observation stations on the moon were doing backflips. Rahellio was still a mess, hadn't ever heard the story like that, and was not paying close attention to the cadets; he struggled with being crybaby Rahellio.

In a flash of action, Vincent had a cadet in his grasp, turned her around, found the blue button, pushed it, and watched the teardrops fall out on her shoulders in a gush. Then the next one, and finally the last queen, who was still crying and was at some sort of a break-even point, one tear in and one tear out, soaked in her own personal flood. The new tears flowed down her jumpsuit and landed on her booties, steaming up in a mist that said the water was hot. Each cadet stood very still for the longest time and then waved in unison at the moon. They looked into each other's eyes, examined the wetness on each other, examined their suits, especially the collars that encircled their necks, and finally nodded at the captain.

"Captain, I'm at a loss for words. I don't know what you've done, but my queens are heartbroken. They need to rest by the fire. They have some questions and comments and will eventually retire into 0 and wait for the morning. I don't know what to say. They want to know how you are. Does it hurt as bad to tell that story as it does to listen to it?"

"Telling the story to others stopped my tears, and I know for a fact that anyone who heard it from me and then became a storyteller themselves also quit crying. The story was meant to be retold. Everyone who hears it is now a storyteller themselves —so are you, and so is Rahellio, and to relieve their anguish, all they have to do is tell it to someone else. I listened to Jude tell that story every day for almost a year—every day, and I cried every time. Never once—even there at the very end after having heard it so many times—never once did I not well up. Never once. I think I hear tears in your voice, my invisible friend."

"You do."

"My dear ladies, come closer to the fire and warm yourselves; that's usually why we have them. We sometimes use them to dry out, front and back." He smiled at all three, got close to their shields, studied those beautiful eyes, looked into them, trying to diagnose their conditions, and found the blackest, most profound, bottomless eyes he'd ever seen. He asked each one personally, face to face, if she was well, stable, and was there anything she needed? Was there anything he could do?

"One of my queens, and I won't mention who, asked if you could step out of the way of the fire. You're blocking the heat."

The vast majority of the heart of the BKPLMOKNAZZZZ systems that were up and running live, viewing Van Vedic tell the cadets the story of Jude, had therefore fallen into the category of future storytellers themselves. The human was making them cry, everywhere in the local galaxy group for sure, with the broadcast streaming at the speed of thought into the depths of it all. Then, they witnessed the three cadets drowning in their own tears live in technicolor, while crying and weeping themselves, unable to do anything about it.

"DO SOMETHING, DIZZY! DO SOMETHING, DIZZY! DO SOMETHING, DIZZY!" All throughout the Universe, "DO SOMETHING, DIZZY!" was plastered on everyone's wristband. He was getting closer and closer to digging GGgvdd Eicccc lilIIoom in the OOOfrTTT SSppprRrR System.

0 reminded him about the blue button, reminded him about the OOOfrTTT SSppprRrR System, and suggested that he do something. So, Dizzy did something and told Vincent Van Vedic, who immortalized himself in the annals of first responders, pushed the three blue buttons, and the rest is history.

Another hour passed, the cadets' helmets cleared up, and their mouth holes started chirping again. They had a long list of questions about being human for both men, thanked them repeatedly for what they were doing, and would appreciate walking around in the morning to regain their prime. There had always been innumerable questions about whether cadets had ever cried in history, what might happen to her if she did, and what would a teardrop from a cadet amount to? All kinds of questions, because no one knew. It had never happened to the best of anyone's knowledge.

It had been a busy day, that was for sure, so when they finally relaxed, Rahellio broke out the cider bottle, two of those tin cups with handles, and their pipes. Dizzy explained to the cadets that the cider was a stimulant, one of many used by humans. The tobacco also stimulated them—the dried leaves they smoked in the pipes, which was why so many humans smelled like smoke. They loved to do it and smoked like crazy everywhere they went. It was so dangerous. Too much of the liquid stimulant caused them to go nuts. The queens were totally dried out by now, stimulated themselves from their environment, and watched the captain and Rahellio roaring and laughing about something the captain had said. They laughed so hard that tears came to their eyes and had to be wiped away. They did it while looking at the moon and laughing out loud, making all sorts of strange male sounds, snorting and slobbering. Every time they looked at each other, they started laughing again, crying again, until it only happened one more time. The happy tears confused the audience significantly, and we're not only talking about the queens. There may have been some doubt about queens having ever cried in history, but for sure, there had never been a queen who laughed until she cried. Dizzy explained to his queens that it was more than likely the result of the stimulant, and the next thing he knew, they wanted to smell it.

"My captain, not to interrupt the party, but my queens wish to smell the cider and are curious if you credit your joy to it?"

The big man looked down at his bartender and proclaimed in a flawless baritone, "YO, HEAVE HO, I'LL HAVE ONE MO'." And they both started laughing again, very near where they had recently left off. More tears while they were pounding on their legs, with the gunslinger shouting, "YOU TELL HER, TELL HER A WEEK!" causing them to roar even louder.

With his bartending duties over, the minstrel started a new song for the time being, and Van Vedic took his twelve-ounce cup of cider over to the ladies. He handed it to The Tall One, but she could have been Two or Three, then begged their forgiveness because he had to relieve himself somewhere nearby. They could smell his cider till he got back. Sarge had found a spot in the sand where the ladies had drip-dried. He had dug it out until it was his perfect body size, and clearly that was where he planned to stay.

"Are you following me?"

Nothing.

"I know you're there; I can't believe you've been there as long as you've been there. How long has it been now? I think you have to answer my questions because if I know about you, any question I ask, you have to answer. Our contract is part of the deal; I get to ask questions because I'll never remember the answers. This is because it's in the *Gold Book* and because X says so! Answer me."

"What are you talking about? It does not say that in the *Gold Book* and the word for God is not X. It is XXXLLLGGJJJXXX."

"I knew you were there. Now get down here. I only have one thing to say about your version of God's name: could you have made it more difficult to say if you tried? Repeat it three times and pretend you have my lips. Go ahead, say it. Don't forget the tongue and the teeth and that little ding-a-ling thing that hangs way back there in our throat. I can't hear you. GOD is so much easier, and besides, I, for one, don't think he cares. Please don't tell me someone's got his ear and God is telling them that he wants to be called XgarblygookX. Never happened!

"Now, every time I've ever taken a piss, you've been there watching?"

"Watching is not even close to how things are in that dimension, but if you insist, the answer is yes. Most intriguing is that you were singled out before you were even born, and this epic tale of yours is challenging to explain. The same holds true for your partner, Father Jude. You've written many times concerning the Y's in the roads you've traveled, said many times that you felt like you were being pushed or pulled; you didn't know which—and you made those decisions in the blink of an eye, no offense intended to anyone listening in, myself included.

"At the end of every segment of your life so far, every chapter, every Y in the road, it was always best for you in that end, always suitable for Captain Vincent Van Vedic. You may never fully understand how important it was for you to find Jude, to steer the boat that took him to his destination, but it was every bit of that; you did good! To make a long story short, your navigation enabled Jude to tell his story to General Patton, who became a storyteller himself. I believe if you scoured your memory of Patton, he might have mentioned other realms that he existed in and different eras that he lived in. Do you remember that? Remember that battle at sea he told you about where they catapulted infected slave bodies onto his boat? That was a true story, and his life, too, was a series of pushes and pulls that got him to the Rock of Gibraltar. Together, they helped save the planet Earth from a guaranteed early demise. They destroyed a drug-crazed German army addicted to methamphetamine, who believed the notion of dying in battle was glorious. Hitler himself was a drug addict, hasn't functioned very well there at the end, and took a coward's way out. You were a part of ending all that, a small but essential piece of a giant jigsaw puzzle—get a messenger, namely Jude, to a man who could make a difference, namely Patton, starting with the moment the message arrives.

"My captain, I've seen you stare into the heart of the BKPLMOKNAZZZZ, heard some of your thoughts on what it might be and how big it is. This blur and slash of stars in the night sky, the ones you've seen so clearly from the bow of your boat on the Black Sea and defined by you humans as the heart of the Milky Way above us. That's where we come from. 'sssLLLOCCCsss,' the fourth planet around the center star of what you call the Belt of Orion. I mentioned this before, and once again, it doesn't matter, but it's okay for you to know. Look at the center star in the Belt of Orion and imagine a dozen planets like Earth rotating around that star and evolving forward like you earthlings, like you humans are doing here. The center of the Orion Constellation is where we all originated, where that evolution has been going on for hundreds of millions of Earth years. Humans have only been at it for fifty thousand of your years."

"I need a sip of my cider, but I want to keep talking about this later on."

"My funny human friend, there might not be time for such talks."

As the navigator came upon the campfire, he made a beeline to the cadets, primarily searching for his cup. There it was on a convenient rock, empty, and he assumed they had managed to spill the whole thing. He shrugged it off, found his bartender, handed him the empty cup, and sang his song. "YO, HEAVE HO, I'LL HAVE ONE MO'."

When the cup was full, instead of handing it to the captain, Rahellio placed it on a rock that caused Van Vedic to bend over and get his face close to his compadre. Then, in a whisper, he noted, "Captain, there is something very, very strange going on with our queens. They are acting like my wife when she's tipsy."

Not knowing a single thing about Orionian jumpsuits for queens, how would the captain have known that their straws were hooked to their mittens and their idea of sniffing the vapors was somewhat different from his concept of sniffing?

"Coouugh."

"Diz."

"My queens are still debating the quality of the cider. They wish to compare a cup of water with a cup of cider."

"Rahellio, my man, I have two requests. A tall cup of fresh water and a tall cup of cider. Por favor."

The bartender went to work, found an extra cup, filled it with well water from Arboles, then filled his cup to the top, taking them both over to the captain.

"Ladies, my queens, we need to have a truth session. The term cider is a misnomer; it's homebrewed tequila in a cider bottle, and even though it may look like water, the taste will confirm which is which."

Throughout the Universe, the wrist bands screamed, "Dizzy, do something. QUEENS HAVE NO TASTEBUDS! YOU IDIOT!"

The cups were close to overflowing, so he handed one queen a cup and then a cup to the other, maybe to Two or The Tall One, or could have been Three, and in that confusion, he lost track of the liquids, as the queens handed the cups back and forth, left-hand, right-hand, Two to The Tall One, back to Three, over to The Tall One, both hands with one behind the neck pass. On that same rock where he had found his first empty cup, he now found three empty cups, one of which was undoubtedly the one he was looking for. They were becoming quite limber, discovered they could stand on one foot, and then they burst into a serenade of eeeees, iiiis, and multiple chirping sessions. Dizzy was trying his best to translate what his queens were chirping, but some of the eeeees and iiiis were brand new sounds for queens, not in his dictionary or the known history banks of queens anywhere. What he could pass on, he did, things the men could understand, added some background strings and drums, with Rahellio doing the guitar. All the captain could do was move his feet and body to this rhythm all around him. To be honest, it went on a little too long, and if you want to talk about "Three-note Dave," the queens have him beat by a mile.

The gravedigger found a new spot near the fire, had his guitar upon his belly, and sang about cowboys in the old days. Then, he would stop the vocals, bend over the tool, close his eyes, and speak through the strings for everyone to hear. He was outstanding.

With no more questions to answer and actually not a part of the party for queens thrown by queens for queens, the experienced campfire guys recognized an old campfire tradition, consisting of knowing that when it's over, it's over. There's work to do in the morning, and we can do this again tomorrow. The party was just getting started for the inexperienced "Campfire Girls." It was as if the cadets couldn't stand still, their arms were in perpetual motion, and from the captain's point of view they seemed to be in love with each other; sisters, fascinated by being a third of a trio and continually looking into each other's eyes. The way triplets love each other. Suddenly one of the queens collapsed in a golden heap of a jumpsuit. To make matters worse, so did the other two. It looked like someone had dumped three golden aliens wearing helmets close by the fire on horse blankets. Obviously over-stimulated.

Starting with the moon and venturing out from there, this election/vote unfolded on most big and small screens out there everywhere in the cosmos, with the ballots filling up in favor of naming the new slide into the GGgvdd Eicccc liIIloom on planet four of the OOOfrTTT SSppprRrR System, 'The Dzzitulatizebistauuugj FfffeekTTTraa Zzucobinnnlll Slide.' Dizzy himself voted no when it came up on his screen.

The captain was all over and around the queens, trying to figure out who was hurt or needed a helping hand, and was as concerned as a man could be. The cadets were chirping, and they told Dizzy to tell him not to worry; there was nothing wrong, and when everyone was back on their feet, they were going back to *0* for a quick cleanse and new helmets. The quick cleanser was a one-seat operation, and they had to work it out as to who went first and who went last. It was customary to make a big deal out of a queen using the quick cleanser, generally speaking about once a cycle, and it was never ever a surprise emergency. At this point in the evening, they broke several cadet records involving speed, distance traveled, and amount of time on the bidet. The last queen took the longest because there wasn't any rush. Between the three, they completely overwhelmed the system *0* was highly proud of, as the quick cleanser recovery tank overflowed for the first time in the history of the *0* models. However, with just a tiny amount of re-plumbing, he solved the problem internally and pissed in the sand between his bottom plates.

CHAPTER SIXTEEN

o IS FREE

When the sun came up that next morning, things were well underway at the rescue site, with 0 finally able to feel the star's heat on his exposed skin. It would take at least three hours or more for him to recharge his energy cells enough to allow him to start his fourth vibration procedure. Rahellio had climbed down into the banana hole and was working on the edges, cleaning up the site and sipping on his coffee; it's a gravedigger thing. The captain was feeding the fire, listening to Dizzy go on and on about the test ahead—for mankind—examining all the rescue hardware, and playing with the dog while the cadets worked their way down to the ground. They seemed none the worse for wear after discovering the tequila the night before, and high up above the gorge, higher than a man could see, the three diamonds were up there, looking down and recording the goings-on. The moon was on the other side of the world and wouldn't be back till sunset, but the diamonds relayed the images to the space stations on the moon, which furthered it out to the rest of the Universe, and most everyone was happy with the way things were going.

0's self-diagnosis was all positive; there was space and light now where it had been pitch black before—his plan was working. He was sinking away from the rock. The sand below his hull was fading towards the river because of WWwWweebbbTmmuumm's powerful gravity, where everything flows downhill, but without the banana, it would have had nowhere to go. He anticipated filling the second to last banana by ten a.m.

0 explained everything to Dizzy, and Dizzy told the men exactly what he said.

"Dizzy."

"Captain."

"I don't carry a watch, and neither does Rahellio."

"Funny human."

Dizzy went on, sometimes chirping, sometimes with music, mainly in Spanish to anyone listening. While he recovered from that ten a.m. effort, they could dig the final pit, he said, and lay out the serpent within it, and in the total exposure to starlight, this sun, *0* would use all his energy one last time to be safely out from under the overhang. Unless there is a complication, perhaps a large stone, blah, blah, blah... Vincent had heard all this before, so he let him speak and tuned out for a bit.

The mighty San Juan drained this side of the mountains, always had, and it had never been this calm and contained before. The San Juan was once a much more powerful river by far, back when winter's snow never melted away completely.

As the *0* crisis developed some five years before, the Watchers found a plan that would include altering the past and forcing Y's in the roads for many different humans, Vincent Van

Vedic for one. That practice was nothing new but gave the Watchers a planning challenge, especially in those systems where things were just getting going. Their purpose was to do everything in a Watcher's power that would hopefully direct the society of creatures they were watching over towards peaceful lives to pass the test when that time came. Decisions were continually being made by the Watchers as to when the creature in question would be genetically modified, the Adam and Eve decision, so that evolution favored the brain and the thumb. In this particular case, the creature became "human." That threshold was reached forty-two thousand years ago on Earth, and that human creation had evolved into what we have today.

The test had begun on WWwWweebbbTmmuumm. The atom was loose in the minds of men. It would exponentially expand their knowledge and understanding of the Universe around them, along with occasional treasures scattered in by the Watchers and the invention of some high-powered telescopes. Throughout the world, at this point in the game, extraterrestrial vehicles would be delivered via crash sites. The most critical eyes would study all of the discovered information, scrap pieces, and even dead bodies. Questions about everything that seems essential would gain new heights, and it would cause this creature to challenge everything it's ever been taught. Of course, wherever that was, the powers that be have always known about the visitors, but they usually tried to hide the truth.

Vincent could see it had already started; the Nazis were reverse-engineering all sorts of things they'd found throughout the world, and their scientists were years ahead of their enemies. It required the Watcher's intervention, it required Patton, along with many others, it required Gibraltar, and it required Jude. The Watchers on Earth were busy going back in time, four hundred years, just to find Patton. The Watchers knew from previous experience that the first nation to acquire and use atomic weapons must have a valid and honest moral compass. A primitive attitude was acceptable, but possessing the peaceful gene was essential; based on the *Gold Book*, that nation must possess the collective nature that respects life. The Nazis did not, the Russians did not, and by fateful direction, both would be prevented from succeeding before the virtuous USA.

Rahellio began his breakfast preparations—pancakes with butter, syrup, bacon slabs, and toast. His coffee was exactly the same every morning, brewed from raw beans, black as night, and dangerously hot. Van Vedic loved it, loved the smell, and always thought of Jude and his morning brew every time he smelled it. So many fond memories of the most saintly man he'd ever known, who told a story, used a cane, and who may have saved the world.

There was a fragrance in the air that grabbed the attention of the queens. They all wanted to hold the cups of coffee and absorb the vapors, chirping on a higher frequency with Dizzy while planning their options with *0*'s next vibration. The sun was hot that early in the day, with crystal-clear skies, three diamonds at a hundred thousand feet, and no wind. *0* was aglow in his skin; every bit of his concentration was focused on the absorption of that energy, filling that skin of his into overflowing with power and moving any extra into storage. He was way past full, resting after the ordeal, and Dizzy started a countdown in minutes for everyone concerned. It was nothing more and nothing less than a moment in time.

The animals sat down and faced *0* from fifty feet away; Sarge found that spot he called home on top of where the queens had cried, where their tears had landed in the sand, and he wasn't going anywhere until the event was over. Same with the horses and the mighty Raton. They were remembering the three times before, what it did to them physically, and seemed to be patiently waiting out the three minutes left, with Dizzy saving the best for last.

The cadets were up near the animals, sitting on large stones Van Vedic had positioned as per their suggestions, causing one to squeak a high-pitched 'eeeeee' when the captain dropped the boulder exactly where she wanted it. Then he twisted the two-hundred-pound bench into the sand, and it was perfectly flat for the lady's rear end. Everything that happened at the site was viewed, recorded, and transmitted at ten times the speed of light. In the case of the queens' seating arrangements, the total weight involved was measured by the Universal score, with Van Vedic breaking several records in specific categories.

He fell into the category of the largest versions of the human species, with his height and weight in the top one percentile. His strength was exceptional. His gun speed was unquestionably as good as men get, accurate to the quarter-inch, a man proven to be deadly many times over and who didn't participate without his firearms strapped to his hips. A rare human being with the right soul and who was physically in tune with the Universal truths concerning justice as if he had memorized the *Gold Book*, Van Vedic was close to what the Watchers wanted for the next evolutionary phase of humans who had entered the 'test' stage for a species, surviving the time when they threaten their enemies with nuclear bombs. Of course, all participants must stay constantly aware of atomic terrorism, an attack from fanatics, and there eventually comes a time when two nuclear-capable countries exchange hydrogen weapons. Before long, everyone on Earth could strike out at their supposed enemies until the Earth is poisoned so badly life fails in all of life's categories and mankind goes back to primitive times if it survives at all.

The portal into *0* slowly closed until the men could not see where the lines used to be, and the many creatures at this event could feel the Earth in their bodies. This tingling vibration was inescapable and made the beings present want to touch the Earth with as much of themselves as possible. The horses lay down, so they only had one eye on the world; all four hooves dug in gently with each beast. The cadets were in a row, sitting quietly and staring at *0*, while Van Vedic and the gravedigger stood on their banana's upper edge and could see the sand vibrating and sliding, filling it in. It was fascinating, watching it flow out from under the bottom of *0*, so much so that when the trench was half full, there was now a measurable space between *0* and the rock ledge he was trapped under.

After thirty human minutes, *0* decreased the vibrations until he quit. A few minutes passed, and he opened the hatch; having wholly filled in the trench, it was time for a recharge. The hottest part of the day was just beginning, and *0* was like a sponge, so much so that he was hot to the touch if you dared touch him. Dizzy was hailing the previous effort in Orionian opera, translated into Spanish that Rahellio might rediscover someday, but it was just background music for now. All the beasts of burden were back on their feet, shaking off the dirt and making horse sounds, listening to Dizzy on that level. Sarge found a new spot in front of his queens and seemed more than content sitting there. His tail was happy.

The plan was simple—do everything just like before, put the snake in the hole this time, and let *0* bury Spaqu's essence with this final effort. Without a doubt, there was now a measurable space all along his buried side hull and center cap. He was falling away from the pinch and would be safely under it all with one more effort, after which his sensors guaranteed that the horses and mule could pull him out from under the predicament. The viewing audience was immeasurable in size, with every conceivable outcome analyzed and scrutinized to the ends of the Universe. Once again, it would take at least four hours for 0 to recharge himself and a bit more than an hour to empty the banana one last time.

Anyone watching this rescue from anywhere in the Universe was informed that there was now open space between the shell of 0 and the rock, where there was none early yesterday. The plan succeeded, and the humans had been priceless to the point of heroic beyond expectation. The queens were safe, unquestionably changed because of the ordeal, and would be on their way wherever that might be within days. Spaqu was now immortalized in the annals of heroes, and 0 was a champion of survival.

It was impossible to exist inside 0 and not trigger sensors and then evaluations, and out of all due respect for the queens, Spaqu was 0's primary field of study. Even though Spaqu never spoke aloud about it, 0 could sense a plan in the making, a willingness to make the ultimate sacrifice, a burning desire for that. His activated wristband was their best chance of being rescued, even better than if one of the queens had died. If Spaqu were to die and his body was to decay without the due processes involving his bracelet, his bracelet would send out a rescue signal for as long as it took, an event noted on plasma, and these cadets were far too young for that. So, they had to be saved at all costs, and Spaqu knew that to his core and believed that more than anything else.

The captain and Rahellio began their dig almost immediately, but there was a new plan for the excavated sand that Dizzy explained to the crew. 0 was looking for a soft runway, creating a sliding ramp of sorts that allowed the beasts to drag 0 smoothly and safely as far from the overhang as possible. It was mathematical, designed down to the number of shovels full of vibrated sand in an exact location so that the structural hubs under 0 had a unique surface to glide on that he himself designed and provided. The men had no trouble hitting their marks that Dizzy showed them with words and let them run with the idea after giving the direction and the lane's ideal depth. It broke the monotony of their work, while this last dig seemed the most effortless of them all, and they acted like they almost didn't want it to end.

By noon the banana was gutted and ready for the snake. A ten-foot-long muscle with two-inch fangs in the head and two gaping holes in its neck, rattles end first, for good luck. It was a record-setting creature that Rahellio respectfully dragged out from behind some rocks and into the open for the queens to examine. Every rattle on its tail counted for a year of its life—sixteen or so—the protective skin was artwork, blended in with the terrain, and they studied it in its death, a state of existence that had never been part of the cadets' world. Nevertheless, they appreciated the evidence that Spaqu was now part of the beast's composition, part of its anatomy, and these conditions were acceptable as his final resting place. The coordinates of this exact spot would be recorded for all times. When the ladies were done with their goodbyes to Spaqu/rattlesnake, they retreated to the campsite, having experienced several firsts in the past so many minutes. Dizzy asked Rahellio for three cups of Arboles well water out of the bag; they loved it the most so far of the human liquids, absorbing the vapors through their mittens, waiting patiently for 0 to be ready again.

Rahellio then dragged the monster tail first down one end of the banana and into the deepest spot there in the middle, threw some shovelfuls of sand on the gunshot holes to dissuade the flies, and then respectfully nodded his head at the scene. He understood entirely what Dizzy said had happened to Spaqu. His essence was throughout the snake, and now he would receive a well-deserved burial and funeral. It was just like his wife always said, "You are what you eat," a saying she frequently used during their discussion of eating week-old elk stew.

The captain sometimes walked back and forth in the banana and alongside the snake. He was trying to see back into those recesses that hadn't been there yesterday. He told Rahellio and Dizzy all about the discovery, gave a thumbs-up to the queens, and patted *0* a few times for a well-done job. When *0* felt the hand tap on his skin, he suddenly experienced an emotion he had never felt before. A human alpha male had congratulated him for his efforts and physically touched the shell, carefully, respectfully, justifying his work and existence. Finally, everything was ready for this final effort.

Dizzy explained that as soon as *0* was done with this last effort, Raton, El Bruto Whetto, and the two powerful pack horses should all be harnessed and ready to step into the position and hook up to one of the circular tie-down ports that *0* would display. Each animal would take out the slack and put tension on the ropes, stepping forward together, nudging and sucking *0* out into the starlight. Each of the beasts had his own harness and pulling assembly strapped to their bodies, and it was as if the animals knew what was happening, taking to those straps and belts without any fuss. They were positioned close by where they would be backed in and attached to *0*, were allowed to turn at the start, and not one fussed in any way; they just stood there patiently waiting. Dizzy started his last countdown at two p.m., told the world, and beyond that, *0* was fully charged and ready to begin. The men kept their eyes on the snake and how the sand was reacting to the barrier, while the diamonds up above focused on the scene down below and successfully transmitted the story all over the known Universe.

Spaqu held his own and maintained his position as the sand pressed up against his body and flowed over it, encasing the other side and filling in that side until things were level and rising. Sand is like water in many ways; it will always find a way to seep through, fill in, and bury something forever if need be. The vibrations went on for another thirty minutes, and when *0* finally stopped, the banana was gone entirely, and he was now over a foot below the rock overhangs.

Rahellio backed the Mighty Raton into place, dragged the harness ropes back to *0*'s underside, and secured them to a beautiful metal circular protrusion that hadn't been there before. The captain backed El Bruto into place and extended his drag ropes, and just like with Rahellio, the perfect hitching port burst out of the spacecraft's hull. It was as if the metal changed and formed the posts as needed. Both pack horses were positioned out on the flanks, and everyone was in place and ready. Each man had two horses' heads with bridals in their grasp, and they asked their animals to move forward a single step in unison. They all did, and Dizzy talked to everyone. The queens were up to speed, and all four beasts and both men knew the score. Another horse step and *0* began to come out of his hole, then another and another, until they were fifty feet from where they'd started.

Finally, *0* was free, resting on the sandbar's downside and filling up his energy tanks. The afternoon sun poured down on the shell, especially the half of him that had been covered for so long. It felt so good, so strong, and his sensors all claimed zero problems so far. All sorts of tests were being done throughout the audience on his condition, but there was one thing for sure: he had survived his entrapment and was ready for a few thousand more cycles. The animals had done their job magnificently, and so had the humans, so the animals were unhitched, had their harnesses removed, and they were regrouped back up by the campfire.

The queens had all been standing during the most exciting parts of the last few minutes; they were chirping with Dizzy and clapping their mittens, obviously excited. Finally, the ladies began to walk down the sandbar as the horses took their steps, and all three now knew for sure that they had been saved. Their vehicle slid along in little jumps, only a couple of feet at a time, until it was out in the sand, flat and level.

0 sat there in front of them, forty feet in diameter, and there was no damage to his buried side; none at all, not even the color of his skin. The portal opened, the steps slid out, and the four hubs that held the tow ropes disappeared into the undercarriage, leaving no trace of where they had been. Then he began to glow as the sun filled his tanks, and Dizzy asked both men to stand close to *0*'s hull and lay their hands on his edge. They both obliged, came up to the portal, and took hold of the seam line. They could see inside, to some extent, could see where the cadets spent their time and where Spaqu had sat at his controls. Vincent Van Vedic knew in his heart that he couldn't even fit inside, and he was sure he wouldn't like the ride; it wasn't made for creatures like him.

The truth of the matter was that *0* was now free, the cadets were not in any danger, and it would only take five or six hours of sunlight to fill him fully. Once he was ready, the queens, along with Dizzy, inside *0* would lift up and away and arrive at the diamonds within seconds of launch, from there to the moon in five minutes, all filmed and recorded and transmitted to the furthermost corners of it all. Everything depended on the humans doing a credible job, a standard that was exceeded by a thousand times, and now it was time to say goodbye.

The moon would rise above the eastern canyon walls as the

sun disappeared, and all of the ridgeline observatories and scenic overlooks on the moon would be able to watch the launch in living color from only a quarter of a million miles away. The timing was perfect; everything was perfect as the viewing audience grew and the goodbyes were begun at the campsite. It started when the three cadets surrounded the dog and seemed to all say goodbye at once. The poor animal was starstruck; you could tell he had been smitten inside out, his tail hung straight down, and he couldn't move.

They left him peaceful and then walked in a short persons' parade directly under the heads of all four of the beasts, touched their shin bones and the bottoms of their chins, chirping, and eeeeeing, ordering Dizzy to tell them how grateful the queens were, and so he did. These enormous animals understood the thank yous on their levels, and instead of only lasting for moments in their minds, this feeling would stay with them for life. It was a gift; all four would pass this gene on to their sons and daughters.

With all the lesser animals taken care of, the queens were confronted with the two humans. The hour for boarding had arrived. *0* had begun a transfer of his existence into mobile prime, and along with that would come his ability to fly immediately, at fantastic speeds. All the while, the moon came up into view, with a thousand viewing platforms watching that spot on the Earth where the drama was taking place. The diamonds waited patiently, just out of visual range, and prepared for the queens to arrive. *0* could lift off and land inside one of the diamonds in a matter of seconds, allowing his queens to wander into that welcoming committee, along with attending the requisite medical checkups. After that reunion, a celebration was planned for inside the moon, where the cadets would acknowledge what had recently happened and teach the lessons learned. These three had experienced things that no queens in recorded history had; they had hibernated three times and then recovered. Most of all, they'd met the captain, but so much else besides him, like Rahellio, the dog, and the horses. The first time for so many things was a very long list, and so much of that was due to him.

Before him, however, stood Rahellio, and he took each queen by the hands and kissed her on the sides of her helmet. Dizzy was chanting how they were so grateful and guaranteeing the man he would never regret his kindness. Each one promised him long life and painless death. He poured each one a cup of Arboles well water from the bag on the side of Raton and wished them good travels. He said it was his honor to have been chosen and, thankfully, able to help. He bowed away and retreated to the horses, as they had decided to camp the night on the outside because *0* would disturb the entire site with his lift-off. They wouldn't be able to breathe for quite a while from the dust, and it would be best for the animals to be at least on the other side of the barrier for the night.

Both men knew the rules from the start; they had never been guaranteed anything except that they wouldn't remember what happened at some point or another.

"Dizzy, Dizzy?"

"Captain."

"I want you down here close by when I talk to the ladies."

He found a spot not too far from the opening portal into *0*. He hated goodbyes and had made a habit of never looking back, except to see Jude that last time. If he knew better who these ladies were, why they were so crucial in the Universe to be rescued like this, it would help him understand. Now that the deed was done, it wasn't that hard to say goodbye, and he'd be glad to see them leave. Unfortunately, Dizzy explained rather abruptly that seeing *0* leave was not in the cards.

"I remember what you said the other day," the captain said. "'Now that I have confided in you a sizeable amount of information about us, you can't be allowed to remember what you've seen and heard last night and today. You knew this. The way it usually works is that when you turn your back towards me and walk away for the last time, a certain percentage of your memory disappears.'

"I don't mind turning and walking away, and I understand that I can't be allowed to remember any of this, but it sure was fun, worth every minute we spent, and I'm so fulfilled, so grateful. So tell them, the powers that be, that's what I think. I know you won't forget to tell them. I promise to keep all this a secret if I'm allowed to remember."

The queens surrounded him, came up to the top of his knees as he sat there, held his hands, rubbed his arms, squeaking and chirping something like a tune. Dizzy talked about admiration and respect, from each of them to him, especially from The Tall One, who was the most grateful of all, though it was very hard to measure. For many minutes they all stood there touching Vincent and *ooohh*ing and chirping. They were in perfect health and about to venture out into a Universe that saw it all and now awaited them.

After only a short time, they were finished with their goodbyes. Dizzy spoke with Van Vedic about how thankful they were, so grateful, and they all wished good things for him. They hoped for a long and robust old age for him and a quiet death when the time was right. The Tall One followed Three, but it could have been Two, away from the captain and up the steps into *0*. When they arrived at their seats, they removed their helmets and mittens, waved to the captain, and brought their hands together in prayer, with there being no doubt about that.

Raton was loaded with all the harnesses and ropes, shovels, and boxes of chain that were never used. It had proved to be the most straightforward rescue the captain had ever participated in, it couldn't have been more simple, and now it was time for them to leave. All the goodbyes were over except for Dizzy's. He had volunteered to walk with them back to the tunnel that went to the outside.

The captain sat high in his saddle and took an inventory of what he was looking at, thinking to himself there was no way he would forget this. *0* had ended up being a beautiful circle of life. It was not a machine in the truest sense of the word, and was primed and ready to leave. The three queens inside were under *0*'s direct control, with the empty pilot's seat waiting for Dizzy to climb on board, even though it wasn't necessary for there to be a pilot. There was also no hurry because *0* wouldn't move if the queens were praying. That they were, still, and looked like it might go on for a while.

Time was irrelevant to their kind.

Time was thus irrelevant to *0*.

Vincent and El Bruto Whetto passed alongside *0*, out a safe distance, and as he looked down on the crown of *0*, he tipped his hat and wished him well.

"Safe travels, my friend. If you ever need a place to land, remember my land. You're always welcome. Peace be with you." He leaned over, ran his hand along the side of *0*, and instantly felt the warmth in the fabric. Whetto kept walking, and the captain saw Rahellio at the bottom of the keyhole, getting ready to lead Raton and the other workhorse up along that distant wall and back to the tunnel.

In his being, something wanted him to turn around and look

back one last time, but he resisted; he and his father would never look back in the old days, so he focused on the bottom landing. He knew that once he got to that point, even if he turned to look back up this side, he wouldn't be able to see *0* or the campsite.

"Dizzy?"

"Captain."

"You are kind of silent. I think I'm gonna miss you, but then again, I'll never know we met."

"That won't be the case on my side of that fence. Everyone who has met you is glad that they did. You and Rahellio have been heroic; your animals were brave, the dog is famous, and we shall not forget you. Of course, you must forget what you've done and seen, but be assured, we never will. You will experience our gratitude in the coming years, over and over, if I know the mind of the powers that be. No doubt in my mind that you will be remembered."

"I remember we talked about this before, and I told you what I thought about that."

"I do remember you said it wasn't necessary, and I passed that information along not long after you said it. So, yes, I remember all that."

"So?"

"So what?"

"So, I'm sure gonna miss you. Gonna miss the queens and *0*. It looks like we've made it to the tunnel, and it won't be long now. I'm thinking you erase my memory when I pop out the other end?"

"Yes, that's close. I'd like for you to be down the clearing quite a ways because when *0* lifts off, there will be lots of dust; some of these cliff faces might break loose and bury their base in rubble and rock."

"No shit!"

"Not today, but someday soon. It will be a mild seismic event, get many people's attention, and the land's actual value will be recognized. Then, oil and gas will start seeping up through cracks in the ground, and the entire countryside will become known as the San Juan oil and gas basin."

"My land?"

"Your land."

"I'm not going to remember this, am I?"

"It's not rocket science, but I'm sure you'll be shown the way. So don't worry, be happy!"

The loud steel hoof sounds disappeared once the yellow horse was out of the tunnel. The captain angled left and picked up his gait, heading for Rahellio a hundred yards ahead.

CHAPTER SEVENTEEN

THE AWAKENING

The brute caught up to Raton, nestled in at the correct pace, with his nose just inches from where the sun don't shine, but the parade suddenly came to a halt. Vincent Van Vedic stopped his horse and turned in his saddle to see what was behind him, Rahellio did the same, and then the men just looked at each other, seeing the unspoken question in the other's eyes. This wasn't the way they usually did things. There was no doubt in their minds as to where they were and the fact that they were looking for a campsite with only an hour of daylight left, looking for a spot that was good enough for the night, with plenty of firewood, and far enough from the river so that it wasn't too noisy. They would finish off the food Rahellio's wife had packed, cook two big rainbow trout per man, and enjoy this campsite in the light of a full moon.

It was near sunset, and the stuck dog issue was over, yet there seemed to be a lot missing, like a night and a day, maybe more, so the captain was looking forward to calling it quits. He wanted to ask Rahellio what they had done that day because he couldn't for the life of himself put his finger on what it was that he had accomplished. It was time for a campfire, a good night's sleep under the stars, but try as he may, he couldn't remember having done anything during the day. Not one single thing, including waking up.

"Rahellio, my man, I don't know about you, but I feel about as good as I've ever felt in my life. My wrist doesn't hurt, my neck doesn't pop, and I can piss like a racehorse. Even my teeth feel clean and strong."

"Si, senor. You know my back problem? It's gone, no mas! Maybe it's because I'm down here by the river; I love the rivers, love being outside at night, and maybe that's why I don't feel the pain, but I don't have any. My back always hurts, but not right now, not at all. I feel strong and almost young. I know I don't look it, but I feel great."

"That's good. You might remember how I favored my middle finger when we met, along with a sad story about chains and fingertips? Remember that? Look at this puppy; totally back to perfect. It was so bad it even affected my grip on the gun, but not anymore."

He showed the mortician his middle fingertip, smiling at his friend while giving him the bird.

"Here we are, here we sit in 1953, and I remember having that accident in 1943 in the Caribbean somewhere, but no one would believe that. Maybe I have had other things on my mind, making me not notice that it healed until now, but it sure as hell has, and I'm thankful for that. I was looking at the three slashes on Sarge, and they too have healed completely—I'm thinking way ahead of schedule—and he doesn't limp at all."

Without any warning whatsoever, a dust cloud exploded

skyward on the other side of the barrier of stones. It rose straight up like a tornado and disappeared all over the top of the canyon walls, blowing in the wind up there and coming back down closer to the river. Neither man had seen such a thing before nor had any idea what it could have been, and as the dust settled, they toyed with their combined knowledge that something extraordinary had just happened. It was as if the Earth had farted, blew dust and dirt all over everything, and now after fifteen minutes, it had all floated back down. Another miracle, like the dog getting out of the rocks; how in the world he'd escaped was also unexplainable and best left alone for the night. Accept it for what it is, don't worry, and be happy about how things turn out. It could have been much worse.

"My first thought, Mr. Candelaria, is where was the noise? I heard the wind and saw the dust, but there was no explosion, no big bang that would have caused that. I'm used to there being fire and smoke when I see clouds of dust like that."

"It didn't bother the animals in the slightest. Raton might have seen something at the start. He seemed to lift his head and stare up at the sky for a few moments before the storm, watching the dust cloud rise as fast as it did. Just like you say, no explosion caused that dust. Maybe it was a rare canyon wind, like a tornado created by the cliffs. A huge dust devil that plummeted over the cliff up there and then sprang back to life in this canyon. It's too bad we can't go any further to see what's on the other side of these boulders—such an obstacle. We could come back someday with rope ladders and climbing equipment and find out what's on the other side. Maybe. I think we should be the ones who do that, not the conservationists. If they find out there is this wall of stones and the drawings, there will never be a Navajo Dam."

"I still can't get over the carvings on the cliff face. The ancient Indians who did the drawings must have felt the same as you, and since they couldn't go any further, they did their pictures here. Let's make camp up closer to the cliffs, and we can take solace in the fact that we won't have been the first. I want to take pictures with my new camera. It came with twenty rolls of film and I'm still on roll one. Then, we can toast the rock carvers with whatever is left of your tequila."

The campfire was roaring and lighting up the corner. The captain was finished with the day; he had a full belly and still had the big question in his mind, even after a couple of hours. He could not remember anything about the day for the life of himself, and it was now beginning to pester him so severely that he needed help. He would try to get Rahellio to comment on what that might be, because he would have been right there with Van Vedic and doing whatever it was right by his side.

"Boy, that sure was something!"

"What's that, my friend?"

"You know."

"Oh yeah, that was something."

"Not the dust cloud just now, earlier today."

"Si, senor, really something."

The captain enjoyed the tequila and a cup of coffee but he still didn't know anything concerning the day. Rahellio was of no help whatsoever and seemed to be evading the subject, doing busy work. So the captain retreated into his gun cleaning mode and could only smile at the cook. The minstrel had his guitar on his lap, both his cups close by his saddle, and seemed happy with the fire. The full moon shone down on the campsite, the temperature was perfect, and the captain asked Rahellio to sing about the moon. Sing a song about love and the full moon.

Unbeknownst to the captain, many of the moon-based observatories scattered along the edge were very much still in the game and recording how the men would handle having their memories erased. On whatever screen was available up there, that viewing audience could see Vincent's face; they could see his eyes were looking directly at them from that canyon floor. Very few creatures from the lower ends had ever had such an impact on the cosmos as these two humans, their dog, mule, and horses. The super networks didn't want the show to end. Everyone knew that it had to, but tonight need not end until the moon left the sky.

The show would be over within hours. The Blue Planet would go back to where it belonged in the news of the Universe and continue with its test. It was all very, very complicated, but many of the resorts on the moon, the cities under the South Pole, and all three of the undersea worlds would go back to the way they were—extended-stay habitats, species-specific paradises that the earthlings knew nothing about.

For now, the captain lounged by the fire. He'd washed his face, hands, and hair in the river and, in so doing, discovered he was one fragrant bunch of male. Back at the campsite, he cleaned and polished his 45s. His mind understood the reason for being in this canyon, and this exact location, these absurd coordinates —because the dog had gotten stuck in the rocks. He remembered finding Rahellio and mustering the animals and their harnesses which would be necessary to pull over a rock. After all that commotion, back and forth, when they'd arrived, the dog was already free, and the chances of that had been deemed a miracle by the first responders. There was that moment when the captain had considered shooting the dog, but he sure didn't want to do that; then, when he looked at the dog's back, he'd seen the possibility of rescue if a particular boulder were toppled. Sarge had, somehow or another, managed to escape his predicament, and that was about where he'd gotten back to as far as remembering what happened went. Sarge was given a thorough inspection by the captain, who searched for broken bones and cuts and bruises, none of which were there, and from that point on, he seemed to have drawn a blank.

"Rahellio, my good friend, I must admit that I'm having trouble with something. I..."

"My captain, you can't remember anything after examining the dog for injuries?"

"Exactly!"

Through all sorts of modern-day gadgetry, and because this was a no-holds-barred event, the cameras on the moon all had acceptable voice-capable contact with these two humans at their campsite. It was either a *0* project, suggested by the queens, or perhaps a Dizzy deal, consisting of a few hidden microphones with long-range capabilities. So, the Universe watched and listened as the two humans toyed with the puzzle.

"Me too. I'm entirely at a loss as to what happened to us from that point on. I did things that I can't remember, said things, played my guitar, and sang. I know that I did. I broke a string. And then a little while ago we were here, on our horses, and I don't know anything that's happened before that. I wasn't on the horse when you caressed your hound. Neither were you."

"I was left with the notion that Sarge getting out of the rocks was a miracle, no ifs, ands, or buts about it. It's a pure and simple miracle, the sort of thing I've believed in all my life. They do happen, and we have to accept that as the only explanation. Miracles make life complicated by happening. I don't remember anything after that inspection. Nothing."

"Senor, we managed to drink half of the tequila, ate the frozen elk steaks, and used up most of the coffee beans. We used all the ropes and harnesses for something because Raton was unpacked and repacked; I remember how we loaded him up at my barn. These animals seem different somehow, and I'm not sure I can explain it, but they've changed. I wish they could talk. My nails are filthy and were not at all when I loaded Raton at my casa. I dislike playing my guitar with dirty hands because I almost always break a string."

Van Vedic told the gravedigger he was also holding a mystery —two mysteries, for that matter. For some strange reason, the cylinders were dirty—not bad or anything, but they hadn't been cleaned since the last firing. Each weapon had four extra cylinders, times six, on their side of the holsters, a spare cylinder with at least one spent casing, each had empty cylinders, and he couldn't remember anything about having fired them. That revelation shook him to his core. It would have been he who'd fired the weapons, and he couldn't remember any of the W's: why, when, where, what, and who—standard stuff. Never before had he disrespected his weapons like this, and he promised the pieces it would never happen again. His hands were clean, and he only cleaned the 45s when his hands were that way first, probably even more so than the guitar player.

"Rahellio, this is not a trick question. When was the last time you remember me firing off these weapons?"

"Hodalay Esse, back two weeks late last month when you were hunting dove."

"I cleaned them later that day. I fired both of these in the last two or three days. I can smell it. Usually, the noise gets everyone's attention, and often times it's one of those life-changing moments. I cannot remember doing that. I can't remember firing my 45s. You can't remember me shooting, but the fact of the matter is that I did. I find it hard to believe that I talked you into going on a fishing trip to this place. I would have thought a person who grew up near this gorge would have a perfectly valid reason for why not to venture down in this far."

"There was a reason for you, senor; that is all I know. You

might remember promising to pay a crazy wage, and from then on, I was all in. I think you wanted to see the middle of the future reservoir and take pictures of the bottomland with your fancy new camera. You wanted to be able to say that you fished the San Juan before it became a lake."

"Doesn't sound like me."

"It was you."

"I fired these weapons, I figure, twenty times. Twice more with the right than the left, changed cylinders three times, and I don't remember doing that. I don't remember hearing you play your guitar, which you generally do at campfires, and I love to listen to you sing. When we packed up, those were brand new shovels, and now they look well used. I damn sure don't remember a party so good we drank half a cider bottle's worth of home-brewed tequila. No sir, don't remember that."

"It was you."

"It's a feeling I have, right now, right this minute, all over my body, like there's a story right on the tip of my tongue, above my eyebrows a smidge. There's a power denying me the ability and the right to remember something—the story of a lifetime. I can feel it; I know there's something there that I need to say. That's what it is; I can't say it. I don't even know how long we've been here. What day is it? I don't know what day it is. I don't remember today or yesterday at all, not any of it. What about the day before that? Fix your guitar, and we'll sing our questions to the moon. We'll head home in the morning."

Most of the critical cosmos watching from above would be curiously waiting for that question. But unfortunately, certain intellectual beings from the higher orders had proven that erasing memories was easier said than done, much easier.

"Senor, you're right. I'm not sure what day this is. I can see you in my memory inspecting the dog, trying like me to understand how it escaped, and nothing after that. It's a white space for my brain, which seems to be trimmed in a light blue. I don't know the date, and we won't know until tomorrow at the earliest. It doesn't matter if it's only a day or two in the truest sense. If we lost a week, it might be a stretch. We'll be able to feel the heat when the dogs discover us at the gates, and if it's been too long, she'll be waiting with her favorite deep-cleaning broom. God, I hope it hasn't been too long. She has all sorts of trick questions. It's a minefield in Spanish. All that aside, I feel great!"

"Me too. I feel full, not even tired. You know, my friend— and I've told you all of this before... Actually, that's not true. Not all of this you've heard before, and the reason I ask you to listen to me once again is that it helps me put the timeline together. I try not to be a bore."

"Mr. Van Vedic, my ears can't get enough of your story."

"Thank you. I have ended the life of many men, evil men in all cases, and none of them haunt me, and I pray there won't be any more, but I do want to be left alone here in my old age. I'm ready to write this story as I remember it, get things done on the ranch, write, fish and camp, write some more and decide precisely how old I am. I'm still not sure. You spoke of a white wall, a white space, and that's good. That's a start. I remember that it was a white space, and I can see the blue. I floated in white space for ten years but then miraculously resurfaced not too long ago. From out of nowhere, me and my *Vanessa* casually found the coast of Texas at Corpus Christi. For days and days, I was adrift in the strangest storm front imaginable, inside a hurricane but not in imminent danger, floating on a calm sea peacefully; that's a moment in my memory. And then, instead, I find myself floating in restricted waters off the coast of Texas with no memory of where I'd been or how long I'd been there.

"The US Coast Guard has pictures. They gave me copies of everything they had, before and after, and it was agreed by all the members of the review board that my *Vanessa* had been doomed inside Hurricane #9, in 1943. The Hurricane Hunter airplane that took all the pictures of the *Vanessa* just barely survived the return trip. The men on board made calculations and measurements, and took wind speeds and barometric pressures that were hard to believe. Parts of the converted war bomber were ripped off, flaps and the like, and the shouting amongst the crew was filled with blame and threats during some of the upside-down turbulent times. Both Colonel Duckworth and his co-pilot had unhitched their seat belts during a calm respite when their fresh pants had arrived, but at the least favorable time possible, the aircraft plummeted over five thousand feet in a minute. Sixty seconds of white eyeball terror. There was good reason to think they wouldn't make it to dawn; just another day in the life of a hurricane hunter.

"The presentation the Coast Guard had for me was overwhelming in every way there was, with many of the flight crew giving their testimony on how things happened. It was an all-afternoon luncheon with lots of tears and apologies, with men hugging and saluting each other and proclaiming that the next Coast Guard vessel would carry the name *Vanessa*. When the war ended, certain historical people gradually rose to the top of the appreciation pyramid, with General George S. Patton being very high on everyone's list. Except for a few, of course. My *Vanessa* had carried Jude to Patton, the general fished off her stern, and their airplane recorded my last known whereabouts with me waving hello or goodbye, depending on your point of view.

"The entire crew experienced weightlessness the whole way down, along with everything else in the plane, most of which moved around quite freely during their death spiral. The navigator was strapped in like a good boy. He caught the pilot, Colonel Duckworth, as he floated by and pushed him back towards his seat, where he regained control and started to unscrew it all. Sure enough, with the co-pilot's help, they pulled out of the dive, got all the engines running, and then burst through the eyewall of # 9 into the peace and quiet of the hurricane's eye with twenty thousand feet to spare. Those lifesaving heroics confirmed what the science suggested. There had to be an eye. And in accomplishing this, the first successful penetration of the eyewall, they also discovered it was no less than fifteen miles in diameter, maybe twenty. It was an entirely different world of peace and tranquility, inside of which they flew in a circle, cut it in half twice, and photographed my *Vanessa* just off the center core from two thousand feet.

"You should have been there. This narrator had a pointer stick, and a projector had magnified the pictures of me on the boat on a huge screen. This part of the presentation came after all the stories concerning what the plane had gone through just to get there, and all of the crew recounted how they were, in fact, only halfway home. Each and every man mentioned that from his point of view, this plane ride had been the scariest thing he had ever done so far, and they were shackled with the knowledge that they had to do it all again. There were lots of people, lots of stories, and a lot of fun for me.

"He told the audience, 'You see here the captain of the *Vanessa*, Captain Van Vedic, standing alongside the bell on the bow of his boat and waving at the airplane. Next picture. Here he put his hands on his hips and watched the plane fly by slowly, two thousand feet above the water. Next picture. Next picture.' Dead silence in the room. He explained how they had no choice but to rock their wings to say goodbye and then started the climb. Some of their last readings of surface conditions detected an undersea volcano that was not on any previous readings, not all that deep in the trenches. Very, very strange that they detected such a thing so close to the surface. They have investigated the exact same coordinates many times since then and cannot find the volcano. That faulty reading has challenged the Coast Guard scientists ever since.

"They circled straight up inside the eye of #9 to thirty-five thousand feet and tried to get above the storm clouds, but they had their limits, and the thunderheads didn't. It was up there at their boundaries that they decided to fly back into the wall of chaos and head for home, with no other options available. Fuel was a concern at the start of the turn, but when the natural lights went out, it was replaced with mountainous lightning storms and a complete loss of visibility at times. Their plane was not designed to fly in this sort of chaos, and at different horrifying times, the forward speed was critically reduced almost to a stall out. They knew exactly how far they had to go on the return trip to get to safety, and those miles passed into the history books. The men on board would become legends in the world of hurricane hunters—if they lived through it and could talk about it —but unfortunately, that white fishing boat they discovered stranded on the surface was doomed.

"That human waving back—namely me, Vincent Van Vedic —in the photographs, smiling and waving to the plane from the front deck of my *Vanessa* on October 14th, 1943? The Coast Guard review board's final judgment about whether I might survive was that there was no way out, with a micro-slim chance, one percent or less, that I might find a cove while the eye was passing over an island.

"Slim to none, and then a great deal of discussion followed about how the boat managed to get there in the first place. I was just off dead-center bullseye of hurricane #9 for that unique photo opportunity. The Coast Guard had no desire whatsoever to ever be where I was. The eye of #9 was no less than fifteen nautical miles in diameter, a new science frontier, with these early crude measurements trying to decide such a thing while the beast was rolling and churning west-northwest at eight knots. This was where *Vanessa* found her groove, where the winds were calm and peaceful, but out on the edge of the eye, eight or more miles away from the circular horizon, the winds were two hundred and fifty miles per hour counterclockwise. None of the Coast Guard boats are any good in those kinds of winds; no boat on the planet could survive those winds and that kind of sea, all of which was unknown information to me. I didn't know where I was!

"The audience was wonderful and gave me standing ovations. They asked questions for an hour. I told them hurricanes were monsters that needed to be avoided, which brought the house down, and if there was one thing for sure, the last direction I would pick was towards that lighting and those boiling storm systems. From the very start, I had lost command of her movement and knew nothing of what was happening around me for the most part. The surface I floated on consisted of small islands of broken vegetation, with the *Vanessa* and everything from the islands floating counterclockwise around a center whirlpool that seemed off to my port. From my bow, I could see to the distant horizon—seven miles, I estimated, in every direction I looked, and that line seemed to be where the storm systems began. After all this time, nothing had changed much; those storms were still far away on the horizon, and I concluded I was moving faster than the far-distant vertical storm walls, but they all looked alike, to be honest.

"The scientists explained how I was trapped inside a demon that only existed on papers that I had never read and occasionally in the memories of the unfortunates on land who found themselves on the land's end of a bullseye. There are many stories of how quiet and peaceful the eye can be, but all hell preceded it slowly, taking its time building up in intensity until the eye arrived, and then the wind stopped, and all the survivors went outside their shelter. But an even worse side of the storm was only a short while away, depending on the diameter of the eye; the flip side is that instantly it seems the same wind speed as before, but from the opposite direction. It seemed to me that the science part of hurricanes had an exceptionally long way to go. No one seemed to have a valid escape route, but they all knew I had escaped. And when they asked me how I did it, I told them I didn't know and, in turn, asked them if they had any ideas.

"I remember being there inside the storm. I remember I wasn't scared or threatened, and then suddenly it was white space."

After a long pause, Vincent said, "I think this question I'm struggling with has something to do with that time. I suppose my subconscious knows what happened. Maybe it will dawn on me someday.

"From 1943 till 1953, I was in that white space. I don't think I aged a minute while I was there in that white-out, and when I found myself bobbing in the Gulf of Mexico a few months ago, those ten years were lost in my memory. That's how I felt about that subject just last month, but now I feel like I know the answer; I just can't speak that language. I know what happened, but I can't think it out of my mouth; the words are too hard to say. It was all part of a contract I agreed to, for some reason. Maybe I was forced into something, forced out of something; I wish I could speak about it. So many things happened in the world during a time I can't remember. I don't remember the Second World War ending. I don't remember the atomic bombs on Japan. I remember being in Puerto Rico and headed for the big republic when a hurricane swallowed me. I concluded that being there, where I was at the time, would be the end of me. Everywhere I looked, I saw mountainous thunderstorms, the likes of which we seldom see on land. I didn't know that the place I was in even existed. I was in the center of a circle, fairly sure of that, and I had been for two or three days. That's where the white-out begins."

The gravedigger sat there listening, trying to understand the mystery and drama his employer was remembering.

"Then I find the Texas shores, 1953, and I can't remember anything that happened in the last ten years. It was, without a doubt, a miracle, and sometimes when miracles happen to us, we have to accept that as the truth and go on about our business. It was a miracle, and that's all there is to it. Those are the facts, and I know that to be true. I cannot explain anything. I smashed my middle finger in 1943, and it still hurt my hand in 1953. I'd say that's a miracle."

"My captain, all I know is you've brought excitement back to the local counties. You brought *Vanessa* all this way, and in front of everyone, you talk about floating around on the future lake, the biggest lake in the west. Well, you can be sure that subject has now been discussed at almost every dinner table for miles in every direction. It will help the close communities, and if they get it done like they say, there will be a lot of it. I can't think of a single reason why they shouldn't flood the whole thing; it's a useless canyon full of big rocks that belong on the bottom of a lake. I hope no one is hurt by it, but there's so much of it there will be pain and loss for ancient families in several places. You told me an information pamphlet you found in Russia talked about the Navajo Dam. Amazing. All the newspaper can talk about is that it will be the biggest earthen dam in the world, which I think is saying something. Biggest in the world!"

Side note: For the sake of the viewing audience, the Superstation replayed on multiple viewing and listening channels the many different angles of the time when *DDccccV* plucked the *Vanessa* out of the way of a mountain of water. That rescue had happened over ten years ago, Earth time. *DDccccV* saved *Vanessa* from the tidal wave they had created. It was almost fluky, how the controlling powers had made all the necessary decisions to save Vincent Van Vedic from something they'd caused. This was a first for the intergalactic travelers, to see how they emerged from the lower depths to find a fishing boat stranded in the center of the eye. Escaping Earth's gravity and starting a trek from WWwWweebbbTmmuumm has always been done through the eye of the storms if possible. The end game turned out to be that their exit wave would kill this human, *DDccccV* caused the tsunami, and there existed a simple remedy, which was to rescue the human immediately. Basic *Gold Book* stuff, with much involvement from the Watchers.

Out of respect for their new hostage, the Watchers did a thorough background check on him and everything on his boat. They read his writing and mind, counted his notches and all his gold, and discovered much. It was a known fact in the world of the Earth Watchers that Van Vedic wanted to own a horse ranch and bury his wife on a hillside with a view. An assortment of rules and regulations governed the Watchers. In pure *Gold Book* logic, it was determined that even though Vincent Van Vedic had to be saved immediately from imminent death caused by *DDccccV*, Mother Nature would have naturally killed him. The Watchers had a great deal of involvement up to this point, trying their best to get him to that homestead he could envision for himself. All he had to do was go home tomorrow if he could get over the notion something was missing—something that mattered immensely and would make everything make sense.

Unbeknownst to these campfire hosts, now it was all over. The cadets were saved, *0* was saved, Spaqu's band was saved, and these two saviors relaxed by their fire and knew nothing about such things—nothing, and there was much about the recent past being kept from their memory.

"In the morning, after breakfast, we'll head back to your casa and find out what day it is. We'll try to coordinate our stories so that your wife and son don't catch us in a lie. If nothing else, at least we'll know how much time we're talking about. You don't remember me shooting off my guns? You don't remember breaking the string, cooking the elk slabs, drinking all that tequila?

The Mexican was plucking at his guitar, a tune he called Clair de Lune, pointing the end of his guitar at the full moon above them.

"Senor, have you ever wondered about the moon? They tell me we only see this side and have never seen the other side. It has a most unusual orbit and is the exact same size as the sun in the sky, causing the total eclipse, but one is a quarter of a million miles away, and the other is ninety million miles away. That's very strange. They tell us the Earth wouldn't exist the way it does without the moon pulling and pushing the Earth the way it must. I think there's something fishy going on up there. I don't know where I heard this or who it was that told me this… Maybe some of the scientists at Los Alamos Laboratories say Martians made the moon. They're the ones who made our atomic bombs. Yep, that's what the weirdos say. The moon came from Mars. Maybe that's where that idea came from? I don't think I've ever thought these thoughts before, but someone told me they knew someone who made the moon. I distinctly remember asking them to say that again, and they did. They said it again, said they made the moon twice. I can't for the life of me remember who that was. I know that's true somehow. I know it."

"I believe you, and I think I remember you asking me if I heard what your friend said. I can hear him, but I can't see him. What was his name? Do you remember his name? I'm going around in a circle; what was his name, what was his name? I'm dizzy. I got dizzy trying to remember your friend's name. I look up there at the moon and see it differently now. I don't know what it is; all that crazy stuff might very well be true, and I try to imagine what the Earth looks like in the moon's day or night sky. They have an Earthrise like we have a Moonrise, and that would be hard to get used to. I understand that there are now missiles that can carry atomic bombs all over the planet, and I just hope that someone is building missiles or rockets that might take a man to the moon. You've got to start somewhere. If we get there and find out there's already somebody there, maybe they will let us stay for a while. Maybe not. I'm not sure anyone really knows what the moon is. Is it possible there might be people like us on the moon who wonder the same things we wonder? They wonder what the Earth is, just like we wonder what the moon is?"

The captain stood up tall with the raging fire at his back lighting up their corner of the canyon like a huge torch lying on the sand. It was almost magical. The moon was full, five hand-spans above the horizon, shining down on the anglers and turning night into day. He spread his feet, tilted back, bellowed "DOVE" at the guitar player, and told the moon to duck. Both 45s erupted in six consecutive shots side by side, one after another, in a perfect sequence of twelve, bullseye, dead center of the moon.

His only audience on Earth, a man who was conditioned by

the word *dove*, could only sit there and strum the perfect final chords when the roaring echoes ultimately stopped in those distant canyons. Rahellio strummed those notes, believing that it was possible and that no one else in the Universe had heard what he had just heard. It was almost musical, raw talent from the world of explosions, projectiles, and bullseyes, which caused him to bloom with pride because he was there to see and hear it happen. A true maestro on stage. Never before and never again.

He couldn't have imagined how wrong he was, because the truth of the matter was the entire Universe, in fact, did experience the surprise of it all. It's essential to recognize that, as the saying goes, "the rest of the Universe" was not conditioned to be ready when Van Vedic said "DOVE." Each and every one of those 45-caliber hollow-point bullets was technically photographed, if that be the right word. From a quarter-million miles away, each bullet was reduced to the moment it exited either one of the cannons and started their spin towards the moon, one after another, one through twelve, huge hollow-tipped bullets, them and nothing else. There may have been as many as two or three thousand high-definition telephoto lenses that were still filming this spectacle at the time, relaying their messages all over the cosmos, when Van Vedic surprised the audience with his late-night quick-draw demonstration. It was how he had always dealt with pent-up anger, and he was angry about being unable to remember the recent past. Way past angry.

"I met an astronomer on an island in the Sea of Marmara. His name was Thousanctus Zerbe, and he said the moon was an unnatural object in the sky and was way out of sync with the other planets and their moons. It was sometimes there in the daytime, sometimes at night, sometimes a slice, sometimes full, and sometimes not. He lives in a place called Tucumcari."

"Tucumcari, New Mexico?"

"There's a Tucumcari in New Mexico?"

"Yes, it's over on the other side of the state, right there on Highway 66."

"No shit!"

"No caca!"

"Goodnight."

Throughout the known Universe, from every corner of the viewing audience, a silence swept through the cosmos, shouting that here was proof once again that particular creatures will regain their memories of something they had been forced to forget. The Watchers were content, at least for the time being, and as the coals of the fishermen's fire died early that next morning, the cadets, *0*, Dizzy, and Spaqu's Life Ring arrived at his memorial site in Orion.

CHAPTER EIGHTEEN

WHAT DAY IS IT

With the sun popping up above the horizon, almost precisely where the moon had done the same thing the night before, Rahellio got the fire going and had a fresh pot of coffee perking on the edge. That smell had woken the captain for decades. That moon was gone, had set behind the cliff face hours before, but there were still secret ears out there close by. There's something spiritual about standing near an early morning fire and being on your feet with so much of the day up ahead. It justifies everything if you are not in any sort of pain. Pain is this one thing that all humans feel, something that we all try to avoid, and here he stood with no pain anywhere in his old body. Nowhere.

There had been that immediate recollection; the first thing debated in his consciousness this morning concerning last night's perplexing question was that he couldn't remember what he did during the previous two or three days.

Rahellio had prayed the rosary before falling asleep. He'd

asked Van Vedic if he could pray it aloud, sing it with his guitar backing him up. Van Vedic sat up and said the answer was for sure; he thought about kneeling for a brief moment but passed on that idea because his common sense had taken over. The captain told a quick story about how Jude did the rosary, and though the words were similar to those Rahellio knew from his childhood, there were differences—but for the most part they were the same.

"I'm very good with the 'Amen' part of any prayer. You can count on it. So take as long as you please. A musical rosary. This will be a first for me."

Rahellio had snuggled up against his saddle, his guitar resting on his thighs, staring straight up at the moon. Then, from his side of the dying fire, a slow procession of chords was followed by his loud proclamation that the purpose of his prayer was that he and his captain could recover their memory of yesterday and the day before—everything that had happened here by the river.

"Amen!"

He even had the beads in his pocket. He took them out, looped them over his guitar's neck, and notched them flawlessly while playing simple chords. It was basically half a dozen different songs, in perfect order, over and over. He didn't cut any corners, so the Universe heard the extended version, known only by certain kinds of Catholics at specific types of funerals, with all due respect.

He was always the man of the hour when one of the nuns died at the cloistered monastery in Waterflow. He took care of everything the sisters couldn't do, and that was where he'd learned the extended version, the monastic funeral version. They were in no hurry to get things done at the monastery when it came to funerals, and a wealthy matriarch down in that valley paid all his expenses on those occasions; she had heard him sing and play at a friend's funeral many, many years before, and when she explained who he was to the grieving Mother Superior, the broken-hearted woman reminded her about the rules. She said no man could speak the male voice inside the boundaries of their holy place. Of course, the gravedigger would be allowed to do just that—dig that grave in their cemetery, play his guitar in the background at the internment, say not a word, nor sing a note, and was sometimes the only outsider there. Quite a few times now, in twice that many years.

"Good morning, Captain. How did you sleep?"

"Sleep? I know I did, but it took a while. I'm waking up today to who knows what day it is, and I don't think it did me any good as far as remembering anything. How about you?"

"I see you rubbing on the dog, checking out his body, talking to it. Then we're on our horses looking for a campsite. There is no doubt in my mind that something happened in between those two visions, but I don't have a clue as to what it was or what we did. I can tell you this: I've never lost a day or two in my fifty-five years so far, and I wouldn't say I like the idea one little bit. I also think that something has happened inside my body. My back no longer hurts, not at all, and it's hurt me badly at times in the recent past, especially after horseback riding, but not this morning. Not at all. I have two teeth that make me cringe, but not at all this morning, for some strange reason. I think there are others, but the day is young."

He handed the captain his oversized coffee mug and watched him sample the brew, waiting for the response from his boss, who stared down into the steam.

"Right around the turn of the century, I killed a man who was about to kill my father. I'd watched my father kill a dozen demon men in the outback country, and then one day, one got the drop on him, and he went down hard. He lived after being shot in the hip in the badlands. I was still a boy, not even thirteen, and at the time, I thought I'd never forget the demon's face. His notch is first on the strong-side cannon, inside grip, one a.m. on the clock. This gun didn't kill that demon, nor the next four notches. A double-barrel shotgun did the trick, but out of respect for the fallen enemy, I etched them on this one. They count just as much as those killed by the strong- or weak-side cannons. My finger pulled the trigger, and my eyes watched them die.

"Russia was a complicated country when I lived there, still is to this day, but back when I was born, the droughts of '91 and '92 brought killer diseases like cholera and smallpox. My birth land, the fertile Volga basin, dried up and became a horrible place to live. Dying of thirst and famine is one of the worst ways for a human to die. Trust me on that one. Where there is no water there's also no food, and it becomes obvious that's what will kill you. In a matter of days, everyone is dead or knocking on death's door. During times like that, during the years preceding the Civil War, the centennial turn times, tools, bridges, buildings, everything it seemed wore out and died. Some were so old they dated back to Catherine the Great. In my world at the time, these two cannons were frequently the only final defining factor. I treasure these two tools; I clean and polish them with all the tender, loving care I can muster, even after all this time, and yet I fired them recently, many times, both pieces, and I don't remember doing that. You know how noisy they are, especially in canyonlands, and yet you don't remember me doing any such thing. If you aren't expecting it, the noise will scare the bejesus out of you."

(((From an earlier chapter. "Gadidg"

Rahellio got back to his feet and was about twenty feet away with his back to Van Vedic when he lost his footing and who knows what else, with substantial white big-eyed eyeballs, as the echoes of those two shots off the canyon walls were many and as loud as could be. When the Captain turned towards where the cadets had been sitting, he found all three standing with really, really, really big eyes. They were blinking like super blinkers, Venetian blinds type blinkers, and two of them had lost their straws.)))

Rahellio saw something there in his recent memory for just a moment. He might have heard something in a far back corner room of his subconsciousness more than saw it. Felt a tremor rip through his body from the backside, out of nowhere, an instantaneous double dose of terror. He shivered head to toe.

"Captain, I just felt something from yesterday or the day before. It scared me bad... might have knocked me down."

"I feel like there's a mirror wall between me and my memory. Someone or something is causing this, causing me to forget. I know that for sure. Since things haven't improved much, I guess we'll break camp and head for your casa. We know what day the dog got stuck after you and your son went home. We know what time it was when we got here and found him safe, the same day —Friday, late afternoon. The only problem is that we don't know what today is. We'll find that out in a few hours. I'm anxious to get back home."

All four animals seemed to instinctively step in the identical hoof prints of the animal in front. The captain led the way with El Bruto Whetto setting a reasonable pace, and the two men talked back and forth constantly about all sorts of things while planning their arrival at Rahellio's ranch. Both men felt like they were way past due, for some reason, and were trying to be reasonable. Yet, each man had lost an unknown amount of his time, his life, days, and nights, for no reason they could find so far, leaving a substantially difficult nagging question mark. *What day is it?*

"We can say we went to my house first and then here. No, no, never mind. I'm anticipating your wife's questions about where we've been. She'll see that the dog is alive, the animals are all just fine, that we're just fine, everything is fine. And maybe she won't say a thing."

"Maybe she won't say a thing? Is that what you said? Maybe she won't say a thing? Raton, did you hear that? Here's a plan: We ride up, and you politely ask, 'What day is it, Mrs. Candelaria?' She'll say something like October twentieth. Maybe she'll say Wednesday or Saturday. Either way, we'll know. At this point, you could scream out something in Russian, turn your horse and race off towards where we came from with the dog in hot pursuit. That would leave me to deal with her, depending on what day it is. What could we have possibly done that we can't remember?"

"I don't know any more than you."

With that, they broke camp, which wasn't much of a bother, and started their journey out of the canyon and back up to the plateau. Neither man had any idea what day it was. The path resembled the term well-worn with horse hooves. In a long straightaway, the captain guided the posse off to the right a few yards and then stopped the procession for a rest. He and Rahellio studied the different prints in the sand. Some were fresh, and the others were days old, but only days. A long trail of horse shit revealed that the insides were still green and less than a week old; horse shit is a science unto itself, using many tools and observations, which allow the investigator to accurately measure their age to the half-day. There had been no rain since they first passed through, and when he thought about it, Vincent knew that a professional tracker could follow these marks a year down the road from now.

He couldn't quit thinking about what Rahellio had said about the conservationists finding the carvings on that cliff face and what they would do when they came to the barricade of boulders, all of which created the possibility that the Navajo Dam would then never be built. That would mean his *Vanessa* would never float again, and that singular thought became his new motivator. He wanted to begin dragging a tree branch behind the horses and burying these tracks immediately. He was now convinced that he had been guided to the drawings on the cliff face and that boulder wall. Who knew why? If his precious *Vanessa* was ever to float again, no other man could discover those drawings. The biggest earthen dam in the entire world must happen; the reservoir was far too necessary not to succeed.

"Rahellio, my man, I've been thinking about what you said about other people finding what we've seen before the dam is built. Let's erase these tracks during the next rainstorm and get rid of them just in case. When I compare these two different tracks, it's hard to tell those tracks over there are older than these tracks we've just made. These might be here a long time. Horse hooves are hard to hide, easy to follow, and we've made a bunch here in the last week or so. This needs to be considered when we meet your wife. Just the two of us, you and I, must come back, drag the trail, and try to hide it from curious eyes. Spend a few days. Maybe make a different trail that goes somewhere else. Let's bring your herd over here and drive them down and back, and instead of a few horses leaving tracks, we have a whole herd of cattle."

"Two men can't handle the herd, but that's a great idea. We might want to consider sheep; they're much more manageable, a lot slower, and democratic. She'll want to know why I would do such a stupid thing on someone else's property. All the neighbors will find out, and they'll talk in the church parking lot. I can hear her now."

"Why in this world will people talk about your herd in the parking lot of St. Rose?"

"Most of my herd is mixed in with about twenty other herds and are grazing up in the high country above Pagosa. Two trailers' worth. My cows look just like everyone else's cows, except for the brand, and if the books say it's time for that cow to get on another trailer, well, then it's time, and there is a cash reward. It's just business, and I hope most of them get on the other semis. We get them back down at this elevation next month, and it would be no problem to graze however many are left in the old pastures. Sheep are a whole different critter. Do you know that sheep can intentionally hide behind large rocks from the shepherd, like children? True stuff. But they can't hide from the dogs. My little herd will destroy these horse tracks. We can do this real soon if you want."

"I do. Soon is best. If I was out on my own, riding along and coming to these tracks, I'd almost certainly follow them to where they led. There's a lot of commotion going on here. I was curious to know if your wife is normally interested in the things that keep you busy. Plus, do you ever graze the sheep on this side of your land? Let's get moving and find out if she does."

Van Vedic listened to the man talk about his sheep like a loving shepherd would speak. He worried about losing one in the rocks, how they got scared and freeze and couldn't be found. Dumb was their middle name, slow was good, and yes, he used to graze them in the canyons, especially in the weeks after a serious rain event. Otherwise, no. What a man did in the rural areas with his herds was primarily unregulated, and subjecting one's herd to the dangers from Mother Nature could be very costly, very costly indeed.

Their trip to the pet gates took two hours, and sure as hell, a mile and a half further, Rahellio's three dogs sensed the visitors,

Sarge sensed them right back, and there was a wonderful reunion of guard dogs with all volumes of barking and howling.

(((They left the river campground at noon on October fifteenth, Vincent Van Vedic's birthday, supposedly his sixty-fifth, but he had his doubts about his body being that old. He now believed without a doubt that he had gone down a drain hole in the ocean in a hurricane, went somewhere for ten years, and on July twenty-seventh, 1953, he popped back to life off the shores of Corpus Christi, Texas. There were pictures of him that saddened the world in 1942, proved where he was in the end, and there was no way out of the eye of Hurricane #9.)))

For mile after mile, the captain and his partner had discussed a dozen different options and scenarios concerning Mrs. Candelaria, none of which held much promise if she became really inquisitive. The best bet was to claim guilty of being old-man lazy, camped near the river, eating trout and rabbit, and wasting time. Rahellio talked about how his wife was so intrigued by the story of the captain hunting dove with a pistol that she damn near called her husband a liar and said she would have to put her fingers in the wound like Doubting Thomas before she'd believe that cock-and-bull story. He described how Van Vedic could blast one dead right there in the front yard of his house if a dove came flying by, which they always did. They could always pretend that they were exhausted and very hungry for her green chili stew and fresh dove. It was one idea after another until both men pretty much had a grip on the upcoming confrontation; they had thought of all sorts of scenes, even considered playing sick if everything else failed.

Their worries were all not for naught as she screamed out, "RAHELLIO, RAHELLIO. It's so good to see you both! Hello, Captain."

As the posse got closer and closer, they both waved at her,

and finally, Rahellio spoke loudly to his wife, "My mariposa, the captain and I aren't sure what day it is. We've lost track. We have a bet that only you can fix with the correct information. So pray tell us what day it is."

"I don't know. I don't care. Where in the holy hell have you been?"

For some strange reason, that particular question had never been phrased quite like that in their planning sessions, which left both men paralyzed from the lips back. Fortunately for almost everyone concerned, two love doves flew by at dove speed. The captain sat up high in the saddle and blew their tiny heads off with the right-side 45. Both their decapitated bodies landed not far from the porch steps, and she shrieked out a long and extended hallelujah. Then, she ran to where their bodies lay and scared off the dogs with a piercing screech while chanting, "Hail Mary, holy Mary, hail Mary, holy Mary," in a whisper for almost a minute. Finally, she returned to the gate with tears in her eyes.

"My precious husband and guardian of this family, I apologize for doubting what you said this man could do with his guns. I'm so ashamed. So ashamed. Please forgive me for those ugly things I said about your eyesight and imagination. I will never doubt your words again in my life. Never. Never again."

Two more doves chanced by and drew the same reward, and now she had enough for dove stew, which was the way it was usually done. Green chili dove stew, fresh tortillas, honey, good food for sure, and then a good night's rest for the campers. Eye contact was virtually nonexistent between the returning mortician and his wife for the present situation. She was the first to realize the problem, a state of affairs she had never appreciated, and which almost always ended up with Rahellio being in the doghouse for something he did or didn't do. The empty fish bucket garnered her attention, which she unlatched and turned upside down. The dove needed her attention, and the two horsemen headed for the corrals with all four animals. They'd managed to survive the initial encounter, but plans had been made to have lunch in an hour, and they could tell her their story over food.

Raton was unloaded of all the harnesses and rigging ropes, his X frame was backed off, and Rahellio polished his skin with a long-handled brush, and combed his hair. The animal had a noticeable air about himself, like he knew he was a different creature than El Bruto Whetto or all the others. He seemed to know. Van Vedic tended to his horse, and while standing directly in front and looking into its eyes, he noticed a look he'd not seen before. Only a man as tall as the captain could hold the horse's head by his cheeks and see it straight on. The massive brute allowed his head to be held, looked straight into the captain's eyes, and the two creatures shared the moment. More like a minute, with vibrations, man and beast touching the earth and feeling something together, with only the beast of burden remembering their encounters with 0 and unable to explain, unable to rise to the moment for his master and be something other than what he was.

The cowboys put it all away, and as they were doing that, Whetto and Raton forced themselves to where all the ropes were piled and then proceeded to smell and lick the ends, a behavior that was as strange as anything either animal had ever done. It didn't go unnoticed as the captain intervened and held those rope ends in his hands. He studied them closely and found them warm to the touch. He mentioned it to Rahellio, and they both agreed there was a warmth and softness to the ends, different from the rest of the coil. The rope ends, over three feet of them, were coated with something, not like oil or tar or any other liquids, but with something indescribable, sweet, soft, visible yet invisible.

All three standard drag harnesses, along with Raton's buggy harness with side poles and drag straps, had been used in the very recent past.

"We used these ropes for something, and that's a fact. They were unwound and then rewound in the sand—it's all over them —and I know that I did these pairs. They're done in my style, and you did all the rest. All the harnesses have been used, and maybe only once, plus there are no injuries to these horses anywhere, none of the minor stuff from a hard day's work. We started off with a full-to-the-cork cider bottle full of homebrew, and now there's only an inch or two left. The water bags are almost empty, and so is the coffee bag. I don't remember any of the past where we drank all that. None of the fishing equipment has been used. The frozen elk slabs are gone. I could understand me not remembering some of the recent past, but in truth, my brain operates on almost total recall. I've never had any complaints about how my thinker worked. Now I'm confronted with the knowledge that you have the exact same problem, which goes against all the rules.

"How come you don't have a radio out here? Will you go ask your wife what day it is? I have to know as soon as possible."

"Ummmmm…"

"Do you want me to go with you?"

"The dog got stuck on Friday, and you and I arrived on the scene later that afternoon, only to find him free. We were prepared to topple a large slab of rock to free the dog, but it wasn't necessary. Then we were on our horses looking for a campsite last night. Something happened at our campsite on Friday night. That's what is missing. Everything from then and there till now is missing. What if it's been a week? What if it's been a year?" The gravedigger was starting to unravel a bit.

"Calm down. I'll go with you, but you lead the way. Don't

you have a favorite song you play and sing when you come home from the trips? Be ready to strum her favorite song of all songs. Keep your guitar close by. I'm guessing today is Tuesday the twentieth, based on that horseshit. She vehemently promised never to doubt you again, which translates into you can tell her just about anything. You can always use that promise down the road."

"I didn't get a good look at her. Could it be ten years, like with you and the hurricane? The barn looks the same. She used holy hell in the same sentence, which is a new term from her if I'm not mistaken. Maybe it's only a few years and nothing much has changed. A couple of months wouldn't be too bad. You think it's Tuesday?"

"I can tell you're not going to do too well with all this, are you? But everything is going to be okay. Let's go."

It hadn't taken long to pack for this rescue, and it didn't take long to unpack. The big question seemed to be the same as it was when they left the river this morning—what day it was. The hundred-foot walk from the barn to the back steps into the kitchen seemed longer than expected, like half a mile, maybe a little less.

The couple had a special seat for the captain at their dining table, having discovered that nothing in their home was made for a man his size in the way of furniture. It resembled something you'd find in the horseshoe barn, only covered with leather, was extra heavy-duty, and sitting there when the two men opened the kitchen door. The smell from her cooking was to die for as the men settled into their spaces, and she poured them both a cup of coffee and brought out a bowl full of fresh biscuits.

"Soooooooooooo?"

"Not even an hour ago, my sweet mariposa, you vowed never

to doubt my word again. So, I'm going to tell you something that you will find very hard to believe, but it will be the truth."

"OOOOOOHHhhhhhKaaaaaayyyyy!"

"We left on Friday to rescue the dog, as you very well remember. When we got to the river, we found that he had escaped somehow, and because it was late, we decided to camp the night. The captain and I cannot remember anything that happened between then and last night. We don't know what day it is. We have amnesia; it's like our memories have been erased."

"You are so cute. I believe you, and I'm pretty sure it's a little past noon on Tuesday the twentieth."

The two men sat and stared at each other, with Rahellio admitting that the captain had been right with his guess. They looked at the parish calendar and could see that they were missing Friday night, Saturday, Sunday, and the better part of Monday. Since today was Tuesday, that meant they'd made camp on Monday night, started remembering things once again at that time, and went to sleep knowing that part of their lives was missing. They discovered that starting before sundown last Friday, they couldn't seem to remember anything over a seventy-two-hour period. They ate, drank almost all their supplies, used their equipment for something, didn't break anything but a guitar string, and left a trail of horse prints they had to deal with immediately. The captain didn't even want to tell the Mrs. about the petroglyphs and explained to her husband that if no one had stumbled across them before now, it could hopefully stay that way until the reservoir filled up. So here they were, enjoying the stew and planning to cover up their tracks from an adventure into the river canyons, knowing full well that the tracks were many and deep, making that task the most urgent of all.

CHAPTER NINETEEN

TO SALVAGE A DREAM

Later that afternoon, Mrs. Candelaria brought out a pitcher of margaritas, along with three salt-rimmed glasses, to the table where the men were sitting. While she filled the glasses with the ice, lemonade, and tequila, her man and the captain talked about the sheep, and she must have missed out on the front part because they seemed to be planning a trip herding sheep here in the back part of their conversation. That was an ordeal Rahellio hadn't participated in for a long time, and raising sheep had been so much fun that their flock was down to ninety-four head compared to over six hundred in the old days.

Generally, after any of his excursions, his many burial trips where he would go to some nearby cemetery or family plot and help dig and then bury someone's dead friend would involve hitching up Raton and his funeral carriage, all of his mortician tools and camping supplies, fishing rods, tackle boxes, and traveling as much as twenty miles by buggy to get the job done.

The dirt roads in those rolling foothills of the Southern Rockies around Arboles and Ignacio lead from one small community to the next, constantly crossing over streams and shallow rivers, with breathtaking scenery in every direction and Mother Nature determining everything. She destroyed county roads like it was the thing to do, sometimes coming as an enormous surprise superstorm from out west, and could ruin any outdoor event.

Most of the people in the valley knew the Candelarias because of the work Rahellio willingly performed with class and dignity and had done so for decades. People always talked about him after the services, spoke about his music, and how he came and went in a carriage drawn by a mule named the Mighty Raton. He was straddling immortality in his small world, the land of seven rivers, with his internment business changing all the time. Every time he participated as the mortician of choice, whether for the young or the old, for forty of his years, he always brought his best work to the gravesite or the altar steps, and his fan club grew big as he aged. Both he and his wife had been born in the lands of the seven rivers, and their parents had been there from the start, sinking family roots dating back into the late eighteen hundreds because of the land grants to the Mexican pioneers.

It was a garden of Eden when it came to raising sheep, except for when the blizzards came, or the pumas, or hungry black bears, and a few other considerations such as wolves and UFOs. A couple of shepherds and a few dogs can manage a flock the size of his with little trouble as long as the grass is thick and that flock can be driven from point A to point B fed by the best grass Mother Nature has to offer, with the sheep having no clue as to what's happening. Their little hooves would justify the horse tracks and leave a broad and thorough sheep track on the land while solving the immediate question of why horse tracks lead down towards the river.

Rahellio had both his sheepdogs at his feet, Fitz was almost asleep down there close by, and he seemed confident in a short speech to Van Vedic that the dogs could keep the sheep in a solid flock out and back. His bartender and barber, chief cook and bottle washer picked up her drink and flowed around the table until she was sitting so close to her husband that the light went out between their bodies.

"I'm sorry, dear. I missed the first part of this story. You seem to want to take the sheep for a long march up onto the plateau and then down one of the canyons to the river. Then you turn around and come back right over the tracks you made today. I need to know why. That must have come up at the beginning of your talk, which I missed while making the margaritas. Pretty good, huh? So, tell me why."

The captain stood up from his bench and turned his back on the woman while he flexed his back and shoulders and then wiggled his holsters into his hips. He was directly alongside the row of mega rocks that bordered Rahellio's driveway, about eight of them that caused the passing dove to fly through with the wind under their wings. Earlier, Rahellio had suggested to the captain that his talented mariposa needed a dozen doves for her dinner plans.

"My dear lady, your husband and I have seen something down by the river that we probably shouldn't have seen. We need to erase our many tracks over the past several days so that no one follows them and sees what we saw. No one would question why a flock of sheep passed over the area, but our procession of horse tracks might arouse the curious. We have decided that whatever we do to cover the tracks should not involve too many others. The world doesn't need to find the petroglyphs we saw. It might be enough to get the reservoir projects delayed, maybe canceled. I can't let that happen."

Just then, a pair of doves came blowing by and ended up headless, with the noise scaring up another couple, who ended up only ten feet from the first two. The Mrs. was distracted for a few moments looking for the dove but she was still involved and wanted to know what they'd seen. She had three out of the four in hand, was close, she knew, to the last one, and shouted at Rahellio, "What in the holy hell is a petroglyph?"

The captain stood ready for more feathered invaders as he explained, "We saw a wall down in the canyon, four hours from here, that had Indian artwork carved into the side of the cliff face and also on some of the big rocks at the base of the cliff. Typical of what they've found in other places. I've thought a lot about this. During a lunch with the mayor of Aztec and a bunch of other folks my last time there, I was treated to the most up-to-date accounting of what was going on with the reservoir. I remember learning about the sacred Navajo ceremonial sites, and he said the subjects had been discussed twice by both the City Council and the environmental impact folks. Some archeologists tried to make it the issue, but there were plenty of other issues, and besides, they had no evidence; none of them had even been there. The University of New Mexico Archeology Department Director, some fellow named Hidden, Doctor Hidden, found a dozen ancient Indian sites in the canyon and took pictures of everything on the rocks and walls. These might be some of the ones he saw. They found a few stone structures in the middle of the deepest parts of the center canyon that were observation platforms but never found any graves of any sort. Hidden was a digger, an archeologist whose claim to fame was that he had found the bones of a lady named Lucile in the Olduvai Gorge in Africa. He didn't find squat in the San Juan River Gorge, nothing but rocks and the raging San Juan. He also insinuated that he and his entire staff and crew had wasted thousands of hours searching for nothing, found a few sites but nothing much—basically a complete washout. When the Navajo Nation was presented with the facts concerning the future dam and the water it would provide them, they voted on it. They decided they needed the water from the reservoir far more than another sacred ceremonial site—which they had far more than necessary, as in thousands. With the Navajos on board, that pretty much sealed the deal and put that issue to rest. I do not want to raise that issue again with anyone. I want to do what I can to remove any temptation for someone to stumble onto our tracks. Our tracks need to be erased, simple as that. They could be there for years if it's left to Mother Nature. For the sake of my *Vanessa* floating again someday and her future, I must insist on this project and try to salvage this dream. Along with that, I'll ask for a vow to maintain our secret as well as possible. That's what I think, and I need your help."

"My captain, I understand, and you can count on my sheep and my husband's dogs to do exactly what you want, but I'm afraid the two of you can't manage them by yourselves. Neither of you knows how to walk with sheep. Rahellio's back will cause him great pain for the next few days, as it has always done in the past after long horse rides. He won't sleep well tonight, so I'll pack extra tequila. How exciting! A good old-fashioned roundup of sheep and moving them to a new pasture. Very exciting. My lips are sealed, and I understand why things should be that way, with no excuses. I could go partway, come back for the night, and go back out and meet you for the return trip. Way out past the critter gates a mile or more."

"My precious mariposa, my back doesn't hurt, and neither does my ankle. I have no idea why, but that's the truth. I'm ready for more."

"So far, the genie is still in the bottle as far as I can tell, and I ask you to stay reasonably close to home and cover our behinds. Rahellio thinks it will take the better part of two days to get them close to the river and then two more days coming back. The whole flock will benefit from the exercise and vegetation along the trail."

"Captain, our Julio is not one bit fond of herding sheep. Young men and boys always ended up with the worst chores on a long move, and he got a good taste of it when he was young. Moaned and groaned like a big baby the whole time, might have been overly fearful of the puma and the bears after seeing what they did to the sheep and heard the crazy stories the old shepherds told. He doesn't even like the cries from the coyotes at night. You will bring a death knell for any big cat or bear that gets too close, but remember, it will scare the sheep half to death. Shooting your guns for any reason near sheep is the very last thing you ever want to do. We'll be looking for those sheep for a month."

Rahellio spoke up, "Captain, I have two Ute shepherds that I know, good men, who I know will help with the drive. Each one has a dog, and they won't have any issues with why we're doing this. They have learned not to question what white men and Mexicans are doing. I know where they are digging a water canal back towards Bayfield, and I'm sure they could use a break. In the distant past, they worked for a wage but also for a pregnant ewe. We'll need them for a week: one ewe each and a hundred dollars. Problem solved. They can cover the entire flock, day and night. We cover what we can with our dogs on horseback. We're basically force-driving say fifty ewes and a few rams and lambs from the side pasture up the road, through the new gates, up onto the plateau, and then down into the river bottomlands. I'll drive down the road and find them this afternoon, and we can plan on leaving in two days. I think we'll be back in three or four days."

The Candelaria woman seemed to have a deeper understanding of the ancient peoples, especially the Mexican side of things, more so than most folks do. She knew where many of his and her people lived and thrived, where they found a canyon somewhere and settled in, and that for the most part they may never talk face to face in their lives. Many of those families ended up all over the foothills of southern Colorado and northern New Mexico. She knew some of her immediate family as far south as Dragon Fly at Cabazon. She also knew some of the Ute Indian women—not too many, but dozens at the trading posts in Ignacio who knew Spanish knew who she was, and sometimes the women would talk about women's things, babies, food, clothes, and medicine.

One spring, she was on a shopping trip to Ignacio and ended up at the parade grounds for the fair. A few dozen women were scattered around in the shade of a cottonwood grove, and some of the very old women started talking about the ancient visitors. One old lady was selling Kachina dolls and telling the stories of who the dolls represented as her sales pitch. It was fascinating to discover a new religion that way. When she realized the Utes had holidays that celebrated beings from another Earth, she became enthralled with the stories. She bought three of the Kachinas just to hear the lady's sales pitch twice. The three Kachinas above her favorite fireplace in the house were guardians of the casa, depictions of Indian travelers with unpronounceable names from the earliest of times who watched over us. They occupied a place in her heart that was different from where she kept Jesus and Mary.

Everything was ready in less than two days, laid out in the barn on the floor and inventoried, lots of time-honored things that shepherds always needed when dealing with sheep. She found the rolled-up plait maps for that general area of the original ranch. These had been used a dozen years ago when the flock was ten times as big as the current one. There was a magnificent art to it, and unfortunately neither of our shepherds possessed that art. This trail ride would be a first for Vincent Van Vedic.

Both the Utes had the small flock moving at sheep speed through the far outback "critter gates," right on time, with Rahellio and the captain leading the way on the two front points. They were just lazily walking their horses and thinking about some areas up ahead where it would be a very tight squeeze for a large group of ignorant creatures. The plan involved getting to that meadow they agreed on that was just a little way down from the ridgeline, and they could rest the night at that point. They remembered a corral of boulders that would trap the flock on three sides, along with a freshwater spring that would tickle their noses. To some degree, those were the instructions from Rahellio to the Utes, for them to follow the tracks from a few days before. This far out, it didn't matter so much, but down inside the gorge, the plan was to disguise those tracks with the sheep prints.

CHAPTER TWENTY

THE DISAPPEARING TRACES

This first campsite was preplanned and just down a few hundred yards from the start of the "steep." That was far enough, plenty for now, and the headcount of sheep was complete. Every living and breathing animal in the caravan drank feverously from the spring once they got there, messed up the whole area with all their pooping and walking, but settled down near a small cluster of boulders and started to fall asleep. The Utes built their fire in a place that prevented the flock from wandering that way. At the same time, Rahellio and his captain guarded the other end along with their dogs and horses. There were only fifty yards between their campsites.

They both knew that things changed for the worst after this flat area near the top of the plateau. The trek down to the river was treacherous at times, with tight passageways. As the captain enjoyed his drinks and dinner by the fire, he rather vividly recalled that one area down half a mile from here, where the horses went through single file. He envisioned the sheep in a procession of two or three abreast in many other spots. Now, after having been with them for a full day, he realized they were very spookish, did not respond to verbal commands very well, and didn't like dogs one little bit. They were low-IQ creatures and required a shepherd or an excellent fence to keep them enclosed, and all the predators out there loved lamb! As the procession had moseyed along, parading directly over the old horse tracks, they obliterated the entire trace and replaced it with their own. Van Vedic was happy with the results.

He was also optimistic that El Bruto Whetto was all eyes, ears, and nostrils at times, somewhat unusual from his natural laid-back self. Still, he was watching the world out there through his horse senses, and especially his ears. Something was going on in the canyons. The same held true for Sarge, but the mane on his neck went away; he wasn't afraid of whatever it was that had gotten their attention. The only creatures at the campfire who weren't involved with the sounds were these humans, but they were both aware that they weren't. There was something out there that had gotten the attention of their animals and wouldn't let go. The dogs would not quit being attentive to something further down in the ravine towards the river, the exact direction they were headed, but the dogs damn sure didn't know that, and neither did the horses.

"I think this is a good thing that we're doing. I feel much better about our progress. Very few people ever come back into this area, and as you said, they come here to hunt. I believe the stories about people getting lost in these canyons and never being found. Someday there will be a lake, and the gorge will be blue instead of yellow rock. I wonder if it will get this deep. Some folks say you can never have enough water, and I know that for a fact. My father and I lived through the Great 1891 Famine in

Russia. My mother and sisters didn't, and just about everyone my father knew died. I didn't know very many people except her and him.

"A drought caused it, killed millions and millions of people from starvation, disease, cholera, and smallpox, and many, many, many died of thirst in a matter of days when the water ran out. There are no words! I was just a boy—maybe four—when it started, but my father fed me bark, among other things, and helped me think it was exactly what I needed. It was the water that mattered most of all at times. We humans don't do very well without it and get flat-out crazy in our efforts to find it and drink it. The same holds true for animals and birds. It's all about the water."

The grave digger settled in not far from the captain and sipped on his coffee while straining his neck to see how the flock was behaving. The weather was a bit of a sundown problem. It was possibly going to be a windy and stormy night, which wasn't a part of anyone's plan, but they would manage. They had four tarps. He could easily remember when he and the captain were first talking about the tracks and how they both agreed it would be beneficial if Mother Nature would rain on their parade route a few times. That would probably be all it would take. At present, he hoped like hell it wasn't one of those really nasty blizzards that occasionally rolled through these foothills, because they weren't exactly prepared for that. There were vantage points throughout the region, from where a person could see a hundred miles to the west, as far as Shiprock and the Chuskas Mountains and watch the storms come from that direction. Sometimes when it was all said and done, people talked about watching the storm grow out there on the plains, which eventually turned into a bad memory.

"Captain, we haven't talked much about the missing time we

lost. I will start off by saying it's, without any doubt, the weirdest, strangest, the most mysterious thing that has ever happened to me. I saw you staring off into the trees today, staring at the back of El Bruto's head, and just now into the coffee mug. I bet a peso that I know what you were thinking about. What do you think could have happened? My wife asked me twice last night if I had any recollection, and she could instantly see in my eyes that I didn't. It's just white space."

"The only thing I know for sure is that I can truthfully say there is nothing wrong with my body. I think I managed to lose weight too. I don't know how much I've lost, because I didn't know how much I weighed in the first place, but my belly is not in the way anymore. I'm somehow as strong as I've ever been. I know I am probably the strongest man you will ever know. My eyes are perfect. I think I was healed from the inside out during the whiteout. My horse is different, and so is my dog. You, my friend, already told your wife that there was nothing wrong with you, and yet here we are, almost old men. That shouldn't be the case, but it is."

Not too far off, it seemed, down through the canyons, miles away they hoped, thunderheads were roaming east like they always did. It was raining and blowing hard, but at their little campsite things were dry with only a light wind. Naturally, sheep don't like lightning any more than the next critter, and none of us like the thunder. There was a bit of that for a while around midnight and then again before dawn, but it never rained a drop on their fire.

Rahellio played his guitar and sang a few ballads he favored, and right in the middle, he would start to strum some chords and then talk about the missing days. He was pressed against his saddle, bathed in the heat from the fire, and as content as a man can be. He was convinced the total number of nights missing was three. Three full days in the sunlight, more or less, and try as he may, he couldn't remember a single detail of anything.

His recollection was now a detailed verbal memory where he knew the exact times for everything, and the reasons they were down there. The first time was to fish for trout because Van Vedic wanted to do that before the lake filled up. It was a crazy thing to want to do, but the man was willing to pay the most incredible wage ever paid to two Mexican guides in the history of North America. Unfortunately, they all got a stomach bug, puked their brains out, and he ended up having to take the boy back to his momma.

Then the captain showed up needing help to save his dog, which would involve pulling over a large stone that would free the poor hound. The captain was sure his plan would work, and if they hurried they might be able to save the dog. Still, the animal was free and unharmed when they got there. Then there was nothing for days. What did they do that they couldn't remember? Then, suddenly, like with a black curtain raising, they regained consciousness and came back to reality from wherever they had been. They were on their horses and looking for a campsite at sundown. They would never do such a thing so late in the day.

It was then that these two men discovered that they didn't know what day it was, a challenging thing to realize about yourself. He told Van Vedic that when he thought about it, he realized something was preventing them from remembering something they did together. How could that be possible? Why?

"You said it all just then. Together—we spent that time together and now, a few days later, we still can't remember. It was the second time for me, and this time it was for only a matter of days, but the first time it lasted for ten years. For that very reason, I believe this is all about me and, secondarily, you— because you were with me, and I must have needed help.

"Our animals are strangely different from what they were a few weeks ago. Then, we used all that equipment for something, but it had nothing to do with tipping over a boulder; it's still there like it was at the time when Sarge was stuck. We ate and drank all our supplies, and I noted that the cider bottle was almost empty. I find that very hard to believe. A gallon of tequila! It's no wonder you broke a guitar string. Let's see here, what else is there? I know there's something else. It's crucial, and I can't remember."

"We are both very healthy. Remember? You don't hurt anywhere, remember? That's hard to keep in mind when you're super healthy like us all of a sudden. I was beginning to fear old age, beginning to ache and pain from a horseback ride, but that's all gone. Of course, the pain might come back someday, but I can pinpoint when it stopped. I can tell you that this fifty-five-year-old body doesn't have a single ache in a joint. Not a headache. Not a pisser problem, and not a problem with the mariposa. I drove the woman berserk the other night, which surprised us both to no end. Not nothing anywhere! And not only that, all my friends at or near my age have lots of pain in their bodies, and I did too, two weeks ago. But not today. It's like all the wear and tear of all those years is gone, and I'm fresh. I'd think about arm wrestling with anybody I know… except you."

"That's sure true enough, and I feel the same. I forgot that. There are basically two living dimensions for us humans, the world of pain and the world of no pain. Pain governs everything about us; if the pain is severe and constant, it makes life hardly worth living. I've sometimes worried that my extra-large size would cause me grief in this life. Sure enough, it has, at times— low doorways, short bed frames, and small bathtubs, to say nothing of me being a huge target in this world.

"Hurrah! I just remembered I fired my cannons, and we don't

remember that. 45-caliber revolvers, twenty times at least, and neither of us two humans remember that? Last weekend!"

"That's not true! I think I remember something like that. I think I was scared half to death by something that would have resembled your six guns going off behind me, assuming I didn't know it was going to happen. Just like when you shot those doves the other day. I wasn't ready for that, and suddenly, '*BOOM BOOM.*' I don't know why, but we shouldn't forget that I think I heard something."

"Fair enough. When I've been permitted to hunt on a man's land, I should prep him one time in advance that these two beasts can come alive at any time. The general area has never been so safe as when I, Vincent Van Vedic, am roaming the vicinity with my pistols on my hips. Woe betides the bad guy who might think he could strong-arm the community because he had a handgun if I'm in the judgment seat. It's hard to say why I would have fired them so many times, and that makes me think I was showing off, perhaps, hopefully entertaining someone other than you.

"Maybe I shot an animal or a snake or some dove, and as you very well know, I'm good at shooting fish from a high-rock overlook. Who knows?

"The truth is they make a lot of noise, yet we don't remember anything. You and I can look around those last two campsites for any evidence we might have left behind. I don't want the Utes down that far; we'll turn the flock way before that and bring them back to the top plateau. We'll have the whole bunch back in their pasture in two more nights. It's raining not far from here—I can smell it—and that's in our favor. I remember many of our trails down to the river were in sandy, dry stream beds. Mother Nature will do the work for us."

Rahellio started to sing about when his father started building their new home after the old one was destroyed. It was his song, and he only shared it with certain people—immediate relatives and the likes of Vincent. If ever there was a masterpiece of guitar music, that song and story would easily be in the running for the title. In the true-to-life ballad, his family was trying to survive a harsh winter. Five people crammed into a shed they called home that was practically made out of hay and straw, two adobe walls so far, when the whole thing caught on fire one night and burned to the ground at three in the morning.

The composer and singer tells how he was six at the time, his sister was seven, and his older brother was eight. When the sun rose that next morning just shy of fifty years ago, 1904, the family was homeless. It only took thirty minutes or less. Not a single neighbor even knew it had happened, but they stood tall in how they helped once they found out.

By the end of the following summer, their casa had six adobe walls and a caleche mud roof on a super sharp commonsense pitch. The place became a model of how to do it, and a company was formed, where all the artisans could build a house in one summer.

The poetry was perfect, line after line, having been practiced and whispered in song for twenty years. A Mexican ballad for the ages that would take him no less than thirty minutes from beginning to end. His mariposa had written it all down over a long period of time, but the only real copy he said was in his head, and so he sang on. Finally, their day was basically over, and when he was done singing, he set his guitar aside and fiddled with the fire. The captain rose to his feet and gently applauded his favorite musical artist, who in turn bowed to his audience and thanked him for his attention.

Van Vedic was enthralled with learning their history and the whole idea of the Mexicans coming here from Old Mexico a long time ago, a hundred years before there was even a state called

New Mexico or Colorado. Santa Fe dated back to before Catherine the Great, and even though he hadn't been there yet, the place was on his list to visit.

Without a moment's hesitation, he flashed back in time. He saw himself riding up on his old homestead north of Pfeiffer, 1941, planning to load his old boat with a few memories and then burn that homestead to the ground. That homestead had been established during a time when life was very harsh in southern Russia. Every rock and timber used in construction had been positioned to last as long as possible in a siege, always be a stable shooting position while providing protection. He burned it all down one night and never looked back on his carnage; his enemies couldn't have his farm, so he set all the delayed firebombs, sailed away, and came to the San Juan River Valley. Rahellio's house—actually, his father's house—had never been designed to be destroyed and probably never would be. That was precisely what Vincent's father said one year. He said the bad times would never be back; the prosperity was here to stay. There was a time when the Fertile Volga Basin was indeed an evolving Garden of Eden for a few very basic reasons and should have never been tampered with. That successful evolution of humans took a hundred years, more or less, to get to the point where Van Vedic's father would say such a thing, and his society should have been a model. Instead, it was attacked and destroyed—the same old story. Totally and completely annihilated.

The morning was ten hours away, and the band of shepherds would start again at sunrise. The plan was to push the sheep down towards the river for five or six hours, turn them around, and return to this exact location tomorrow evening. The night so far had been uneventful, except when the lightning and thunder were at their peak and keeping the campers awake because it didn't seem all that far away. Of course, it's hard to tell at night in the canyonlands exactly how far off the storms are, but in the wee hours of the morning, it felt like they were going to end up wet for sure. Yet nothing happened, not a drop, and the animals stayed calm.

That was until the ground began to shake. From out of nowhere, the earthquake began to rumble, shift rock ledges and slide boulders off balance, with a mighty earthen bellow that was indescribable when it was all over, twenty seconds from start to finish. Both campers were on their feet. The fire was somewhat overloaded right off the start, and the flames grew as they analyzed what had just happened.

"That was an earthquake, senor! I have felt it three times now in my life, and this was bigger than all the rest. We believe it's our Mother Earth rearranging the mountains."

The noise that belched out all over the land had come from somewhere down close by the river, at least a mile away as the crow flies, in the exact direction they were headed. The sound of a mountain falling, a tremendous landslide—and one thing for sure, it wasn't thunder! The commotion began at around three that morning, and even though it didn't last all that long or cause any problems, it aroused both campfires along with all the sheep and horses. With their fire roaring, the men walked over and visited with the Utes, who weren't too excited about spending another night on the trail. They were into signs, aware of the signs, and this earthquake was not only a sign but a first for the ditch digger. In the end, it turned out to simply be a question of money. When the captain was finished being generous with the two shepherds, they decided to stay as long as needed. For only being a country bumpkin, as he claimed to be, Rahellio rattled off a rather lengthy and explicit oration of what an earthquake was for both of his Ute friends. They listened intently and then explained to the white men what the definition of a sign is, was, and ever will be. That included forever. They went back to sleep, got two hours maybe, and the next day lit up the eastern lip of the sprawling canyon right on time.

Not needing any sort of an alarm clock except for enough light to start looking for grass, all the sheep were awake and walking soft, stepping in the same direction, along with their many shepherds and dogs. From out of the haze, Rahellio's bride rode up on her pony with burritos and coffee, along with a story she had heard on the radio that morning. Fifty thousand watts, KOB out of Albuquerque had breaking news.

"There has been a slight earthquake somewhere in the general area between Durango and the New Mexico border early this morning, causing things to fall off shelves and scaring everyone who felt it half to death!"

She was not one of them, hadn't felt a thing during the night, and nothing fell off her shelves. She headed out for the critter gates as the faint light of sunrise hinted from the horizon that everyone would get at least one more day.

Dawn is one of the hardest parts of herding sheep. The shepherds go from sound asleep to following and guiding sheep without any warmup period.

It only took an hour or so at a mild trot to find the flock and deliver the hot coffee to both men, precisely the way they liked it, with two substantial breakfast burritos wrapped up in expensive aluminum foil. She told them the day before to expect it, be ready in the morning, and not waste time making breakfast or even coffee. Even though they told her it wasn't necessary, she told them one more time and used certain time-honored facial expressions and inflections in her voice that Rahellio had learned from previous experiences, which meant that that was that! She carefully unpackaged the burritos, smelled them from end to end, and felt their warmth before giving the men their rolled-up pies.

The aluminum foil was carefully flattened out and folded in half and then in half again and one more time. This new invention was remarkable and well worth protecting and using repeatedly.

The captain was enjoying his breakfast in the saddle, quite a way in front of the flock, lazily walking along until he had come to the end of the long meadow they were in. He stayed directly on top of the trail they had all made the week before, lots of tracks going in both directions, six or seven distinct trips, and was thinking this plan to erase the tracks was moving along nicely.

Things tightened up a great deal at the bottom of the clearing. The sheep would have to be pushed through two tight spots, after which the flock would be in another long, narrow glade.

He rode up close to Mrs. Candelaria and told her the burrito she made him was quite possibly the most wonderful thing he had ever eaten in the morning so far in his entire life, and the coffee was perfect. He thanked her once again and then told Rahellio and his Mrs. that he wanted to ride ahead and get some idea of what to expect. He'd be just up in front a way. Then he took off at a gallop.

The terrain was not exactly friendly at this point. He knew they were still at least a couple of miles from the river when he found himself on the edge of the second meadow. These meadows were the reason why Rahellio had chosen this particular canyon to work their way down to the river. It had rained really hard in this area last night; there wasn't much standing water in a place like this—too much sand—but the tracks he was following had been duly affected by the downpour. That realization made him feel good about the tracks being erased by Mother Nature and solving the problem.

He was riding high in the saddle, daydreaming about who knew what, smelling the wetness, whistling, watching the hawks and things, when he discovered that he had lost the trail completely. El Bruto Whetto's tracks and Sarge's were the only tracks in the sand.

He couldn't believe it. He had gone entirely brain dead, who knew how far back, and as he turned the horse, he was thoroughly embarrassed about his miserable tracking skills. When they got this far, he would concentrate the sheep all over the mistake area. He wasn't sure he was ever going to tell anyone about it. Now he was following his own tracks from a few minutes before, and they seemed to be all there was, all the way back to the second tight squeeze.

He must have gotten off course coming out of that cluster of boulders, turned too soon or too late or too something. Now he was confused by his environment, and the massive boulders had tricked him into thinking he was right when he should have been left. So finally, after roaming around in a sense, his animals walked out into a clearing. There was Rahellio and his wife headed his way, with the whole flock nibbling at their heels, so to speak, and the Utes bringing up the rear. Off to his left a short distance was the trail they were trying to erase, and somehow or another, when he went through those boulders, he got crossways and lost the course. He rode out in front of the flock and stopped Rahellio in his tracks, pulling up alongside him and confessing his sin of getting lost like he did. The man was worried that if it could happen to him, it could indeed happen to the sheep, and so, before they got in there, he wanted to inspect it and figure out what had happened.

The two men left the flock and rode up to the boulders and the wide opening where all the horse prints ended up in a single file lane with few options to turn left or right for what seemed like fifty yards. Rahellio took the lead, and his horse jumped up a slight ledge, following the tracks left by Van Vedic thirty minutes before. When the climb was over, those were the only tracks anywhere around. He had evidently done the same thing the captain had done, got sidetracked somehow. When the captain pulled up alongside once again, he had a mischievous smile on his face. He hadn't been paying any attention, so he couldn't explain why the mortician had also gotten lost.

They knew there was no point following the only tracks they could see, which were Van Vedic's from a while before, so they angled right and eventually walked into a dead end. This dead-end routine had happened to them at least fifteen times when they tried to get to the river the first time a week ago. Dead end after dead end, always something blocking their way until, finally, they made it. For both these men, the time they spent there by the river together had managed to include a massive hole in the middle of their memories, and they couldn't remember anything that happened for three days. Presently, there were no options other than to work their way back to where they first entered the megalithic maze, find the flock, and never do anything like this again. That would be easier said than done, because with Van Vedic in the lead this time, following his tracks from earlier, he ended up walking in a circle until they found themselves standing on top of their tracks, going the other way.

It didn't take long for the funny part of their situation to wear off as both men now understood that the previous fifteen minutes were not a normal part of how they went about their business. It's one thing to get a little off course, but it's a whole different matter to do it three times. Eventually, the captain guided El Bruto through a tight spot between two massive bottomland boulders that rubbed the sides of his boots because he could see that trail once again on the other end. He approached the long narrow gap the way humans do, which is oftentimes not even close to the way a horse does, and the beast didn't like it one little bit, but the reward was that they could now see the flock far off to their left. It was unbelievable! They weren't even close, a hundred yards off to the right of where the others sat waiting. When all the dogs recognized each other, the mariposa jumped to her feet and squealed something resembling Rahellio's name. She was as surprised as she'd been lately and was anxious as could be to hear what the scouts had found out.

"You got lost, didn't you? You two horsemen got lost. I can't believe it."

"Yes, we did, and I love you too. I got us lost, and then the captain got us lost, and then we got even more lost together, and to be honest, I thought I might never see you again. It ranks right up there with several other reasons why I will never come down here again. So, let's turn them around and retrace our steps. We could be at the critter gate by sundown. Something tells me men shouldn't be in this leg of the canyon."

She interrupted, "When we first talked about this drive, it caused me to remember some of those drives where we covered ten miles alongside the big rocks. Terribly difficult stuff, horrible weather, mostly women and boys and girls, few men, and only honest shepherds know this to be true. A fundamental rule that sheep know nothing of says, stay away from the rocks you can't see over."

"My dear lady, I've been on horseback since I was four. I rode a horse into the Tunguska wilderness, found a treasure, and we walked out in the name of God, but they made us give it up.

"It was such a waste of man and beast, but it taught me that men are savages at times. I and some others escaped the wrath of money-hungry savage barbarians and fled from there, traveled a thousand miles west on one horse, across the frozen Volga and to a village in Southern Russia. I left that horse there and still miss him. His name was Brutus. He was much the match of El Bruto

Whetto that I'm sitting on. A horse has to be this big and strong to carry my weight like it should. My point is simple, and I only speak for myself, but something is blocking my way on the other side of those rocks right there. Something made us make the wrong turn, miss the sign, left instead of right; who knows? Most important of all, I now know what that is. Rahellio, my friend, you know, don't you? It's whatever erased our memories. That power is keeping us from going back there again."

The captain motioned for one of the Utes to catch up, and they explained that they had decided to turn the herd back and retrace their steps to the other side of the critter gate by sundown. The man was in total agreement, knew exactly which two ewes to strap the stupid carrot to, and that guaranteed a straight line. No problems, no pressure, good plan to pay attention to the signs. The shepherd went back to his brother and told him about the change of plans, and immediately the flock was turned back on itself in an instant by their dogs.

"We got one visit to where we were, and that one time seems to be a time that we won't be able to remember. One time only. This gentle sign to us says go away and don't come back. Leave that sleeping dog alone. Those petroglyphs are safe, and I'm comfortable with this turnaround. I'm no longer worried, and I believe my *Vanessa* will float again someday. If we can't go any further, I would have to believe that no one else after us will be able to get any closer than we just got. I know for a fact that I will seldom ever even think about this excursion in the future, and I hope both of you honor our code of silence. Silence is golden. Tell no one, please! If you remember anything at all, please come and tell me, and I'll do the same."

All three of the horsemen guarded the side of the flock while the Utes guided the nose, and at a snail's pace, they worked their way to lunch at the top of the plateau. They talked about all sorts of things and made plans for a future payday, because there was an immediate end to all this shepherding for the captain at the top of the steep. He would turn left and head for his home a few miles south along the rim, and they would turn right, pass through the critter gate in the afternoon, and be home by sunset. He was going home to a place he hadn't been to in well over a week.

All of this drama was supposedly caused by his desire to fish in a raging torrent. After having seen the river and stood by it, he wasn't sure he'd actually fished in it. He had to conclude that there had to have been something else involved. This wasn't his first river. He generally didn't give a spit about fishing in raging rivers, and as far as big rivers are concerned, the Mighty San Juan didn't hold a twiffel to the Mighty Don.

If there was one thing he was looking forward to, it was checking on his three different favorite locations that he was just now getting used to. He loved the view from her gravesite looking west at sunset, and he also loved the eastern site that looked out over the empty expanse that would someday be the lake. He seemed to be at that location at sunset more often than at her site. It was bizarre, but he knew he hadn't seen a sunset in quite some time. Now that he thought about it, he hadn't been there to watch the sunrise, but he always looked north at sunset. He loved his house already, had big plans to renovate it, and now he was comfortable with where his boat was and her chances of floating again, he felt very good about everything.

CHAPTER TWENTY-ONE

NAPPING WAS NOT IT

It wasn't but half a mile after he said goodbye that Vincent found himself on a far distant lookout point where he could see all sorts of things, front and back, left and right. His land was just ahead a few miles and then all over the place. Finally, he turned and saw the small herd headed north, almost out of sight on the end of the plateau. Rahellio and his Mrs. were in front, small figurines on horseback, and the two Utes were on the bottom end of the circle of living things. At that distance, it was hard to tell they were moving, but they were, and in not too long, they would disappear out of view and be past the critter gates in only a few hours. He didn't know when he'd see those people again, but it probably wouldn't be all that long, because Rahellio was constantly checking on the captain like it was the thing to do, and he appreciated that safety net to no end.

It was just like the mortician always told Van Vedic. When it was up to him to conclude someone's life at a funeral—one where he was paid to perform, for people he didn't really know all that well if at all—the driver of the hearse pulled by the mighty Raton, he had a time-honored playlist. He would sing certain ballads designed for funerals, old favorites, and tell and sing simple stories with faultless chords involved. He was a hard act to follow whether he knew you all that well or not.

He had a favorite story among many, the one of the ship heading for the horizon; that ship leaves this harbor where it's very well known, travels to the horizon, and disappears from view. Past the horizon, on the other side and on the most distant shoreline, that ship comes into view, new to this sea, very much alive in that new world. It's there, on that new sea, where we find an even more glorious harbor than any ever imagined or wished for.

The story always took the audience of grievers to a spot many of them had never actually been—a seashore, the edge of the ocean—but everyone knew what it would look like. Waves gently massaging the shoreline, beautiful boats bobbing in the surf, and in all cases, this family of mourners watching the ship leave the cove and head for the horizon with their loved one sleeping peacefully on the boat's bow. A million, maybe a billion thoughts and memories constituted the deceased's life, concealed for the most part from view but there nonetheless. When he finished his song about horizons and shorelines, Rahellio would keep playing and strumming his guitar while his audience put their thoughts on top of his chords, and their weeping was encouraged.

It had been a while since Vincent was alone like this, just sitting on a saddle on El Bruto Whetto with Sarge leading the way as if he knew where they were going. In this case, he was walking home with all his thoughts and recent memories taking up space in his mind, a big question mark that wasn't fading in the least and demanded something, an answer, anything—but he just couldn't be sure what to ask for.

El Bruto Whetto, the mellow yellow mountain of muscle, was a different animal from the one that went the other way a week or more ago. It was hard to explain; something to feel, to see in those giant eyeballs. It was different, and it was too bad the beast couldn't talk.

The same held true for the dog on an even greater level. Man's best friend was there for it all, saw everything his masters did and spoke, knew everything that happened when it was awake, and would have more than likely been close underfoot like always.

Meanwhile Rahellio, miles away, stood in the barn, helping to unpack Raton. The beast looked at him as if it were the smartest gigantic jackass to ever pack a load, two thousand pounds, with there being two things to note after the trip. First, Raton had tangled with barbed wire not long ago, and two of the gashes were refusing to heal. They had Rahellio worried, so he'd wrapped them, applied his most trusted horse liniments and paste, and paid attention because those kinds of lesions can take a horse to the grave. The mortician was shocked to discover that both lacerations had sealed themselves over and were already at the white scar stage, remnants of disturbing things of the past. So, there was no need for fresh bandages.

All the animals had managed to get rid of two or three different ears, nostrils, and teeth problems. The teeth on all four were astounding, white, up to the gums, clean, and instead of jerking their heads away when the cowboys tried to look in their mouths, they actually assisted and opened wider. It made it look like they were all smiling.

Rahellio had ridden his stallion for the longest time. They knew each other well, plus Rahellio mentioned how his horse and the stud pack horse were, among other things, a great deal more mellow, not quite so dangerous and kick-happy now. Not at all, for that matter. All that is nothing more than feelings, a human feeling an emotion about an animal, and with animals this big, one can never get too casual, but now the mortician felt entirely at ease around them both.

Vincent felt as though a difficult period in his life had seemingly come and gone, and the only problem was that he was not quite sure what that was. Among many different issues concerning a wide variety of subjects, such as time and space, he now found himself alone and at peace and didn't even know without a doubt how old he was.

There in his mind were those rock carvings, all over that cliff face, way up the side, with some being fifty feet from the ground and quite the trick for whoever did them. He figured they either had all sorts of scaffolding of some sort or, somehow or another, they might have lowered themselves down from the top. An impenetrable wall of boulders at least twenty feet tall prevented him and Rahellio from seeing any more of the carving, but he was positive there were more because the cliff face went around the corner out of view—and why wouldn't there be?

He could see himself straddling that small crevasse Sarge slid down into and got stuck. To free the dog, he had to pull over a tall slab of rock, and he could slide the dog out of the pinch he was in. The fact was that the tall slab of rock had to go away, tip over somehow. He saw it lying on the ground, pulled over by the horses, and it was too bad he didn't have a decent rope or he would have tried with just El Bruto; that's how easy it looked. So off he'd gone rapidly, following Rahellio, his son, and the mighty Raton from the day before. He'd had no trouble convincing Rahellio of the urgency, and lo and behold, when they got back to the site of the rescue, the dog was already free.

Both he and Rahellio concurred that it was starting at that moment when they couldn't remember a single thing for the next three days. When they finally got back to the reality of life, they were in the exact same area and looking for a campsite while on horseback. The examination of the dog was on Friday early evening, and they were looking for a campsite three days later on Monday evening.

He smiled a grin when he thought about realizing he couldn't remember a single thing from that day and tried to trick Rahellio into saying something that would unlock his frozen memory. It took hours for these grown men to acknowledge that something was happening to both of them simultaneously involving the exact same time period, and you didn't need to be an Einstein rocket scientist to know that was as remarkable as remarkable gets.

Then they'd discovered that they didn't know what day it was, didn't know at the time if it was Tuesday or Sunday, the fifth, eighteenth or twenty-sixth, and that was a hard thing for an intelligent human being to do, a hard something to admit about oneself, and then, of course, the fear sets in, when suddenly one realizes the consequences of such a thing. When you stare into a fire with a good friend, and you both know that you share such a secret, that something is preventing you from remembering something that you did together, well, it gets hold of the thought process and won't let go.

What was it? What did you do? Then also you ask, what has happened to the bodies—the captain's body, Rahellio's body, the animals, all the living creatures that went fishing and which were now different, indescribably different, and healthy beyond good. No complaints except that they didn't know why, whom to thank, or even whom to ask.

On their way back to Rahellio's casa, the men agreed that the world need not know about the petroglyphs, about the twenty-foot tall mountain of boulders, about any of that area they had just visited because if the world found out, they'd want to investigate it to no end and probably cancel the entire project. If they didn't build the dam, *Vanessa* would never float again, and that couldn't happen. The only things they could do to prevent someone from seeing what they had seen were to erase their hoof prints as best they could and, most importantly, not discuss the subject with anyone until there was a massive reservoir. Ten years at the most.

Fortunately, there in his saddlebag was his modern-day 35mm camera, which had thirty-six pictures per roll, and he'd taken a whole roll of everything he could see from their campsite. He wouldn't see the results until he went to Aztec again, to the drug store where they developed the pictures in only two days—and a thought crossed his mind concerning who the developer would be and what he'd see in the prints.

His camera even had a telephoto feature that magnified the drawings that were higher off the ground than the tallest of the cottonwoods anywhere nearby, some of those trees he knew to be fifty or sixty feet tall, maybe more. Two carvings, in particular, were the most difficult to see, and of course, they were so high up the side he wondered why anyone would have bothered. Nonetheless, the figurines had their heads in a box, and it damn sure looked like they had two long antennas instead of ears. There was no doubt in his mind at what he was seeing, so he'd taken two or three pictures of that. Very weird, very strange, and he remembered asking himself at the time why the artists would do that. Why do it down here in this river gorge, and why the box for a head? Why so far up the cliff face and almost out of view, why this and why that, and when he got confused, he took a picture of it and actually wrote down in the diary that came with the camera the details of each photograph, long before it made it to the developer's studio. If a man gives a petroglyph five minutes of his time and attention and considers all the things to consider, such as who pounded the handheld rock into the cliff that many times to draw a figurine that looked like a man but had a square head, he would realize men don't have square heads, and that's all there is to it.

From the edge of their campfire, he had studied that cliff face for hours and hours that evening, actually rubbed his fingers in the grooves of some of the drawings, and when you do that, you realize how hard that is to do. Pound a stone into a larger stone until you leave a substantial mark, a groove, and that's how they did it. If there's one thing for sure, and he'd tested his theory by pounding the hell out of a slab of the cliff face that had fallen off the edge a few million years ago. It took him at least a hundred impacts to make a mark an inch long. It's not one bit easy to scratch one's favorite figurine into granite and sandstone, and from the looks of the petroglyph wall, because there were so many carvings, he had to assume they must have had big parties where everybody got together and pounded the hell out of the rocks. When he was finally finished with his experiment, Vincent had warned Rahellio that he was about to make a lot of noise, spun around, and blasted a dozen 45-caliber hollow points into a pattern on the cliff face fifty feet away, two twelve-inch V's as clear as could be. They would be there forever.

With that in mind and hardly any downtime, the next thing that happened was that Rahellio's small herd of sheep went back and forth all over their earlier tracks and erased that evidence down to the far end of the second pasture. That was where the warning took place—that was what he called it now; the warning. It was where the two great horsemen got lost following their own tracks three different times, and it wasn't a joke. Not funny, not one little bit, and a bit of a slap in the face once they thought about it. That "something" that was erasing their memories wouldn't let them follow their own horse tracks from only days before, and now, all these days later, the questions that hadn't been answered sat there at the front of his mind, on his tongue, everywhere.

There were so many questions in his mind that he started to sing a song he remembered from many years before that turned the mind off in a sense, a simple song in Russian, three and four-note phrases that the caravan used to sing as they walked out of Tunguska. Two abreast, side by side alongside the train tracks, sometimes eighteen hours a day, depending on the tone of the rumors coming up, the procession trying to stay ahead of the barbarians and the butchers. The convoy was rumored to be ten miles long, headed west towards the Volga region in spring that year and hopefully to better weather. People got so tired of being frozen all the time, so tired of being scared, so tired of being so tired, and most of all, the mosquitos; why in the name of OGDY was it necessary to create the mosquitos? Their Siberian horses could not fall because if they did, that rider also fell, and it was against the law to ride two to a horse. The riders chanted just to stay awake and hopefully change the subject in their minds, a topic that was filled with terror.

Hours and hours of trudging along, tied to the saddle and hoping beyond hope that this animal you were tied to wouldn't drop over dead. It's always strange how ancient memories flash back into our visions if we allow it to happen.

In this case, by him simply riding the saddle, the present situation disappeared and memory took its place. A memory of just him and Brutus, with them both walking at a snail's pace, two or three abreast, out of Tunguska. It was like that a lot of the time, where he walked or jogged so as not to wear out his beast, and so did everyone else with him, never actually knowing how far it was to the front of the column, what was slowing things down and they didn't know how far back the chaos was happening. Miles and miles behind them was a ravenous mob of savages. A swarm of humans who existed at the end of the ten- or even twenty-mile-long caravan forced it to exist, caused it to keep moving, and by its very nature, it created deadly rules within itself that couldn't be broken. One person to a horse, for example. He was returning to his childhood home at the time after his one last mission for his bishop. His beloved wife Vanessa had recently died, and he had her preserved so he could bury her somewhere else when he returned.

At the time, he had been recruited from the ranks of the living guardsmen as the only man who could succeed with the mission. He and the bishop figured it would take four years or so to go back and forth through a dozen time zones, but it took the prime of his life, from 1926 to '41. It involved him traversing Russia, all expenses paid, with the primary objective of meeting some very primitive mountain people in the Tunguska region. People who had a box containing an object that fell from the sky one day and who had shown it to some Catholic priests who happened to stop by about twenty years after the event.

The group was spreading the good word, saving souls, and trying to overcome people's mystical beliefs about who was God and who wasn't. They had proof about God, spoke his name with sheer reverence. It was a deity they called OGDY. The high priests of the PMP had a ritual that involved certain people being able to hold the stone. As one stared into the pitch-black surface, one would see the face of OGDY. It happened to almost everyone, and when it happened to you, you became a believer and worthy for all time.

The priests requested demonstrations, and before the night

was over, all three and a few camp hands had burnt their hands so badly, primarily because they couldn't let go of the one-hundred-and-four-degree rock. That doesn't sound like much, but you lose that vision of OGDY if you lose your grip on the piece of shiny pitch-black mirror, seeing OGDY's face in their momentary agony.

For the most part, their personal conversations hadn't really changed anything but had reinforced it a thousand times. The incredible truth is that just about everyone knows the face of Jesus, but his Father is a different issue. That was what the priests saw, and the fact their hands would be useless for a few months was a small price to pay for the vision. It seemed to be proof of something or another, and the truth of the matter was Van Vedic never was sure. The PMPs didn't really want it, but they had their standards, so they made the rules for who had the best plan for the stone. To keep from being burned themselves, they made the box that prevented that, and when the time came, they willingly set it down at Vincent's boot tips and backed away.

He had absolutely no intention whatsoever of burning his hands, and so not to spoil anyone's plans, he set out to deliver it to another bishop on the Pacific coast, who in turn would take it from there. The box was the size of a small suitcase, had a very sturdy handle, two latches, two hinges, was not too heavy, thirty pounds or so, and certain powers that be somewhere had decided that the object in the box could not remain in Russia. For the longest time, the enormous man made his way east on the Siberian railroad that was almost always under construction. He only had two pieces of luggage, and as the Russian Revolution tried to destroy the motherland, he worked his way east to a seaside bungalow where the good bishop would be found. Most estimates suggested it could take many years. It was an unknown, but one thing was for sure—the man would be on his own all through the Great Depression in one of the most depressing places in all the world.

Vincent looked around. He was getting closer to that dropdown where the faint trail left the plateau and descended down into the river bottom areas and eventually the road leading to the switchbacks up to his casa. For the most part, he was exploring his neighborhood, trying to understand where he was in relation to the many geographical features all around him and how most of the canyons and gullies were difficult obstacles. After his dismal tracking experiences earlier that morning, he was most attentive to what he was looking for. There it was up ahead, so he allowed Sarge to lead the way down to some extent, with there being many areas where it was a lot easier than walking out the way they had last week. Rahellio had invented that trail after looking at the maps Van Vedic had acquired and seemed to think he knew the best place to try to get down to the river, to fish in the wild and raging torrent. It never failed, and it hadn't failed to be true every time the captain thought about this entire adventure; all of the questions, all of the circumstances, all of the mystery were caused and happened because of why?

Why? Because the captain told Rahellio he had to go trout fishing in the raging San Juan River before everything became a lake. He had a real hard time believing that was the real reason; in his self-evaluation, it didn't sound like him at all, not one little bit. Now, at this point in the game, he had to conclude that discovering the real reason would answer all the questions. That idea didn't hold water. He didn't even know how Rahellio came up with that exact location, and that now seemed to be the question that needed an answer. Why did they really go down there? Why there?

The captain of the *Vanessa* had fished ever since he was a boy, fished from trawlers, fished off the stern of the *Vanessa* from the Mighty Don River in Russia to Corpus Christi, Texas, ten thousand miles to the west, fished the whole way and ate fish half the time in his life and caught everything he ever ate, almost. He watched General George S. Patton almost catch a five-hundred-pound tuna off the stern of his *Vanessa* not too far from the Moroccan coast, and the whole experience was now embedded in his memory. You would have had to have been there. It was an extraordinary, extra-terrestrial experience and involved two of the most remarkable men living at the time, a destiny of sorts, way out past the supernatural. The captain witnessed Jude catch several exotic fish during a cyclone in the Sea of Azov, which broke every rule there was and forced the captain to conclude that his passenger had mystical and saintly powers.

Those were some of his fishing stories, and Lord knows all fishermen have fishing stories, but if there was ever one man who had plenty of fishing stories, it was Vincent Van Vedic, and him needing to fish the San Juan River before it became a lake was ten thousand feet below believable. No siree Babou Louie! That song and dance didn't really float his boat.

Even though it was hopefully temporary, this amnesia bug that had bit both him and Rahellio would haunt them both until the day they died. There had to be a reason for going where they went that didn't have anything to do with fishing. Perhaps it had something to do with the petroglyphs and the boulder wall. For some strange reason, whenever he turned his head up to and over his right shoulder, something happened to his equilibrium, and he would actually say the word "Dizzy" for some crazy reason. He wasn't dizzy and had developed this new nervous twitch where he'd glance up at something behind him. Very weird.

When the captain and his stallion were down alongside the river and headed towards where he knew *Vanessa* would be off to his right and up the ravine a way, he started redesigning the riverbank from back where the tent was pitched to where the creek flowed out from where *Vanessa* sat parked under that cottonwood. He would need to be able to drive his deuce-and-a-half that far to be able to load the bell and at least two dozen large boxes and barrels into the truck to be taken to his casa on the plateau up above.

It would be a big job, lots of work for a two-man crew of laborers, and he was thinking about all the safety concerns. Keeping the knowledge of the treasure a secret was always sitting in the back of his mind, the incredible treasure locked away throughout Vanessa's being here, there, and everywhere throughout her shell. He was trying to remember back when they loaded *Vanessa* in Pfeiffer that day, at least a dozen years ago. Two different loads of treasure, along with the bell itself, from the ruins of Saint Francis Church down to the secret harbor where *Vanessa* was docked and waiting. Boxes and barrels came on board that day, and not only had Basil packaged them years before, but he couldn't remember what was inside each one any more than Van Vedic could remember what the priest said that day. He was guesstimating the weights of things at the time and was striving to give each item its correct spot in the hierarchy of what weighed what and where it went. He would leave a light chalk mark on the container stating his guess, which was close enough to the truth.

First, he would check on *Vanessa* and see how things were at her location, sleep on the boat for two days and get a feeling for that.

El Bruto Whetto had plenty of grass to fatten up on, the trout were waiting to be caught, and he was ready to be done with the saddle. So when he rode the yellow horse up to the boat's bow, the brute rested his nose against the bow point and seemed to say hello again. She was just fine, almost as if she had been dry-docked for some reason and would be none the worse for wear, even if it took ten years—or hopefully less.

That was when the captain noticed that the bell on the bow of his boat was no longer there. He sailed off El Bruto Whetto as if he had been catapulted somehow, clambered up onto the stern, and raced to the mid-deck. The bell was gone. Everything was gone. The pallet was not there, neither was Hammer's Hammer, and that stack of boxes that the bell had surrounded were nowhere to be seen. Basil's epiphany had vanished. The hatch was undone at all the eight latch points, and he was able to open the doors and stare down into a deep, empty catch bin. All six of the king's lockers were missing, and the four boxes of books and coins that he remembered sitting on top of the lockers... well, you know.

His mind was not prepared for such an assault, and since the deck was now a blinding question mark, he decided to see what was left of things that had been kept inside *Vanessa*, the crew quarters, and the engine room. All the barrels were gone, and he had very little knowledge of what was actually in them. He'd taken the lid off one long ago and could see more treasure in the form of coins or jars of valuable gems and things. He'd put the top back on and quoted Basil, "More of the same." The barrels were converted flour drums weighing thirty-five pounds each, more or less. They were gone. Four boxes that were precisely the same size had been kept in the engine room and were strapped down tight, with toolboxes strapped on top of them. All four were practically empty anyhow, because that was what he'd plundered to make his gift boxes on the trip. That was where he found all those bars of gold, dozens and dozens that lined the bottom row of stuff in all four containers. They looked like little solid gold candy bars. Even though they were empty, they were gone, and the toolboxes were now on the floor.

Basil would always say, "More of the same," every time the captain asked him what was in any vessel they ever looked at. More of the same—must have said it fifty times, and like with the king's lockers, he got all giddy when he tried to explain what some of it looked like. Another one of his favorites was, "Heavy gold and silver. Heavy." It was like a warning so as not to strain someone's back. Because they did everything they did in a hurry-up and fast mode, Basil would hand a container from the wagon to Jude, who in turn would feel its weight and hand it to the captain of the boat, who would decide where it went on the inside of his *Vanessa*, with his verbal guesstimate as to its weight. Many of the early ones were a two-man job just to get it to him. He picked up the king's lockers as if they were lightweight, held them in front of his body for a moment, and asked Basil to keep track of the weights of things. One-oh-seven, one-twelve, and so on until he finally positioned the top four and closed up the hatch. He suggested that he needed to know the weight of all the things they brought aboard, and between the three and their undivided attention, they all agreed it was a boatload.

At the time of the launch, Van Vedic remembered how he was very concerned about all sorts of things that he had no control over whatsoever, such as how much weight she could take. During the loading process, he felt like they went right by the maximum load without even knowing what it was, and at the time, the bell was still in the wagon. The captain and his first mate Jude had busied themselves with putting everything away and securing it as best they could. The captain looked and pointed at one of four beautiful, two-foot-tall, handcrafted wooden waterproof boxes that he guessed to weigh one hundred pounds each, each probably full to the top with who knew what, and asked for the umpteenth time, "Good Father, what's in these containers?"

"Heavy gold and silver. Heavy." Then the Wolverine shrugged his shoulders a tad as if apologizing for those boxes breaking his personal load limit rules, about them being too much for one man to handle. When he watched Van Vedic decide they belonged in the engine room where they could be raided and given to the poor, he nodded his head that that was just perfect. Basil eventually ended up with nothing to do, so he sat with his cane, and then it was time for goodbye.

Just like the day when *Vanessa* broke free from the hitch and sailed off on her own down the hillside like a destined maniac. At the time he ended up sitting down on the edge of the road, wondering to himself how such a thing could happen. In the end, that following day, everything proved to be all right; everything appeared to be where it belonged.

Here he was again, only this time at the bottom of the hill, and once again, he wondered how such a remarkable thing could happen. He stood there on the bow point of his undamaged *Vanessa* and could almost see down to the river. He could hear the river relatively clearly compared to a week or so ago, hear it clear as a bell for that matter. The captain scanned both side areas for tracks of any sort, but there were none. No other horse but the brute had walked up from down there. So, he walked from the bow to the stern, not fast, had that over-the-shoulder twitch three times, and concluded the thieves had probably come down from up above like the trailer had a while back. Not only was that not true, but in many spots, the vegetation had already stood back up and had new growth everywhere in the damaged zones.

Once again, as in not that fast, he left the stern, passed by the door to the pilothouse back towards the bow, had two twitches, stopped in the mid-deck, and stared at the spot where the bell used to be. The bell on the bow was gone. It had disappeared.

His mind was whipping back and forth. Not only his bell on his bow, but it and everything else along with it had up and disappeared, and whatever happened didn't even leave a scratch mark on the handrails or a footprint in the sand. Perhaps a ton of things that he had looked at for a long time, had constantly considered what to do with—and now the entire inventory had vanished.

Fortunately, the thieves weren't into deck furniture and had left everything Thousanctus and his artisans had created. He folded it all out, made it into his bed, and wouldn't you know it, the cabinet was empty, so he decided to close his eyes and nap, clear his head, and hope for inspiration.

About ten minutes into his rest, suddenly, from out of nowhere, El Bruto Whetto started baying at the top of his lungs; he sounded like a dying mule. Then the dog chimed in, sounding even worse than when he'd gotten stuck in the rocks.

It was all taking place up there in front of the boat somewhere, and Van Vedic had both pistols out and was way past ready to kill whatever was killing his horse and his dog. It had to be a giant grizzly bear or some such thing, maybe two of them. He gained his feet, found a pistol, and prepared to fire, but instead found both his fishing buddies standing together about twenty yards off his bow point and very calmly looking at their master. In return, Van Vedic found himself looking at two lesser animals that were evidently thinking the exact same thought, staring straight at the man and forcing him to feel like them, forcing him to do the right thing. Napping was not it.

CHAPTER TWENTY-TWO

GONE

Here the captain was again, sitting back in his well-worn lounge chair in the middle of her front deck, a few hours away from calling it a day and trying to make a little sense of it all. He was facing the river, which was not too far away, with that being the closest water to him other than his canteen. His *Vanessa* was as long as that peaceful mountain river was wide, and this would be *Vanessa*'s home for a long time to come. What could have been a complete disaster when it happened turned out to be a godsend of sorts, with everything being better in every way over the first plan.

That had been the case a week ago when the fishing party left for the San Juan. For some ungodly reason, it appeared that he'd developed some harebrained scheme to fish the big river, a belief he wasn't so sure about and was getting more and more unsure of with every passing minute. So, for the present time, he decided to start a list of everything he had issues with over the last week or so and put question marks and stars, check marks, and parentheses next to every subject. Perhaps that might help him make some sense of his life.

He planned to sleep here on the deck for a couple of nights and decide on his actions starting in the morning. Being one hundred percent overwhelmed by the missing inventory, he had no choice except to lie back, stare up into the cottonwood, and rest his mind from all the problems.

In seemingly no time at all he had a long list of the questions in a semblance of their importance, but each line was a showstopper, and there were two pages of them.

What should have been blocking his view was gone, not there anymore, disappeared; a five-foot-tall, six-hundred-pound church bell. The T-shaped gong filled with gold and jewels was also missing, and everything else on the inventory was too. He was convinced that something supernatural was happening; something not of this world was pushing and pulling him, changing his life, and causing him to do things that he may never be able to explain. Most notable of all was that he had no complaints whatsoever. The list of things to consider that he had memorized and categorized was daunting, but on the other side of the scales of justice were a few facts that couldn't be ignored.

First of all, he wasn't scared in any way, not fearful or anxious about all the things on the list, because he had been all those three things, and much more, way back when he lived in Russia and the times were very hard and violent. Once upon a time, he knew all about being scared, fearful, and anxious. He was a fourth-degree Knight of the Guardsmen, his code name was 'Gunslinger,' and he made his living hauling freight for the bishop. It was a world he had lived in for twenty-five years, where he became a legend by simply doing his work. His Spivey sense had not been triggered, and that feeling he'd felt in the past when there was a dangerous enemy close by didn't keep him awake or tie up his thoughts. In this valley, he had no enemies, and he didn't believe there were any from coast to coast—or so they say in America, though life had taught him over and over that there are always evil men in the shadows.

So, his not being anxious was actually very good for everyone else around him. He was truly at peace with the world out there, and he hid nothing. One thing was for sure—he knew practically nothing about his new country, and instead of life being really simple in his isolation, for some strange reason, it seemed life was very complicated and confusing, with long questions and more of the lost-time issues.

Number two, for some weird off-the-wall reason, he had developed a neck twitch that didn't hurt but happened all the time and caused him to lift his chin slightly up and to his right, and his lips seemed to whisper a hissing sound with an 'e' on the end. It was new and on the list of weird stuff, but for now, it was totally unexplainable and painless.

Lastly, or maybe next to the last, was the health issue he is very aware of. There was no pain in his life, and that was a condition that a painless person must consciously bring to mind. You have to ask yourself sometimes if you're in pain because you don't think about it when you're not.

Besides those many subjects, he knew something was going on with the animals, which was very hard to explain even to himself, but his horse and dog were different and unique in a good way. Neither of his animals were in any sort of pain or having any trouble being their selves, including the idea that Sarge had only three very faint chevrons on his shoulder from the time that cat had laid him open. It should have laid him up for a lot longer than it had. Sometimes when he caught the canine looking at him, he could see something in those eyes that simply couldn't be read.

It was essential to realize that even though the missing time was all too apparent to both the captain and Rahellio, it happened to all the animals at the same time as well. They all knew exactly what happened, and just like normal, they couldn't talk about it. Every army he ever knew anything about spent almost half of its efforts on taking care of horses and trying to understand horses and how they deal with war, with the smells, the noise, the screams, because all the animals really want to do is run away from there. Horses are everything, and Vincent always tried to bond with his personal beast. They couldn carry you to safety when you need it most. El Bruto Whetto knew what happened to his master.

Way up there on the list, of course, was the fact that everything had vanished, and yet he wasn't the least bit concerned this particular evening. It fell into the category of all that other stuff that had happened to him over the last ten years at least, and he had no complaints about anything that transpired or the way things had turned out. Not a single complaint about anything. This would clearly affect his bottom line, but truth be known, everything was paid for, and that bottom line only existed in the world of dreams so far.

Well, that was not exactly true, because the subject of the missing three days still ranked up there as the number-one question of all questions. Twice while he was meditating on the circumstances, he had the twitch, which seemed to cause him to conclude a thought on something, and that problem went away. What made the missing time so important was that it had happened to Rahellio besides himself this time, and that proved something, but he hadn't put his finger on it just yet, and neither had Rahellio or his wife. He and the mortician had mulled over the subject constantly until it became monotonous, and they ended up feeling so helpless, so malleable, by only who knew what—and who knew why? As a matter of fact, he wasn't any closer to filling in the blanks any more than he had been able to over the past few days, when they were all together thinking and talking about it. At least now, Rahellio could better understand why the missing ten years were so important, when he had been swallowed by a hurricane in 1942 and disappeared until this past summer, and was resurrected off the coast of Texas, which had always been his destination, even though he wasn't quite sure exactly what harbor he was headed for. The priorities for the voyage had been redefined throughout the trip, but once Father Jude met General Patton, that ended those tasks, and in a sense, the *Vanessa* was set free. The next thing he knew, he was riding on the bow of the Pilldersleeve and headed for Venezuela, courtesy of the US Army. At the time and from his lofty perch there in *Vanessa*'s pilothouse, he studied the maps that showed a route from Texas to Kansas, and he now knew where New Mexico was. All he knew for sure was the most logical point would have been in the Gulf of Mexico, somewhere along the Texas coast, and he'd worry about that when he got there.

Whatever power had abducted him had never harmed him. If anything, they seemed to have cleansed both men of any ailment they may have had. Even the scars from the shrapnel wounds on his forearms had wholly disappeared, and for some reason, it seemed to know the captain's most secret thoughts and aspirations, almost as if their power could read his mind all the way back to when he was a child. It was very hard to explain because it was a feeling. It was as if a being was watching him— not God or anything like that; more like just a part of an entity that only has eyes and can't talk. With that thought in his mind, he turned his head to the right and up, and looked hard for any trace of those eyes in the space he studied, but it was empty.

"I know you're there. I can feel you." The captain spoke to no one besides the dog, who got all excited about the attention.

The supply of 45-caliber bullets on the *Vanessa* restocked his pistol belt, and that, above all other things, underlined the question of what they did that they couldn't remember. How could he have fired these two cannons that many times and not remember what the targets were? If he tried, he could remember the country fair in Pfeiffer, Russia, 1912, where he scored 59 out of 60, took first place, and could still remember every single target, where it popped up, and which gun he used to take it out. But he couldn't remember firing them just last week?

He could still see the pirates scattered about on their pirate ship. It was dawn, near sunrise, on the edge of Turkey in the Black Sea, 1942. The group had all fired their initial shots at once in the first three seconds and were screaming across the side rails at no one in particular while trying to slide their action in and out. Too late! We do not scream during a gunfight if possible. You scream after the gunfight if possible. Fourteen dead pirates in fifteen seconds with eleven bullets, and after all these years, not only could he remember every second, but he could also still smell it and feel the heat from their blood. Every detail of that firefight had played in his mind like a movie in slow motion, where they attacked and fired first, and missed, and then Van Vedic emptied his guns save for one while he reloaded in an instant. He fired eleven times at three groups of pirates on purpose, killing two at a time at the very start when they were all lined up. Jude had thrown the second 'gotcha bag' and dove for cover along the starboard guard rail wall and watched his captain kill every member of the pirate crew so fast they all entered eternity on the same raft.

In the logbook he kept, which would rank right up there near the top of the ten best journals ever kept, there would have been a long and involved passage where he wrote about that last day in Pfeiffer and the two wagon loads of supplies and cargo they'd loaded on the *Vanessa* that afternoon. Basil's inventory list consisted of twenty-four lines, giving every container a number and its measurements, estimated weight, a description of tie-down features, and what percent he thought it might be waterproof. Almost everything was rated seaworthy, watertight, sealed, and latched, out in the open or protected for sure. Virtually every container ended up protected from the elements, inside *Vanessa* somewhere, strapped down tight as could be and frequently inspected just in case.

Unfortunately, that memory has been warped by the time in between now and then, and because he had nothing to do with getting it all ready in the first place, the treasure rode the waves with him and became a mystery as to precisely what it was, and in that respect, a mystery of its worth. When he would study the bell, check the clamps and tie-downs, making sure it was secure and not loose in any way, it was easy to forget that the bell surrounded the pyramid inside itself and weighted down the lid to the catch bin. The catch bin went from empty to full to having the wedges slammed into place, and the catch cover lid latched and locked in less than twenty minutes. It happened so fast and so smooth that when the bell was shackled down, he almost forgot there was a catch bin. The truth of the matter was that bell covered a treasure that could handle the expenses of the world's greatest philanthropist and finance any dream ever dreamt, and that was a little more than half of what was packed all over her shell. However, it all seemed to be missing, and there was no trace of anyone having been anywhere near this boat except for the captain, his dog, and his horse. If they left any evidence of who or what they were, he hadn't found it yet, and to understand what all was missing and what it would take to haul it away, it was like a running tab in the brain, a total of things, and when it comes to brains, his worked really well for the most part and always had. This did not make any sense at all. It went way past surreal within minutes of his investigation beginning. The logistics, the weights, and the time, all piled up on his scales of justice and left him so amazed that he realized he didn't even know the correct question, didn't know where to start, and relinquished his authority to whatever superpower took it away.

Thinking back on that afternoon at the dock there in Pfeiffer, he remembered juggling the boxes Basil had prepared and deciding where to put them throughout the boat; Father Jude would huff and puff up and down the stairs while the captain loaded the catch bin with the six kings' chests, and four smaller boxes on top, totaling hundreds of pounds of treasure from the south corridor in the basement. He closed and latched the cover and set the pallet in place; Basil stacked his pyramid of treasure boxes that had to be set precisely for the bell to cover them correctly. It was a considerable amount of humorous hot air, but the captain and Jude played along as the bell came on board, hovered over his pyramid, and then descended for a perfect fit. For two hours, Van Vedic secured his cargo as only an experienced seaman can do with all due respect for the way Mother Nature treats her seas and rivers, the likes of the Mighty Don, the Sea of Azov, and the Black Sea. Then, unsure about what lay ahead, he had to ensure the cargo wasn't going anywhere when the waves got tall. It's rule number two—tie it down good and tight, with rule number one being for the captain of the boat to avoid the angry seas. It has to be a trusted instinct, a feeling from the heart and soul to stay out of her way when she's windy.

His *Vanessa* had been scoured of the fortune now, as if a being had come on board while he was on the fishing trip and, without disturbing anything nor leaving the slightest trace of who or what they or it were, but in so doing managed to remove just about everything the voyage was all about. They took the bell. They gutted the *Vanessa* of everything Father Basil had packaged, and the only thing left to prove it once existed was the list of all the containers and their dimensions, and in several places, a slight discoloration confirmed something had once sat there—a ghost.

As his scales of justice were filling up, one thing sprang to mind right off the bat concerning his things-to-do list: he could remove the task that demanded getting everything off his *Vanessa* and somewhere else, somewhere where he could look at it, polish it, stack it, and count it. He had to assume that the moving company took it all from here and put it there, and now he must try to find it and ask for it back. The idea that someone had done him a favor started to sneak around the edges of his calculations, and because he had always handled big and heavy loads, he understood to some degree how strong a creature would need to be to move the bell. The logistics of everything had overwhelmed him. In a sense, he was physically exhausted, and he hadn't lifted a thing.

When the animals got his attention, he tended to the business of El Bruto's saddle and a fresh bag of oats, and they all walked down to the river where he caught dinner for himself and the dog. Soon the trout was cooked to perfection, the meat just falling away from the bones, and the captain decided Sarge was getting to the point where he wasn't such a gluttonous wild animal anymore. He watched his dog spit out a stray bone, which was an excellent sign. He treated Sarge's trout the same way he treated his own trout, and never let the canine be a pig.

Through some creative design work, he assembled a staircase of a sort up onto the bow for both himself and the dog, and the brute had a small little grotto of sand and grass that he rolled around in and claimed for his own. As the evening settled in and he stared at the burning logs, his peace and quiet were interrupted when an entire flock of turkeys, maybe as many as thirty birds, decided to fly up to the lowest branches and then work their way to the tops of the cottonwoods. This roosting tree may have a history that goes back fifty years, where hundreds if not thousands of this family have come and gone every day, just like the seconds on a clock. At the same time every day, they position themselves on the hillsides nearby, where they can take a few turkey hops and launch themselves into the trees, where they find the same branch to roost on until the morning. They can't see very well after dark, and now after ten days or so, they hadn't abandoned this site simply because of the man, his dog, his horse, and his boat. The cooking fire and smoke didn't seem to cause them any grief, and so far, there wasn't much turkey shit on his vessel anywhere.

He wanted to cover every square inch of her with tarps and sheets of corrugated metal siding carried to the site by who knows who, and that project needed to start as soon as possible. It ranked right up there near the top of the to-do list, and when the owner of the small hardware store and lumber yard said if given enough time, he could have some of the most modern construction materials delivered to the base of the switchbacks for a nominal fee, Vincent sat there in the man's tiny office at the time before the *Vanessa* sailed over the edge and down into a hidden oblivion of sorts and understood that his deuce could haul anything the man delivered up the trail to his future ranch house. He pictured a construction site full of building boards, sheets of plywood, bags of cement if you could believe it, and all the nails and screws he would ever need.

It wasn't all that far, half a mile or more from where the tent was pitched to the ravine where *Vanessa* sat hidden. The terrain had forced the ancient shepherds to start the switchbacks where they did because the banks of the river became giant boulders one after another or dense forests of scrub oak and impenetrable berry bushes that can't be controlled. At least that's how it was back when this all started, probably back in the early twenties, and until recently, that dense forest of acorn and scrub oak hadn't ever met a front-end loader. They were about to.

He must have had fifteen different projects going in his mind at any one time, and for him to have convinced Rahellio to go fishing down inside the canyon was almost absurd. Why in the world would he have stopped everything he was doing, all those many projects that would take up all sorts of time? Why would he go fishing? It didn't make any sense at all, and now it appeared that neither he nor the mortician could remember anything from a seventy-two-hour period right in the middle of that week where he fired his weapons twenty times. That was what didn't make sense most of all. Those two guns with all the notches had been the center of his life for forty years or more, with stories at almost every notch concerning the end of a bad boy's life. Every single one was either an enemy or an evil waste of skin, and in the end, it was always the last resort, loud, final, and absolutely necessary. Twenty times last week he'd pulled those triggers, and he didn't know why. The world out there was as distant as any place he had ever been before, even more so than the deep outback south of Moscow, where nobody lived. He now owned a good-sized piece of land that will soon border a giant reservoir and has found that place he dreamed about here on the western side of northern New Mexico, right on the

Colorado borderline. The northwest plateau region was mostly empty of people, showing lots of promise in certain ways, and Vincent was more than content.

Just when he couldn't spare a single extra minute, according to everyone concerned, he decided to go on a fishing and camping excursion into the heart of a rock wilderness that everyone agreed should be underwater. Why in the world did he do such a thing, and now, to discover the missing inventory?

It was all so insane. Gradually the night closed in, and he went to sleep in his favorite deck chair just like he'd done who knew how many times before. Nowadays, after learning from the Coast Guard what they witnessed, he seemed to relive those nights in the hurricane, where he went to sleep in this very same deck lounge like there was nothing wrong on the horizon. So many memories like Thousanctus and his carpenters there in Tucumcari and how they hand-made the deck furniture just for him and one guest.

At the break of day, not to make a big deal about it, the captain stirred about and had a percolator doing its best to mimic either Jude or Rahellio, but in fact, it wasn't like that. He would never complain about the morning brew someone else prepared because coffee was an art form. Coffee was an idea, a smell, a taste to be appreciated for the moment, and there was nothing wrong with additives if they were at the table. Sugar was one of those and always available.

His plan was relatively simple—tighten down the latches for *Vanessa*, get on El Bruto Whetto, and climb the switchbacks to his casa. There was no point in staying another night on his *Vanessa*. Nothing much he could do that couldn't wait, and he needed to sleep up there and try to get his bearings a little better. He hoped so anyhow because it sure hadn't happened since he climbed up on her bow and found everything missing. As he tightened the saddle and explained exactly what was happening to the horse and dog, it suddenly occurred to him that maybe the moving company took his mighty deuce-and-a-half along with everything else. He shivered on that one and had a pretty serious twitch, but then it was over. He didn't want to think about someone taking his truck. That would not be good. For a few brief minutes there, he must have had five or six twitches in a row, kind of like sneezes, until he felt dizzy and actually said the word aloud.

"Dizzy." Like he was talking to himself and described his state of mind in one word or less. Strange as it was and not like it hadn't happened before, but when he said the word, it was followed by an echo of his own name spoken in a question from up and to the right.

He was undoubtedly guilty of a syndrome hermits are afflicted with, which causes them to either talk to themselves or an entity of their creation who is invisible to dogs and horses and generally doesn't talk back. Actually, if he were to take it all the way back as far as he could, he'd find himself alone for long periods of time in his past and he often times talked to himself on the Orient Express, which went on forever. He'd done it twice just making a delivery and then going back home. Ten time zones, at a snail's pace for the most part. At times the train would stop and fail to move for a week, and after a while no one bothered to ask why it was stalled or how long it would be till it moved again. The Orient Express was such a terrible experience, and he constantly tried to appreciate just how difficult it was to run and maintain train tracks that far.

Besides that memory, there were many others where he lived on the saddle and learned how to sleep on a horse that was following the trail. His whole life revolved around his animals, and he could readily remember at least a dozen different horses he had trained and trusted throughout life. He never felt truly alone, even though he was, and was always singing at the wheel of *Vanessa*, singing while holding the reins to a team of horses pulling the wagons, he and his dad, humming and whistling. All of those sounds were nothing more than talking to oneself.

To take it one step further, he had to conclude that something or someone was watching him go through life, something had manipulated him for as long as he could remember, always there at critical moments—left or right, stop or go—and for all intents and purposes, he couldn't remember ever making a bad decision. He'd always felt it up there. All through life, he'd always made the right decision and, in many cases, survived many a near-death experience that required an instant decision, almost as if he was sometimes seeing around the corner or a few seconds ahead of right now. You wouldn't believe how many times in the past when the gunslinger did a head nod up and to the right just before the cannons came alive, either on the trail or in the wars, and now at this age, he seems to have become aware of his companion.

All of that experience piled up on his scales of justice and convinced him that there was some kind of spirit up and over his right shoulder, which manifested itself in his life periodically, wasn't all that pushy and didn't seem to need much. There were stories upon stories in his journals that talked about those gun battles where his opponent always died, and there were things in common that he noted and wrote about. He decided to name it. It was a revelation of sorts, nothing short of a creation, a birth, with all due respect and every bit his equal mentally and probably physically. Most of all, this being was like a brother—more than a brother if there is such a thing. A twin brother who shared at least his heart with the captain. Yes, it had taken a while, but now there would be four souls at least at any of his fires. The dog, the horse, Vincent Van Vedic, and his not-so-new friend, Dizzy.

"Dizzy. I know you're there. Do you know what else I know? I know that you know what happened last week. I know that it's probably you who won't let me remember. Friday night, all of Saturday and Sunday, and most of Monday. I'm not kidding about it being you. I'll tell you something else. I am a smart man, I'm honest, I'm true to the righteous side of humanity, and I don't tolerate my fellow men being animals. I don't kill dogs, I kill animals, and I've killed many in my life so far. If you bleed, you should be extremely cautious when it comes to dealing with me. Don't sneak up on me now that I know you exist. I'll do my level best to figure out the answers. You should help me every chance you get. I can keep a secret if it comes to that. Dizzy! You hear me? Dizzy?"

CHAPTER TWENTY-THREE

A FAIR TRADE

As he coaxed the brute alongside the edge of the Los Pinos River, Vincent kept in mind that Sarge would also have a rough time because of the impenetrable acorn and scrub oak forests that existed if there weren't any boulders. Sometimes the brute was in shallow water, but that was only for a short while, and the dog found his way through all the vegetation along the riverbanks once he knew where they were going.

The last switchback corner was far above him on the hillside, totally out of view. When the trailer went over the edge, it had plowed its way down the corner ravine until it stopped fifty yards from the edge of the bustling little mountain river that eventually mingled with the Mighty San Juan deep inside the gorge. When he and the dog had walked out the morning after the accident, his understanding of the topography led him to think it was a half mile on a very, very seldom used animal trail to where he pitched his army tent. So, when he was coming in to find *Vanessa* on horseback, it was somewhat challenging the first time, because there was a lot of guesswork going on as to which ravine held his lady. Then, sure enough, he spotted the top of her cabin way back in there, but that was all of her you could see from the river, and you had to be on horseback.

The captain had slept in the tent frequently while working on the switchbacks. El Bruto Whetto was free to roam around the tent area, and the captain appreciated right away that he always stayed close by once the day was over. Sarge was in perpetual forward and covered the entire area back and forth, over and over. He seldom stopped for long, knew every chipmunk and lizard living near the tent, and was getting close to catching one.

Back when this all started, *Vanessa* sat nearby on her trailer and was pointed towards that first uphill straight-away, a three-hundred-yards-long ramp to that first U-turn, the first of five, with the last one peeking out on the plateau where the casa was built. Sometimes he slept on *Vanessa*'s bow in the recliner, but the dog caused issues that didn't exist when he slept in the tent, and not only that, but he had also built a tarp bed that was ten feet long and six feet wide, covered in pillows and blankets, was easy to climb onto and hard to climb out of. All in all, the switchbacks were an engineering masterpiece that started out as a pedestrian walk, then a horse trail, a sheep trail, and now it was what it was.

If a person wanted to go from down along the river up the side of the canyon wall and onto the plateau up above, this switchback was the only way to do that. But, as fate and time would dramatically prove, an army deuce-and-a-half pulling a heavy fifty-foot-long trailer might be too much for the engineering masterpiece to accommodate. On the afternoon in question, as everything jackknifed and went to hell on that fourth switchback corner, where the ball hitch shattered and *Vanessa* disappeared down the ravine in the bat of an eye, this total failure was caused by the only person present. The captain was tired of the predicament and rationalized that it was time; he knew all the dangers and understood all that, but he did it anyway. For a brief time after the trailer was gone, it appeared to be the worst disaster of his entire life from his vantage point there on the road. He had gambled and lost. Too bad, so sad.

"Dizzy? Dizzy? I'm thinking you're some sort of dodecahedron. What do you think of that? I'm waiting for an answer. Dodecahedron! I can't believe I know such a word, and I know I didn't know it last month. How'd that happened? Did I dream it? It's all about twelve, isn't it? Twelve bullets in my two guns, twelve faces at the world. Twelve, twelve, twelve."

At a post-event workshop on the moon, a small contingent of studio personnel posted this quote from Vincent Van Vedic at something or someone up and over his right shoulder. He was talking to Dizzy and if there was one entity in all of this, of all the entities who every single entity in the known universe knew about, it was the entity known as Dizzy. The human who had been the star of the show for so long, last whenever as the time frames obviously varied throughout the cosmos, and in some cases, they obviously won't start the series for a questionable amount of time, but everyone already knew that. The hero of the epic involving the three cadets, the human who'd had his memory erased had just discovered and said out loud that he remembered something from deep inside that seventy-two hours. Something that the experts said couldn't and shouldn't happen. It now appeared he knew of a geometric pattern he'd learned in the canyon but didn't know why. Dodecahedron! Whatever next!

.   .   .

By noon the captain, his horse, dog, and imaginary sidekick Dizzy finally came out of a thick pinon forest alongside the river and into the clearing where his tent was standing. It was secure and hadn't been tampered with by the animals, so he didn't stay long. Once he was underway again, that first long switchback trail was up where the rider can study the terrain and estimate distances and depths, because about halfway to the first hairpin, the trail ended higher than the giant cottonwoods.

There were four corners, U-turns of a sort, and nothing for El Bruto Whetto to negotiate. Doing the switchbacks on horseback was one hundred percent different from doing it from the front seat of his deuce. That position allowed for no judgment errors, sightseeing, or bullshashiska. The last time he rode in the saddle to the adobe casa, he realized how pleasant that was and how incredible the sightseeing. Unfortunately, this whole valley would be underwater someday in the near future, and there won't be an access road from this side of his property. He needed to make a new road out the back side of his ranch someday soon that solved all sorts of problems, and since he seemed to have satisfied his desire to fish the Mighty San Juan, he could start getting to all those projects now.

Considering the notion of fishing the untamed river once again, as he enjoyed his saddle time, it occurred to him that he had no memory whatsoever of having done any fishing at all in the recent past except for when he fed himself and Sarge. Not only could he not remember firing his weapons, but he also couldn't remember fishing, and that was weird enough, since that was why they supposedly went there in the first place. To go through all that trouble, all those animals, harnesses, tequila, and what in the world was the point of having Rahellio and his son bring their horses up to his casa first when they could have met at the critter gate and saved a whole day? That was flat-out dumb!

Any time he dwelt on that particular subject, he could only wag his head side to side as he recognized how absurd that was, for Rahellio and the boy to first come to his house and then they would retrace their tracks and go all the way back to the where they would try to find a way down through one of the many canyons available. It was all so strange, so unreasonable, but when Rahellio talked about it, for him, it didn't matter; he and his son were making a very nice wage, and whatever the boss man needed doing would get done his way. "No problemo."

As the captain watched the two Candelarias ride away from their first encampment, he'd wondered what could have possibly made them all so violently sick. Even though he had retched with the best of them, when it was over, he felt fine. He understood the necessity of taking the boy to his mother, but that didn't mean he had to abandon the fishing trip. At least that thought bounced around in his memory, and then the dog got stuck, requiring him to race to Rahellio's house for help. They were going to pull over a tall, thin boulder that would then allow him to rescue the dog.

This question-and-answer thing had been going on for many days now, since that campfire on Monday night a week ago. It took a while for him to review the calendar the mariposa had drawn up, where each day was a single page and everything that happened that day by the hour was filled in, with room for additions as they were hopefully remembered. On that Friday afternoon, the two men and their four beasts of burden arrived at a location deep inside the canyon to rescue Sarge. This was a place where no men had been in the longest time. It now appeared that the gatekeepers won't let anyone back in down there; you would get lost, won't be able to find the river, and would always end up back where you started until you finally gave up in total frustration.

They discovered that the dog had managed to escape its

predicament, and they credited the understanding of how he did it to it being a miracle. There was absolutely no way the mind of man—make that two men—could understand how that animal climbed out of that trap that Mother Nature had created. It fell into the category of a miracle, and while the captain was caressing his dog, Sarge, and Rahellio was watching him do that, their memory ceased, replaced with a bright light and trimmed in blue.

Both men agreed it was at that moment when something happened; the light went on, a bright light beyond whiteout. They made a note of the fact that neither man was on his horse at the moment, but as it turned out, three days later, they found themselves looking for a campsite just down the way from where the dog was trapped, on horseback. At a precise moment in time that afternoon, they stopped, turned in their saddles, and reentered reality. The light dimmed back to normal, and their questions and reasoning did the same; in essence, they had no memory of a shared seventy-two-hour period. The critical truth was that they did it together and had no knowledge of what that might have been, and when they finally talked about what was happening to them, that was when they realized they didn't know what day it was. Finally, after walking out and arriving at Rahellio's ranch, they learned it was Tuesday, and it turned out to be three days lost, from Friday night to Monday night.

It wasn't long until the party reached that fourth switchback corner, and the captain guided the brute up to the exact spot where the wheels on the trailer had left those two tracks over the side and virtually instantly disappeared, hitch first in fast forward, see you later.

"DIZZY! You up there? This is the spot where *Vanessa* dove over the edge. Right here."

From that vantage point he could see down a way, but there

wasn't a lot of information on what may have happened other than corner and road improvement debris, and not too much of that. Rahellio and his son had passed by the spot twice on horseback and never noticed a thing, never asked about the boat and trailer, and probably thought it was up by his casa sitting according to plan and waiting for the dam to lift it off the trailer.

On the moon, that small contingent had grown into a huge contingent of former studio personnel, because there was only so much news going on on the back side of the moon, and now that Vincent Van Vedic had broken the rules at least three times through no fault of his own, an APB went out on the whereabouts of Dizzy.

Knowing the captain had literally changed the Candelarias' lives, with Rahellio handing his wife large sums of money for the work he was doing—and not only that but she also got paid for all of her switchback work, which was the first time she had ever been paid for any work. That may or may not have been verified, but her reaction was such that one could easily believe she was making a huge deal out of a paycheck, a paper she cashed at the First National Bank of Ignacio, which also had a couple of Vincent's accounts. His combined accounts had been started with his contract agreements with the bank's owners, consisting of gold coins and an assortment of gems and diamonds they promised to have evaluated. From the initial one, the drop of the jaw evaluation, they started off with fifty thousand in his savings account and whatever he needed in his checking account. He just wanted to ensure folks like the Candelarias could take a paper check into the bank and cash it with little to no hassles, no matter the amount. That meeting had lasted for about an hour, and the captain was as relaxed as ever, expecting it to take some time for things to go through the process. They took pictures of all the coins and gems, gave him a really fancy checkbook binder, and he accepted the system and treated it as his local business account. He had another one in Aztec.

He crested the hilltop and could see to his excitement that his beautiful deuce was still sitting there by the side of his casa. When the thought first rumbled around in his brain that the "movers" might have also taken the truck, he was greeted with a flurry of twitches, almost like a spanking for thinking stupid. He could go on and on, but none of that mattered because there she sat, a little on the dusty side but ready for his next trip to Aztec. The only thing wrong with his vision from a quarter mile away was that he knew he hadn't parked it like that; he always parked his trucks pointed at sunrise, an old Russian trick that helped in the wintertime. This forward-facing thing just went against the rules. He doubted that anyone but he could start it in the first place—because of some simple rewiring issues. As the brute got closer to his stable, his passenger felt a twitch—not a Spivey sense, just a serious twitch—which set him ready in the saddle for whatever might be next.

He'd always been deadly from the saddle, but in this case he was walking straight into an ambush if there was danger up ahead. His Spivey sense was nowhere to be sensed, so the truck issue stayed on the front burner, with his mind guaranteeing that he had parked it more or less in that spot the last time he drove it but parked it going in the other direction. The truth was, as he walked up to the driver's door, he could put that information on the list of weird things that had happened recently. 'The truck is pointed in the wrong direction.' There were so many things to think about.

Just for the hell of it and because it was good practice, he decided to turn her on, let her idle for a while, mix her oil, and check for mice. With her purring on the high side, he set off to take care of the brute and gave him a huge helping of oats and alfalfa. His water tank was full, and the animal brushed his master with his nose in an apparent thank you. Van Vedic turned in an evident huff, his chest a mere foot or so from those flexing nostrils when El Bruto Whetto nosed him once again and held a stare-down for a few moments. Then he went back to his oats.

Standing moderately close, Sarge barked out two barks, and with the horse and his master's undivided attention, he did a half bark and went back to his slab of elk thigh. It was hard to say what that was all about, but the captain was treated to two double twitches, and if anyone were watching all this, they'd have to conclude there was something seriously wrong with the human.

With the brute content and Sarge busy, the captain headed back to the truck. As he walked up on it from the rear, he could see it better and knew what he could barely see in the canvas-covered deuce. The tailgate was up and closed, and there, resting in the very middle of the cargo bay, sat the bell that had been on his bow. What was lost had now been found.

Even though Vincent Van Vedic was tall enough to see over the top of a deuce-and-a-half tailgate, in order to see the cargo bay in its essence, it was best to have the tailgate down, and so it was lowered. There on its original pallet, the bell sat strapped and centered, waiting for a set of forklift tongs to pull the cargo out from its sheltered cove. Whoever managed this superhuman feat had cleaned and polished it first—which wouldn't be evident or fully appreciated for some time to come but, out in the sunlight, the thing was basically dazzling.

As the captain climbed on board to investigate things further, he noticed the T-clangor was completely refreshed, not even strapped to the front of the pallet, and it was empty. With one hand, he examined it up close and personal, decided it weighed about thirty pounds, and seemed ready to be attached up inside the guts of the bell someday soon. It was a moderately complicated device, had a great deal to do with the quality of the sound, was governed entirely by the rope, and whatever had filled the tubes was gone.

He remembered it being almost a two-handed job when he'd shackled it down the first time, a hundred pounds or more, and knowing full well what Basil said was inside the tubes. He laughed at the memory of Basil talking about almost freezing to death in the winter, but he'd stayed alive, melting down the gold and filling the tubes an inch at a time. Then he'd drop in diamonds and gems, hoping they would survive as the gold cooled down. He had a routine of things that had to be done to the gold to get it ready to melt, rituals according to volumes of ancient texts that treated the subjects of how to deal with gold and do it right. It was pretty simple to take a golden candle holder and turn it into an ingot, a standard size that the books told him was accepted worldwide. Each one had a stamped impression that told its weight and quality, was poured into a precise and registered size, ready for the world market that would determine its value at any point in time.

The coins were a different matter; their value hinged on many variables, but seldom was it a disadvantage to be the owner of such things. Van Vedic had more coins from ancient times than anybody in the neighborhood, and without doubt, deciding what something like that would be worth in the San Juan Basin was stretching the limits of the local gold coin community, as he'd seen when dealing with the Bank President, a friendly sit down where the captain was opening his account by laying out solid gold coins, silver coins, diamonds, rubies, things like that that almost always worked. So far, he didn't want to mess with gold coins and diamonds any more than a man in the moon.

He felt a twitch for some reason, but it was true. From the very start of this excursion, all the way back to when that first switchback on the Illava erased Pfeiffer and Saint Francis from his vision, he began to deal with the notion that he was, in fact, a very wealthy man. How rich, he had not a clue other than to believe it huge. For the most part, all he knew for sure was that Father Basil had packaged a couple dozen containers full of things from the two treasure rooms at the end of the south corridor. He was now also in possession of an ancient library of first-time publications. According to Basil, although there were only forty volumes in the collection, they were forty scarce and famous first-time books. He joked during his discussion of the subject that Van Vedic should try his best to not let them get wet.

Basil had been as thoughtful as he could possibly be while he packaged up the many containers, and using only his imagination, he packaged four large one cubic yard waterproof containers, full of things he found that he hoped the generous inheritor would use to give away to people he might meet along the way to America. He could give away bars of gold and fists full of diamonds and never even know the items were gone.

Father Basil had been organizing the treasure room across the hall from Treasure Room Number One, which held a fantastic assortment of fortune, wall to wall, a thousand keepsakes if not ten times that. Things ended up in that room because of many descriptions that got a yes or a no answer. Once things got to a certain point, it turned out to be put it here or put it there, and some of those things never got moved again. Expediency was undoubtedly one of them, each and every time. Sometimes it was a difficult subject for the Van Vedics and Father Hammer, three a.m., and they finally had the wagon empty.

"What is this? Where does it go?" Two or three men asking each other over and over until, now and again, they couldn't see straight. Eventually, the floor in the central lobby of Saint Francis would be back to normal. Down where the elevator stopped were boxes full of things from a church that had been disintegrated, and all of the parishioners had been savaged. The whole community was finished. As they brought things down the elevator to the basement, Hammer was always there to help in every way he could, but the idea at the time had always been to get things put away, at least into the rooms where they belonged, and let the Van Vedics get back to the highway. The definition of something's value became lost in the fact that, as often as not, the item in question was just one of many that people save for generations, and each wagon load of relics was actually a copy of the previous loads. It was always full of the same things, the beautiful crucifixes, the altar paraphernalia, the pictures and artwork, musical instruments and sheet music, and old church records with the names of the people. Old churches were full of artifacts and artworks that dated far back in their histories. It never failed; no matter the church, there would be a closet or two chocked full of things that never got seen by the congregation but fell into the category of "DO NOT LEAVE THIS BEHIND!" In most cases, those kinds of things ended up in the wagon the Van Vedics drove to Pfeiffer.

One of those things that Basil found one day was a rather large suitcase that contained everything some ancient goldsmith had regarding anything gold. The 'how to' book of all times on how to deal with gold. How to make small manageable fire boxes, time-tested techniques, and charts that knew exactly the right amount of time when it came to the stamp. Inside the case and probably most important of all were the array of molds and the proper stamps, along with the scales and the counterweights, things that made his ingots beautiful. To call it a wintertime hobby was fair and reasonable, but the end result was that there were up to six rows of gold bars on the bottom of every single one of the saddlebags, just about every box and barrel he packed, and the king's chests were weighted out at a hundred pounds max, no more, too awkward, but they were brought up to weight with small bars of gold tucked in here and there. Depending on what day of the week it was, he could mold up twenty-four bars in an evening, play the piano for from two to ten hours, and build and work on a new box after starting the Mass not long after waking up. Usually, his Mass was a solemn high event with lots of piano music, and singing had no time limit whatsoever, and in the winter months, he usually got it done before the day was over. It was a mental thing in many cases, knowing exactly where he was in the liturgy, and considering that he treated the entire basement from wall to wall as nothing more than an extension of his altar there in the chapel, his basement church was all that a priest could ever need. One or two parishioners would be nice, but those days were over for St. Francis, and sometimes when he could get out into the countryside as the winter lost its grip, he would sometimes travel twenty miles just to find the first senior Russian officers of the new season. Sometimes the wolverine, Pocomaxa, would look hard at the senior NCO's, the bullies, and the assholes, and was considering a change of philosophy, which would change who was eligible.

The captain climbed out of the truck, turned around, and closed up the tailgate while staring at the bell with stunned being an appropriate word to describe him at the moment, but there was a great deal more to his discovery. He hadn't made it inside his casa just yet but needed a tall glass of water from the spring, so he filled up the water bags and headed for the front door. When he pushed it open, he staggered once again. Unbelievable!

There in the middle of his living room stood the entire assortment of missing containers. Some were obviously king's travel chests, some were barrels, some were boxes, but one thing for sure, all the containers that had been scattered throughout the *Vanessa* were now very neatly stacked together up against the long wall, upside down and empty. All except for two. Both were king's chests, and whoever had decided what to leave behind had picked some fancy books, stunning pictures in picture frames, salt and pepper shakers, along with all sorts of window ornaments. For the most part, it seemed logical, but there would be no way he would read all the books, and he wasn't into paintings any more than the next guy.

The questions were just beginning to form in his mind as he got the fire started and made coffee. That was when he noticed a standard-size business briefcase—two matching latching straps, solid leather, excellent work and trim, and a small gold medallion with the raised letters VVV. It was obviously his, even though he had never owned such a thing in the past, and when he opened it up, he found a simple business-type letter addressed to him.

"Dear Captain Vincent Van Vedic."

The letter was four pages long, very technical, seemed to have been written by someone who had nothing but the captain's best interests in mind, and after a short discussion concerning what had been in the containers and what sorts of dilemmas their very existence created. After some lengthy discussion, the experts had all agreed on a plan. The best strategy for almost all of his cargo was to let the experts deal with it and distribute it out into the world markets, using the wisdom of the ages concerning such things, all the while assuming that the captain, a true expert if there ever was one, would agree wholeheartedly and thank them hand over fist. The many historic crowns from the two kingdoms, along with the many other ancient artifacts, were returned to their rightful places, and everyone was thrilled with the discoveries. Most importantly, not one single item on the list was attributed to the captain in any way, shape or form.

There was a law firm printed on the front page, two names listed who would handle all the technicalities of his estate if he so chose and approved, but let it be known that the captain was officially a wealthy man. The entire treasure was sold to a company that paid an undisclosed amount, but a total was guessed to be in the hundreds of millions of dollars, maybe more. That money was used to set up accounts in his name here and there, throughout the world. The banks were all listed in a monthly report with their interest rates posted, and all the contracts had been established with the sole purpose of making a decent profit.

All of the accounts in a dozen major worldwide banking institutions were created in the name of Vincent Van Vedic. Each would begin receiving quarterly deposits of at least a million dollars from an international organization that manufactured who knew what. Very hush-hush sort of thing but totally transparent, like few other companies in the entire world. The system was untested in the North American investment circles, with immediate totals that would justify the revolutionary methods, and Vincent would not have do a single thing to keep it all running smoothly. A banking genius seemed to be in charge, almost like a wizard, a mind that seemed to be out of this world, and the results were that Van Vedic's Corporation had been set up in only a week, with different experts ready to answer any questions the captain might have over the phone or in person. The offices were in Aztec and New York City. The Aztec office was staffed, and the back of the building was being turned into a private office for the captain, along with a plush apartment on the XXXL side, just in case he ever came to town.

Most important of all, the bell on the bow of his boat was now the bell in the back of his truck. Since none of the experts had been privy to how he would get it to Pfeiffer, Kansas, they thought that since they had it out and about there for a while, they might as well clean it up, polish it a bit, and there was some work done on the clangor as well. It was now sheltered from the storm, ready for transport off the plateau and back to Aztec once again, where his many different options were laid out on his table. As he filled up his coffee thermos, his plan was to visit Vanessa and watch the sun go down. He decided to read her the letter, and they could discuss it together. It seemed like a long time since he had done that, and he knew it wasn't true but he still questioned the emotion. As he sat there with his bride, he seemed to want to go to the other lookouts on the eastern edge that watch the sunrise for some strange reason.

If there was one thing apparent from the four-page letter, it was that the folks responsible for just about everything involved in this saga seemed to think that Vincent Van Vedic was the cat's meow, the bee's knees, and they could not do enough to celebrate his life and the things he did to get to the point where he was now.

When it came to declaring all the things proclaimed in the letter, and then in the most general of terms, he never actually recognized a single thing in particular. Starting with the first paragraph, the letter talked about what a fabulous human being the captain had proven to be. At least a half dozen more super-vague generalities with similar very high accomplishments followed, so much so that he found himself humbled beyond humble. Right from the start, he understood that whoever was capable of all this existed in a world not of this world, from outer space maybe, and the only problem his mind was dealing with was that he didn't know why. There was a list that accompanied the why, who, how, when, and all the rest.

There was nothing wrong with anything that was happening, nothing he could have possibly done about anything, and now it appeared that all he had to show for the last twenty years was held inside his fancy new briefcase. His fortune appeared to be a perpetual motion money-making machine, consisting of methods and techniques that were unheard of in the business and banking worlds, untested before the VVV Corporation had been filed and listed.

"DIZZY. Okay, no yelling. Dizzy, do you know why? Take your time; I'll wait."

"He did it again!" was the headline for the message that went out universally from the back side of the moon, from the new chairman of the new panel of "concerned personnel" concerning Captain Vincent Van Vedic shedding the vail that protected his memory.

After only a short time and not even resorting to making a list, Vincent made a Russian blend of vodka and things that he kept in his liquor closet, which he'd patiently waited for. He enjoyed the tequila in this region and the feelings from that drink. He loved beer and wine, but he'd been raised on vodka, and it was a taste that God gave to man to take his mind off the shithole world they lived in. And up to this point in time, the world had proved to be harsh for the common man and his woman; nothing comes easily for almost everyone.

It had been a while since he'd camped out in his own living room, had a friendly fire going, had his dog nearby, and had a favorite drink in hand while he surveyed his wall full of empty containers. Not even Basil had ever seen them like that. He made the boxes, or so he said, one at a time, to specific measurements and had the six king's chests as examples of master box-making techniques. They had been buried in the sand during a great flood, and even though there was serious damage to the outsides, because of the way they were crafted, the contents never suffered any damage. He opened them all, repackaged them to some degree, kept their weight to a hundred pounds or less, and used gold ingots to raise their weights to his standard.

This living room—in particular, this couch, the fireplace—seemed to mellow him out faster than any room he'd been in lately, causing his mind to enter a state of thanksgiving for everything that had happened not only recently but back throughout his whole life. Whoever had done this, whoever wrote the letter and emptied the boxes and barrels, had miraculously lifted all those burdens of what to do with the contents. They must have sold everything and dispersed all the treasure as if it were air to who knew where, except for two boxes full of an assortment of mementos and keepsakes.

The captain sat by the fireplace and remembered lowering the bell over Basil's epiphany of treasure boxes around New Year's 1941, at least a dozen years ago. As the boxes disappeared, Van Vedic realized he had no idea what was under that bell. A baker's dozen of containers full of golden artifacts and all sorts of handpicked treasure, packaged by Basil with great pride and as much forethought as possible. It was a strange scene—the man, his dog, and a room full of empty boxes except for two.

"Hey, DIZZY! Sorry, I forgot. Mr. Dizzy? Mr. Dizzy, sir? Do you know anything about these empty boxes? I think you do. I bet we had a contract of some sort. I've always had contracts when I dealt with folks, things between men, mano a mano."

Dinner was pretty simple: lots of meat, two potatoes, corn, and big T-bones for the dog. Vincent was done for the day. He took a coffee out onto the porch and looked up at the moon.

"Mr. Dizzy, sir, tell them thank you from me."

"He did it again!"

CHAPTER TWENTY-FOUR

THE BELL IN THE BOX

Van Vedic knew his deuce could be in Aztec in a couple of hours with the bell in the back, and he knew that the train station could handle the load. The bell on his bow had become the bell in his deuce and soon to be the bell on its way to Pfeiffer. Here it was, the end of October, and as far as the captain could tell, everything was far better than he could have ever imagined. After a bona fide full-blown disaster—or so he'd thought when the trailer broke loose—everything seemed to have turned out just shy of perfect three months later, sitting near his newly found favorite fireplace, sipping on a tall vodka and chewing elk jerky.

He watched his dog look at him like he had a secret to tell and would if he could, but he couldn't, and the drool slobber off his jaws indicated he would accept a bribe of elk meat anytime. The captain knew that fact was true; he knew the dog knew what he wished he knew. Sarge had been there at his feet all during that three-day period that he and Rahellio couldn't remember. At this point in the game, he understood that there was one thing for sure above and beyond everything else that he knew anything about, and that was that he wasn't in charge of anything except for his new ranch and his pets. He was exactly where his mind had envisioned to be the perfect place for him, it seemed, in an adobe ranch house on the edge of a future reservoir. He'd dreamed up that image ten thousand miles ago in Russia, long before he was rich, and this was his new reality.

Recently, he and his friend Rahellio had both experienced a life-altering three-day weekend together and now couldn't remember anything that happened during that time. It was proving to be anything but easy on the mental side of who and what Van Vedic was turning out to be. This was now the second time the captain has seemingly entered a place where he did things, ate, fired his cannons at least twenty times, for crying out loud, drank tequila like it was going out of style, and slept, but he couldn't remember a single detail. The first time around, which seems to have lasted for ten years or more, involved him and his boat disappearing into a world that didn't hurt him, released him very near where he had always intended to go, and just like that, he came back to life exactly where he needed to be. Who in the world could complain about that outcome? And it appeared Vincent was allowed to remember everything that happened right up to a point where a massive wave would have swallowed his *Vanessa* like a moth by the ferocious storm. He had found himself inside the eye of a hurricane, and he didn't even know there were such things. After a day or two floating counterclockwise inside the eye, something must have taken a turn for the worse, and his mind got a bit hazy at this juncture, but he could suddenly see that wave in the distance. It seemed to have burst up out of very calm waters, fifty feet high and only a few short moments away from killing him, and since no man would want to see the apparent end face to face, he turned away and waited in the doorway to his cabin, but that's when things went white. Time must have stopped, a period that lasted until 1953. From 1943 to 1953, and then poof, the *Vanessa* pops back to life off the coast of Corpus Christi.

Because of his odyssey with Hurricane Number 9, and the fact there were pictures to prove where he was when the hurricane hunters took his picture, and then over ten years later when they took his picture once again, he knew he hadn't aged at all, or so he believed and had proof because he'd hurt his finger pretty bad in Puerto Rico before he ran into the hurricane. That same finger was still hurt badly enough to get his attention while they waited for the Admiral of the Coast Guard to show up with dinner on his first day back. Having been born in '88, he would supposedly be sixty-five years young, but his finger didn't heal at all during that same time, and he reasoned his body didn't age or change. It was as if he went into hibernation like the bears and came out of it just like when he went in. So there was no doubt in his mind that he was fifty-five, didn't need a discount or anything like that, at least not yet, and was convinced the missing ten years hadn't been counted against his life clock. Nothing more or less as an example of his idle mind playing with numbers.

Everything on his calendar had changed because someone else had taken all the cargo off the *Vanessa* and evidently sold it, saving him a big job that he wasn't looking forward to in the slightest. Not only that, and even more astounding, someone had taken the bell off the bow, even used the same pallet assembly, and stuck the unit in the back of the deuce. That all by itself seemed to indicate that the bell belonged somewhere down the road and not on the plateau. No more lallygagging around. It was one of those signs that he always paid attention to, and so he put that goal at the top of his list. When that goal was accomplished, when the bell was finally at the bottom of the bell tower of Holy Cross, the captain of the *Vanessa* will have been set free of all the promises he made back where he came from, promises made and promises kept to Basil and Jude, and as a result, Hammer's dream for the bell was now almost a reality.

One thing that had captured Vincent's imagination a couple of months back was Vannie, that lovely woman who lived in Aztec, only sixty miles away using dirt county roads. When he first met her, she managed to instantly take over his mind, but he had to leave her and finish the switchbacks, get the trailer to the top of the plateau, and then he could return to eat in her café again anytime he liked. He supposedly now had an office on the end of Main Street that he planned to visit. He would take his new briefcase to prove to whoever staffed the place that he was who he said he was. In addition, he needed a driver's license, one of Vannie's haircuts, and a whole long list of products delivered to his ranch.

Without any trouble at all, he remembered how she had overwhelmed him there in her barber's chair and at a number of other locations right from their first eye contact. It shed a new light on everything he was thinking and doing when his plan for the boat was finished. First things first, and Vannie begrudgingly agreed with a smile on her lips that melted him like butter, approved of the man's plan, and wished him well. She wasn't going anywhere, and if and when he thought it might be right, she would love to ride in the deuce and see the views. They were both sort of star-struck, and he would slowly discover that a lot of the locals had already decided the captain was a little bit overboard on his grand plans.

Not only did he come up with a few legitimate reasons to leave, he must go for now but would be back soon, and finally, after a couple months of hard work, he hitched up to the trailer and attacked that last U-turn. When he was almost there, halfway through the last corner of the switchbacks, the whole kit and kaboodle, trailer and boat, went sailing over the ledge and plummeted down the ravine to the edge of the river a few hundred yards below. Bow first, bell second, treasure third, finally resting under a tree, undamaged and very hard to get to. The descent was only witnessed by God, so it was hard to say exactly what happened, but she arrived intact, which was way beyond crucial. *Vanessa* sat sheltered and stranded under a mighty cottonwood tree, and she would be there until the water lifted her off the trailer. When he pictured that scene someday in the future, where he'd be dealing with the rising water, he joyfully realized that she would float again much sooner and way ahead of schedule, years ahead of his original plans.

So, then what happened? Instead of getting started with any of at least a dozen super important projects, what did the captain do? It's hard to fathom (an ancient sailors term for someone being stupid), but it's like everyone knows and is almost impossible to fathom; the captain of the *Vanessa* decided to go fishing in the raging torrent known as the San Juan River in the middle of the gorge. Nobody in their right mind fished the San Juan River for a whole slew of issues that lined up below the number one question: Why would you ever want to do such a stupid ass thing? WHY, WHY, WHY, and not only that, he managed to drag his good friend and neighbor Rahellio and his son along for the adventure. That was, in fact, a simple matter concerning their wages, extreme wages in anybody's book, twenty-four hours a day, for a week or two, they weren't quite sure, and then after the last three days or more, it all seemed to be over, with the captain and his first mate still missing those three days from their memory.

It can get so dark at times there in the canyons that a person can't see their hand in front of their face. There are other times, like during the full moon stages, when the weather is perfect, and the land is lit up like a bright light bulb is floating across the sky, and some people can function really well in that kind of light. Armies can move across the land under the moonlight, just like during the day, without the scalding sun, if things are planned correctly. It crossed his mind as he leaned against the wall, staring into the fire, that all of his stories and adventures, especially the wars and those memories, everything about his life had led him to this wall, and in fact, his life was beginning again. Here he was starting all over, could do it here or there or anywhere, and was gradually piecing it all together as to precisely what had happened to his tiny world. According to the information in his briefcase, his wealth was hard to measure; it grew exponentially every day, developed on top of itself, and forced itself to grow. One of the things that made it so successful was that it happened to a greater degree to everyone involved in any way, shape, or form in the operation. While reading the back of the third page, he felt as if he was reading something that had never been printed before, a form that took the proceeds from the treasure, creating this bud of a business. This revolutionary business opportunity was hard to describe, like a one in a trillion sort of a thing, hard to measure, and luckily for the captain of the *Vanessa*, a legendary man who guided her to her present location, he was in the right place at the right time. *Vanessa* sat laden with a great treasure on board, twenty-four containers of priceless artifacts and the like from antiquity. Without even knowing it happened and a myriad of questions with few answers, during the fishing trip to the raging torrent, something happened, and the trip got all messed up. The trio got sick, the dog got stuck, and it was right then and there when they both agreed they couldn't remember much for the next three days, seventy-two hours; they couldn't remember squat.

The one crucial thing that he knew for a fact was that they had seen petroglyphs on the walls where they camped and decided the rest of the world didn't need to reinvestigate the place; it could cancel the entire project, Navajo Dam would never happen, and *Vanessa* would never float again. With those conditions filling up the scales of justice, the Candelarias agreed to graze their flock south of the critter gate and down into the canyon where it was hard on sheep, but nothing erases horse prints like a herd of lambs and ewes. So Rahellio and his wife, along with two Ute shepherds and Van Vedic, erased their former horse prints, and at one point two days ago, both he and Rahellio got totally lost following their own tracks. Got lost a few times, gave up, turned around, and left the valley for good. They talked about it, tried to figure out how true horsemen like themselves could get lost like that, no bullshashiska in Espanol, and then it clicked. Some great power was keeping them out, they would never be allowed back in that bottomland ever again, and that was just fine and dandy with Vincent. Neither man liked the idea that they shared such an amnesia, and since they had such limited resources, it seemed they would be forced into submission and just let it be. Just like Tommy said, 'move on.'

A furniture store there in Arboles was beautifully crafting all of his furniture out of cedar and pine and had delivered quite a bit of it to the bottom of the switchbacks, with the agreement that the captain would load it in his deuce and haul it up the switchbacks himself. The lead carpenter and owner was himself a big fella and had designed Van Vedic's bed with a firm understanding of what that meant if one is three hundred pounds and two and a half meters long. His furnishings were somewhat lacking, and there was good reason for that, but the kitchen table and three chairs were a welcome addition, which he had converted into his desk. He began to study the pages Rahellio's wife had drawn up that showed how both the captain and her husband quit remembering what they were doing around five in the afternoon on Friday and re-entered a conscious state on Monday about the same time.

"Dizzy?" The room was very quiet, the fire was silent, and when he looked up above his right shoulder and said that word without any warning, someone up there whispered his title, very faint, distant, "Captain," in response. It was a test and proved there was someone close by, watching, listening, so he repeated it. "Dizzy?" Nothing could be heard the second time. "DIZZY!" Nor the third.

On the back side of the moon, the chatter and chaos were in full swing, and from there on out, it had the Universe in a five-alarm fire. No one knew precisely why. What was all the fuss, what seemed to be the problem? One extremely powerful legal faction stated over and over that Van Vedic had promised not to tell what he wasn't supposed to tell, and all of the naysayers were to remember that the Watchers let it be known the captain had been awarded a #1 rating for having saved the queens. The #1 rating had only been given to a dozen humans over the last thirty-six thousand years, with Vincent Van Vedic creating a dodecahedron of #1s. The Universal odds makers had been sitting on eleven #1s for so long that most constituents gave up on the wait and turned into non-believers who claimed it would never happen again. When *0* lifted off the Earth with the queens, those two humans became cosmic legends. For the Universe, that meant something. A really big deal. It might even involve naming a mandatory Universal holiday after the captain. "THE SNAKE SLAYER FOUR-DAY WEEKEND." (Note: That would be a standard four-day weekend according to the original third planet mean-time Oranian.)

The real question seemed to be, should Dizzy be allowed to say hello? The arguments against breaking the time-honored rules of the *Gold Book* versus the well-known fact that, more than likely, complete contact was just around the corner for this planet and its inhabitants were being bandied about from all corners of the Universe. The captain was, by all standards, really close to what the experts were looking for in a test they planned to use someday soon. This year, 1953, the Nobel Prize went to the discoverers of the double helix, even though mankind didn't know exactly what it meant. The two men had only gone and discovered the double-helix structure of the DNA and life itself. That was big, very big. Vincent Van Vedic seeing the blue light was also big, just as big, and saving the queens was the biggest of all.

Since he got no answer, or so he thought, Vincent went back to writing about what had happened to the treasure and the bell, where he was in the process, and how he would leave for Aztec in a day or two. High on his imaginary friends' list was the entity that had emptied the *Vanessa* and brought the bell and the empty boxes to his casa. That being (or beings) hadn't come from here, weren't earthlings, but they seemed to understand big earthlings like the captain. The logistics of what had happened to everything had humbled the big man to the point where he was stupefied by the magnitude of it all, all the gold and silver that was in the boxes and barrels, all the jewels and coins, the crowns, and tonight, the results of the inventory indicated almost all of it had vanished. Unbelievable!

Then, and quite possibly most important, was the bell itself. What could a person say about that bell? It had been picked up and brought to the deuce, a mere six hundred pounds plus, polished like an eating utensil, and was shackled down tight to the pallet Van Vedic had made for it back in Russia. The only person on the planet who would ever understand and appreciate all this would be him.

The complexity of what he understood the treasure to be had been simplified to four pages in a briefcase. All that work, all that worry and difficulties had vanished, and he'd been left with one more task to fulfill. Even that had been simplified to the most simple—all he had left to do was put the truck in gear and deliver the pallet to the train yard in Aztec. They should enclose it in a box of plywood, protect it from the rain, and he could ride along in the passenger cars, personally deliver the bell to Holy Cross, stay as long they allowed, and then ride the train back. There were few other options.

CHAPTER TWENTY-FIVE

A GOLDEN NEW BELL

In no time at all, Vincent arrived in Aztec with a long list of things to do, but when he got to the station, all his plans changed. He discovered that the only train meeting his needs was arriving in a few hours and then leaving immediately for the hazardous journey over the two passes and arriving in Walsenburg, where he'd have to change trains and climb aboard the Super Chief. The complication was that with it being late October, the weather could change on a dime and an early winter storm could close things down till spring.

While he stood at the ticket counter and listened to the manager talk about his incredibly lucky timing and the possibility of it being the last train that way this year, none of that news made Vincent feel all that lucky. He felt rushed, cramped, and all sorts of no good, but then he realized this was typical. Everything that was happening had probably been arranged by the same entity who had organized everything else

375

along the way. He always came up with that logic that justified the predestination of it all, and just like that, he was waiting at this train station. No point in wasting time. He bought the ticket, paid the freight charge, and then paid a steward twenty dollars to take a message to Vannie as fast as he could. The telephone operator said Vannie was out of her shop and they didn't know where she was. They'd keep trying to get her on the line somewhere.

"Ugh, Dizzy, Dizzy, you up there? A little help if you don't mind."

He hastily wrote her a message that asked her to come to the railyard and see the bell. The train was on its way, had passed through Farmington, and would be in Aztec in forty-five minutes or so. Time was up, and the yard hands had to box it up for the trip to Kansas, get it up on the dock and ready to be loaded. The same held true for the passengers. The long-haul conductors on the "ten-car choo-choos" seemed to think they owned the terminals they were passing through. There were stops along the line that proved they needed extra time and patience, sometimes stopping for twenty or thirty minutes, but Aztec wasn't one of them. It was against the superintendents' better instincts to waste time waiting when they didn't have all that much in the first place, and this operation wasn't allowing for any complications. It was all pretty straightforward. Box it up and prepare it because these guys don't waste time waiting on coulda, shoulda, or woulda.

Vincent and the yard superintendent talked for a while as soon as the captain entered the yard, with him going from very casual and laid back as he explained what he was doing, where he was going, and what he needed done with the bell to rushed like crazy.

First things first. He needed a large packing blanket, because he didn't want the world to see what he had done to the bell.

The super had seen it when the *Vanessa* was unloaded that day it arrived a few months before, and being the sort of man who understood heavy steel and things like railroad ties, he looked at the bell for a few moments and then practically fell out of the truck.

When he returned with the blanket, he handed it to the captain and didn't say a word. He tilted his head to one side, and his eyes screamed a dozen questions without him actually saying something. Sitting under the rear window was the HDLPA, and that was precisely where Van Vedic put it when the super said he could have it. It hadn't been moved, and people who are familiar with six-hundred-pound bells and HDLPAs know that they go hand in hand —very carefully, cautiously, because of all sorts of reasons. It was the nature of the beast for the super to question everything about how and when and where, and all the others, like why the bell ended up coated in some sort of golden paint. Its wooden collar was of the finest workmanship possible, and there was no doubt the T-clangor was a unique piece of hardware that needed to be absolutely secure.

Building freight boxes is an art form for the railroads; they are designed around the idea of forklifts loading and unloading four-foot square boxes really fast at any station along the way. The plan was pretty simple. Cover the bell with the blanket, pull it out from under the canvass, and attach all four side sheets to themselves and to the oak pallet. Cover it with a cap sheet and call it a done deal with time to spare.

The super was disappointed for Van Vedic, because someone he was waiting for never showed up. Too bad, so sad.

They loaded the bell in about five minutes, took the captain's ticket stub, along with quite a few others, and the train whistled that sound that wouldn't be heard again in the not-so-distant future. The narrow gage lines were almost things of the past unless it was for tourists.

Vincent's accommodations were perfect, practically a rolling leisure lounge with food and beverage and periodic stops in small towns. In many cases, the train rolled through the towns but never stopped. Unfortunately, he'd had to make this journey at night, but the only light in the sky turned out to be a spectacular full moon the world had always dubbed the harvest moon for obvious reasons.

His conductor never rested through the night and the very early morning hours, passing through the car and making small talk with the captain, who seemed mesmerized by the scenery. He acted like a tour guide; he'd found a passenger who didn't know much about the countryside or any of the famous names of places and the histories of the many towns they passed through. Before long, the whole lounge car was full of passengers drinking and chatting and listening to stories from the conductor.

Van Vedic started a story about riding the Siberian railroad from one side of Russia to the other, ten time zones, and his audience and new-found friends couldn't get enough of either man or their laurels. In some stretches through high mountain passes, the train literally crawled along as the stories kept coming. Without the input from a friendly conductor, those long slow climbs could become very tedious. Still, this guy had all that stuff timed and could help the passengers know that it wouldn't be long and this little locomotive would be churning through the flat lands between Wolf Creek Pass and La Veta Pass. Both had always represented major obstacles to man's ability to cross over and through the Rockies, peaks that top out at fourteen thousand feet or better. Almost all the roads are tenuous at best, especially in the winter, and sometimes they say there is no gas available when the cars and trucks need it most.

Vincent considered he might have to cross that bridge in his future, but he'd have to have a car or a truck, and currently, as they pulled into the Walsenburg terminal, he was as excited as he'd ever been about anything. His conductor told them all about the Chief, how it veered off the main line from Albuquerque to Denver and headed across Kansas straight for Hays and Victoria. He was about to go faster than he'd ever gone in his life, a hundred miles an hour at times, inside the Santa Fe Super Chief.

Periodically during the nighttime voyage, the captain had napped and might have even snored a bit, but his seat in the lounge car was made for his derriere, and the bartender had only been a high wave away when he was awake. He had a compartment that was made for Jimmy Durante. It had a door that was just barely wide enough if he turned sideways, and the toilet was so small it forced him to piss in that area between the cars when he went for a walk. A person could stand safely in the space between the cars, lean out over the safety chains and see the engine blowing smoke, the coal car, and two freight cars ahead of the sleeping compartments car, or look back in time and see the caboose five cars in the rear.

Vincent had a fantastic dinner that took two hours to finish, and during that time the moon came up and showered the pitch-black countryside with as bright a light as was possible from such an unnatural object. While staring at the moon at two a.m. that morning, he kept having twitches and felt like there was someone on the moon looking straight at him. He'd never had that thought before, never thought of the moon as a place where other beings lived. It lit away the darkness as it rose and then set, rose again, and set behind some distant Rocky Mountain peak. Finally, it rose for good, and for extended periods it seemed to center itself in the upper arch of his window, all because of the way the train was traveling, lighting the landscape that flowed by his huge private window with a light all its own. When the grade was not in her favor, the Rio Grande Northern putted along at times at only ten or fifteen miles an hour, but she had a faster side when things were flat and level.

The wait in Walsenburg was only an hour. A small crowd with their luggage waited for the Super Chief that was coming up from Albuquerque. It would stop briefly in Walsenburg, then again in Pueblo and finally Colorado Springs, where the beautiful train turned due east and out onto the Kansas plains. It was three hundred and fifty miles, somewhat downhill, and there were stretches in there where the four engines up front would pull the load at over a hundred and ten miles per hour. All in all, the captain estimated the journey would take eighteen to twenty hours, maybe more, maybe less, but he was positive he didn't care about the time in the slightest. When he got to Hays, he'd be there, not too soon and not too late, and the only person who knew he was coming was himself.

He could only hope that a small welcoming committee would be available to take possession of the bell, and he pictured unboxing the jewel with his well-rehearsed speech as to what it was and where it had come from. He had been able to arrange for a delivery service to pick up the box, and there was one other thing he was positive about—that he could have never driven the deuce through those mountains or on that highway that paralleled the train tracks. The train would often go considerably faster than the cars, and the roads didn't look all that great. The one thing he had noticed so far was that everything in America was a hundred times better than back in Russia.

The Santa Fe Super Chief was a state-of-the-art machine that rolled out of Colorado Springs and raced from one stop to the next before the Victoria station covering the long stretches like a red-nosed bullet. The observation cars had speedometers on the walls that kept the passengers' attention. As the train got closer and closer to a hundred miles per hour, the passengers would start to raise the noise level, whistle, and shout out famous three-worders. Some folks were screaming. The only way to go any faster would require wings, and that's not the same.

Just like on the Rocky Mountain Northern, the much larger cars on the Super Chief had half doors on both sides, front and back, between the cars, where speed buffs could stand and smoke and feel the wind when the beast was cooking out on the plains. Trying to keep up with the aerodynamic silver streak on Highway 40 was futile, but it sure was fun to watch the boy racers.

Traditionally railroad cars had a "Conductor," whose job was to frequently walk through the cars and announce to everyone the name of the station just up ahead and how long the stop would be. They knew everything about everything and kept a tight ship if they could. Van Vedic was staring out the windows of the lounge car once again and knew he was getting close to his destination when he heard the shout, "Next station, Victoria, Kansas, thirty minutes, please, thirty minutes."

His suitcase was full of clothes he had acquired in Corpus Christi, held an extra pair of boots, and the thing only weighed fifty pounds. Usually, he kept things simple regarding clothes, and if and when he needed new things, he would find a seamstress who would clean it first and then duplicate the piece so that he had extras, and they always fit the same. Same with pants and socks. Six foot eight, three hundred pounds, those clothes weren't on the rack. He climbed off the train and onto a long boardwalk that led to the freight office. The bell in the box was sitting under a canopy that protected freight from whatever, with a big painted sign that said, "Ring the ding-a-ling at the counter if you need assistance." The simple fact that the bell had beat him to this spot proved this bell had a mind all its own and couldn't wait to be hung once again, but even though the captain lost the race to get to the loading dock first, he was very happy about that, happy the bell was here first. It would be a shame and a tragedy if anything should go wrong from here on out, and the captain assured the bell in the box that he was close by and things were under control.

The train had pulled into one of the longest train yards out west, a few miles past Hays and halfway to Victoria, and around nine a.m. that day unloaded a small amount of freight, including the captain's four-by-four plywood mystery box, along with the captain himself and a few others. A few folks got on, and then the Santa Fe Super Chief whistled goodbye; she was gone out of sight and sound after only a twenty-minute stop, headed for Topeka and the start of the bridges that take the tracks over the rivers, on its way to Chicago and Philadelphia.

Theoretically, the final destination was only ten miles due south from this platform on a county road called Pfeiffer Avenue, believe it or not, straight like an arrow across flat land, just like back in the fertile Volga Basin in Russia. According to his directions, Vincent would be passing intersections with street names just like back in Russia, one after another. Dirt roads that met Pfeiffer Avenue with stop signs for everyone, even if no one was coming. Every side road went to the horizon, with names like Kamshyn, Schoenchen, or other familiar Russian names, with the instructions saying "…just keep going straight down Pfeiffer, and I don't mean maybe. Straight south on Pfeiffer to the horizon, and then the next horizon, and finally to the hill overlooking Pfeiffer, where Holy Cross Church stands like a beacon down in the river valley."

Holy Cross was on the Smokey Hill River, where the original settlers made their home back in the 1880s. It was a story very similar to Saint Francis of Assisi on the Illava River in Russia one hundred years before, in the 1770s. The patriarch of the entire clan, Johan Adam Thomae, traveled from his village named Lohr am Main, somewhere in the northern Rhineland, to their new village, Pfeiffer on the Illava. That epoch journey took two years for Thomae, and his descendants would live in that garden of Eden until insanity took over Russia. There near the end, during the 1880s and early 1890s, all of Thomae's fourth and fifth-generation children left the fertile Volga Basin and fled to America, to Kansas, to where the buffalo roamed, where the tornados came down from heaven, where the bugs tried to eat them alive, and scraping out a living was one way of saying it.

Van Vedic had gotten off the train and watched as the bell in the box was unloaded from one of the freight cars. The forklift guy sat it down carefully at the end of a loading platform while this gigantic smiling Texan watched him do his job. Vincent walked over to where it sat and signed a ticket saying it wasn't damaged in any way and he accepted the charge. Right on time, he ended up being described as the tall man with a suitcase and a plywood box on the platform and waiting for a ride. The bell from Saint Francis was now only ten miles from the end of the road, so to speak. The captain was optimistic, at the time, that the freight company had received their assignment to pick up the package at the station and deliver it to the rectory at Holy Cross Catholic Church in Pfeifer. He was assured of the pickup date and time with a receipt via Western Union that explained the bill, including a trip charge of forty-five miles from shop to shop. Fortunately, or unfortunately, it hadn't been determined just yet that the captain was the only person who didn't have a ride in all this, and as fate would have it, the freight company was having several issues and would probably be late. There was mass confusion by all sorts of people. The Atchison, Topeka and Santa Fe staff didn't even know that the train had come and gone, so Vincent walked off to find a car.

From this point on, he knew he had a few options, one of which was to ride the train back to where he had come from and rent a car for a few days while doing his business. Another one, and the one he liked the most, was the one where he drove his own car. He'd never owned one, and he had learned from the railyard hands in Aztec that one of the best places to get a new car was in Victoria, Kansas. The car lots were everywhere on the highway back to Hays, fascinating places where new cars were lined up side by side, row after row. He'd never seen anything like it. There were Fords and Chevrolets, plus Plymouth and many others. He was trying to digest this new country he was in, every window full, and so far, almost every town was a new frontier. He had missed so much of the countryside because he had traveled at night, but what he had seen had been glorious, and the train was on schedule like a timepiece.

The train had crept through Hays, from one side to the other, down the tracks a way to the new terminal complex. The old terminal had been used back in the civil war times and was where all the immigrants got off back in the 1890s when there was free land. The old terminal was where Desch and Domme ended up, Christmas 1892, together with their families, along with everyone else who had climbed on board the SS Foust Bismarck out of Hamburg who survived the transatlantic trip, and then the train trip from Philadelphia to Hays. They all showed up in the late fall of 1892, got off the train, and started to walk. They would have called first, but you know how it goes. They would have written, but you know how that works.

All the men and women who left in that caravan, all their

children and little suitcases, hundreds and hundreds of Pfeiffer peasants, illiterate old-world Catholics and immediate relatives, doubling the population at the wilderness commune one freezing cold late November afternoon. The commune council of concerned local Catholics had evaluated everything at their disposal not even a week before their in-laws and relatives had arrived, and produced a report. You talk about a sad report— well, this report was really sad, and the council suggested that everyone plan on having a very hard winter in 1892. The winters on the Kansas plains were horrible, but now, after twenty years since the first settlers had arrived, they had learned all sorts of things and would probably survive. For the most part, the Civil War fighting was over, but there were still crazy factions roaming the territory, but for the most part, it seemed as though the Indians were gone. Sometimes the buffalo wandered across the hillsides on the other side of the river, but they were so dumb and so scary it was best that they stayed over there.

The modern-day loading docks at the train station seemed to be the unloading dock for every car dealership in central Kansas, along with just about everything else made east of the Missouri river. As he watched the beautiful new cars rolling off the distant railcar, Vincent instantly fell in love with one particular model. They parked her at the end of the last row of dirty and dusty new arrivals, a Plymouth Cranbrook Belvedere two-door sedan. It was a two-tone model, dark forest green on top, hood to trunk, and light forest green on both sides, front to back, with the whole puppy being trimmed in half-inch wide stainless steel skirting and molding. The future owner followed on foot to a storage lot at the end of the street, caught the driver by surprise, and wanted to know everything about that car the boy had just parked.

The young shuttle driver, Lloyd Junior, was the son of the man who owned the dealership. He began to list everything about the Belvedere that a sixteen-year-old might know. She had a flathead six-cylinder engine that could generate a hundred and four horsepower, a twenty-two-gallon gas tank, with the whole thing weighing two tons or more, and even had two spare tires. The seats were the finest naugahyde available and guaranteed not to shrink, crack, or ever wear out.

Van Vedic examined the engine, the dash, and the trunk, got in on the shotgun side and told the lad to take him and the car to see his daddy.

He loved her the minute he saw her and felt she could make it over the mountains on his way home. She even had seat belts, a built-in radio, an excellent heater, and a cigar lighter. It looked like she could go a hundred miles an hour, had a three-on-the-tree transmission, and the front seat went back almost far enough for a man his size. He would not be needing the pillow.

At the local car dealership, the owner, Lloyd McKee, sold him the 1953 Plymouth, the first one to make it this far west, slid the seat back as far as possible, had the captain climb in, and they went for a test drive. Lloyd flowed through the gears and explained the clutch to the truck driver—a much different feeling from that of a deuce. What a smooth-running machine it was. When Vincent admitted to many never haves and first times, the consummate salesman slowed things down and taught his best class.

The inside smelled like nothing he'd ever smelled before, and it was virtually quiet running down the road. For the most part, it was an easy sell once the captain found the driver's seat, got her going, and practiced all sorts of things on a back country road under Lloyd's direction. Eventually, his face relaxed, and his hands on the huge round steering wheel calmed down, so much so that he rolled down the window and put his elbow out into the wind. When he stepped on the gas, they were going sixty miles an hour in no time at all. The speedometer suggested it could go a hundred, but it wasn't a very good idea.

McKee got a smile on his face, and you could tell he liked speed; he cautioned the driver about that and told him how speed kills people like crazy in the cities. Speed, liquor, and lousy roads and mud, and then said a wise man always buys the best tires made in Topeka and always has two spares. On the way back to his office, he started talking about how all the big car makers were getting away from flatheads and converting to V8s. It would change everything, but for now, the big flathead 6 was the best he had for sale. Forty miles to a gallon of gas, a very simple engine to work on, and the interior was a heavy-duty modern-day fabric that takes a beating but still looks nice. Sold!

This would turn out to be as fateful as all the other encounters concerning the bell in the box, because McKee was married into a huge family of Catholics who were parishioners of Holy Cross in Pfeiffer. The man owned a large tract of land just west of Pfeiffer, had a big family, and they had electricity and a community phone line. When he heard why Van Vedic was visiting and the plans for delivering the bell to Holy Cross, he became overwhelmed and collapsed in his new sales room. He didn't hurt himself; just sat there refusing help of any sort. He had sort of slid down the wall looking at his customer.

"I understood you to say you lived in New Mexico."

"I do."

"You have brought a church bell from Pfeiffer, Russia, via New Mexico, and your plan is to deliver it to Holy Cross there in Pfeiffer. Free of charge? Is that what's in the big box? I'm a parishioner there. I'm active, very active, and I don't believe we knew you were coming. No sir, if we did, I'd have known about it. How big is this bell? Desch and some of the others are going to go apeshit!"

The captain reached down and helped McKee to his feet.

"My friend, it's roughly four feet tall and is, in fact, the original bell from Saint Francis of Assisi on the Illava, in Pfeiffer, Russia. The church burned down in 1928. It's a very long story, and I'll be able to tell it to you and any others when we get there today. Briefly, however, to help you wrap your mind around all this, I can tell you I've just arrived in the USA back in July. After a long trip getting to America, I bought some land in northern New Mexico, and now I have a ranch there that I need to eventually get back to before winter sets in."

"Is this a joke?"

"Absolutely not. There is no obligation or charge. It's exactly what I say."

"The bell in our beautiful church has cracked up the side and has been rendered useless. It's no longer a bell—more like a gong—and seems to be unsalvageable. We've despaired to some degree over the situation. The bell has always been used to call the faithful, and in these flat lands, the sound travels for miles and miles from a high bell tower like the one at Holy Cross."

"Do these people remember where they came from?"

"Many are gone, and you can be sure of that. The men had to go where the jobs were, and the World War caused us all sorts of grief, unearned grief. Those who are still left—and to be honest, there aren't many—those people live it and breathe it daily. Many still speak the language from the old world, although the government forbid such talk during the war. Ragas German, they call it, but it's mingled and blended by a hundred and twenty-five years of living in Russia."

"There's nothing left of such things over there in the Illava valley anymore, and fortunately, one of the evilest of them all was gone earlier this year—so they say. The monster Stalin will be hard to forget, but I'm certain they will replace him with his equal, if not worse."

"Mister Van Vedic, may I offer my services to you. I am a former parish council president, and I can get our pastor on the line before we head that way. I would be honored to ride with you to the side of our church and help unload that crate. I wonder where the delivery company is that you said was supposed to be here."

"They must have broken down somewhere. Here's my Western Union letter. It seems to be some guy named Basgall. Basgall's LBA freight and baggage."

"Whoa there, cowboy. Basgall, you say? He's a baseball player from Pfeiffer, and that LBA stands for low batting average. Plus, I know him. He's just about the greatest, the only guy who ever made a name for himself, and it ain't over yet. He's tied up coaching, and I think you have an old contract here. If I may, may I take care of everything from here on out? You just get comfortable in that driver's seat, get used to the Belvedere, and I'll get you to the church on time. Wait till you see Holy Cross. It's a beautiful church and is only thirty minutes down the road here a way. I do it twice a day, almost every day."

After signing all the papers and the captain paying cash for the car, the men got in and headed for the outskirts of Victoria for a test drive and beginner-driver's lessons for the buyer, it would turn out. They took dirt county roads to Hays and back, practiced all sorts of driving skills, and with the captain totally lost, they found themselves at the far end of a dirt road back in Victoria.

Lloyd always took his customers through the same course of streets and straight county roads where they would let it out, so to speak. Far in front, Vincent could see two enormous church steeples out the car's front window, which readily confused him, because he thought there was only one. There was only one bell in the box, and the driver couldn't remember the church being so close to the railroad tracks. Due to the fact that he was totally lost, he thought he was already there, which got a laugh out of Lloyd. His guide explained the confusion and said that what he was seeing was the top of the Cathedral on the Plains, not Holy Cross. Holy Cross was over the second horizon due south, maybe ten miles.

"The Cathedral on the Plains is one of the wonders of Kansas and is as magnificent a church as anyone can find. It's the biggest there is and has far and away the most parishioners, who come from all over the county for the services. In fact, big, beautiful Catholic churches are all over the place. Every town has one, and every church steeple has a bell. The Cathedral in Victoria has two large bells, and some say those bells can be heard from fifty miles away, especially when considering the collection plates of all the neighboring churches. Have you gone through a lot of trouble to get the bell here to Victoria?"

"Trouble? What trouble?"

Lloyd made a few phone calls while they waited for the bell in the box to be loaded into an open-air small delivery truck that would take the package to its final destination. Lloyd was one of those people who just couldn't do enough when the situation needed somebody to step up and do something. One call was to his pastor, who had fortunately set that afternoon aside for his nap; one quickie to his brother Richard, who had all sorts of hidden talents; and one was to Desch, who would know what to do from the Parish Council point of view.

The captain was now down to ten miles or less and counting down towards completing his mission of delivering the church bell from Saint Francis to the doorsteps of Holy Cross in Pfeiffer, Kansas. The captain instantly flashed back in time to 1941, when he and Father Jude pulled away from Father Basil there at the secret dock in Pfeiffer, Russia. He and Jude floated away from that chaos, and the story of Jude continued that day. One thing he remembered was how it was just like now, ten miles down the Illava, and they would float out into the Mighty Don and be on their way to the Mighty San Juan. Father Hammer had hoped and wished and dreamed that the bell might find such a step in the Kansas land, he'd told all that to Father Basil, who in turn told Van Vedic, and the rest is history.

His newfound tour guide was wrapping things up at the loading dock. The delivery truck would lead the way, driven by Lloyd's service and parts manager, a hard-nosed relative named LeoDan the Man, who didn't put up with no bullshashiska whatsoever from anyone at the thriving dealership. Unbeknownst to LeoDan the Man, the captain was listening when he mentioned to his two helping hands that he didn't need any "bullshashiska" during the loading procedures, and the word so shook him when it arrived that he wilted where he stood. He had never liked a man so fast and so much.

So the Belvedere would follow under the expert pilotmanship of Captain Vincent Van Vedic, following at a leisurely pace until he got the hang of things. It was just like that old letter said— Pfeiffer was as straight a road as a road could be. The intersecting streets were named after places and streets back in Russia near Pfeiffer, and they too were as straight as could be.

From out of nowhere, an emotion washed over the captain as he realized where he was. A small sign went by, advertising a store in Pfeiffer only five miles ahead, and at the next stop sign, the captain honked at the truck driver in front to stop.

They all sat at the intersection for twenty minutes, maybe, and Van Vedic asked Lloyd and LeoDan to walk to the top of the hill they were on and talk about what was out there in those fields. Van Vedic wanted to know everything. Who lived in those farmhouses they'd been passing and seeing here and there throughout the countryside? There were a lot of other questions, deep stuff, numbers of this, that, and the other, and the captain wanted their opinions about all sorts of things.

An ancient memory sat there on his shoulders, surrounded by the chaos of his own personal childhood insanity—him being only four years old, watching men driving away with his father's favorite horses, almost all of them, and also the wagons. Those men needed the wagons and horses to take their families to Hamburg and eventually to this dirt road in the heart of Kansas, USA. No one explained any of that to his tiny self, and all sorts of other horrors followed for years and years until things got better. It always works that way—things get better, and it's hard to remember the hard times.

He went and stood next to a sandstone pillar that was maybe five feet tall, sixteen inches square, two or three or even five hundred pounds, standing there angled in the dirt; they were all angled in the ground, but that was a result of time, and there were hundreds of them in an acre, pointing every which way except perfectly straight up. Once upon a time, they had, back when Alice lived in Wonderland in the next county and things didn't weigh as much as they do today. Thousands of them forming fence rows, corners, and edges, everywhere at the intersection and on all the right-angle corners of the intersecting two-lane dirt roads. Yellow stone pillars, heavy as all get-out. Lloyd said they dated back to a time when men didn't make mistakes when it came to marking the edges and corners of one man's world in relation to his brother. When they got here, they brought the idea from Russia, split up the land with a Godly honesty to the whole thing, and nothing had ever changed. Those ancient forefathers went through a lot of trouble to set corner posts and straight-line edges that couldn't be easily changed. As they engineered their acres, they wrote it all down, recorded it, and so be it.

Van Vedic was encouraging both his guides to teach him everything they thought he might want to know about all those people who had come here before the bell. Neither man had seen it yet, could only use their imagination as to what it might look like, and sure as all get-out, it weighed in at an even six hundred and eighty pounds, including the packaging. So here they were, standing on a straight-as-an-arrow two-lane dirt road, sharing stories. After listening to both storytellers and their tales of what mattered, the captain was satisfied that his effort had been worth it, with only five more miles to go until they got there. Pfeiffer was just over the next horizon.

CHAPTER TWENTY-SIX

FIVE MORE MILES TO GO

Father Christian Foy of Holy Cross was looking forward to his nap when the phone began to ring in the office. The operator said it was Lloyd McKee calling from his car lot in Victoria, and his tone was guarded; there was no telling which operator was plugging in the lines on the community line. McKee mumbled something about the pastor not leaving because he was bringing a surprise guest, and said they'd be there in an hour or so. The car dealer asked the reverend if he wanted one of the sandwiches from the hamburger joint everyone used, to which he said, "Yes, only make it two; the double-decker with cheese."

The captain was treated to a couple of good old-fashioned smothered hamburgers with all sorts of trimmings, and four-inch long French fries with brown gravy. A fellow named Old McDonald had a farm, but he retired from that. He built a restaurant on the edge of town, and they specialized in doing it fast, no bullshashiska, get them made and out the door hot. Rumor had it that McDonald was considering putting one in Hays and some more in two or three other spots in the area. LeoDan the Man insisted they stop there on their way out of town. It was way past lunchtime, after all.

By the time McKee finished his calls he had orders from everyone, totaling twenty burgers and all sorts of other eatables and drinks. They planned to eat at the church there just off the right side front steps in an hour. Desch would notify a few of his staff, and his brother did the same. All the guests were left guessing about everything except the food. It was just like McKee to bait them all, tickle their curiosities, and insist on their attendance no matter what. He had raised the rally flag, and all the Knights of the Pfeiffer Council were to convene at the church as soon as possible. Word went out from the parish office via the phone channels to an extensive list of active church members; not an emergency but a come-and-see request.

After the brief chat on the side of the road, they continued south on Pfeiffer Avenue, stirring up dust and getting closer by the minute. The captain's forearms were tingling, and the goosebumps were everywhere after McKee said they would see the church in one more moment off to the right and down in the river valley. Still half a mile away, he could see how the bell tower seemed to rise a hundred and fifty feet, maybe more, and would be a fitting location for the bell in the box.

The moment the captain first saw it, he honked for LeoDan to stop, parked the Belvedere on the side of the road, got out at the top of the turn, and took pictures of the village from up there. In one snapshot, he silhouetted the church and its steeple with the plywood box in the back of the delivery truck. For the longest time, he was guilty of just standing in the middle of the road, and the traveler let his mind retrace some of the places and faces, and memories preceding this hour in time.

The journey for this bell started when the bell tower collapsed during the fire in 1928. It lay in a hole in the floor of the church until around New Year's weekend, 1942, when it was resurrected, put on the captain's boat, and brought to America. That ten-thousand-mile-long journey was now ending on this late October afternoon 1953.

His two new friends were only partially understanding what the moment was all about, but since there was no traffic whatsoever, his fan club gave the cowboy all the time he needed. Besides all that, after having known the man for a few hours now, both Lloyd and LeoDan the Man had noticed that captain had a twitch of some sort up and to his right that he twitched periodically. When it happened the third time inside the Belvedere, Van Vedic gave a mischievous smile at his passenger and said, "I got it during the war. It won't go away."

"Sorry. May I ask which war?"

"World War One in Ukraine, then the Russian Revolution at the end of that war, on the red side, and we won. Then, a campaign to open up the railroad in the east that lasted for three years in the early thirties and is unknown to history, all for no glory, where men fought and died for and against the railroad. No one knew why they opposed the idea with such a passion, but they did. They just fought and died and then quit. Stupid! I inherited the bell in the box in Pfeiffer, Russia, at the end of 1941. A priest named Jude and I floated down the Don river before Operation Barbarossa got there a few months after we left. The Battle of Stalingrad, quite possibly the greatest battle in the history of mankind, happened fifty miles south of Pfeiffer during the winter of '42. It might be a while before the west appreciates that battle and how decisive it was, because the west wasn't there. There were no Allies in that battle, just Russians and Germans, and without a doubt, it was a turning point. Our beloved sister city was way too close, totally and completely obliterated in two separate artillery battles. I'm planning to go back and visit the area if the officials will let me. I have to know what happened and find out what's left.

"There were other reasons for my voyage besides bringing the bell to this church—that we may or may not get into on this trip. I plan to write and publish a chronicle of the journey, detailing everything, and of course, what happens here in Kansas is an integral part of the saga. Besides the bell, I have some of the church records from Saint Francis of Assisi Catholic Church that I am positive folks like yourselves have never seen. Unfortunately, the minor basilica where so many of this community's forefathers and mothers were baptized, confirmed, married, and buried was burned to its floorboards on Easter Sunday 1928, but these records survived, and you'll be glad they did. To be honest, I didn't even know we had packed them."

CHAPTER TWENTY-SEVEN

YOURE THE GUNSLINGER, AREN'T YOU

The Holy Cross Church was one of the architectural wonders of Kansas, its style Gothic, with a matching rectory, convent, and schoolhouse, but there was one thing missing from that vantage point on the road: the town. Where was it? There were ten or twenty buildings here and there, but nothing close to what Vincent was expecting. He could see houses with small garages and barns on some of the streets, and a few storefronts down on all four corners of an intersection of two dirt roads. The river's edge was the end of the community to the south and was the main reason why Pfeiffer Avenue detoured off a perfectly straight line and down into the river valley after ten miles.

It sure was pretty, very peaceful, and small, much smaller than he had imagined. Perhaps there was more to it than he could see. These people had one spectacular church, and that was for sure. Not as big as the Cathedral on the Plains but just about as lovely a church as a person could bend a knee in. Spectacular in every way—and now they would have a bell to match their altar.

LeoDan the Man was leaning against the side of his truck, his arms folded, staring at the church from a vantage point he had actually never appreciated in his past. He had not once stopped on the road like this, and now was seeing Pfeiffer through Van Vedic's eyes.

"Does this view remind you of the old world church? You were there in your youth?" he asked the captain.

"I was baptized at Saint Francis, born about ten miles north of Pfeiffer, and I survived the famine. This place I'm looking at only existed in my imagination until this moment, and I'm very pleased with the vision. I've always wondered where they went and what they made when they got there. Saint Francis was a big church with a triple bell tower, one big bell tower with two smaller bells tiered just below, just like what I'm looking at, except the building was made of wood. I see peace and tranquility with only half a mile to go, and I hope that's how things are going for these people. It's none of my business, I'm just a delivery boy, but I can tell you Pfeiffer, Russia, was in the way of the Russian Revolution, and worst of all, as everyone knows, fifty miles north of Stalingrad. Operation Barbarossa ended on the edge of Pfeiffer, which ended Pfeiffer as a place. When the Germans first arrived in the general area of Pfeiffer in the early fall of 1942, they destroyed the 'front' with artillery and aerial bombardment, all guided by 'forward observers.' Soldiers who were far out in front of the tanks and infantry and adjusted the big guns' points of impact. It is a military art form, and the good ones are very good at pinpointing the shells in the flatlands because they can see so far. The teams would find a hilltop from where to see all over everything and would then tell their gunners the adjustments until the distant target was no longer there. The guns were miles behind, constantly moving forward and systematically blowing everything to kingdom come. Pfeiffer and some other villages along the Illava River were blown to smithereens by German howitzers ten miles away.

"A few months later, in late November, the Russian army flowed right over the top of Pfeiffer, north to south, in a spectacular pincer movement known as Operation Uranus, led by more long-range artillery and dive bombers, acting like the icing on the cake if the idea was to turn the land into a desert. Only the Russians could understand their anger and hatred of the Germans for what they had done. In this case, they'd trapped the Hun in Stalingrad and turned the beast into a creature that ate itself, ate their fellow dead, drank their own piss, and surrendered in mass on the second of February 1943. What an insult to their pride and their honor. The dead Germans far outnumbered the survivors, and most of them would live to regret the fact they had survived. The Russians captured a hundred and some odd thousand Germans when it was all said and done, and those prisoners were marched up the western side of the Volga, passed by the grotto of where Saint Francis once stood, and were marched off north into the gulag of Siberia. I doubt they'll ever be seen again. No sir, they won't ever be back."

"Mr. Van Vedic, you speak English as well as any human I've ever talked to!"

"I speak several languages, thank you very much. It's not that difficult to erase the accents of both German and Russian. I'm sure you understand, because I know you folks were questioned about your patriotism if they sensed that German inflection in your speech. I have my pictures now, so we can go whenever you want and unload this gift."

"You can see the parking lot with those cars on the side of the church? That's where we're going. It looks to me like they're hungry. I can't wait to get there."

Off they went, down to the corner and turned left, with LeoDan pulling in backward up to the right rear steps that led up into the vestibule, where he came to a stop. The bell on the bow was now sitting at the foot of the beautiful bell tower of Holy Cross, and the resemblance to the exact same steps of Saint Francis had the captain's head in a whirl.

Vincent had parked the wagon in this very spot when they pulled the bell out of the hole it had been hidden in for over thirteen years with the two mystical war horses who made it look easy. The church had disintegrated, of course, and he remembered how the bell came up out of the hole, filthy dirty, covered in sludge, and then slid across the ancient black remnants of Saint Francis and dropped into the back of the wagon like it had a mind all its own and wanted to start its journey. There was no resistance from the marooned metal mass as it glided across the thirty-foot space, up to the edge, and over. It was a fulfilling first thought that the welcoming committee couldn't share. So far, they didn't know who he was or what was in the box. McKee never told them anything.

Once the Belvedere was parked, Lloyd told Vincent that none of them bit, and smiled. It wasn't but a few brief moments later, and the captain found himself surrounded by eight parishioners along with the pastor; everyone was smiling, ready to shake hands, and Lloyd did a miserable job of introducing the crowd to Mr. Vincent Van Vedic. Wearing a modest white cowboy hat that put him up near seven feet tall, he qualified right off the bat as the biggest male human being that had ever graced the community. Four nuns from the convent, including the mother superior, were very excited, standing off and out of the way, because this was how most of the statuary had arrived in the past.

Usually, they knew what it was, had been notified beforehand that something was on its way, but evidently not this time. This would be a total surprise.

Lloyd passed out all the remaining hamburgers and had to lie to several parish council members that he'd heard they only wanted one burger and not two. Sorry 'bout that. LeoDan had eaten four already, had number five in his hand, and was acting like the long stain of mustard on his belly was from yesterday. No one believed him, and Father Foy actually blessed him. McKee repeated the captain's name and suggested that the honored guest show and tell everyone exactly what was in the box and where it had come from.

Before he could start the introduction he had rehearsed quite a few times, a hard-looking sixty-year-old Kansas farmer dressed in overalls, with a corncob pipe sticking out of a unique sleeve there on his chest, a fairly dumbass straw hat if there ever was one adorning his head, and an empty holster there on his hip stepped forward.

"Mr. Van Vedic, I think I know who you are, and I am honored to be here and meet you. You're the Gunslinger, aren't you? My name is Xander Aloysius Desch the Third. Your father gave my father six horses and a new wagon so he could take grandma to Hamburg in 1891. Our family branch survived because of his generosity, and I can truthfully say the Desch family has, for the most part, been very happy in the new world. Not many of us left here in Pfeiffer, but it's a big family, and they're spread out all over the place. My father's best friend, Peter Aloysius Domme, left Russia during the drought and famine of 1891, dead last in the convoy that was leaving, and showed up here in 1892 with a wife and two kids, and now that family is as big as they get. There are many other household names who would all say the same thing. This is so wonderful. Welcome."

"Nice to meet you, and yes, I am who you said. Let the truth be known; I was there that day when two men came to our house and left with the horses and wagons. They were crying at the time, and I remember crying because I'd never seen men cry before. I was hoping to leave that nickname over there, but my love for the pistols will never leave, and I can't wait to find a range. It's a small world; we all know that. What goes around comes around, and there are a thousand other old sayings that help explain the past and the way things happen. Perhaps we could arrange for a group get-together after this initial presentation and I'll be able to fill in some of the gaps and answer some questions. For now, all I would need is a crowbar if someone might have such a tool in their truck."

LeoDan the Man had one out of his toolbox in no time at all, and Van Vedic recalled a trick the carpenters in the Aztec trainyard had taught him, for getting the plywood up and over the bell. A crowbar in four particular spots on the bottom edge of the pallet freed up everything, the bottom straps broke loose, and all that was left was for the plywood box to be lifted up and off to the side somewhere. The captain had one side of the square, LeoDan the Man had the other side, and they raised it up and away together. The crowd surged forward a bit, but the bell was also covered with a railroad-protective shipping blanket that still hid the contents.

The captain reached down and pulled the blanket away, revealing a glorious golden bell that was staggeringly brilliant to everyone. The surface was dazzling, unlike any other bell any of these people had ever seen, and the wooden collar at the top was also polished, a piece of work most carpenters would be hard-pressed to duplicate. The T-clangor was also a work of art, a bright shiny golden T-bone, but everyone was sure it was paint and nothing more, which underlines the old adage that warns about people thinking they know what they're looking at when, in fact, they are as wrong as can be. Often times that's best.

In the bright sun, like it was, there was the possibility that the reflection could damage one's eyes, but there was one thing for sure: it was the exact right size for their church, not too big and not too small. It would be hidden from view when it was finally mounted, but for now, it was simply beautiful.

The audience was mute for the longest time. They all found places to stand and gawk at the bell and looked like they might be doing so forever. Fortunately, the side steps of the church were excellent for viewing it. Every man and woman came up to the side of the truck and examined the bell up close, including the captain—he ran his hand across the bell, signaling to all the others that it was okay with him if they wanted to touch it. It was no longer his in the truest sense—it was theirs, and it always had been. It was up to the council to decide if the people could touch it between now and when they got it up to the top of the tower.

Some of the folks didn't need to touch the bell, but some did, and in no time, a bundle of baby diapers showed up on the tailgate and gave everyone something to wipe off their prints. For some incredible unknown reason, their fingerprints seemed to seep into the golden surface as if underneath a glass film, and when they tried to rub it off, it wouldn't erase. The prints began to mingle as the many hands left their marks, and as they did, a form of texture appeared all over the surface of the bell. It made it even more beautiful, as if the fingerprints bled out in golden veins that mingled with the other prints nearby. They could see it happen. It was irreversible and didn't happen on the second touch, only on the first. That knowledge became an understood fact to everyone. One touch anywhere left a mark on the bell that disappeared into the collage of other prints.

Soon a line formed, and everyone there left their prints for the time being.

Vincent hadn't said much after the blanket came off. He let the locals savor the moment while he saw every day of the journey. This golden bell, created during the fishing trip period two weeks before, was as beautiful a church bell as any other bell anywhere. Mystifying. Someone had taken the bell off *Vanessa*'s bow, cleaned it up to this golden sheen, and then put it in the back of his deuce. In only three days, the captain had moved the bell from the plateau where he lived down past Gomez's place where he told him of his plans—and could he check on the horse in a few days? From there, at the state line, all the way to Aztec, and all during that phase, he wasn't in any sort of a hurry, drove his big rig like he owned the county, safe and friendly, and sometimes when he saw people he'd wave and they'd be excited as if they saw a celebrity. Something inside himself demanded that he get things in gear, and when he got to the train yard without much of a plan, he'd discovered that everything was already in motion for his departure.

Those kinds of thoughts bounced around in his memory as he watched the reactions this first group was having. It settled in quick for some of them, especially the older ones. According to Father Foy and McKee, there were dozens of living senior people out in the boondocks, five horizons in every direction. There were some who were close to the end of their lives but had started their lives in and around Pfeiffer, Russia, went to Mass at Saint Francis, and more than likely went to school there in the old school house. They would have heard this same bell on the morning they were baptized or had their first communion, and for some, it might have rung at their wedding. Those realizations were happening to all of them to one degree or another. Some of the records concerning the history of Saint Francis suggested that this golden bell was well over a hundred years old, but it looked like it had been made last month.

Vincent was sure there were those who might doubt the whole truth about what he was saying, and he'd have to convince them somehow that everything was way above board. Perhaps the bell would sound exactly the same as it did in those ancient times, with the same tone, the same resonance, same pitch. What's the word that explains how we recognize the sound of our favorite church bell? They're all different, but all unforgettable to the critical ear.

The bell could and should sell itself, and when the elders heard it the first time, they'd know. They'd know. When the bell rang that first time for the faithful, when those grandparents listened to it, they'd know, react, and justify this community, these people, and everything about them.

The captain himself would be the judge of all that. The sound the bell would make would explain everything. He was willing to challenge their ears, their memories, and like Basil had said, "Father Hammer wanted the bell to ring over in the new world in memory of the old world. That's all there is left of those times, the sound of a bell once again, and heard this time by great-great-grandbabies."

"Dizzy? A little strength and support, if you don't mind." Double-twitch. Deep breath.

"Ladies and gentlemen, my name is Vincent Van Vedic. My father decided to stay behind in 1891 for several reasons. Instead of leaving like everyone else, our family had to stay. My mother was sick, and so were my sisters. All three died during that first deadly winter. There were survivors besides him and me. We started life again, hauling freight and moving animals. Gradually life came back in that fertile Volga Basin, but there had been tremendous damage to everything that mattered. So much death shattered humans who might have gotten to the edge of starvation and then come back to life. It was a well-worn belief by those who were forced to stay behind that those who left for Kansas in 1891 were very lucky and fortunate souls.

"Do any of you remember Father Carl Hammer? This bell is his gift to you from those ancient times. I swear. He was pastor of Saint Francis for the longest time and was there the day when those fortunate souls walked away from the old Pfeiffer and into the jaws of a monster, with no guarantee of any sort. They were terrified and trying to escape the impending drought, famine, widespread disease, and sickness. When it was over a vast swath of southern Russia, the Fertile Volga Basin had been ruined and decimated. Catherine the Great, Czarina of Russia, promised freedom to our forefathers with few strings attached, and they, in turn, turned it into a garden of Eden. That is true. Our surviving elders talk about how things bloomed in that entire basin after a hundred years, and if only the government had left things alone, it would still be that way today. What incredible pioneers our forefathers and our grandparents all turned out to be. Men and women both, along with their large families, survived here in Kansas when things were anything but easy.

"On Easter Sunday, 1928, Father Hammer and Father Basil celebrated the last Easter Sunrise High Mass in front of an insane communist colonel and his band of pyromaniacs. Mr. Desch, I do believe your grand uncle was there at that Mass. I could be wrong, but I heard from Father Basil himself a fantastic story about Secretary Desch. I'll tell it to you in private as best I can recall. I'm sure many of your older relatives may have talked about the Diamond Teardrop appearing in Mother Mary's eye in the stained glass windows up and behind the altar during the consecration of that Mass. That miracle had been celebrated at Saint Francis for a long, long time. The communists wanted that section of the beautiful stained glass backdrop that had the miracle glass, the exact place where the diamond appeared, and they had to be sure; they had to see it themselves. The only way to do that was to have our dear old pastor Father Hammer and his assistant celebrate the Mass precisely the way it was always done in the past, and they even filmed it. I myself saw the Diamond Teardrop many times when I lived there. I knew exactly where to look, and the only time the diamond ever happened was on Easter Sunday morning, assuming the sun was shining.

"Later that morning, the colonel ordered that his soldiers loot and vandalize the church for hours, destroying almost everything not worth hauling away. Without intentionally telling the world he was insane, the insane director saved the big confessional booth in the front foyer of the church for both priests. He forced Hammer into the center booth, demanded Basil get in one side, and mockingly stepped into the other unit. Then, with both priests inside their respective coffins, he had his assistant chain the doors closed from the outside and screamed his hatred at the men before he left. Once outside, he had his soldiers light the magnificent church on fire with flame throwers, and the basilica burned to its floorboards.

"During the rampage inside the church, the colonel believed there had to be a basement, so he put his men to work digging a hole ten feet down in the main center walkway of the place. They found nothing but foundation material and gave up. As the church burned that evening, the magnificent bell tower leaned into the conflagration and fell towards the altar, with this beautiful bell landing dead center of the hole they'd dug, a bulls-eye if ever there was one. It lay there buried under the rubble for the next thirteen years. When the tower fell, the lunatic was positive that the confessional and its occupants had been cremated in a blinding fireball. All that was true from his vantage point, but there just so happened to be a secret escape hatch at Hammer's feet that went straight down twenty feet to a spectacular survival shelter. The sliding window between the units came out, and Basil climbed through, down the escape hatch, followed by Father Hammer. The pastor was unfortunately fatally attacked and severely injured after the Mass and would die two long days later peacefully. During his dying times, he told his assistant, Father Basil, that if he could, perhaps he should find a way to get the bell to Pfeiffer, Kansas. I can't tell you how much I loved Father Hammer.

"They had both been cowering down there in the basement while the church was burning down on top of them when suddenly a tremendous impact and vibration rattled the shelter they were in, made dust bounce off rafters, and scared them both half to death. Actually, they had already been scared half to death twice, if not five times, and this just frightened them a little more. They got over it quickly. Hammer instantly diagnosed it as the entire bell tower falling towards the altar in the chaos of what was going on up above.

"As a mental hobby, he knew all the mathematics of the construction of the magnificent church, the exact lengths and widths of everything. He understood how it would burn, how the walls would cave in, and how the bell tower would be pulled toward the center of the church. The genius knew how high his Bell Tower was; he knew the length of his main aisle walkway as if it were embedded in his being, inside his spirit, every time he walked that walk up to his altar and said the Mass. Every day of his priestly life, he walked the walk, and instinctively counted the steps from back to front. He could do it with a blindfold on. He could read the readings without the book, and most of all, he was positive about what he heard that evening. From out of nowhere, a crashing boom. The entire bell tower itself fell towards the altar and landed in the hole by the communion rail, which meant the monsters would never find it. They didn't have time to wait, as the site would take a week to burn out and cool down. They wouldn't be able to turn it into bullets; they'd never see it in the hole they themselves dug.

"There was nothing left of religion in Russia in 1928 when Father Hammer died. The communists had saved Saint Francis of Assisi on the Illava to be the last Catholic church they intended to burn down there in the entire Fertile Volga Basin. They would film the last Mass, film the rape of the inside of the church, film themselves stealing the glass panels of the stained glass windows, and of course, filmed the fire that brought it all down. However, Father Hammer was brilliant and knew in his soul that all those people who had left the village in 1891 would take their religion with them, hopefully stay together, and start again. So the faith would survive somewhere else, and if possible, so should the bell if Basil could do his part. Father Edward Basil took Hammer's dream and devoted his life to getting everything ready for when I got there."

Starting later that afternoon and lasting for a week, the captain found himself the honored guest of two huge picnics and all sorts of visits to neighboring homes out on the plains, courtesy of Desch and McKee, visiting people's homes and their farms spread out all over the countryside. Everyone had a station wagon, a tractor or two or three, lots of kids, and they were Catholic for the most part. He discovered that just like back in Russia, there were Mennonites, Methodists, and Lutherans out on the fringes, and the Kansas plains were providing for the people much better than he could have ever imagined. He also discovered these people had a fear of Mother Nature he found hard to explain. They were fearful of her storming side, and it kept them awake during the thunder. He learned about tornados, a spiraling horror that dropped out of thunderstorms and ate the ground. So far, he hadn't ever seen one and was positive he didn't want to. Except for that, these people were very content and thankful to live where they were.

The very next day, experts began figuring out what it would take to get the old bell down and the new bell up where it belonged. Somewhere during the debates, someone suggested that what they needed was a pulley assembly of some sort, something that could handle the weight, and thus it would have to be heavy-duty. They set the new bell on the walkway leading into the church and erected a large tent that covered it but allowed the throngs to pass by close and leave their marks or just stare at the thing and let their personal thoughts run away with the moment. For the young, this was a history lesson many had never known about, and the bell seemed to be proof of something significant, but they weren't quite sure exactly what. The nuns had set up a table that showed where Pfeiffer Russia was, and one of the artists traced on a large globe the exact route Mr. Van Vedic had traveled and, last of all, where he lived in New Mexico. People started bringing pictures of the old country, the town of Pfeiffer, and lots of pictures of Saint Francis Church, taken by cameras that were virtually brand new toys back then.

On Wednesday, the old bell was lowered down into the lobby using an HDLPA. It was like an awakening for the people as the carpenters started a quick remake of the bell room, new paneling and shutters, a new floor, and paint all the way around, including the narrow little staircase that led to the chamber. The steeple itself rose to a hundred and sixty feet, looked out over the parish like a watchdog, and seemed empty for only a little while.

All the work was done in two days. On that second Sunday

morning, Foy said a Mass in celebration of the bell arriving, after which all sorts of things happened.

Next came the baptism of four local babies, and along with that, the bell would be rung for the first time after that ceremony to celebrate the noon hour.

The parish picnic was massive, had been organized within hours of the bell first arriving, and the construction men all agreed they'd have things in place by the second Sunday at noon. It was one of the biggest picnics ever, and the captain was the honored guest the whole time. It was announced at the two early masses that they would start off the afternoon's festivities with the ringing of the new bell. It was quite possibly the biggest social gathering in a very long time, and the road into the village was a gridlock all the way back to who knew where.

As the noon hour drew near, the atmosphere was electric, the folks were on edge, the minutes passed like hours, and finally, all the hands on the clock pointed straight up, and the bell began to ring. It was beautiful, loud, over and over and over, a dozen times to celebrate the noon hour. At the same time, the two lower bells chimed in, and the valley was washed in a melody that had each and every one of the seniors crying in their hankies like anguished mourners. But plastered across their faces was a smile, on every single one. Their hands were raised, and they were so happy. So very happy.

Every hour on the hour, the bell would ring the total. It had done that since the first day so long ago, and now the tradition could continue. The locals had missed that timepiece like a long-lost love, and now it was back. The sound was the same, just like it rang back in the old Pfeiffer, and those ears that heard it way back then all agreed in unison that the sound was exactly the same. The captain agreed too. He had stood there listening and nodding his head with each clang from the tower, waved his hand out to his side as if he was conducting the echo, smiling, with his eyes closed, until it ended. That was all the pay he needed for his effort, the sound he remembered from when he and his father stood under the tower on their way into Saint Francis for Mass.

The captain's father, Aloysius, had many friends back in the old world, and there were a few very old men living in the parish who had worked for him, drove his wagons, and wanted to see his boy. The captain heard stories from half a dozen ninety-year-old veterans, who were perfectly lucid, funny, and full of memories about his father before he was born. Van Vedic listened like a bloodhound for sound.

The God of Reply was sitting on his shoulders and caused him to remember virtually everything. Besides all that, he kept a ledger of the people he talked with, their names, addresses, and where they had come from. One very old guy talked about all the missions the Knights went on from 1876 and about church councils and how they kept things together when all of Catherine the Great's guarantees ran out. This old man talked about men like Aloysius Van Vedic killing traitors and scum, gangs of men who preyed on the society from the edge and got away with it sometimes—and then the hammer would fall, the bullet would fly, or the knife would stab and slice. In the Fertile Volga Basin, the headhunters handed down justice in a world that didn't have much justice; they were more than fair and reasonable, and traveling for hundreds of miles on horseback was nothing to kill a pig, nothing. The headhunters would leave their mark along with a declaration to that community that condemned the pig for a simple charge, and the assassins were very quick with their sword.

McKee had organized seven family name gatherings at people's houses out in the country. There were so many names and family traditions that he found it hard to do it right, but the plan was pretty simple and had been agreed to by former council decisions.

One example was the Dommes. You talk about a wild clan of hooligans; they were it. Of course the entire clan would gather at Grandpa Peter's empty house a mile down the ditch row street from the church, right there on the backside of Pfeiffer. Now that Grandma Katy was gone, their home was in transition, with lots of empty rooms and camping spots. That couple brought ten babies into this world. He died a year after the world war ended in '46, she died a year before the bell arrived, and they were both buried side by side in a Topeka cemetery. They would meet at Peter's house—no guns, and no one paid any attention to that rule. It would be a bring your own food, bring your own booze, and bring your own family.

There was plenty of parking, all kinds of charcoal grills, barrels boiling corn on the cob, and watermelons everywhere. It was definitely not a good place to be a chicken. All these families that showed up were super glad and proud to be Americans, and were one and all ready to begin the most remarkable transformation of people in the history of the world, ready to be the superpower of the world, and happy to have the captain come to their Grandpa's home.

Peter Aloysius Domme was the one who did it all. He kept the Domme name alive, gently threw his wife and two kids in a wagon in 1891, and rolled out of a brown village in Russia with literally nothing in their bags, no money, no nothing, except for hope and a few dreams. It's really hard to start out in life that way, but lots of people do. Life is a long journey, and a person should never give up. Aloysius Van Vedic and Peter Aloysius Domme were best of friends when they were children and grew up to be best friends when they were men, and a time came when one had to do for the other what only a best friend can do.

"You can have my twelve horses, and you can have my two wagons. I want you and Desch to take this gift and go with it. Run with it. Make it worth what it should be worth. Start all over in the New World and never look back. Never look back. Back is gone, erased, and forgotten. It's always that way. No matter how hard we hope and pray that this time it won't be that way, in fact it is. Too bad, so sad."

At the Domme shindig, they all brought country cooking of one plate or another, pies, and for the most part, there were seldom any tears about how difficult some of this has been. Some of this had been horribly difficult. But these people were enjoying the fruits of the gamble. There might have been ten different families with up to ten kids each and two or three branches, all still living in the general area. Several families had rushed in from Topeka when they got the news, and the veterans from both World War Two and Korea were celebrated over and over.

The captain greeted all those men and gave each one a chance to tell his or her story of what happened in the last ten years. One thing that seemed to happen over and over to people was that they watched people telling their story, whatever it was, to this giant of a man, and there he sat looking at them, glued to their words and everything they were saying. He had a little preamble that he used on people, "Tell me a story that you remember that you want the world to know. I'll likely remember it, and it might end up on the world's playlist." He would adjust himself, set his notepad on his thigh, look them in the eye, nod his head a tad and wait. They would stare for a moment and then tell a brief story that they thought might be worth the world's time. Before long, a beautiful verbal history of the whole valley around Pfeiffer had been relayed to the captain as he sat there greeting the guests just past the entrance table.

When this party was over—and it was one of the most fantastic parties ever, no kidding; just great, no fighting and no gunplay whatsoever—and while these people were leaving and going back to their lives, Van Vedic too would go back to his and start his life once again. How many times did that make it? Maybe it wasn't a start-over, just a continuation, another chapter, but for the most part, he was looking at the sunset that day and that was where he was headed—into the sunset, back to the reservoir, and hopefully the dam. The party had been fun, with a wonderful family with all sorts of roots, and everyone he had talked to was optimistic and excited about the future. There were a few devils on the horizon, but the people at this party were not afraid of them. They'd won the second World War and they knew it. They were good people, they were honest, and they knew that. For the most part, they were pretty content with life, and besides all that, Harry Truman came from Kansas. The Atchison, Topeka and Santa Fe had pulled a large segment of the Dommes to Albuquerque just because Aloysius had become a superintendent of construction at the shops on Second Street. It was a task to feed so many children, and it was hard to stay Catholic, and the Great Depression forced people to suffer in the slums of the bottom lands of Albuquerque. Some of those folks rode up free of charge when news reached the downtown area; they jumped on board and were in Hays within thirty hours.

A local band played all afternoon, played Hank Williams music, and every time they did, the whole crowd went wild, crazy, nuts, and exhibited strange behavior for white people. The captain was slightly confused, because he had never heard of Hank Williams. Then the band of guitar players and singers started singing a song that the lead spokesman said everyone would know. "Your cheating heart." At which point, all hell broke loose. Van Vedic was spellbound. Every single solitary person in this huge crowd started screaming at the top of their lungs all the words to this song by Hank Williams.

"Your cheating heart will pine someday and crave the love you've thrown away."

Just like that, and at the top of their lungs, the whole ensemble was screaming this number-one hit on the charts at everyone listening nearby. Every AM station in the valley played the song at least every hour, and for some, it had already outworn its welcome. It seemed to Van Vedic that someone had made a big deal out of the Hank Williams fellow, and if that's the way they did things, well, so be it. It was time to leave. Follow the maps and go back to where he came from, back to Aztec, and back to the plateau.

In the morning, just past sunrise, the captain would point the Belvedere in the direction of Colorado and retrace the train tracks back to Colorado Springs. He knew the route. All his new friends and advisors had shown him the way, showed him how to get to Walsenburg and then all the way to Durango. It would take a few days, lots of questionable areas where he'd be at the mercy of Mother Nature, but if none of that got in his way, he'd be back in Ignacio by Sunday.

It was time to go, close the door, and start the car. He had a full tank of gas that would get him to the Springs, or so McKee had said, and he would be on his own from there on down to Walsenburg and beyond. He'd been advised to fill up every chance he had in the mountains, and not only that, keep a five-gallon Jerry can in the trunk just in case, maybe even two. The weather was beautiful, the roads were plenty good enough, and the Belvedere coasted along at fifty miles an hour until he got close to Walsenburg and started the climb. It was nothing, dry roads over the La Veta Pass, and when he began the downhill grade towards Alamosa, he knew he had dodged a bullet. He could see the train tracks out of his left side window, the ones he had been on only a few days before.

After a long two-lane road from Alamosa to South Fork, he found himself at the bottom of the incline leading up to the Wolf Creek Pass. It was open, had no snow, and required good tires—that was all. Those he had, and he even had snow chains that he wouldn't need. The pass was beautiful and spectacular, with all kinds of hip-hip-hurray for Mother Nature. At the top of Wolf Creek, he stopped and took a lot of pictures.

The Forest Service had set up an information station at the top of the pass that cautioned the explorer about excessive speed going down the dirt mountain road into Pagosa Springs, a beautiful mountain resort that was less than thirty miles from his home. The county roads were basic, slow, and steady, with the driver being cautious of road washouts all the way to Durango. He would turn long before that, at the Chimney Rock turn off, and hope for the best. No car like the Belvedere had ever ventured this far off the main line. When he came upon the State line five miles south, he turned left and crossed over the bridge that led to Gomez's ranch. Once on the straightaway, he passed by the small sign on the side of the road he was looking for, "GOMEZ, 2 MILES."

CHAPTER TWENTY-EIGHT

PROMISES MADE AND PROMISES KEPT

Gomez and Feddy were working in their garden when the captain drove up in the Belvedere. They had never seen such a machine, two different colors, and it almost looked like a race car in the magazines. As he got closer, and them not knowing who it was, they finally saw him smiling and waving as he pulled up to their porch. That had been a long journey, and here he was with his new car somewhat dirty, finished for the time being, and yes, he was hungry, yes, he had delivered the bell successfully, and for the most part, he wanted to climb the switchbacks and be home in a few hours. He got out, got a hug and a shake, and let his neighbor study the most modern-day state-of-the-art vehicle being sold these days. Sarge came running up, ready to kill the driver; his mane was bristling, and then his master came full into view. From there on out, he went into a full-blown crazy dog incident where he ran off his version of a four-leaf clover at thirty miles an hour. Then he came over near his master, stood about ten or fifteen feet off and to the captain's right side, did two complete backflips, perfect backflips, and then stood there panting and acting really strange, staring at something in the air up above the captain. All three humans wrote it down as a first, and then he wove himself in and out of all their legs until he sat down at the captain's feet and swished his tail like a broom. The man went to a knee and held his dog's face to his, and all they did was stare at each other, with the captain whispering a short Russian chant into Sarge's forehead. Basically, "Calm down, you idiot. Dizzy! Leave this sleeping dog alone." He said it in Russian, and Gomez didn't do much Russian.

This was probably the only new Belvedere in the entire state of New Mexico; it had snuck in the back door, so to speak, and was now parked in Gomez's front yard. Fetty did it to him every time he came around and was able to stay a while and would feed him his favorite food. Her huevos rancheros were now unforgettable to his taste buds, and her early lunch would hold him till the next day. They sat on the porch, and he told them about Kansas, the trains, and how fulfilled he felt. He wanted to sit by Vanessa's grave that very evening and then at his table and write. There was a fantastic story to tell, and he'd been somewhat lax in his attention to that subject lately.

The captain filled up his tank in Pagosa at a gas station that charged a little extra. The owner explained very politely that it cost a little extra to get the gas to his station, and he had to pass it along. Van Vedic assured him that he understood and thanked him for being open so early with a smile on his face. Out along the byways he had been on for the last few days, gas was thirty to forty cents a gallon. In Pagosa, it came in at two gallons for a dollar, and his fancy gas gauge said he needed sixteen gallons to fill it up, so that's what he told the owner he needed. "Top it off, check all the fluids and tires and such, and I'll be back when you show me where the pisser is."

He handed the guy a twenty and headed for the outdoor shitter that didn't even have a door, but it did have a view. When he returned to the gas pump, he could see that it took exactly that. A tiny fella about five feet five and a hundred and fifty pounds rattled off a list of all the things he checked, tires, oil, and antifreeze, all good, windows, clean, headlamps washed, and when he was done, he handed the captain a ten and two ones.

"Keep the change."

For the young man, the tip was a full day's wages, and before the captain could get settled in his seat, the kid had wiped down all sorts of chrome edging he hadn't already cleaned and had a smile that couldn't be beat.

A crowd had gathered around to look at his car. The captain told them where he was going and if they had any thoughts on the road ahead, he'd love to hear what they knew. The worst part was over, him having made it over Wolf Creek Pass. The road from Pagosa to Durango was easy. For him to get to Arboles, he had to turn south about twenty miles outside Pagosa at a landmark called Chimney Rock, travel another twenty miles, and he'd be close to the Candelarias and the Gomezes. Even though they were only ten miles apart if you were a crow, to get from Rahellio's house to the Gomez house ended up being twenty miles if you were a car. It was basically a two-hour ride by horse, and so far, even after all these years, there still wasn't a manageable road that went from Arboles to anywhere near Gomez's.

The sheriff was ogling the beautiful car. He told Van Vedic not to turn at Chimney Rock but to keep on going until eventually he'd come to Bayfield—that's where he should turn south. He said there was a crummy mountain county road that rumbled alongside the Los Pinos river all the way to Ignacio, and from there, he'd know how to get to Gomez's house.

"I've been to their house. I can draw you a route on your map. You should be there in a couple hours. Don't be out on those roads in a big heavy tank like this when it's pouring down rain. On the far side of Ignacio, there's a turn-off—I think we've named it the Indian Highway. That's the one that takes you to the Aztec highway. That's the road that goes north to Durango or south to Aztec. You're almost home. I'll check that route later to see if you made it."

"Thank you, Officer. I'll do just like you say."

"Plymouth is in the running for our new squad cars. I was wondering what you thought of this model."

"To be honest, I wouldn't know what to compare it to, but it ran like a top from Hays, Kansas, to here. Do you want to drive it? I'm in no hurry."

"No, thanks. I pretty much know how it would feel, and besides, our model is usually a little more souped-up than your average getaway car. It's all about traction. Always have good tires. They say someday they'll have four-wheel-drive cars and trucks. That will make life in the mountains much simpler, I hope."

"I have an army deuce-and-a-half that I brought with me from Texas. It's all-wheel drive and just a beast on these questionable roads. I live in New Mexico, just over the state line. I bought the land from a man you might know named Gomez."

"I know all about it. I know who you are, and I know about your boat. I know your big truck is in the railyard there in Aztec. Please don't feel any pressure whatsoever. The only reason I know anything is because I have good friends on the New Mexico side of law and order. Plus, I'm a vet. I drove the deuce in the big war. All the good men I know like to talk about deuces, and I and almost everyone I know who knows anything about deuces has stood by your truck. Your beast is the talk of that town. I'll bet that's where you're going."

"Well, don't that beat all. I'm glad to meet you. I'm Vincent Van Vedic." He stuck out his hand. "So, I'm evidently about forty miles from Bayfield, where I start following one of my favorite little mountain rivers, the Los Pinos, south ten miles to Ignacio, another ten miles alongside said river to the New Mexico state line, and there's a bridge there. The road to Gomez's place, and in fact, my place. There's a small sign, Gomez 2 miles. I bought about two and half thousand acres from Gomez, down on the south end of his property. Currently, the only way to get to my land is a rather primitive road out the back side of Gomez's ranch house. It follows the river for quite a few miles and then, at a dead end, a five-cornered switchback climbs out of the valley and up onto a plateau which is where my house is. It's exactly where I want to live. Kind of primitive, but that's quite all right. My big deuce does the climb without any problem, and I'm hoping my new fancy chariot makes it up there just once. First, I need to check on the place and feed my horse. Then after a couple of days, I'm headed for Aztec to retrieve my truck and get a haircut."

"Unfortunately, I have some bad news for you. Your truck won't start, for some ungodly reason. Someone wanted to drive the truck to the hardware store and fill it up with your order, but it just won't start. Also, there are other issues in the background concerning the Gomez family, including Gomez's problem child 'sweetie pie,' who is married to an even bigger problem. Those two thieves steal every chance they get. I talked him and her into surrendering to the police because they were talking crazy at the time. They were both screaming about suicide over being caught stealing easy money, and it was really nothing.

Embarrassing, yes; criminal, yes; worth dying over, absolutely not.

"The Gomezes are fantastic people, and they've told everyone they know that you bought their land and plan to float that boat of yours on a great lake that forms after the dam is built. I've heard people praise everything about you, and I offer you my hand. You should be there by noon. Tell Gomez hello for me when you see him. Be careful on the switchbacks. Tell Vannie hello for me also. She's my cousin."

"How'd you know she is my barber?"

"Let's just say virtually everything you've done since you arrived in this area is, was, and probably will be talked about on many different levels of this local society for quite some time to come. Vannie is a local treasure. You, my new friend, are the first man she's allowed into her life, and those of us who treasure her hope you're as good as you should be. People talk, and all I've heard are good things about all this Navajo Dam commotion. The only way to top what you've done for our community, in general, would be for the construction of something relevant to an earthen dam to get started—anything to begin."

The weather was great, and the roads were well maintained and hard. Usually two lanes, and the speed limit was safe and reasonable. He didn't know who had thought that one up, 'safe and reasonable,' because there were quite a few folks out there who were neither. People would pass him like they were immune to having a wreck or causing one, and the speeders were flat-out stupid. Many of the cars were older models; invariably there would be something slowing things down to ten or fifteen miles an hour, and all you could do was go that speed and enjoy the mountain air and the scenery.

In his daydreams for the last six hundred miles, he was comparing his new life with his old life. The problem was his new life was approximately three months old, and his old life had stopped ten years ago in Russia. An example of comparison would be these roads he's been on, not one bit bad for such rugged terrain, and the traffic was moving along, and he was getting where he was going. That didn't happen in the Russia he grew up in, and he knew all about roads and wagons and things like that, especially horses. He hauled freight for his bishop.

One thing that was playing hard on his mind was the fact that he didn't wear his guns anymore. Here he was, ending a long trip, and he hadn't worn them once. He hadn't ever needed them, and that was much different from his life in the Mother Land. Perhaps he was done killing men and wouldn't ever have to do it again, but there had been peaceful times in the Fertile Volga Basin when the Gunslinger walked around with his guns hanging near the front door of his house. That might have been a daydream because there were stretches in his life back then where someone needed to be killed at least once a month, masochists who came looking to die within a couple hundred miles of Pfeiffer—and all that aside, within fifty feet of Vincent, which meant you were too close and you got to die.

Delivering the bell via the route he'd used taught him a ton about America, or at least southern Colorado and western Kansas. Only the police carried guns for the most part. It wasn't against the law to carry a handgun outside your clothing so everyone could see it, but no one did, primarily because it wasn't one bit necessary. These were peaceful people, much more so than his homeland, where vendettas and honor killings dragged on for decades. Pure insanity, perhaps never-ending. There was no doubt in the captain's mind that in some of the social circles back in his homeland, there were men who would kill him if they had a chance because the Gunslinger might have killed one of their in-laws, father, brother, uncle, or son, who knows and when he looked back on his life as the Gunslinger, he knew in his heart that he only killed the bad guys, only the enemy, and that's the way it goes in this life. There had never been any guarantees in his gun fights, with all sorts of possibilities ever present, but the cards always fell in his favor no matter the odds.

Ignacio was as old a town as any in that general area, and he had visited it briefly a month or so before, when he and Rahellio had gone there shopping for supplies they needed on the switchbacks. Among many other things, he'd set up a checking account at the bank and found a gun store where he bought all the 45 ammo they had on the shelf. The store was right there on the side of the road, so he stopped and cleaned out the house once again.

He headed for the state line on an even more narrow county road that needed a blade in the worst way. He came to that bridge he remembered so fondly, that last one with the trailer and boat in tow. It took a while to line everything up, and he remembered how he had creaked across, testing the creation as seriously as it had ever been tried in the past, but it passed the challenge and became part of the folklore about it all.

This time he came at the bridge from the opposite direction, and the Belvedere hardly even rattled the timbers as the captain got to the other side, stopped to take a piss, and listened to the river. The Los Pinos River was tiny by all standards. It didn't matter that she had a raging side in the late spring and early summer; it was still tiny, and the truth of the matter was, tiny or not, everything depended on how strong the bridge turned out to be. The locals had named it Anna Marie's bridge and built a grotto out of large river rocks above the flood line in memory of something that happened to her here at the bridge in 1908. There were candle holders, flower pots full of reasonably fresh flowers, and beautiful budding cacti. Her picture—a gorgeous dark-haired beauty—was painted on a ceramic plate, her dates, separated by a dash, proved she had died young, and rosaries dangled from different rock corners inside her grotto, rocks that were put there just for that. Not many of us get such a shrine after we die, even if it didn't cost all that much to create such a memorial.

Vincent was back in that world he lived in where he only spoke Spanish, back where there were very few people. He and his horse and his dog lived together quite nicely, relatively quietly, and he was ready for that to begin again in earnest and for it to be like he had always dreamed it would be. The sooner, the better. He had a story to tell and a book to write, maybe two books, perhaps a trilogy. But there were other things to do right away at both the ranch house and then down in Aztec, and to be perfectly honest with both his dog or his horse, there was one thing right there at the top of his list for sure: seeing Vannie. Gomez had checked on the horse every other day or so, took care of Sarge without batting an eye, and was glad to have the captain back.

He left the lovebirds behind, thanked them for breakfast for taking care of his animals, and drove away, headed for that distant corner of their back property where the road headed for the switchbacks and his casa. Sarge was running alongside the car, happy as a dog could be, and so far, so good for the Belvedere. For the most part, the road was not that bad, but some spots would be challenging if it got wet. That didn't seem to be in their future, and in no time at all, he found himself at his army tent. He intentionally parked it headed for that long first ramp of the switchbacks, got out, and he and the dog went for a walk about a half mile further along the river bank to that ravine where the trailer and boat finally stopped, where she sat waiting. His *Vanessa* was safe and sound, a long way from being ready for winter, but he still had a month left before things get nasty, and there were tarps on the shelves there at the hardware store in Aztec, already paid for and waiting for the tailgate of the deuce to show itself at the loading dock. He was headed that way.

The going was slow, only five or ten miles an hour. He could have gone faster if need be. However, there was no need. Besides, it was only ten miles, maybe eight. On one of these trips, he planned to note the mileage at the start and then the finish, from Gomez's front porch to his front porch, after which he'd know exactly how far it was. Now, mind you, these thoughts were constantly going on in the man's mind, plus, a dog was running alongside the car somewhere— a dog that had been known by the name "Stupid" in the past. He didn't want to run over him. Even though he was stupid, he knew stuff and might spill the beans someday. Honestly, both he and the horse knew all kinds of stuff. Slowly, it seemed to be sinking in that he had all the time in the world to do everything he needed to and so wasn't in a big hurry about any of it except seeing Vannie.

He pulled to a stop and gave the hound a break, let him splash in the river, lie down in the shallow water and get a drink. The property line passed through this area—metal T posts along with thick cedar posts ten feet apart, with three strands of barbed wire separating the captain's land from the Gomez estate.

For now, the challenge would be these switchbacks and whether his car with only two-wheel drive could make the grade and handle the corners. It had a powerful flathead six-cylinder engine delivering a hundred horsepower, and as good as all that sounded, he knew it was nothing compared to his deuce, a beast the army called their M35 6x6. It doesn't take long to learn how to drive the M35, and once a person does know how, there are few vehicles near that much fun to drive. He simply felt good in the driver's seat; it was where he belonged.

Now, after running his beast back and forth to Aztec a couple times, up and down and back and forth on the switchbacks who knows how many times, he had actually driven the truck to the northwest of his casa, just out a bit from Vanessa's grave for about a mile across uncharted barren land until he came to an impassable arroyo that now carried the name the Embudo. His common sense told him not to do it, DO NOT DRIVE INTO THE EMBUDO, and just to prove to Vanessa that he wasn't an idiot, he came back the next day and surveyed the other side of the Embudo while on the brute, and started planning the new trail out the back side of his land instead.

More than likely, he would build the road from the county road to his west towards his casa. It really wasn't all that big a deal using modern-day tractors and dozers. The only reason there wasn't a road there already was because there hadn't been a need. His presence provided a big need for an electrical and phone line coming off the county line no less than ten miles west and on the other side of the Los Pinos. He was positive the issue would turn out to be money—hundreds of telephone poles, the lines themselves, hours of labor, and most importantly the route they chose.

While sitting on his horse at this one particular lookout point about two miles west of his house, he realized he would need it all surveyed by experts, and probably the smartest route would be outside his vision. He intended to pay for everything and do it as quietly as possible. He'd leave it in the hands of the folks in his office—two gals whom he hadn't met just yet, Roberta and Bonita. They would make all the contacts and do his bidding like the pros they were. They were out of touch when he came in with the bell, so he left a note saying he'd see them next time he came to town.

His things-to-do list included all sorts of things, which is precisely where things belong, and all during the trip to Kansas, he accumulated more things to do, but he now approached life through a new set of fancy sunglasses that the admiral gave him in Corpus Christi. They gave the captain a military physical for free that included an eye exam that he passed with a 20:20 score. "Aviators" they called them. For that matter, he obliterated the Coast Guard standards for male magnificence, strength, size, and width, and when the tests were over, the admiral bought him lunch one last time. Another thing that had set in was the concept and understanding that he was incredibly wealthy and the world was his for the taking. This beautiful Belvedere came in at a little less than two thousand dollars, and when he wrote that check, he realized that was an unbelievable amount of money in that world he had once lived in. In that world, people built the roads by hand, using mules, and oxen, sometimes twenty or thirty beasts, all pulling drags and plows to make a trail wider and turn it into a road. How old-world, how primitive, and probably still going on that way back where Pfeiffer, Russia, used to be. It was all over back there, ancient history, and now it appeared that at least the bell had been reunited with the people who cherished its sound. Going back to Pfeiffer, back to where Saint Francis Church used to stand, was on his list to visit again someday for sure. With any sort of luck at all, Basil might still be alive.

It was time, and he planned to do the first three corners and pull over in that same spot he used with the trailer, at which point he would get out and have a look at that fourth corner on foot. The fifth corner was at the top of everything and wasn't a problem at all; it never had been. It was number four that challenged life, and for sure, the last thing he wanted to do was commit that same sin again. If he chickened out or the Belvedere proved incapable, he could turn it all around right there and go back to Aztec.

Sarge was in the shotgun seat now, smiling at the captain, and off they went, up that first incline without any problem in the slightest. The corner was nothing, and she flowed around it like it wasn't even there. Another long climb straightaway led to turn two, and this time the right rear wheel would make a much sharper turn and carry the whole load, but just like in turn one, she handled it just fine in second gear. The incline to turn three was steeper than the others so far, and the turn itself was identical to turn one. After making it, he pulled over.

Once again, he and the dog went for a walk to look at turn four. There was the usual wet spot that made a mess of the exact area where the right rear wheel did all its work, but it wasn't too bad, and when he stood there near the spot where the trailer went over, already there was evidence of Mother Nature building it all back.

As far as he could tell, this fourth corner was no worse than two, but he planned to do it in first gear this time. Instead of a running start, he planned to take it slow and easy, try to get that drive wheel into the dry area and just go for it.

He went around four like it wasn't even there, shifted into second, and came up on that fifth corner like he owned the place. What a relief it was to crest that final corner, and when he did, he stopped to smell the cacti.

This corner had a view of the switchbacks that usually only lasted for a brief time in a person's mind if he were headed down on either his horse or the deuce, and not really at all when he crested it like this unless he stopped. It was an example of missing the obvious unless we force ourselves to do something different. LeoDan the Man had said it while they were stopped along the road looking down at the church there in Pfeiffer. He'd driven down the hill who knew how many times and had never stopped to smell the roses, which the captain made him do. For all intents and purposes, we never really quit learning until our brain dies, and as he stood there, Vincent knew in his heart and soul that he was beginning a new life once again.

How many did this make? How many start-overs? As he studied the distant valley from this corner perch, he could see better how high the water would rise in this area. He imagined the fourth turn of the switchbacks being the water's edge, and this last ramp he had just climbed someday lead to a boat ramp. That was the sort of learning he was thinking about—thinking ahead and seeing water instead of the forest, the trees, and the river valley. It all had to go under the water someday in the future, with some of the information he'd read suggesting that the reservoir would be four hundred feet deep in some places. This far from the dam, it could get as deep as two hundred feet.

All of his promises to different entities had been kept. He had promised Vanessa a special spot somewhere in the new world, and now she had a view she had died for. That alone made him smile. It was so hard to remember specifics, and any memory of those times was very challenging to recall; they have become a faded and foggy recollection. Those times were as many as forty years ago, and the place where all those memories were formed had been entirely destroyed over that time; there was nothing left, and he knew it.

The promise to Basil and the commitment to Father Hammer had been fulfilled, and the fruits of that promise were ringing every hour of every day for as long as Holy Cross remained a Catholic Church.

He drove away from there with his spirit overflowing, knowing those people who left Russia when they did had found a new home and a new place to do what they did in the old place, only this time in a land that was based on Christian values and traditions. America was about to bloom like countries very seldom do, and the ride toward the next century would indeed be glorious. The US Constitution was a powerful document, and when he read it the first time, he imagined people from another universe having written it. At the time, he was resting with some local officials of Aztec, and while they waited for something, Van Vedic started reading it. He became totally submerged in page after page concerning the writing and the history of the document. The article started with headlines asking, "Would you die for this Constitution?" All of the witnesses, all of the persons who responded and screamed out a positive response, were KIA victims of some of the previous wars the United States had participated in. "KIA. KILLED IN ACTION." It was a clever article that lionized people, men and women both, who went off to war and left their living spirit on a battlefield somewhere. He truly loved being an American and loved everything about it so far.

The captain parked the Belvedere where he always parked the deuce, turned it off, and sat quietly in his seat. That had been the longest trip he had ever made in three days. He went from never owning a car to driving his first one almost a thousand miles up over the top of the world at Wolf Creek and down the western slope of the Rockies to his new doorstep. As he crested the fifth corner, suddenly, his radio had found a signal from Albuquerque, KOB; it was a welcome addition to his life, with good music and a strong reception.

Nonetheless, he turned it off, and another thing that caught his eye and then amazed him was the fuel gage. All this milage from Pagosa to this spot had lowered his gas gage about a needle's width worth, which seemed to confirm what McKee had said about the gas milage being as good as it got.

His plan was relatively straightforward from here on out, and he didn't plan to stay too long. It was essential to get to Aztec, retrieve his deuce, fill it full of supplies, get back up here, and take care of his boat. When a man loved to ride as much as he did, his priorities changed. Instead of going in his house and looking it over, he walked real fast to El Bruto Whetto's corral and greeted the beast with many pats and whispers, set up his bridal and climbed on board. No one had ever ridden the brute bareback; no one ever even tried before the captain did it. Before he did, he and the horse had a 'come to Jesus meeting.' During that first meeting, the horse relayed the thought that if the captain wanted to ride bareback, that was just fine with him. Get up there, big fella.

On this particular occasion, and having only sat there for a few moments, he decided to use one of the fancy new saddles. That, too, was fine with the brute. The threesome headed west towards the grave site, and when they got there, he dismounted and tied the brute to a stump. He sat down for the longest time and stared out over the vast northwestern New Mexico desert, talking out loud at times so Vanessa and the horse and the dog, of course, could all hear what he was thinking about.

Even though his personal financial situation had changed dramatically, so far, it hadn't affected him all that much, and he hoped like hell it wouldn't turn him into something he wasn't ever supposed to be. There were times in his past when he had no money; he had a suitcase and a satchel, his guns, and a mission at the time, but money was nowhere to be found. It was hard to remember the situations exactly, but something always came along, each and every time, that replenished the pockets, and his journey went on. His travels were often altered for one reason or another, but in every case, it ended up being advantageous. In those gun battles where the difference between life and death is measured in fractions of seconds, in split seconds, requiring patience and concentration in order to survive, close-quarter combat where there is no room for mistakes, and in his case, he never made one.

He rode on and noticed survey stakes embedded in the ground running across his land from back up near his casa to the Embudo arroyo. He came up on one for a closer examination, and the first thing he noticed was there was not a single boot print anywhere near the stake. He pulled it out of the ground and examined the stake, discovering a flawless piece of wood, perfect cuts and edges, no knots or flaws, and most intriguing of all was a set of numbers that he instantly recognized as global coordinates, an elevation measurement in feet and inches, and an official stamp from some outfit he'd never heard of. There were quite a few visible to his left and right, about a hundred feet apart, and reasonably new to the area.

If there's one thing for sure, when a man finds survey stakes on his land that he didn't authorize, or at least he can't remember sanctioning, he is obligated to find out just what the holy hell is going on. He was quoting Rahellio's wife because he had fallen in love with the saying. "What in the holy hell is going on? Where in the holy hell have you been?" He couldn't remember exactly what she'd said for sure, but that was what he thought when he first saw the stakes.

There they were in this long row. He could actually see six stakes from the one he was at, headed for the county line maybe ten miles up to the northwest, just over and around the rock escarpments, arroyos, and other obstacles. Without any trouble, he crested a corner after walking alongside twenty stakes so far and became transformed, seeing thirty-foot-tall telephone poles instead of thirty-six-inch two-by-fours. It was a hallucination, like a mirage in the desert, but they were telephone poles in this case instead of a water hole. With his untrained eye, he envisioned the service road that would follow that line of stakes, just like El Bruto Whetto was doing. Most interesting of all, the stakes were evidently not cheap, because they were perfect, identical to each other. In some areas, there were more than plenty, complicated paths around obstacles, narrow in some places, but the right choice, no doubt.

The whole idea had been to map and plot a two-lane rural country road paralleling the telephone poles that brought in electricity and the telephone line. He had never lived with such things back in Russia. Ten or twenty times so far he had been startled when people turned on the lights there in Aztec. He had taken several shits in total darkness, because he didn't know about the light switch and how things worked. The phone lines were very impressive, the way they connected people, even though he didn't know whom to call or why he would want to call someone a thousand miles away in the first place—just to say he did it because they did that kind of stuff in America? He just didn't know anybody... and then he remembered how the Fleet Admiral of the Coast Guard told him to call any time. Many things were going on in his mind as his horse made the only prints in the dirt.

Stake after stake protruded precisely three feet out of the ground. The one and only extraction showed it had been buried eighteen inches in the ground, with no point on the end of the shaft. These stakes were going nowhere without him pulling like crazy, and his effort reminded him of a story, a sword in a stone that only stupid men tried to pull out of the rock. It was arrogant and foolish, and no matter how strong a man might be, it was in there too deep. He tried it once with the first stake and found out it would come out of the ground, but that got him nowhere because everything he discovered when he held it in his hands, he could have learned by just looking at it and deciphering what all the letters and numbers meant. Except, of course, the fact there was no point on the stake, which took it out of the stake department and put it somewhere else. He was positive the definition of a stake involved the word 'point.'

When he came to the Embudo arroyo, the stakes guided him through the best area with the most rock-hard ground and the least amount of sand. Mother Nature seemed to be guarding the route through the Embudo by laying down a rock-hard surface that stayed free of sand for the most part and crossed over to the other side of the arroyo to where the stakes continued northwest.

There were about two dozen markers through the Embudo that seemed to be perfectly balanced on this solid sandstone ledge that ran for at least two hundred yards through the arroyo, actually a two-lane sandstone roadway built by Mother Nature for Vincent Van Vedic's road. There was absolutely no reason whatsoever why they shouldn't all fall down immediately, if not yesterday, and even though it was against his basic instincts to mess with survey stakes, just to prove a point and answer the question, he softly nudged one over with the side of his stirrup. Sure as hell, it wasn't embedded in the sandstone; it kind of ricocheted off the stirrup and started to spin like a top out and away from the horse and rider, spinning and twirling, almost tumbling twice as the vandal rode away, but it wouldn't fall. The captain broke a rule about never looking back, and when he did, he saw it spin to the very edge of the rock surface, but instead of stopping and falling over, it flowed down a slight embankment, picked up speed, bounced over a substantial crack, wiggled itself through a long sand pile back up onto the original rock in question, and stopped spinning gradually in you know where.

All the survey work had been done, or so it seemed, by people who didn't leave tracks, didn't mark the ground in any way, and didn't leave a trace of who they were or how many on the crew. When it came to doing surveys through virgin territory like this, it would take ten people, horses, lots of tracks, and proof they were doing what surveyors do.

At one point along the route where the view to the west was stunning, the captain stopped alongside a stake and actually looped El Bruto's reins around it. On all four sides of each and every stake was all sorts of information with a progressive number at the top. When he set his compass on top of the stake, he discovered there was a north side, east, south, and west side, and not only that, the elevation actually changed over a hundred yards or so. Every single stake was perfect on its own north, east, south and west alignment.

The quality of the survey was stunning. Once upon a time, while he was riding and working on the Trans-Siberian Railroad, Vincent learned all about such matters. Many men died over such things as surveys, and over there, at the time, they never used stakes like these. He had been employed to assist in protecting the rail line from rebels, who pulled up stakes and ambushed surveyors, frequently leaving scalped victims whom they had impaled with survey stakes. It so angered the civilized side of the local community that they declared war on the savages and erased them from the picture. It's intriguing to consider the things that trigger our memories. It was a rather vulgar way of filling his money belt, but it had been forced on him every time. The train would be stopped for who knew how long, and quite a ways up in front, there were 'savages' terrorizing the countryside. In the haste of an impending battle, train officials ran through the stalled cars and declared a Stage 1 Emergency, bounties on barbarians. In not too long, thirty minutes maybe, the Gunslinger and two backups followed along the cars and killed the savages one a minute for half an hour. A few ran off into deep snow, and the backups tracked them down and killed them. The Trans-Siberian Railroad Company honored their policy, and the captain's personal Trans-Siberian checking and savings accounts flourished from then on.

The captain turned the brute back towards his home, recognizing that the horse was getting plenty of exercise, and so was the dog. Who could have possibly put down those stakes? The road idea had been a whim that he'd whimmed about a few times already, one of many, many whims, a project that would require some professionals who knew how to survey, put down stakes, and get the job done. He might have confided the need to his horse and perhaps spoke out loud in front of Sarge, but that would be it. He told Rahellio one night that he didn't even want to think about the road out the backside, but it had to happen. The only way up to his casa, the road to the bottom of the switchbacks along with four of the five switchbacks, would all be underwater someday. If a man wants to live in the outback, he needs to make a road that can handle the load.

Back at his casa, Vincent fixed a few shutters and the front door, unpacked the car, and piled his stuff on his porch. Then, with all the necessary candles lighting up his kitchen and living room, he sat down at the table and wrote till dawn. Outlines of chapters, short groups of words that recalled someone, something, from somewhere along the road, all waiting for more and more words. There is a limit to everything written. We can only read so much, only write so much, and every one of us is a chalice that can only hold so much.

The Bell on the Bow had been delivered, and the people of Pfeiffer had been most appreciative, which made it all worthwhile. Their smiles, their hugs and handshakes, and especially the children, everywhere, all ages, babies everywhere. Everything about the entire reunion was flawless and worked out perfect in his judgment. Especially the food. Everything was grown on their farms, orchards and gardens, fields of corn and wheat that went over the horizon any which way one looked. And "bestest, mostest, goodest of all" were the slabs of beef they laid on his plates. The Belvedere was now full of jarred foods, a basket load of the best tasting corn on the cobb he had ever eaten, lots of things he remembered from the fields in the Mother Land and cooked by women who were artists with food. It seemed like every time he put something in his mouth, women watched his every mouthful, looking for a reaction of some sort, and he played his role to the hilt, *ooh*ing and moaning at times, constantly smiling and thanking them for their hospitality. He said it over and over there in Pfeiffer that a man his size needed special foods, apologized that he couldn't accept things that spoiled and failed, but managed to fill up the backseat with all sorts of stuff because everyone had these food baskets. The Belvedere had an area they called the trunk, and it too was full of two spare tires, two five-gallon jerries of gasoline, some luggage, and his 45s. It had the best crank-up jack he had ever handled, and he loved it. In his past life, he was the jack, would lift the trailers a few inches at a time, and his helpers would slide in wooden blocks to change wagon wheels.

Everything, absolutely everything—except for that bell—was destroyed after all those refugees fled out and away from their old Pfeiffer. The Russian Revolution, the Second World War, along with the Great Depression erased Pfeiffer from the face of the earth, but as fate would have it and just in the nick of time, a considerable percentage of the town gathered themselves together and walked away from all that in 1892, the great Russian famine of 1891/92, do or die, leave for good and don't look back. Their government had failed them, and things were only getting worse by the day and the week until finally, decisions were made, and they picked a day when everyone would leave. He now knew hundreds and hundreds of stories of families that were in the caravan from the very start. Peter Aloysius Domme's wife Katherine had a son named Aloysius John, who was three when their first daughter came along in 1891. They'd had her baptized in Pfeiffer, Russia, but she celebrated her first birthday in Pfeiffer, Kansas, United States of America. The first leg of their journey would cover two thousand miles, and they took care of each other every step of the way, the long wagon trains out of Russia, across Ukraine, Slovakia, to Hamburg, Germany. From there, across the ocean on the SS Furst Bismarck to Ellis Island in America. They stayed together; the whole village of Pfeiffer Russia was still together—without a few, no doubt, but intact—and somehow or another, managed a group train ride from Philadelphia to Hays, Kansas, a thousand miles due west in the fall of 1891. That's a good parlor trick in anybody's book.

There were many husbands and wives who talked about being so poor from the very start that they were in perpetual starvation, always thirsty on the journey, never eating with any sort of regularity, and hoarding biscuits and pig fat. The thirst was the worst because it never seemed to end, and the people always knew exactly how much water they had left in their containers, treasured it, and that attitude never stopped. The caravan left Pfeiffer, Russia, in the spring of 1891. Seventy-five percent of the town's population, including all their children and necessary animals, walked into the sunsets like many other communities without much water. The great Russian famine and drought was well underway, with all of the usual accompanying plagues and diseases such as cholera and smallpox, just to mention a couple, and this nastiness would ravage the Fertile Volga Basin like few barbarians had ever managed. Truth be known, it was just the start of the hard times, and even though people survived the famine and tried to put things back together, the damage was severe and deadly. At the turn of the century in the Volga Basin, life was just a few steps above medieval, and the chaos of the monarchy would doom the country into a state of communism by 1920. It was, in fact, a great place to be from, and the homeland, the Mother Land, the land called Pfeiffer, was no more. Only one man, Father Edward Basil, survived past the Easter Sunday fire in 1928, hid the bell from prying eyes, and prepared the two dozen boxes for Vincent when he came.

The captain spent a lot of his mental wanderings back in the 1890s, enjoyed revisiting his childhood and remembering he and his father hauling freight for the bishop. His recall was moderately vague in its accuracy, foggy, recalling distant places deep in the outback, where he and his father arrived and then left in a whirl. They were always Catholic churches that were dying for one reason or another, might have been already dead, and the contents of a single heavy-duty long haul trailer would be loaded with church treasures, the hidden closets were emptied, and then the contents were driven to Pfeiffer, unloaded in a matter of hours, and for the most part, no one knew it had happened. Literally hundreds of times. The last thirty years of the eighteen hundreds left a severe mark on the evolution of mankind on almost every continent except Antarctica, with Russia being no exception to that rule. There had been so much inbreeding in the European monarchies that everyone with a broken heart died by the fireplace from internal bleeding. All over the world, men and women, children, pity the child, one and all suffered greatly in one of the most insane periods ever lived and died in. For the folks in the Fertile Volga Basin, it was one thing after another, a drought, a famine, a plague, government soldiers, wild barbarians, insane and drugged-out gypsies, and even if not worse wild dogs. Packs of vicious and starving wild dogs clawed at the doors and the windows for sometimes hours, terrifying the household, and then the men would start shooting. No one ever knew how many were in a pack but if that pack came down your road, do your best to save the children, don't waste ammo, and try not to panic. If you think they're gone, think again, the dogs smell blood, and their memories are short. You might have to kill them all.

After only two days at his beautiful adobe casa, he was ready to drive down the switchbacks and head for Aztec, knowing full well that the Belvedere might not ever be back once it got him to the Aztec rail yards. For the most part, he had a plan and a schedule of sorts. He had a dozen pies to give away, a deuce-and-a-half to fill up with winter supplies, and most important of all, right up there near the very top of his things-to-do list was getting his haircut.

Rahellio was coming for the brute and would keep him till he got a telegram. The captain only had the dog to worry about, and he wouldn't leave Sarge behind. Van Vedic explained all that to El Bruto Whetto in Russian, told him he was the one, he was the horse, the real deal, and that Rahellio loved him almost as much as his master did, and when they came to get him, he should know that in his heart. Rahellio was a good man.

Suddenly there were like eight twitches in a row. Dittz, dittz, dittz, over and over, upper right-hand corner of his world, five or so feet above his right shoulder. Then the horse started clearing his nostrils, sucking, and blowing, slobbering, and acting like he was ready to sneeze, all the while making the only human on that end of the reins afraid for himself and trying to stand out of the way. This perfect animal knew in its guts about the twitches, spoke with Dizzy several times on their level, and now, El Bruto Whetto possessed an unusual gene that should be passed along. The captain stared into the horse's face, trying to cross that barrier, but it didn't happen.

With everything secured as best as possible, he drove away, leaving the horse in good shelter till Rahellio came to take him to Arboles. Unbeknownst to the massive yellow muscle, Rahellio and company had a contract that assured the brute's genes would spread around the local community. It was hoped he would cooperate and not turn into an unmanageable beast. There was no doubt about him having lady friends at Rahellio's and at least two of the neighboring spreads upwind from the Candelarias.

Heading down the switchbacks was not all that exciting after all the improvements he'd made. He knew the car wouldn't have made it up or back down without them, and that made him smile. When they reached the very bottom and he came up on the tent, he stopped and took a moment to let the dog out so he could run along in front part of the way to Gomez's.

After saying hello and goodbye once again to the Gomezes, he headed for Anna Marie's bridge, turned left on the county road, drove a few miles, and immediately got lost. So lost that he started worrying about finding a way out of this desolate desert he had driven into. It was humbling to realize that he was as lost as he'd ever been, and when he thought about it once again, he remembered being lost in the rocks when they were erasing their tracks, and he couldn't explain that one any more than this one. He hated being lost. One thing was sure; it was impossible to backtrack out to where he made his first wrong turn. He had come to many intersections, Y's in the road, circle drives, dead ends, and long straightaways that went to who knew where, making totally irrational decisions at each juncture just to do something. The only thing he hadn't done was stop—until now, maybe three hours later.

He came to the conclusion he had been pushed, or pulled, to an unknown location out in the middle of nowhere. His beautiful car was covered in dust and looked like it had been around the block a few too many times, having gone from a brand new 53 model to a worn out 1950 model in Tijuana, and they'd only stopped because the Belvedere just stopped running. The passengers got out and went for a walk. Truth be known, one went for a walk, and one went for a run.

All over the hillside, it looked like someone had driven big trucks from one end to the other, made lots of marks, and crushed down a couple of acres of sagebrush and pinon trees— everything, for that matter. Then they must have dragged spiked field drags all over the area, trying to put things back together and pretend that nothing happened.

He found a sign lying in the brush alongside the road that said, 'HART CANYON UFO CRASH SITE. NO PICTURES!' Line after line, warnings and consequences for almost everything a human could do at this location. The sign was actually spotted by Sarge. It had been blown over by the wind and was buried in the center of a sagebrush bush that was half the size of his car. He dug it out, didn't get gouged by the sagebrush spikes, and eventually placed it in the trunk. He couldn't help himself, and since he was the only person in the general area, he got out his camera and took pictures of everything, including the sign. He absolutely hated three-letter definitions of things and kept dreaming up words that went with UFO. Maybe UFO was the name of a plane?

During his walk, he took pictures of the strangest views, assuming that an airplane must have crashed here in the recent past and it took a while to clean it all up. On one hillside corner in particular, he felt like he was going to lift up backward and fly straight back to where he'd just came from. He could feel it—go from here to there in seconds and stay for almost, almost, almost, almost forever. He was having twitches like breathing in and out.

445

His subconscious companion was causing all this, and that was a fact.

"DIZZY! DIZZY! What is this? I know you're there. You know I know you know I know you're there! I'll bet a buck you know what UFO means. Tell me what UFO means! I know this! TALK TO ME! What is this place, and why did you bring me here? I know you know, I know. I get it. Holy cow, I get it! I figured it out… sort of… maybe. You brought me here because it was the only way you could get here. You're stuck with me, and you have to go where I go. You made me come here so that you could see this place again. You've been here before? I don't think so. I've never been here before, and you've been with me since forever, watching me piss. I still can't believe it. Watching me piss is weird! I told you; I know shit. I get it again! You brought us here so other eyes can see this place through your eyes and feel it through my body. Good trick. We'll stay as long as you want. Tell me where to go and tell me what to do."

It was a fantastic emotion that swept over the man from fingertip to toe point; his whole body, eyes, nose, and tongue were all involved in the walk. He ended up standing in a dozen distinctively different locations on two different spots along the hillside like he was on a sightseeing bus, some close to each other and others alone. The whole time he stood at each location, he slowly turned his body in a circle, looked at everything close by, and then moved to the next one. Eventually, he was freed from the constant subconscious direction, and in the end, almost an hour later and fifty pictures or more, he found himself positioned in front of his car with his dog by his side. Finally, the encounter was over. He climbed into his car and started to follow the road due west, coming out onto the Aztec Highway five miles outside of town. He crested that one last hill on the east side of town and could see Saint Joseph's Church up ahead on his left. It was close to the turn that led to Main Street, and down that street was where his offices were, or so they said.

With a big smile on his face, he pulled the Belvedere up to the only parking spot left in front of the building. A small sign pointed the directions to VVV Enterprises. No sooner had he finished reading it than two unknown faces came into view at the door, smiled, and gave him a wave. He was the width of the sidewalk from meeting his staff. Both of them had waited for quite some time for this moment. They were somewhat giddy once they discovered who was behind the wheel of that filthy dirty wreck, and once they did, their pre-planned greeting kicked into gear. There was not a single thing they hadn't thought of, and after the introductions, it became apparent they had been groomed for their positions and responsibilities that included anything that would make the captain more comfortable and his life stress-free.

They seemed to have his entire whim list written on a huge chalkboard in a glassed-in conference room that seated a dozen or so, although it appeared to have been designed in some other time and place—New York City? Some different world? All the whims were listed and described in exquisite penmanship, every whim he had whimmed lately, and where things had progressed to since he'd first whimmed the whim. Some of the whims seemed to have been written on the boards with two or three different shades of chalk and thickness, then had as many as five identical descending square boxes with perfectly identical green check marks in the boxes. That whim was the one about getting a road and an electrical line with a telephone line from the county line to his house. All those things he wanted to get done for all those people around him were also listed, and there was even an entire projected quantity and cost for everything list that had a check in the box for, among other things, eight hundred new state-of-the-art telephone poles. The order was already contracted, and deliveries would start arriving in the next two months.

After only a few minutes of studying the whim boards, he looked at both the women, asking profound questions with his eyes only. No words, haunting moments between the three where the man realized these whims spelled out on the boards have never been discussed with anyone of consequence, other than perhaps the horse and the dog—and Dizzy for sure. Someone had been reading his mind.

"Ladies, I have a question about a place I visited on the outskirts of town when I was coming here."

Bonita was almost four feet ten inches tall and might have weighed in at ninety pounds. In the most petite voice imaginable, she looked way up at his chin and said, "Unidentified Flying Object."

"My dear lady, I didn't ask the question yet. How did you know what I was planning to ask?"

"I'm a good guesser. Was I close? People see big highway billboard signs around this area talking about the future National Monument at the UFO crash site, and very few folks know what a UFO is. The rumor suggests that a huge submarine-sized space ship crashed there in 1948, far up Hart Canyon in that desolate wilderness you just drove through. The Federal Government stepped in, sealed off the whole area, built a siding off the rail line out in that area, and then the army came in, filled a dozen train cars full of something after cleaning up the site, and hauled all the wreckage back through Aztec at three in the morning."

"Yes, Ms. Bonita, you nailed that response. You don't have to answer this one, but are you two reading my mind?"

She smiled at him and disappeared into the kitchen, singing like a little bird. As the greeting party wore on, some of his most cherished nibbles and dips were brought into the room, old-world momma-made home-cooked treats on platters that he remembered. A glass pitcher full of ice water sat on a nearby table, an empty glass was there as well for if and when needed, and from out of nowhere, his first late-afternoon Russian Martini arrived, with the first taste ranking it right up there with one other as the top two Martinis ever made. On a coffee table alongside his magnificent chair was everything he needed for the next hour, a splendid lumberman's smoking pipe, smooth pipe tobacco, and plenty of wooden matches.

While he sat there sipping and nibbling, he thought back on that morning when all the food and water had come on board the *Struma*. Here he was, ten years later at least, and he wondered what may have happened to those people. What happened to the *Macedonia*? That place was on his list to visit someday soon. There must have been a thousand things for him to think about, to recall, and there was no better time to start than now.

The ladies showed him his unit—the bedroom, the bath, and the closet—excellent in every way, and after the tour one thing was sure; everything they made and designed for him was made on the XXX side of things. Before anything else, he needed a wash. After four days of very little attention, he was ripe, so the women started him a bath. They had prepared a fine closet with shirts, pants, socks, boots, a few hats, and when he had finished inspecting the living quarters, he closed his eyes for a little while.

On the whim boards was the one concerning the deuce, along with the theme of filling it full of all the stuff from the hardware store, the grocery store, some furniture, a state-of-the-art radio, and the neatest of all for this trip back was a small trailer with dual axels filled with a wind generator that anyone could assemble in three hours or less. It also had a Briggs and Stratton two-stroke engine with two coils of wire, gas cans, and light fixtures. The invention was the rage of the land; people could now run small electrical lights and radios out in the country where there were no power lines.

Something had malfunctioned on the deuce after the captain had parked it. It just would not start, so all of the supplies were brought to the truck and loaded with a precision that made future unloading a snap, all sorts of things the captain may have dreamed about or paused about, whimmed about for sure, and no matter what it all ended up on the whim board and almost all of it now had a green check mark in one of those perfect little boxes. There was one box that hadn't been checked, the one that said, 'Start the truck and check the fluids.' The ladies had brought in the most experienced army deuce-and-a-half mechanics and operators from as far as the rumor would carry to help start the truck. There was no key, just a push button start, but nothing ever worked. No one ever sat in the driver's seat who weighed as much as him, and that's what flipped a little switch.

After his bath and a brief nap, wearing all his new duds, new boots, socks, a fancy cream-colored cowboy hat that fit perfectly from Jack Candy's Leather and Boot Barn, handmade underpants, and a T-shirt that fit wonderfully, great slacks and a fabulous dress shirt, leather vest, and classy belt, the only thing he needed was a haircut and a great shave. While he had been inside getting all spruced up himself, the entire boys' baseball team came running by on their exercise run, surrounded the car when they realized what it was, and insisted on cleaning it up like it had never been cleaned before. When they were done, no one could believe what a beautiful car lay under all that road filth and mud. It was astounding. The boys buzzed around the car like their daddies owned it, cleaned it with a fine tooth comb, but had to run along and missed seeing the captain. Roberta and Bonita, the two whim-board artists, thanked the boys to no end, got all their names, and would cover that thank-you base but good. The lads had hit a team grand-slam homerun, way, way over the fence, and they didn't even know it. Sometime later, VVV Enterprises granted a perpetually growing financial package to the Aztec Schools athletic department that paid for just about everything they would ever need from that time on.

According to the whim-board ladies, it appeared that just about everything they hoped and planned for had come to pass. First on the captain's agenda was to drive the Belvedere down to the corner, turn right, go three blocks, and he'd be at Vannie's Hair Salon and Nails. His appointment was set for four, and his ticket proved he'd ordered the number one treatment, which demanded the customer not to be in a hurry. The job could take as long as the artist and sculptor needed to clean up his head and his hands, usually an hour or so. He had dinner reservations later that evening, and the keys to the building were on his chain. Sarge had a dog door out the back door, onto a beautiful, elegant redwood porch, then into a grassed yard he couldn't get out of.

When those first few days were over, when all the things on his things-to-do list were started or finished or moved along up or down, he had a chance to meet with the whim girls, and together they made a pretty good plan for how the man would deal with the winter. With things being the way they were, he planned to make it back and forth from Aztec to his casa, three weeks at home on the plateau, and one week in the Aztec valley with all the churches and church-going people.

While eating with Vannie one evening, she explained to the captain how people were watching their every move, their every moment together, and for that, she apologized. There was no need for that, and they decided to do things the right way all the time. She overwhelmed him once again. He did the same to her, and she ended up with the Belvedere parked in her driveway after he was gone, and she could tell the curious whatever she wanted. He rolled out of Aztec in the deuce, Sarge was riding shotgun, and the M35 was full of supplies. Hopefully, Rahellio would be at the army tent, waiting to help in every way he could. They had a boat to cover and a truck to unload, so Rahellio was asked to bring the brute, bring Raton, and plan to spend a few days helping his boss get ready for winter.

CHAPTER TWENTY-NINE

THE JOURNEY BACK 1956

Vincent Van Vedic had probably outlived everyone from those glory days back during the wars in the Fertile Volga Basin lands and spent half of 1956 touring his former life— Europe, the Black Sea, the Sea of Marmara, the Don River, and many other places after starting off in Russia, visiting his homestead north of Pfeiffer.

His contact in Russia had guaranteed his ability to visit the gravesite of his companion, Jude, in a severely closed-up society. He was allowed to see Jude's grave in that cemetery at St. Michael's in Czechoslovakia in '56, a country that had become an unwilling satellite of Russia, the USSR, the United Soviet Socialist Republic. The exact same outfit that owned the two submarines he'd sunk back in '42. This beautiful country was now communist, with a flair for a revolution in its quietest of corners, a muffled mumble against Moscow's totalitarian domination; but that was all it turned out to be—barking at the wind.

He was ashamed to discover firsthand what the Czechs suffered because of their location. While he was there grieving at Jude's memorial, his former homeland, Mother Russia, rolled into Hungary and obliterated the ideas of a democratic revolution. That country was just down the road and was attacked big time, including world-shocking pictures with tanks, infantry, and lots of bullets. It had repercussions in all the countries nearby and brought the world to the brink of all-out nuclear war. It would be another forty years before Hungary was free again.

The captain was granted permission to walk the entire way back down to the train station from the semi-uninhabited old castle gates, unescorted, after spending a few hours one afternoon at Jude's headstone. His driver was told to report to the police station precisely what time he dropped the captain off, he was to make sure the tourist knew where the headstone was located, and when he made his report, the police chief corrected his drop-off time by three minutes and suggested the man be more exact in the future so that his statements always matched the other reports. The local officials had no clue why this Russian wanted to see such a thing, but it was harmless in the whole scheme of things, and their orders were specific. The man was to be allowed to fulfill this request and not be interfered with. Inside the order packet that explained who Van Vedic was and how he should be treated was a formal letter from Nikita Khrushchev himself, simplifying how those suspicious eyes were to treat this hero.

"Watch him all you should but do it from a distance and let him be, let him visit the dead for whatever reason, watch him until he leaves, and report back when he's gone."

Nestled back in a far corner of the ancient unkept graveyard was where the last and most recent graves had been dug by the local folks who lived down by the river bridge and periodically unloaded caskets at the train station. The mortician families had old memories from ancient times, from when the seminary was a holy place and had priests, nuns, and church bells up there in the higher country. Some of the local family names went back in history so far that they even mentioned in their bibles when the King of Germany gave his castle to the Catholic bishops, which changed the valley for the next two hundred years. The churches had extensive records, family histories, and genealogies, but some of the places lost their names after the war, and the stories about what went on there got erased from history. That part of the world, the center of Europe around Saint Michael's Seminary, was where the Second World War first arrived in the spring of '39 and then hovered over that valley even to the very end, when the Russians came back through with vengeance in their eyes.

The morticians in that community, families who had practiced the art forever, had records that no one would ever see that spoke about times in the far distant past when they understood and believed with all their hearts that God lived in their valley, lived in their churches—and now he was gone. He never came back after the war was over. His people tried to bring him back, worked hard at it, and when some of the faithful died trying hard, it became a new day. Enough dying. The God they had prayed to all through the war, everyone's different version of who and what He was, that God got lots of prayers before, during, and after the war, but then praying became illegal. When it was all over and communism became the law of the lands, that part of the world, the Eastern Bloc countries discovered that God was against the law, just like in Russia. Praying to God, at least in public, was prohibited, which meant many Czechoslovakians had to do it in guarded secrecy. They managed to keep certain beliefs alive, at least for a while. They were destined to wander in the desert like Moses for a long, long time.

Those plain caskets were treated with all due respect once they hit that train station platform and were then buried in private not long after dawn by the mortician's sons-in-law and grandsons, who dug the grave in shifts. They spent hours and hours, before the sun came up, preparing Mother Earth for another soulless body, usually within hours of when the unannounced casket had arrived, and every shovelful of dirt had a brief prayer attached. Those honored men became the pallbearers for those caskets. They participated in a funeral ritual twelve times in about that many years, a ritual that would never be repeated again because everyone who had been endowed was now present, and all the gravesites were full. Essentially, the Twelve Apostles were all back at the Last Supper table once again and together. A dodecahedron of endowed apostles, and it didn't go unnoticed.

Both of the patriarchs of those two families had their stories to tell at the start of each ceremony and explained what they both saw that day up at the seminary in 1939. Both were on the doorsteps of being ordained Catholic priests at the time, which would have happened within the year. At that precise moment in time, they were actually burying the very popular yard dog on the other side of this exact hedgerow when the monsters drove onto the main seminary grounds. The anger, the fear, and the instant terror engulfed them while they froze solid and stared through the rocks and bushes at the chaos only three hundred yards away. They cowered behind the same hedgerow they now stood in front of and watched that afternoon gathering with Reinhardt Heydrich, repeating what they heard, both crying manly tears, with trembling voices, and very, very scared.

As the sun set that day, Josef and Josef would have known all those priests and monks they saw standing in that circular crowd. Both would have known the sisters and even the cooks and gardeners. They knew them all because the seminary had been their home for the last seven years. Then, with no warning whatsoever, with the ferocity of a raging pack of lions, the most diabolical monster on Planet Earth had found the esteemed Saint Michael's Catholic Seminary and University. These two young men vowed to each other as they slipped away that night to never forget that name, Reinhard Heydrich, and somehow or another exact justice, find a way to fill Reinhard full of septicemia. They became underground soldiers, no longer seminarians, and would lose their callings together because they were now needed somewhere else.

Each pallbearer had a memorized graveside eulogy consisting of hushed, quiet, almost whispered prayers for the dead, each one a song in words about eternity, grief, and hope, along with several other consequences to life.

Mr. Denemarek himself miraculously escaped suspicion and survived. But, in a final ironic twist, after the war, he was accused by the communists of being a Nazi collaborator. "Most Czechoslovaks were paralyzed by a feeling of defeat and humiliation," he told the BBC. "The killing of Heydrich roused the people into standing up to the Nazis. It showed we were not a nation of enslaved people."

The human cost was enormous. The men's families were rounded up and shot. The Czech villages of Lidice and Lezaky—based on flawed intelligence reports linking them to the parachutists—were razed, and their inhabitants were shot or sent to the camps. Another 15,000 people met the same fate.

"Of course, it was worth it, killing Heydrich," Mr. Denemarek told the BBC. "Even though it cost the lives of my family, my brother, my mother, my father, and hundreds, thousands of other people. "But as I always say—that's nothing compared to the losses we would have suffered if Heydrich had been allowed to live."

Funerals had become godless, just the end of something insignificant, no discussion about a soul living forever, no eternity, only the end for a citizen, a body, a human that had once done things. Not worth talking about. To receive a civilized funeral in those years just after the war turned out to be a blessing that at least the grief-stricken appreciated if they could.

Almost everyone now knew what the war had cost in the number of dead, or so they thought, rough estimates, but no less than twenty million, maybe thirty, with there being a feeling in the air that it was still going on behind the wall. Some in the West believed that fifty million people had died worldwide, with the final numbers taking generations to be revealed. The worst cataclysm in human history, no doubt about that.

All those combined silent memories of the past, subjects only spoken about in absolute secrecy, passed down through the generations and became closely guarded secrets in those two families of undertakers—both men and women who knew the backroom business of burying the dead.

These two older morticians experienced a living visual memory together; both shared a nightmare in their minds. They were raised together, taught about God together, found their priestly vocations, and in their mid-twenties, they were being educated side by side at Saint Michael's when the Germans arrived that Easter in '39. Both young men had once cowered behind the hedgerow, two senior seminarians at the renowned institution hiding in terror when the Germans arrived that day. Half a mile away in the distance, they froze and watched it all happen. Shivered while they eyed that monster, German Colonel Heydrich, as he killed the headmaster, shot him in the head, and then shot someone nearby, which ended their education at Saint Michael's. The two men watched it all, saw the Saint Michael Statue explode from the heavy gunfire, and used those unholy loud moments to turn and run into the mountains they knew so well. They escaped together, as usual, and disappeared into the underground while creating much work for the German morticians who followed the invasion.

They both survived the Second World War, and because of their birth records they were allowed to further their father's business, the business of burying the dead, which most folks didn't like to do anyway. There had always been a great need for their services, and they did so in strict accordance with many new rules in the society that allowed them to live and exist near where they were born and hope for better times. Communism had arrived in full force. That ancient knowledge those prior morticians harbored and saved, the codes, the things about bodies that only they knew, all of that lay buried inside their circles just like the dead.

The train brought half the caskets, freight trucks brought in three, one came on the bus, and two were left on the morticians' doorsteps. No matter what the case, no matter anything, in total secrecy inside the families, they understood instantly what a casket with just a single name addressed to this railroad station demanded. As morticians, they accepted the body from the officials and took the caskets to a particular burial site reserved for people with only one name. Both morticians remembered Jude instantly from their years at the seminary, knowing that the final grave would be his, the last of the twelve, the only name not accounted for on their list, the guest list at the Last Supper, not counting Jesus. The Endowed Ones.

When those caskets had arrived throughout the years, each was buried in that outermost row by the hedgerow. The available information was stored in an envelope inside the coffin, along with the man's walking cane taped to the outside handles. The word "JUDE" was carved into the wood instead of a metal plate, engraved deep by a wood artist who knew his work would get covered with dirt but did an excellent job just the same. The gravediggers and pallbearers laid a thick piece of treated leather over that carving and then placed a square copper sheet over the leather.

The information available was an estimate of when the priest had died; why, how, and what happened had not been decided but was under investigation. It was a standard form used by the government as a death certificate for an unknown person— bureaucratic talk, a document that provided few answers other than to say the enclosed body died during protests at the gates to Theresienstadt only a hundred miles west of this station, and not long after the war was over. He was imprisoned for a brief time, during which time he died. However, he was able to write his last wishes for his body, and there in the envelope was a letter to Vincent, saying goodbye and congratulations on a job well done. Everything was duplicated, recorded in the mortician's logbook, along with the codes for who dug the grave, the pallbearers, and the date they buried a man named Jude.

Much like all others, there was little information about this man's death and what happened to him, including a note with his body that quoted his final three wishes. One. That he be interred in the cemetery at St. Michael's Seminary in northern Czechoslovakia. Two. That his trusty cane should rest on the casket lid when they covered him over. His final wish was that the enclosed envelope be held for a man named Vincent Van Vedic, who would stop by someday to visit and pray at the grave. That worn-out cane and the envelope were the only things the man appeared to own, so they did it his way.

No one seemed to want the stick as it looked worn out, had been used to a frazzle at the handgrip, and was starting to resemble a long club. Not only that, but it was also covered with some kind of slop all over the top of the handle; it almost looked like a woodborer bug was inside and spitting out the waste that dried like cement. It was taped to the coffin just under the left side pallbearer handle, didn't get in the way of those handgrips, and arrived intact at the gravesite, where it was placed where Jude wanted it. They performed their last ceremony at the hedgerow, said their many prayers in the sunrise, and layered the hundreds of shovels full of fresh dirt on top of the cane and the copper sheet down along the sides of the box until it all disappeared. A long mound of earth, along with a large flat headstone, was all that was left when they were gone.

The envelope was set on the shelf by the mortician's logbook, sealed with a few drops of wax, and stamped, "HOLD FOR VINCENT VAN VEDIC."

The captain traveled in a lavish cabin cruiser riverboat from Rostov-on-Don to Pfeiffer, three hundred miles to where the Illava merged with the Don. From there, they plowed up the Illava to Pfeiffer and then ten miles further up the river to where his home once stood, a place he himself had burned down in '41.

There was nothing much there—another graveyard and down the vanishing road a way, all over the meadow's high side, were the remnants of his homestead. It was almost gone from view, overwhelmed with vegetation except for the fireplace his grandpa had built. Family legend had it that the oldest Van Vedic of all set the cornerstone to the chimney of his new home the week after they set the cornerstone for St. Francis of Assisi church in Pfeiffer, ten miles away. The year was 1846. The entire homestead was surrounded by healthy young pines at the time, trees that hadn't fallen over in a hundred years, and now the estate was more a meadow than anything. Fifteen years after the fire, the forest was everywhere it could be, taking it back completely.

His companion for the trip had arranged everything the men would need for their voyage, their visit into the past, especially concerning their appetites and liquid refreshments and fishing poles. Now one of the closest advisors to Nikita himself, he could order for the moon to be full, and people would do what they could to make that happen. The conversation would focus on a specific point in time, a battlefield on the western edge of the Great Open Waters.

In that valley, Vincent carried the secretary off the battlefield, one of the last of the rebel battles, The Reds versus The Whites, and the last of the whites for good. A monument to that time had become a favorite tourist attraction and was planned as an overnight stop when they arrived.

. . .

At Saint Michael's Seminary, or what was left of it, while standing at the foot of Jude's stone, Vincent kept hearing Jude's voice in his memories, the priest's voice, that voice that told the story of all stories. A man who lived by the motto of "don't worry, be happy" said it repeatedly until it finally caught on.

As he stood there thinking about the past, the ground slowly split open as if the wind had pushed a razor blade from toe to head on the grave mound. The dirt moved away but didn't pile upon itself—a slash from an invisible sword, six inches wide and straight down into deep darkness. The miracle manifested itself there before the captain's eyes as the sacred cane rose up to the surface, the ground closing back together underneath it, leaving no evidence that anything had been disturbed.

He reached down, picked up the cane with all due respect, and let it fill his hands.

It was in bad shape. The face of Jesus was covered in a sludge of some sort, which made it look like the stick had been used to stir something foul, and he said a brief prayer that it wasn't ruined, because it looked like it might be.

When he bent over to pick it up, as his hand got close, the cane rose a few inches and attached itself to his palm. His body began to change as he clutched it with both hands, just the way Jude used to hold it. For almost an hour, he stood at attention just out from Jude's feet, holding the cane to his breastbone the whole time while absorbing the air, the silence, the trees and plants, the earth. It was as if his toes woke up. Each one wanted to wiggle in the dirt, and because of the cane, he could feel their yearnings. He and his toes had never bonded much unless he smashed one. He'd never gotten that close to the critters, and now they were like long-lost friends. He was levitating, barely touching the ground, eyes closed, when a request came into his mind—to be humble, to accept this challenge, and to continue to be worthy of all this attention. Be worthy of the cane, and thank God. Always, always, always be worthy of it, treasure it, and realize from the very start that in the future, someone would come looking for it, claim it as per his right, and Van Vedic might have to give it up. As he stood there, his soul agreed to always be worthy.

After standing still for so long, his first movement was to kneel while holding his new cane on both knees—and no butt on the heels. In front of distant secret watchful government eyes, the captain knelt in the gravel and stayed in that position for thirty more minutes. The spies were tired of watching; they couldn't believe a human being could stand that straight for that long and then kneel like it was the only way to pose. They didn't realize that the giant was practically levitating as he stared into those eyes on the end of the cane and almost went to sleep kneeling down. He could see Hammer holding the cane, Basil and the cane, then the eleven months with Jude and how he held the cane. Now the wooden miracle was Van Vedic's, and he had a new walking stick as he finally rose and turned to leave. Perhaps there was a new mission in his life. He wasn't quite sure what it was, but the cane would help him figure that out.

From the spies' point of view, their report noted that finally (capital letters and underlined), the tourist rose to his feet with the help of a tree branch he had found close by, a ready-made walking stick. The man nodded a final goodbye to the chosen stone, turned to leave St. Michael's, and began walking down that road to the train station as he'd promised.

They didn't know he was reliving Saint Michael's exodus that fateful day in March 1939. It now seems that he alone knew the story about the priests and nuns, cooks, and monks pushed into oblivion, forced down the road, and murdered along the way one after another until the survivors were ultimately crammed into cattle cars. They were loaded into the boxcars by violent soldiers at the train station and then hauled to the Theresienstadt Concentration Camp a hundred miles west.

That was where they were all worked to death. The Germans called the place many things and continuously lied to the world as to what it was. The Germans told the Red Cross it was a sanctuary, showed the inspectors a fairytale land, and the Red Cross went away, never seeing the place for what it was. It was a death camp, one of many such hellholes, and almost impossible to escape from. Almost.

Jude had shared that experience many times with the captain, took him down that road at a campfire one night. Not long after their journey began, he sat there holding the cane, and with perfect total recall, he remembered that walk into hell while tearing the captain's heart apart. Jude told the captain what every step had felt like, what the guns' explosions sounded like to clergy-type people, the screaming women, the yelling from insane soldiers, their eyes, and all the other details. Jude described the guards as being in another dimension, howling at times, staring into the forest at nothing, and then murdering a human being in cold blood. They were on drugs—methamphetamine. The German Army soldiers seemed to function in a trance, continually screaming, even talking to the people they had murdered. It was so horrifyingly obvious.

The story Jude told always started at St. Michael's, but he gave his average audience only a few minutes of the total horror of that very first day, which started them crying, then moved on to talk about the compound itself, Theresienstadt, which upped the crying times five. Their world had gone from sane to utterly insane in twenty-four hours or less. St. Michael's people disappeared from their homes in only one day, and the terrified survivors then vanished from each other by the end of the week.

On an individual basis, each person disappeared into the camp somewhere, never to be seen again by anyone from the seminary.

There was another version that Jude only shared with a few confidants, but you had to be very strong because it took two hours and was crushing. There was a version that remembered every single step. Basil and his cane heard it by the Grotto one afternoon when he and Jude were alone, and then Basil wrote a masterpiece the world might never hear. Several folks in Tucumcari were overwhelmed with that extended version, including Thousanctus and David. General George S. Patton walked down that mountain road with Jude as the *Vanessa* cornered the tip of Africa and sat paralyzed there on the bow, shattered by the graphics, unable to move.

The general had heard of the drug use, knew it was something some soldiers needed, and German soldiers' autopsies found large quantities of a stimulant called methamphetamine in their blood. Sometimes there was no food in their gut, and other times there were reports of severe wounds that didn't slow them down. That army was being drugged from the top down, including Hitler himself; they were all addicts. They might have known what had happened, how entire units were turned into addicts and given additives to help them stay awake, brave, and focused.

Methamphetamine is so potent that it blocks out all reason, makes a man invincible, makes him invisible, and makes dying much easier.

The captain would now walk that walk physically for his first and only time, feel it to his core through every single toe tip, every step—total recall through Jude's eyes. Do it just like in Jude's story and do it with the cane in hand, a first and last for both entities, and both had already walked it spiritually so many, many times.

All dozen graves represented men who had staggered down that same road in 1939, made it to the train station, and caught a hop to Theresienstadt. He only knew Jude in life's reality but listened to him talk about these other eleven men, often the funny stories. Jude loved to talk about them, how they all met, how they were released together, were endowed together, sanctified in their existence, and were only together a short while before they all went their separate ways with the one basic story. "Surely, God is with us and not them!" They were all back together again, lined up just like at the Last Supper. The one thing the captain knew better than anything else he'd ever known was The Story of Jude. He knew that story better than any man alive and told The Story of Jude to thousands of future storytellers before it all ended.

The cab driver parked on the side of the narrow road when he got up close to the collapsed front gates of the old castle. From that spot, Van Vedic could see to the furthest back corners of the property and discovered that there was no back wall to the castle. Over the years, the blocks had been taken down and used as foundations for other buildings, classrooms, living quarters, and other uses on the property behind this front wall.

"Mr. Van Vedic, do you still want to walk back down to the train station now that you know how far it is? I can wait. I was often reminded that you must be on that train that leaves the station at five p.m."

"No, my good friend. I'll walk, and there's a reason I want to do that—pure nostalgia. Just to be able to say that I did. And it's not all that far. I'll be at the station in plenty of time, but I want to be alone for now. You know full well that I'm here to visit a grave, and when I find it, I intend to say my prayers and remember a man. After I've spent my time there with an old friend, I'll go back home."

The cab driver left with a final goodbye. Vincent found the cemetery without any trouble, an ancient few acres that were on the verge of being forgotten, a concept the mourners vowed over and over and promised at the time would never ever happen. Hundreds of tombstones and markers were scattered over the three-acre hillside, creating a problem because he realized he didn't know where to look. As he stood just past the falling down entrance archway, a spirit of some sort touched him; a force was pulling his face, pushing on the back of his head, directing him to the distant hedgerows.

In a beautifully shaded back corner, on the edge of the forest, overlooking everything worth looking at, was a long row of graves. A few were obviously fresher than all the others, and the one on the far end was the most recent, the one that said "Jude."

"Hello, Father."

Whenever we find an old friend from our life in a cemetery, it takes a while to start the conversation, especially the first time and, in this case, the last time, and since most greetings aren't appropriate, we do what we can.

"Hey, what's up? How's it going?" Those greetings just don't work. "Hello, Father," did, and just like we all do when we're talking to the dead, we can say about anything there is to say, relive anything worth reliving, and the whole time treat our audience like they don't know what's happened.

We don't even need to say it out loud; mental telepathy works just fine, and in almost all cases, the conversation is usually a one-way street. The captain talked about how he had been swallowed in a hurricane in the fall of '43, disappeared for ten years, and only recently came back to life.

"Father, you wouldn't by any chance have any idea what's been going on with me and my life here recently? Perhaps this cane will help in that regard. Something has stolen three days from another gentleman and me a few years ago and won't let us remember very much about what happened, to say nothing about me and my boat disappearing for ten years. I don't know if you know about me and my boat and what happened? Wait till you hear this one. I have a companion these days wherever I go, and like you, he's a spirit. I named him Dizzy. I was questioning why I was having these mental failings; I don't know what else to call them. Very strange, and I'm open to any suggestion."

That conversation was followed by many more rambling orations while he was standing and kneeling, until the well went dry and there was nothing else to talk about.

As usual under those circumstances, the conversation is always a one-way street; there are never any answers, no yeses, no nos, and not even an echo. Finally, the captain rose and said his goodbyes.

He tapped his cane on the ground and nodded his head many times, knowing he had the walk in front of him and the knowledge that he'd never be back here again. "Goodbye, dear friend. Thanks for the cane, and may you rest in peace forever."

Because of that invasion in Hungary, all foreigners were immediately ordered out of all the other Eastern Bloc countries, which forced him back to the same terminal from where he had come. All he had done so far was ride the train a hundred miles north along the German border to a train station only a few miles from what remained of Saint Michael's and then he took a waiting cab to the gates of the abandoned school. It was a complicated mental matter when he left that cemetery and began the walk with Jude's cane and his memory of that man. When he had first planned all this, he planned how he would walk down the mountain, all the way on that rural country road, like he was back in 1939 and doing it with Jude. The only thing he hadn't planned on was doing it with the cane.

Somewhere along the road, he could see and feel Father Peter Whelan raising his hands to heaven and telling all his companions that, "Surely, God is with us and not them!"

The captain could hear the silent echoes from the gunshots that killed all those holy people way back then as he walked along with the cane. His body was overwhelmed with feelings, almost like the trees were talking to him. His senses were magnified beyond double or triple, if there was such a thing; his muscles flexed, and his toes were acting like fingers. He had over an hour to walk a few miles, so early on, the first hundred yards or so, he stopped by the stream that was talking to him as well; a vein of life that was flowing then, where all the blood went, off the road and into the creek. His new cane had pulled him there, made him stand in the water, and caused him to get those toes wet while blending and bonding with Mother Nature. In the spring, she was there that day, 1939, when the war started, watching the road, recording what happened, hearing those screams from the nuns, people dying like trees falling in the forest that no ears hear. Screams that were embedded in the trees' bark, in the skin on the rocks, and even into the dirt. And she always would be watching the road. He saw it through someone else's memory, saw the stream had turned red once upon a horror time in the spring of 1939.

Dozens of human beings had been shot, beaten unconscious, and thrown down the embankment, where they bled out in the stream. Only two weeks into the Germans' invasion of the Sudeten Lands, Saint Michael's Seminary was discovered and liquidated in only a day. Their war had just begun, but for these unlucky Catholics, it wouldn't last long.

His hearing was everything—the forest's sound, the wind in the trees, the rustling leaves, the sound of water, and when he looked at the clouds, he could hear them puffing. The world had become a symphony of natural noise, all because of this cane. Off in the thick forest, the spirits of the dead rustled the trees and forced a vibration down their trunks to the stream.

No one ever really knew how many people died along the road, one after another, murdered and then flung off to the side of the road, starting at the front gates to the seminary and then all the way to that train station. His new cane kept pulling him down the mountain, energizing him with a better understanding of what it had been like, enhancing his senses and teaching him what to feel for.

Without any warning, the cane lunged to a spot in the road, and Van Vedic never let go while discovering that he was welded to the handle, stuck there standing perfectly still. Sitting there on the side of the road were three nuns, more like shadows. Slowly they faded back into the forest. He knew their names because they were friends of Jude. He'd seen what had happened to them, talked about them in different stories, and the cane now projected a mental image for the captain.

Twice more, he was overwhelmed with a memory that the cane allowed him to see so clearly, in slow motion. Each time it pulled him to an exact spot on the roadway where the tip of the cane would scarcely touch the surface but was unmovable, and he heard an echo of sorts on both sides of the road, something clear, "Surely, God is with us and not them!" At that point in his walk, he was totally overcome with emotion. He had walked alongside Jude all the way down the mountain and saw all that carnage through some magical mystery memory tool, namely the cane. When Jude told Van Vedic the more extended version one day out on the Black Sea, he winked and assured the captain he would probably walk that walk someday and know the feeling firsthand.

There were three unmarked police cars, three unmarked

police trucks, and two motorcycles parked in the small trainyard parking lot when the captain walked out of the forest and headed for the platform an hour ahead of schedule. He was handed his ticket at the check-in counter and was very discretely given an envelope, courtesy of the local mortician who had dealt with Jude's casket.

"Captain Vincent Van Vedic, we have waited for you to visit our tiny community and visit the grave of your friend. I see that you salvaged his walking stick, and my question of how need not be asked. My questions from long ago have all been answered now. Dear Sir, this envelope came with his casket, and as you can see, it's addressed to you. I worry about the police taking it from you for some harebrained reason. I do believe we could smuggle it through to France or anywhere you wish."

"That won't be necessary. I'll tuck it into my waistband. I have a letter in my satchel that comes from a very renowned member of the Communist Party of the USSR in Moscow, and I enjoy watching the local police chief read it. I'll be where I belong within a few days, and I'm so anxious to find out what's in there. Father Jude was the most extraordinary man I've ever known. A walking miracle. Do you know any more about where his casket came from?"

"We paid the charges for his delivery here, and that fee went to the station you just came from. The same one you're going back to. Theresienstadt."

"I sure appreciate this funeral information. We can write back and forth as I try to interpret the code of characters. I so despise the communists. Those twelve priests you buried up there, side by side with each other, all survived and escaped from the Theresienstadt Concentration Camp, a hundred miles west of here, in 1941. They all lived at the seminary and walked down the mountain, just like I did today, to this very station and were then crammed into cattle cars. That's where I'm going. It's next on my list."

"I know. We all know. I doubt we'll ever be the same again. The only way to forget the horror of it all is to die. Have a long and safe life, Mr. Van Vedic. We'll talk again someday. You have my numbers."

Vincent saw the main gates and a memorial to the Theresienstadt Concentration Camp. An eternal monument proclaimed the Germans lied about it being a resort for old and retired Jews, tricked the Red Cross into believing that lie just once, and then used the place to work people to death.

He'd started his train ride to Saint Michael's from the modernized railroad station platforms that probably stood exactly where those boxcars Jude had talked about were located, the ones he was loaded into fifteen years before. The train headed north towards Poland, and after a hundred miles, he'd gotten off and spent the day with Jude.

While he toured the Theresienstadt countryside, he told his cab driver he needed information and wanted to find a place called "Potato Farm #6." The cabbie drove to a small police station for directions to the said farm, but the ever-suspicious and angry local officials said there was no such place and never had been. The police started watching him immediately, asking questions about why he was there and did he have papers, why-why-why, and he was happy to leave if they didn't mind. He was escorted to the border checkpoint between Czechoslovakia and West Germany, was held for three more days, and was finally allowed to leave the socialist nightmare.

CHAPTER THIRTY

BURIED ALIVE

Van Vedic was surreptitiously slid a note from a police shift supervisor at the hotel he was confined to there in the town plaza. The memo said he was the son of Colonel Desch.

To deal with the boredom, seven foreigners played a five-card poker game for hours, which involved a dealer who didn't play and a sizeable pot of money in the middle of the table. All these men were leaving the country by order of the government immediately, if not sooner.

The card players were in Lovosice, Czechoslovakia, for various reasons, all legitimate business concerns except for the Russian Texan, who was apparently visiting the dead and looking for make-believe potato fields out in the countryside. One and all, they spoke their versions of English and understood the rules and all its odds and consequences, with the captain sometimes cursing in Louisianner, Russian, Spanish, and Kansas English.

All foreigners on temporary visas were ordered to leave the

Soviet Bloc countries immediately, report to the local police station, and be prepared to never return. The United Soviet Socialist Republic-slash-Russia was having trouble with one of the members, the one right next door to Czechoslovakia, and was preparing to slam the hammer and slash the sickle down on a rebellion that was continually smoldering. Van Vedic's timing was undoubtedly meant to be, and now that he had a new cane, he was finished with his visit. As the crisis was developing all over the region, most folks preferred to be on the western side of it all, while the authorities on the eastern side needed no extra baggage anywhere close to the fire. Foreigners were considered excess baggage, troublemakers, spies, and persons to be watched the entire time they were about their business, so the fewer, the better.

Not only did the police want everyone gone, but some were leaving as fast as they could and trying to be gone. The captain had discovered a land, namely Czechoslovakia, that had been savaged for centuries, war after war, time after time, until it may have lost its soul.

The Soviets in 1956 were ferocious and intimidating towards everyone they dealt with. They encouraged communist revolution everywhere in the world, had a space program of all things, and, most intimidating of all, had set off their own hydrogen bomb one year before.

The captain had read the article himself. *"On November 1, 1952, the United States successfully detonated 'Mike,' the world's first hydrogen bomb, on the Elugelab Atoll in the Pacific Marshall Islands. The 10.4-megaton thermonuclear device instantly vaporized an entire island and left behind a crater more than a mile wide. Three years later, on November 22, 1955, the Soviet Union detonated its first hydrogen bomb on the same principle of radiation implosion. Both superpowers are now in possession of the so-called 'super bomb,' and the world lives under the threat of thermonuclear war for the first time in history."*

The note said, "I saw the priest Jude one day in the compound talking with my father. I always have dinner at the diner next door, and you shall meet me there for our interrogation."

In badly broken English, the policeman told Vincent there would be one last interrogation, nothing serious, with drinks and food, before he left for West Germany at four that afternoon. The police captain had a few last questions concerning the ideas of the Russian Texan admitting to being an author, and more provoking was him writing about Theresienstadt, a place he seemed to know a great deal about. In front of many subordinates, the head policeman confronted Van Vedic and all the other card players in a most aggressive manner. He insisted on one final interview for everyone to ensure they understood the Czech point of view concerning what was happening.

The police were highly suspicious of this group of foreigners who appeared addicted to gambling and had played for eight straight hours twice in the lobby while waiting for their permission to leave. They hardly spoke to each other during the games and occasionally yelled at the cards. That instantly excited the door guards. Because so many of the players were constantly looking up during the hands, the guards assumed there was someone up on the ceiling who seemed to be looking down and paying attention. So the guards continued to glance at the ceiling for whatever the card players could see. Since they don't play five-card in the police barracks, the guards had nothing to relate to. Nonetheless, all seven were interviewed for three hours, at separate tables, by one or two or more members of the security police. It appeared to have something to do with the table size, and Van Vedic turned his table for three into a table for two.

Just Vincent and Captain Desch, the interrogator who seldom asked a question but rambled on and on about the past, about being a young boy and living with the commandant, his father. He insinuated that he was a lesser-degree knight in the dying Templar tradition and that the only two others he had ever known, his father and his father's driver, simply disappeared one morning.

First out of his mouth was a story about having gone fishing with his father and the other man one day in the spring of '41 and how they stopped at an old barn a long way from the prison on their way home. As a confused and fledgling teenager, he saw those faces in those windows of the grange, saw his father bless them like he was a priest, and told the captain he had never seen his father do that before, never. Of course, many immediately blessed him back, and then he and their truck driver crisscrossed themselves. Those were the same faces he saw at the compound at Theresienstadt whenever he went there. They were the faces of prisoners, and he never liked looking at them because he knew in his heart and his soul, and his mind, that everything about the place was wrong, no good, and dishonorable.

There had been terrible consequences to that encounter, a long, turbulent time that resulted in him never seeing his father again. Then the family disappeared into a ghetto for widows with children on the German border near the railroad crossing. It was a horrible place, but they managed to survive. All these widows were not responsible for any of the horrors all around. He wanted someone to know, namely Van Vedic, that he had seen those people in that building, had never told anyone before, and couldn't tell anyone now, except this historian who just happened to be passing through. Van Vedic was a God-sent messenger, a miracle, and he so badly wanted Van Vedic to know he had seen them, seen their faces.

Not long into the interview, he beseeched the grieving traveler, "Please write it down and tell the truth. I'll never speak of this again! I hope this admission confirms other stories you may have heard. My story is true. I saw them and knew who they were and where they were going. It was their first day of freedom, and they looked at my father, me, and our driver with those huge question-mark-filled eyes. In my memories of that horrible place, the prisoners all had the same eyes, that look of horror, the question of why without words. Why me? Then I watched my father bless them, and they all blessed him back. I didn't know he could do that, and then best of all, he blessed me and asked me to forgive him for what he's done when that time came. When it did, I did. I forgave him, and so did my mother."

Desch wanted the tourist to remember that most of all. He recalled in great detail how he confronted his father for a truthful answer by doing nothing more than standing there in the driveway. When they got home, their eyes met, him looking up into the eyes of his adoring father with a question mark all over his face.

"Father, please don't lie to me; I'll know if it's a lie. You told me to make sure I found the truth in this life. You said that. Make sure! Truth is truth."

That evening by their fireplace in the Commandant's quarters, military housing of the finest fittings and amenities imaginable, the boy and his parents entered the world of a harsh reality. They crossed a line where a Fourth Degree Templar Knight initiated his only son into a rare tradition. It might or might not run to fruition, but it was a start. The boy would have complete control of his destiny, a guided path if anyone lived through all this, a young stallion at fifteen years with nothing but sad memories of his youth. Knighthood is supervised and supported by any of the surviving Knights; it's an ancient tradition. The boy had to abide by a list of rules from the start, the underground laws, the guiding lines for the Knights Templar, that had to be sworn to. After he had, he got far more than he had bargained for, learned the truth about who those faces were, and saw his father look him in the eyes and tell him he hated Adolph Hitler and despised everything Nazi. Nothing would ever be the same again.

The man never stopped talking for damn near three hours, read from his pocket binder without looking up, and when he was done, he slid the memoir under a napkin to the traveler, hoping beyond hope that he wasn't being filmed this late in the afternoon. His stories of Theresienstadt came one after another, scenes he witnessed as a boy, murders, beatings, and horrible happenings that shook him deeply. He told how he didn't really sleep in this life. He would get close, but then jerk awake with his eyes wide open, and see hollow, sunken eyes asking why. Finally, there came that time in the mid-forties, at the end, when it was just him and his mother and two sick sisters, and the war was over.

Colonel Desch, his father, had simply disappeared, vanished one day when so many other German officers in the area did the same, and the only people who suspected that were those men's wives. Rumor flourished in the case of Colonel Desch that he left both his Lugers still in their holsters hanging there in his office. But unfortunately, that was all his son would ever know about the day his father disappeared. That was what someone told his mother. The beast that devoured the German Army was labeled the Eastern Front and was the destiny of so many German soldiers. They all knew it—no matter who you were, no matter the rank, any soldier in the service could end up on that front.

Now, after years of rehearsals caused by a premonition the policeman had, an idea he entertained for years, where he was waiting for this interview, and then suddenly Van Vedic was there and able to hear it all. Early in the interrogation and in response to the rumor that the Russian/Texan possessed a photographic memory, he told the policeman that it wasn't that; it was just a brief exchange where he spoke of his belief in his God of Reply sitting by his side.

"If you believe in the God of Reply," he said, "it sometimes allows you to know that things that are being told, things that are confessed, matters from the heart will be remembered flawlessly."

The policeman stared up into the captain's eyes for the longest minute until he finally asked if the man had heard all that he said. He was instantly consoled by the captain giving him a long series of slow and easy head nods. His eyes said it all.

"They tell me you spent all your time at the headstone for the priest Father Jude. He's the one you knew best? Was he special? Jude was the most treasured of them all to my father; he talked about Jude the last morning I saw him. My father believed he had seen a saint in Father Jude. A one in a million man. My dad told our mother and us every single day that he was done with what was happening; his soul was destroyed, and he was so full of regret and terribly ashamed. Without saying so in so many words, he was trying to save us. He understood that he couldn't save himself, but with luck and understanding, he might be able to save his family from extinction. Those exact words are very hard to breathe out at the breakfast table. Then my father walked away like he always did, down to his car, where they drove him to work. We never saw the man again."

Vincent Van Vedic found himself about to help a man sleep soundly from that night on. After a small preamble, the captain decided to turn Desch into a modern-day storyteller, and with the policeman's permission, he told the most current and up-to-date version of the story of Jude. One interpretation would be that the world would survive because Jude was set free, and the man who did that deserved all of heaven's glory.

When the nods were over, the policeman said Van Vedic could leave. His bus ride was waiting outside. That notepad binder fit in the corner of his jacket like that was where it belonged, and he and the other poker players were dropped off at the train gate headed into freedom, and when they got there, they all went on with their business. The captain had a mountain of information stored away in his library, and from deep down inside himself, he was consoled in his mental arrogance that everything he had recently experienced was just sitting there on the tip of his tongue, so to speak. He would feel it all once again in perfect detail, everything, when the time would come again that he could sit down and write about it. He now lived in a world that worshiped the God of Reply.

He visited Patton's grave not too far away in the Rhineland, in Luxenberg, one of over five thousand markers in that cemetery. The general's memorial was set aside, solitary, impressive. A warrior general was buried there, with the irony being that he'd died from a car accident after all the shooting had stopped. Patton took his last quadriplegic breath at noon on the Winter Solstice in 1945, just like he had feared, just like he knew, just like he'd done before. Jude's marker would last at least as long as that cemetery did and be seen by few as per his request, the epitome of humility. There had been few mourners at his interment.

On the other hand, Patton's grave was destined to last forever if there is such a time, and be visited by millions. They also made a shrine at his alma mater, the West Point Military Academy on the Hudson. In that graveyard near the entrance, they immortalized one of their own, and behind the general lay the remains of thousands of his fellow knights in armor. He wouldn't have wanted it any other way.

The first country Van Vedic visited in '56 was Russia. He eventually landed in Rostov-on-Don, and after a wonderful reunion with old friends that lasted a few days, he found himself the honored guest on a riverboat fishing cruise up the three hundred miles of the Don River to where the Illava merged and mingled, a trip he had made no less than a dozen times in his youth. The yacht was a fisherman's dream boat and a gift to Van Vedic for as long as he needed it, including food, furnishings, and a crew. It resulted from him writing a letter to an old friend and announcing he was coming home for a visit. That old friend had demanded that if Vincent ever came back to Russia, they should meet and say hello once again, one last time, for ancient times' sake.

"Please, please, please?"

They did just that in Rostov for a few days, reminiscing on that week they had spent in hell together, while the son of a man Van Vedic once carried off a battlefield learned the story his disabled father never talked about. He was allowed to sit close by and listen and cried manly tears while holding his father's damaged hand. That severely mangled hero and father of his had survived his injuries because of Vincent's bandages. He had been carried for miles through minefields in a mummy bag, laid across Van Vedic's back like a sack of potatoes. That bag of spuds became one of the most influential of all of Stalin's confidants, an advisory position that he had also survived. Whenever he received an award, gave a speech, or talked about the party, he credited everything about his long life to Vincent Van Vedic, his version of a true Russian hero, an ordinary man of the highest and largest order. Van Vedic's wish was his command.

"Don't give up on me. Please, please don't quit." (SHOTS FIRED) "Not much further... It can't be much further, can't be much colder..." (SHOTS FIRED. MORE SHOTS FIRED) The words seemed to freeze, and then they came back—over and over, they came back, "Don't give up on me. Please, please don't quit." (SHOTS FIRED) "Not much further." (SHOTS FIRED) "It can't be much further." Then silence from the backpacked human. Moments would pass, many steps in the snow. "Don't give up on me. Please, please don't quit. Not much further. It can't be much further." (MANY SHOTS FIRED)

Two miles later, the future war hero was laid on a gurney, saved by Van Vedic's effort, and destined for greatness.

With the promise to do it again in a month when the cruise was over, Van Vedic boarded the yacht with its crew of three and a stout Russian woman who loved to cook. The ship's captain was a retired KGB colonel who answered to 'Sir,' and only 'Sir,' carried a sidearm and promised Van Vedic that no one would interfere with their fishing trip three hundred miles up the Don River to the ruins of St. Francis of Assisi Church on the Illava, guaranteed it, and then casually saluted the giant Russian hero.

When they were out on the great open waters, the KGB colonel allowed Van Vedic to play with his 45 revolvers because it was in the contract and part of the plan. They had goose guns, boxes and boxes of ammo, because Sir had been told that Van

Vedic's nickname was "The Gunslinger" back in the day, and in no time at all, he became a believer.

After one of Van Vedic's demonstrations, while he was reloading the smoking beasts, Sir had to look down the barrels of his own 45s for some strange reason. The gunslinger blasted everything the crew had thrown in the water to kingdom come. Every single can sank, every bottle shattered, and sometimes he shot the cans a second time when they exploded up out of the water. It didn't matter in the slightest when Vincent changed hands. He explained to Sir while he was changing cylinders that it was only fair that he alternated so that both fists got equal practice, usually sixty rounds each hand or until they ran out of things that floated and were almost out of ammo.

Sir had come close to the target several times, tried to hold his cannon steady in the slightly rocking boat with both hands and balance himself, zero in on the target like a pure gold 007 the KGB would be proud of, and fire his weapon. Most shooters have their eyes closed at that moment and miss the impact moment. It would have shown Sir that he was close, but they weren't playing close. His comrades would toss the floating target ten feet out, off the starboard bow, while the yacht headed north at a few knots. When he fired, there were no explosions of the mark, so his comrades threw a broken lounge chair tied to a white life ring, which he miraculously destroyed on the second shot.

Their vessel stopped at a lavish Sports and Hunting Resort where they resupplied themselves courtesy of the local KGB authority. They were only a hundred miles from the turn onto the Illava, then ten miles to Pfeiffer.

Van Vedic remembered it all from fifteen years before when he and Jude went the other way on the *Vanessa* in early January of 1941. It was late afternoon when they came up on the Illava, but they found it full and manageable. Then, after churning up the Illava for an hour, Van Vedic stood on the bow and remembered the upcoming bend where he would see the black monolith, the Grotto sitting atop that hillside. That was where the church used to be.

It wasn't there like before. Part of it was, but the upper half was gone and replaced with a gigantic bronze clenched fist. He walked up the road alone while they docked the boat for the night. He found the entire ancient foundation of St. Francis surrounded by a concrete sidewalk platform with memorial plaques telling stories of the Volga Basin, the people who settled the region, and the battle plan for Operation Uranus. The most prominent plaque of all talked about Operation Uranus, November 19, 1942, and how a million hardened Russian Red Army infantry poured through this entire area and headed south.

The grotto that had sheltered the statue of St. Francis was filled in entirely with black granite chunks that had been stacked on purpose to make it look like it had been that way forever. Concrete embedded everything that was loose, a typical post-war memorial celebrating the heroes who may have died in this valley. That high-point pasture had become a World War Two Russian Memorial, the genius of Operation Uranus, a pincer movement that trapped the German 6th Army in Stalingrad and turned the war around on the banks of the Volga.

"The greatest battle in the history of mankind," the Battle of Stalingrad, had danced the war of death right on top of Pfeiffer for a few days in late November of 1942, and the disturbed foundation blocks of St. Francis of Assisi were all that was left of Pfeiffer.

The monument and memorial committees had decided to destroy the top half of the monolith, use all that material as fill, and mount a spectacular bronze fist sticking up into the sky at the top of what was left. They placed all the broken and blasted black granite chunks inside the confines of the massive foundation blocks that were surrounded by sidewalks. It was someone's idea of art—an elongated rectangle of nothing, with a fabricated lie telling the tourists and veterans that the war killed whatever had stood there. What in truth had stood there was the last vestige of the German Volga Catholics, St Francis of Assisi on the Illava, and nowhere was it mentioned that Uranus had rolled over a Catholic Church—in this case, that had actually been burned down in 1928 by communist pyromaniacs.

Basil had survived it all up to that point, lived in the basement quite comfortably, and became a very refined Pocomaxa who saw Uranus from many different angles when it flowed through. It's somewhat difficult to look through the cracks of foundation blocks and conclude too much about what's happening outside. It was almost divine construction of a sort, the way the debris from the firestorms during the bombardments landed all over the statue of Saint Francis and disguised it, hid it, and turned it into something it wasn't. From a distance, the grotto stood alone, covered in ashes, and because it was so dull and featureless, it enabled the Wolverine to stand back in the shadows during the day and watch the army as if he were invisible. The grotto looked like a burned to a frazzle black thing sticking out of the ground.

He hadn't done it in a while but went out into the chaos of the past two weeks, leaving very early in the mornings, and would be back by dawn when the army started waking up. It seemed that the war machine was everywhere, and he could watch just a small part of the army come through the Pfeiffer area in a busy swarm headed for Stalingrad fifty miles south. He felt obligated to stand there and count things and estimate numbers since they willingly allowed him to do that. It was impossible to come up with any sort of an accurate number, more like dozens, hundreds, and thousands of everything, especially infantry troops. Still, he thought that maybe a hundred thousand soldiers marched out of the outback and passed by the grotto just like Van Vedic had done. As he, Pocomaxa, very well knew, there were many other areas along the thirty-mile-wide corridor where tens of thousands more troops were passing through.

The wolverine knew where they were coming from, and he had to assume they had crossed over the Volga somewhere upriver, where it froze over early. It's hard to believe that such a magnificent river can freeze solid, bank to bank many miles wide, but it does, and it's sometimes considered normal if you talk to the locals. For the most part, the columns of men and tanks and trucks stayed a half-mile away because of the way the road went, but the procession never ended; day after day, all day and sometimes all night, thousands and thousands kept coming out of the outback like a faucet of Russian infantry soldiers was open out there somewhere and running full blast. As the days and hours passed, he analyzed what he saw, trying to imagine where these men were going and why. Basil knew precisely what was in front of them as far as the lay of the land was concerned, and at some point down there, in twenty or thirty miles, they would run into Germans.

In one harebrained extension of it all, he envisioned a similar army coming up from the distant south to meet with this army coming down from the north. Hypothetically, that would trap all the Germans who had made it to Stalingrad, and this country they had invaded was notorious for having long and nasty first-class winters. These snowstoppers put mankind to the test, and you'd better be ready because if you're not, you die.

All that aside, when they were gone, they were all gone, and for three nights in a row, he stole things from the rear troops, like papers and documents that seemed to explain everything about what was happening. He enhanced his pistol collection by one because he witnessed the execution of sick and injured Russian soldiers by their own colonel. He was an easy target, slept outside, and woke everyone up for a mile. It just so happened that Pocomaxa found an outcrop of sandstone on a nearby canyon ledge about an hour after the medics hauled the colonel away. He was halfway home and debatably within earshot of five thousand troops, so he held the sides of his face at the start and roared the roar of Pocomaxa like he had never roared before. By dawn, by first light, it was as if the entire army had disappeared, crossed over the Illava, and flowed south into the regions that bordered the outer edges of Stalingrad. Word spread rapidly throughout the upper ranks that there had been a confirmed icepick assassination in the forbidden zone. The information was proclaimed as a joke in the Officers' Club tents, but no one laughed very loud.

They returned five years later and unknowingly trapped Pocomaxa with their presence, showing up one spring day in 1947 as a small, well-organized army of engineers and veteran construction workers ready to build a reminder. They were there to make a war monument, one of many monuments, had a basic plan in mind, and had no intention of the project taking too long, even bringing their own cement truck and cement-making machine. Both were a first for the area. Their plan was pretty simple and was time-honored; it focused on the idea that a collective group of concerned neighbors and veterans could design the memorial once they got there and, after walking around the site, were able to develop a feel for the location, what did the land contribute and there ended up being a long list of commie bullshashiska heaped on top of every meeting. After a hard day's work, there was generally a good dinner for everyone, and plenty of vodkas washed it down. That was when most of the serious design discussions took place until finally, all the campfires went out, and they all went to sleep. On the third night, they got his attention when they set off high explosives around the top of the grotto, systematically blew it in half, and turned the statue of Saint Francis into a pile of shattered marble. They picked up all the black granite pieces and filled in the cavity like they were artists of stonework, trapping Pocomaxa, trapping the priest deep underground, and unwittingly burying him alive.

Basil thought about escaping through one of the four ports he knew about, but the risk of them discovering the basement because of his effort seemed too high a price to pay. In the first few days, he listened through the cracks in the foundation blocks to the two architects while they talked to the engineers about what they had in mind. Fortunately for the spy, they set up their workstation tables and chairs about twenty feet out from Basil's favorite crack of them all. In those casual sidewalk discussions, Basil learned everything he needed to know. He could see in his imagination the drawings those men were looking at, and his conclusion was the monument would be the foundation blocks for Saint Francis, encased in cement on both sides, with a thunderous bronze fist rising out from the top of the grotto at the top of the hill. There would be gardens along the sidewalks that eventually encircled the fist, many trees, two large parking lots, and a public restroom at the very start, with water.

From there, inside the upper rafters of the basement, in four different corners, narrow channels climbed up between giant round support pillars to a spot where one could see through a small crack in the enormous foundation blocks. He had to climb a ladder, ten feet or so, and stick his head into a box that surrounded the crack. Basil would wait, watch and listen by any one of the four cracks to learn what was going on at that spot

489

when the one by the old front steps disappeared one afternoon and liquid cement poured through for a bit. That crack he knew to be eight inches above level ground was now officially sealed. Within days, all four cracks had turned black, and finally, one day, the ground quit rumbling; they'd turned off their cement machine, which had run from sunup to sundown for two straight weeks.

Nothing had changed as far as life in the basement was concerned, with the breeze from the tunnel that led to the grotto keeping things fresh. The door to the passageway was never closed. Basil would walk that walk like he'd always done, but when he got to the right rear corner of the back side of where the St. Francis statue used to be, his lantern showed where liquid cement had poured through in many, many places where the granite had been packed in place. A loader farm tractor dropped huge chunks of granite into the cavity first after the dynamite, and then some workers filled in all the spaces with the smaller pieces. It took about a week, and he listened every day until he couldn't hear them anymore. He pictured an angled wall of granite pieces leading up the side of the grotto, with the whole area cemented in by sidewalks and gardens. A strong breeze flowed through the entire area, bringing the air from inside the basement to this spot, where it flowed through the granite chunks like an air filter. The cellar was breathing somehow, sucking in air and expelling it through many ports. So far, his air was as breathable as it had always been, and his candles constantly flickered towards the passageway.

His life had had two stages—the first twenty-six years spent becoming the man in the mirror, and then twenty-six more, at least, at Saint Francis on the Illava. It was now apparent that there was no construction going on above his shelter. Many of the vehicles involved in the construction of the memorial vibrated their existence down through the timbers. He could tell when their workday started and when it was over. Without any doubt whatsoever, he was now trapped for the rest of his life in the basement. In those first days after that realization, he had drawn up a mental list of just some of the benefits of that. He had plenty of books to read, plenty of songs to play, a ton of candles, and more food than he could ever eat. Plus, a small tributary flowed through his living room. What more could a man need?

One of his many talents was drawing landscapes, and he started a new one concerning a birds-eye view of this unique monument he was trapped inside. He heard them talking about where the placards would be set, what would be placed where, how wide the sidewalks would be, how deep, and everything about the shrine. It would be a cold day in hell when the Russians would ever forget what happened to their country during the war, and it was a well-healed opinion that the more war monuments there were, the better. Every town and village had one, and every battlefield had one. This one surrounding the old church blocks was made of thick concrete and destined to be there awhile. When he was finished, not only was he proud of his work, but it helped him accept his fate. Who would have ever thought?

Pocomaxa died right around those times, and it was hard to tell it had even happened; it might have had something to do with him putting his icepick in a drawer and closing it while thinking to himself he'd never kill again. In the world of the Russian Army, in the world of senior officers colonels and above, there would always exist an area on their maps where only fools commanded at their leisure, and if they did and lived to tell about it, they were more lucky that smart. A Russian colonel had succumbed to an ear invasion in the midst of Operation Uranus, a complete flaming asshole by all accounts, and no one showed up when the fossdick was hauled away the day after he went tits up. So far, he was the last one, the most recent icepick assassination, not necessarily the last, and the military high command had been taught a lesson. There's a place down in southern Russia, between both of the great rivers down there, a stretch of land fifty miles wide and a hundred miles long where a mystic wolverine prowled the countryside and stabbed military colonels and generals in their right ear with an ice pick. They never died right away but in time they did. They were protected, should have been safe deep inside the unit and resting for the night, when something penetrated the defenses and assassinated the highest ranking officer of the unit, right in front of his defenders, and then escaped every single time like it were invisible, like a ghost, like a blur. Then, as everyone sat back and tried to recover from the traumatic events of seeing their commanding officer go tits up total for who knew what reason or who knew why, and some banshee of a demon out in the woods would scream out this howl of a wail like its balls were on fire and it needed meat to eat immediately. This sound would scare the shit out of every human anywhere at any time. No questions asked, bring me my fresh pants. That was Pocomaxa's trademark, his favorite howl, the one he knew caused them to grab their shorts, shiver their length, and they would sit where they were the whole night and hardly move a muscle. All through dawn they would sit there and tremble and sometimes be glad they hadn't been promoted.

The assistant pastor had gone from prowling the countryside and covering dozens of miles in any direction he chose to not going anywhere. Worst of all, and he knew it, was the fact he'd never see the sun another time, never fish again, never look at the moon again. There was no such thing as the morning, noon, or night anymore, and for some strange reason, he wound all the springs on the grandfather clock that ensured it would run for a year. Sitting down in one of his favorite chairs by the waterfall and listening to that sound again, the Diamond Teardrop poured out a melody that never got old, and for that reason, he decided to make this chair his home base as long as he was alive. Behind him was his chapel that harbored the Eucharist and his bath and bed were next door to that. Further down was the crypt that had his name on it and his mind became flushed with the ideas of how he would manage that feat. During those mental discussions, he prepared that end of the hallway as best he could for an eventuality that was hard to predict. The idea of him being dead inside that coffin, inside that crypt, and then the lids closing down tight, was hard to conclude. It appeared to be a two-man job and with him being the dead man, he concluded he wouldn't be able to help much, smiled at his hermit humor, and everyone knows, you would have had to have been there.

The stream in front of his chair was a few feet wide, a few inches deep at the most, and it disappeared in the cracks in the floor right before the wall of timbers that held up this end of the roof. Even in the worst drought times, Hammer always had a trickle in front of his chair, except in '91, after everyone had gone. They lived out of vases and jars till things changed and it rained again.

He had turned the other side of the creek into his study, where he read and wrote and meditated on what he thought. It was the quietest study in the history of studies, with plenty of paper and pens, pencils, and whatever. Next came a kitchen with more food than he would or could ever eat. It had been packaged by people who understood such things, how long things could last, and what was good for a human to eat. And when he meditated on the kitchen, he thought of all the things he'd never eat or taste again. He was pretty much done with fresh fruits and veggies, although there was plenty of canned and jarred green things that he had always ignored. In the past he could find most of that hanging or growing on the ground on his nightly excursions, but those days were over, and he would have to make do.

There was actually only one room that had what he needed down that southern corridor. He had no need for vestments and such and no need for gold and silver. All the boxes he'd ever made were gone, and his tool room candles hadn't lit the room in quite some time. He needed his piano. He never seemed to get tired of it, constantly writing and creating new music of the highest degree. He created at least a hundred masterpieces, some way too big, some just right, and all of it was dutifully written down in a flawless pen, very fast and one time only, with no corrections. One a month, it seemed, manuscripts of music that he signed and dated, clipped all the pages together and left the document in a stack that might be found someday in the far distant future. It's hard to explain, but he and his piano were an entity unto themselves, a state of being that lasted for hours; with no such thing as daylight or nighttime, and the weather never changing, he played for God in a small concert room third door down on the southern corridor.

It doesn't take long for a man to change for the worse under sunless conditions. No rain or thunder, no wind, and right up there near the top of the wish list would be to hear the birds one more time. All of nature had disappeared from his world, and there were a host of fur babies out there that he had partially bonded with over the years. They might have wondered where he went, especially the jay birds that had kept him company on so many of his walks. There was a world up above him that he had once owned and, as fate would have it and through no fault of his own, that world vanished in a day, disappeared in its entirety. All of the sounds and the visions, everything about the world vanished, and when it did, that meant Basil had only so much time left until he too would vanish. In his never-ending genius state of mind, he calculated that he had to make up for the isolation with a very sophisticated routine of exercise and good habits that might keep his body alive as long as possible. It was Basil against the silent world that he lived in, totally silent unless he made music, or sang out loud or sneezed or sat mesmerized by the Diamond Teardrop waterfall. Time passed in a myriad of ways, including when he slept, most often while sitting at the piano, or there in his chair by the waterfall, at his desk on the other side of the stream, or sometimes in the kitchen, just him and a few candles all sharing a fresh cup of coffee.

There are a lot of ways to go out in this life, lots of ways, and there's one thing for sure when you think about it, when it's over it's over and for everybody that has ever existed, there came a time when that body died, and it quit making music. When we die we're done, no more fun, no more games, nothing. We get cold, real cold, we start to get hard, we change really fast when our hearts stop and for a brief period of time, the world out there can see us and remember who we were. It don't take long and all of that changes, man or woman, beast or fowl, when we're dead we're done and the earth must deal with us in a most rude and undignified manner. Fast, it all happens fast and the body goes from what it once was to something no one wants around. Please.

CHAPTER THIRTY-ONE

RAHELLIO'S LAST GOODBYE

With his back to the Shale Rock grave piles, Rahellio let the sunset shine on his throat and began singing an old gunfighter ballad about a famous New Mexico gunslinger, a marshal named Elfego Baca. He killed bad hombres and cowboys along the Rio Grande almost seventy years before. It seemed fitting. In the ballad, Baca, as an older man, relived how he never wanted to kill anyone.

"...but if a man had it in his mind to kill me, I made it my business to kill him first."

It was almost verbatim to something Vincent Van Vedic had told the mortician so many years before, over a tequila campfire down where the stone carvings were etched all over the cliff walls. Way back in the autumn of 1953, a time that changed his life forever.

There had been thousands of bonfires in Rahellio's life before that week, but the horseback trip to where the petroglyphs were, where that white-out occurred, and where he and the captain had lost their memory turned out to be the campfires he always remembered, his most unforgettable.

Now, with the captain dead and buried next to his wife, the crooner was the only mind left to remember those campsites, currently a hundred feet underwater. After the lake filled up and became a huge success, Rahellio would often fish off the stern of his cabin cruiser directly over those locations to the best of his judgment. To this day, he had never told the world what he and Van Vedic did or what they saw. He left that up to the captain because he had made the arrangements. The captain wrote a letter that put in writing his promise and Rahellio's, and lo and behold, his memory came back about some of the things that happened that weekend—everything from that time, three days in his life where he did things with the captain, and where for a time neither could remember what happened.

Life went on, and here he was, a very old, widowed mortician, singing like a wounded angel at a funeral for his best friend. Completely brokenhearted. Both he and his captain had developed a friendship that went as deep as two widowers can get. As little as a year ago, they sat together at the beautiful Eastern Overlook, looking out over that gorgeous lake towards Colorado, and talked about the blue lights in 1953. It was a subject they could talk about with each other. Neither made much mention of it to their other friends, as in almost not at all.

Among many other things, they talked about how good they felt. Neither man suffered from even the most basic ailments, and they would often reminisce on having discussed that very subject in those days immediately after that fishing trip. Even though the captain walked with a cane, he didn't really need it because all he ever did was lean on it and talk to it. Now it was part of his estate and part of *Vanessa*; they stayed together in the will.

497

Standing there, playing his six-string in front of the gravesites, the sounds from his guitar and his ballad spread out to the west, where he could see a hundred miles out above the water, looking directly at the setting sun over the Chuskas. The view was to die for. The reservoir had filled in all the river valleys, became the most substantial body of water in an otherwise bone-dry region, and Vincent Van Vedic had built his horse ranch on one of the most scenic corner outlooks of all. He invested in mineral rights everywhere they were for sale, bought more land, and built his new road to the county road that went north to Ignacio or south to Aztec.

Vincent was gone. His life had been well lived, had lasted for over ninety years, until he went to sleep one night, exhausted— bandaged from two bullet holes but recovering nicely at the time —when on his birthday, of all days, he simply never woke up. October 16th, 1979. He'd died in his sleep, which the mortician put on his death certificate.

The gang of robbers who put the bullets in him all died here and there along the long private dirt road that led to his country home. They'd disguised themselves as a busload of stuck-in-the-road tourists, attempted to lure him to their stranded vehicle with the hopes of killing him there at the scene, out in the middle of nowhere, and then search his home for whatever it was that made him so wealthy.

His trip to Europe and Russia in '56 had lasted for months, seemed to have fulfilled him, and while on that trip, he started using the cane. It was perfect for his size and had the most unbelievable carving at the top, the head of Jesus, front and back. When he was walking alone for exercise, full stride and fast with the cane, it was like watching a machine, and the only way an ordinary soul would be able to keep up would be if they were jogging.

In 1957, after his trip to Europe that had lasted for months, the captain started a construction company and assigned his first four employees from Arboles to build that road across his property, then onto a grateful neighbor's property, a long stretch of "forest service land down to the river and up to the bridge at the La Boca crossing." He paid each man a thousand dollars a month. When they were finished a year later, they named it "County Road 4000." The number 4,000 was a special dedication on their part, as every payday, the captain would hand each man fifty twenty-dollar bills. Obviously, news of the workers going from poor to semi-wealthy in less than a year had spread and attracted the wrong kind of attention, if his cane was right—and it always was.

The out-of-shape young man standing in the driveway that day had an accent from somewhere in Europe, and this woman he claimed was his wife was not in love with the windbag. They didn't wear wedding rings, and the captain could tell all that without proof because he'd always trusted his gut and felt they were somehow up to no good. His Spivey sense, coupled with his cane's vibrations, started with the first words from the heavy breather's mouth.

"HELLO, HELLO IN THERE. MAY WE COME ABOARD?" After hearing the hail, the captain walked out on his porch, instinctively taken aback by the loud greeting. Not the way to talk to a cowboy in the desert. Everything about this guy was wrong; it showed in his manner, voice, and appearance.

"This angle is plenty good enough, and so what can I do for you?"

"We were trying to turn around on the road to this house, trying to go back to the county road we had been on when we ended up sideways. Now we're stuck in the middle of the road a couple of miles that way. Our back wheels are buried in a little ditch, and we eight together couldn't push it out. We were hoping to find some help or maybe use your phone?"

They told the ninety-year-old man they had walked for who knew how far from where they were stuck, left all the rest of their companions behind to wait for help and quizzed him about living alone in this outback country.

"I've always been an outback sort of guy, and I'm not near as alone as it appears. Can you young folks describe the area where ya all got buried? Describe it a bit, so I understand what we're up against? Back two miles or more, you say?"

They described the Embudo arroyo down that road at least that far, a problem area for sure, and a long way from the county road he was talking about. They had driven by dozens of places before getting stuck where they could have turned around and gone back safely, huge turnarounds for the water trucks and the drilling rigs. However, the captain knew full well that getting from one side of the Embudo to the other had always been an issue. It was well over a hundred yards wide, full of sand and easily manipulated by Mother Nature when she rained hard. Vincent had paid for the narrow little two-lane—sometimes one-lane—road that traveled from his garage doors to La Boca Road. It was not an inch short of a dozen miles, with many, many turn-offs, Ys in the road with no signs, but the oil field people in their one-ton trucks always knew where they were going. The 'patch hands' had been known to find survivors, people who ran out of gas while lost and thought they could walk out. Fishermen try to come in the back door, so to speak, they try to get to the lakeshore from the north, but most folks get lost in no time. The Ute Indians frown on it with all their might and diligently patrol their property. County Road 4000 was the only way in or out and had to be perpetually maintained and repaired after any rain worth talking about.

The captain knew that road as well as any path he'd ever walked, knew it like the back of his hand, and knew that getting where they were stuck could only mean they were trying hard to find the reservoir. His Spivey sense was itching like poison sumac. His cane became hot to the touch.

"I have a fabulous yellow backhoe that can get anything out of anywhere. We can use that. I haven't driven it in a week. I use it to get to my exercise class, which doesn't mean I can't get my exercise today on the way back. It only seats one, but you two can ride in the bucket. The phone is out; it's oftentimes out and pisses this elderly gentleman off but good when it is. I'm sure glad to have a phone, and I can only hope the service will be better in the future. Sorry. Why don't you young'uns grab a couple of those cushions out of those chairs over there to sit on and go wait for me inside the bucket of that yellow tractor on the side of the barn?"

He pointed with his cane.

"I've got to take a pill, take a piss, find a coat, the keys, and I'll be right with you. I can grab you both a tab if you like soda."

The two begging strangers were now dealing with a host of questions and answers; they saw the cushions, turned, and saw the backhoe on the side of a building quite a way away. Finally, from the top of the porch, he directed his last comments on the subject toward the bottom steps, where his guests didn't seem to want a tab.

"Kids, I've got to take a piss," he said from the top of his porch. "I'll be right back. Usually, the dogs don't bother strangers, but I don't know where they are; probably down by the lake. The big red one is my favorite because he's big and red and seems to answer to 'Big Red.' He's different from the others; you'll recognize him instantly, if you know what I mean. When my phone works, he hears the bell inside the house even when the tractor is running and all the rest are yapping. If you're sitting in the bucket, they won't bother you. No matter about that, I'll be a few minutes. It's nice to have visitors."

He hadn't packed so many lies into a twenty-second speech in a long time, but he also hadn't felt this uneasy in an equally long time. Before they could answer or object, he left the porch and went inside, acting every bit like the ancient man he was. They had no choice but to do what he said. They did it quickly, eighty yards across the large driveway in thirty seconds to the yellow thing and struggling with their cushions while running. He watched them through the window, watched her scold Windbag all the way to the tractor for some reason, and watched him tap his right side waistband while dusting off his fancy boots. He was glaring at her the whole time while she glared back.

Windbag did not seem concerned that she couldn't climb into the shovel bucket without his help, with its ugly, dirty front lip three feet off the ground. Primarily because he became immediately concerned about the oversized "Doberman Pincher Guard Dog" warning signs she pointed to all along the barn wall.

Actually, the term warning might be a stretch; it was more like a mural of the family pets, an introduction of sorts. The characters looked like portraits of Dobermans, six altogether, with each one's name clearly printed on the frame's bottom board. "Guts," "Lash," and "Wonder Dog" had their portraits on the left side of the barn; all three were what the casual observer would describe as your above-average Doberman Pincher with teeth. Each barn door had a portrait of an entire horse, a big head, big muscles, and that animal's name, "Brutus" and "El Bruto Whetto," with three more dog portraits on the other end of the barn. The middle picture of the three was "Big Red," a fitting name, maybe even the perfect name, and there wouldn't be anything wrong with making mention of jaw muscles and teeth. The first painting, "Sappo," was just about as red, a belligerent-looking red, and could be mistaken for Big Red if it was someone's first encounter. The last picture showed more of the same, only the dog was blond and had a handsome head, glaring eyes, shoulder muscles, and pointed ears. "Sarge." Every portrait was from a photo that a Indian artist friend had painted, and each of the images took Wilson a sunup to sundown day to finish. He would cover an area along the side of the barn with two four-by-eight sheets of quality plywood per portrait and then use the very best paints available. All of the animals had been a part of the captain's life once upon a time, but these days they lived only in his memory banks, and all were long gone.

While inside, looking out, the captain started an old tradition at about one-tenth the speed of the glory days. With his eyes wide open the whole time, he hung the forty-five caliber cannons on his hips with his Spivey sense tingling through his neck hair. In his old age, he wore them much higher than back in his gunslinger days, still strapped the holsters' tips to his somewhat shrunken thighs. He hadn't practiced his quick draw in many years, always considered the fact he could possibly dislocate a shoulder on either side if he tried too hard, and at this late age, it didn't matter; the holsters were now only suitcases that carried the beasts to his weekly exercise class that sometimes lasted for hours. Nevertheless, he still loved to wear them just for the feel. His leather coat had recently been modified for his old age, weight loss, and the fact that he was six feet six and shrinking, but he wore it very well; he didn't even limp unless on purpose, and still had eighteen of his teeth.

The coat, of course, was nothing more than perfect for disguising the exercise equipment. When he left his house and walked to the tractor, his tourists were sitting on their cushions, plotting and planning their ambush against their savior.

She acted a bit impatient as he walked up. "Sure hope this doesn't put you out too much, old man. My name's Rowena. You got one?"

"Old man will not do! Most folks hereabouts call me Captain; I have a boat on the lake. Back in the big war, I was captain of said boat when I got tangled up with some submariners who didn't respect their elders, hated other people for no reason, but called me old man one too many times and shit. That was almost forty years ago. When I think about it, I wasn't even old back then!"

"ROWENA, HONEY, are you taking notes?"

"No, dear. I can remember anything this captain can remember!" After that, she re-adjusted herself to better look at Van Vedic with all her glare. "I don't need a history lesson; I NEED A RIDE! Next thing you know, he'll be making up some bullshit story about sinking a submarine and saving the world. GADS! Could we get moving?"

All conversation was almost over as he showed her those remaining front teeth in something like a smile, then slowly tipped his hat to the lady while asking one final question.

"Were ya'll just trying to get down to the edge of Navajo to fish or something?"

Rowena was almost touching the steel inside the bucket wall, hanging onto the back and the lip and not liking it one bit, while Gabby the Windbag was on the other side, doing the same.

"Do I look like I fish? Does he look like he fishes? I have not a clue what the edge of Navajo might mean, but I would appreciate it if you could get this thing in gear! Thank you!"

After that statement, she ignored the cab driver but started a new conversation with Gabby mumbling something about assholes, fuddy-duddy, and Gabby having been right.

That brief exchange convinced Van Vedic that she had been evidently mistreated somewhere along the way, was incapable of interaction with humans, didn't fish, and didn't know that Navajo Lake had an edge, so he instantly decided to de-friend her. It was a term the Knights used during the hard times at the turn of the century back in Russia. The Headhunters and the Guardsmen used the term "de-friended" to explain why so-and-so was dead. Of course, he and she weren't actually friends to begin with; he felt like he had been forced into it, had plenty of friends already, more than enough of those, and was now on a personal mission to help get this bitch out of the county.

Since she didn't want to chat, he climbed into the cab and started the beast. His jacket had done the trick, and not only that, he wore the time-worn, out-of-shape original cowboy hat that more or less made him look like a really tall, ridiculous, extremely old long-haired hippy cowboy. It had been some time since anyone had called him "old man" to his face, as most folks had more respect than that, and if they did say such a thing, it was preceded by "dear."

Rowena and Gabby held on tight to the heavy-gauge steel dirty corners on the bucket while instantly appreciating how necessary the cushions might actually be, assuming they ever got out of the panicked crouch they had immediately taken.

The craft's pilot didn't honk the horn to warn them, didn't tap on the window. He simply turned it on and tilted the bucket back further at the very start. The captain grabbed that handle rather violently, which scared them both half to death, and allowed the screaming engine to drown out their initial comments. After just a few seconds, he raised their reserved seat almost six feet up over the driver for better visibility while putting the monster in gear at the same time. The whole moment was enhanced when he ran over the two railroad ties on which the bucket had rested. Two small obstacles that generally turned a standard backhoe into a bouncing, bucking-bronco backhoe, resulting in more screaming from the gallery.

He churned down the gravel driveway in first gear, a few thousand RPMs too many, with his engine screaming for him to shift to second, but for some reason he wouldn't do it, stayed in low first gear the whole time. The muffler was blowing pitch-black diesel exhaust straight up in the air but, fortunately, well over a yard behind their open-air balcony. All in all, everything around them sounded like a volcano was going off, and the smoke proved it, shooting twenty feet up in the air behind them. When they dared peek down at the madman, he seemed oblivious to almost everything, focused on sliding through his magnificent central gate creation at fifteen miles an hour. After all, as Gabby mentioned, they were in a hurry, and time was a-wasting. His two massive rod iron gates were hinged far wider than necessary, with the left side permanently closed and the other side always open, accurately illustrating the notion of "overkill." His passengers were immediately aware that it was an arched gateway of sorts, made out of three-foot-in-diameter vertical white cottonwood timbers, with massive horizontal timbers thirty feet long, about as high off the ground as the top of the bucket, give or take, depending on how the machine was reacting to the dishpan road surface.

As time was running out, the high-altitude spotters became insanely aware of what they hadn't noticed when they'd walked under it. Being in the bucket this time would give them a new appreciation for Van Vedic's heavy timberwork. Maybe fifty yards from impact, the tourists peeked over the bucket's edge with huge eyes, twice, and appeared to be screaming for joy.

Unfortunately, it was hard to hear with the engine making all that noise, and being an old man, all their tour guide could manage was two thumbs up, for way too long, with no hands on the wheel while mouthing, "Don't worry, be happy."

The backhoe rattled over the cattle guard—consisting of an elaborate concrete box with a drain hole that housed and supported a dozen twenty-eight-foot-long steel railroad rails spanning from one side to the other. The tracks were so heavy that they were merely laid in place, side by side, with steel spacers to terrify cattle. As a result, it was safe for heavy vehicles to drive over at reasonable speeds, cement trucks, drilling rigs, and the like. he eased off at the end, slowed her down to ten, and sailed through the tight right side, slamming the rails together and creating an exploding steel sound that few tourists had ever heard. It was possibly the loudest, scariest, most deafening noise the pedestrians had heard so far in their lives, much like the end of the world would sound, perhaps. The bucket sailed—or slid might be the better description—under those cross-beam timbers with well over a foot and a half to spare, and he picked up speed when the road widened. They had a long way to go yet.

When they'd come up, most of that last uphill mile they had moaned and groaned about. It was now the first downhill mile, and the whole time the captain waited for them to appear but they never did. He assumed the entire time they were leaning over the front of the bucket and watching the country go by. Then, slowly, like really slow, an inch a minute or so, Rowena's hair came into view above the bucket's lip a few feet higher than the top of the window. Eight dainty fingers grasped the yellow steel from the other side. Finally, her giant round white eyeballs appeared above the bucket's backside. She had been on the other side when they first left the yard a while back. Then Gabby showed his frightened face too.

From their elevated vantage point, they both insinuated from their gestures that they were almost there and could see the bus a long way up ahead. There appeared to be prayers involved. They had magically fallen back in love on this brief tour, as they were obviously kneeling on the cushions, hugging each other, maybe singing God Bless America from the looks on their faces, and then hugging some more.

Van Vedic shifted into second.

CHAPTER THIRTY-TWO

SEVEN MORE NOTCHES

On the other side of the dry arroyo, a gray VW bus was sideways in the road. The lovers had suddenly become suspicious and bossy. They wanted him to stop the tractor long before necessary. The captain could tell that for the last few hundred yards, four sets of footprints had headed back the other way. It was not easy being a legendary tracker from the cab of a Caterpillar tractor, but someone had to do it. In this case, it was easy, because it's impossible to walk along the road in a desert arroyo and not leave footprints. Coming or going, we always leave footprints in the sand that point which way we went. But, in this case, and past the halfway point, no prints returned to where they'd started.

Whatever he may have looked like to the average lost tourist was one thing, but he was sure he didn't look a fool, because a fool he wasn't. He paid attention to such things. His exercise programs kept him more than able in many regards. He had no interest in dying young, still fed himself every day the right way, and used 45 revolvers like dumbbells before and after emptying them both at targets from up close or a hundred feet away. Of course, he missed the targets a lot these days, because the guns had gotten so much more cumbersome, but he still loved the thunder. In his glory days, he kept track of sixty rounds, but he concentrated on the first twelve. They were all that ever mattered. Everything after the first two cylinders had always been just for fun, except in the war.

He stopped the tractor and slowly lowered the bucket, but he didn't turn it off and let her rumble while his passengers found safe footing and were immediately greeted by four of their friends. Van Vedic opened the glass door and stepped out onto the running board while leaning on his cane, giving a wave to the group, who were anything but friendly.

Rowena started the reunion by saying, "We found this old man and his tractor, and he volunteered to help us."

But instead of being greeted with perhaps a wave or an introduction to the foursome, not a one seemed surprised that he existed, the group of four men acting distant from the start, cautious, giving him that nervous eye contact thing he had seen dozens of times in his life. It caused his Spivey sense to instantly flare once again across his shoulders, that feeling he abruptly remembered, an atmosphere that is impossible to forget if you've ever felt it. If another man on earth might have felt it more than him from so many personal bad and deadly times in his past, he didn't know who that might be. 'Spivey sense' was what he nicknamed that sensation, that tingle that flies up the backbone, ruffles those neck hairs right before the shit hits the fan, and a feeling he had felt many, many times throughout his life, many times.

Later on, after he'd notched the consequences and would then write about those encounters in his journal, he coined the term 'Spivey sense' and vowed to trust that feeling, a vow from way back when, to recognize it instantly, trust it just like he did the 45's. Of course, that feeling had always preceded everything in the past, even in the wars, and every time, people died.

The cane was hot. It turned in his hands and pulled his gaze to the cane's eyes for an instant. Then it turned back to record what was happening. Here he was, on the edge of as old as we get and soaked through in his Spivey sense one more time.

"ROWENA? Rowena? I thought you two said eight folks were on the bus, but I only counted six."

She turned and glared at him, just like she had done with Gabby, and for more than a second, he saw on her face that same look he saw in the men.

"Don't worry, old man. The missing two went the other way for the same reason we went towards you. It shouldn't take a wizard to figure that one out. But, geez! Why don't you stick to worrying about how to get us going, huh? Why don't you just do that, get down from there and hook up a chain or something? How about we get this done?"

With the married couple just off his left front tire, four dark-looking strangers directly in front of his bucket, and two off over the hill somewhere, not in front but behind, he once again found himself in charge of things.

Due to the fact that this wasn't the captain's first rescue, he let those old instincts take over. Any time he was involved in such a thing, he always took charge. The evaluations concerning why there was a need for a rescue usually only take a moment or so after the rescuers arrive. Any relief always starts with the basics. In this particular case, the fundamental problem was, as he had been told earlier, that the rear wheels of a small bus were stuck in a ditch. That was the reason for everything—the long walk, the sad story—but from his vantage point on the running board, he could see none of that was true. The bus was intentionally blocking the road, was not stuck in any way, and could go forward or back without a problem.

That analysis might have taken up the first fifteen seconds, with all the introductions going on, but when they saw their savior point at the right rear tire and then crinkle his old face into a visual, "What's that all about," with no words, the lizard was now out in the open.

The next thing he knew, Gabby had pulled a small handgun, raised it, and shot it four times at the open door. All sorts of the tractor protected Van Vedic—the door itself, a large air filter assembly, wheels all over the place—and a certain percentage of all that created the ricochet effect, and that's what got him. He slid down the cane in a crunch and almost let go, but he didn't, and then he felt a surge of strength.

Those first bullets made the older man mad, shot by a small-caliber handgun, but to add insult to injury, he suffered more shame knowing that it was second hand, a ricochet that nicked him on the thigh. He still went down hard on the running board, but on the way, he found his left-hand 45. His assailant came running forward with the clear plan in mind to shoot him dead for good, but when the assassin discovered his best angle, he also found someone already there with a much bigger gun. The living sometimes debate what the victim might have been aware of in that last split second of their life before the bullet arrives and literally removes the 'plan in mind' from the chess board.

As far as Gabby was concerned, if he recognized and understood what the barrel of a 45 revolver looked like from his vantage point, it would have been the last time he ever realized anything. Instead, his friends watched his head lift off his body in a cloud of something unrecognizable, which caused all five to race to their bus to gather all their guns and immediately start shooting at the tractor.

The captain's wound was virtually painless. The bullet hadn't hit the bone, and of that he was sure. It wasn't even bleeding all that bad as he returned fire.

Rowena was screaming, "Gimme a gun, gimme a gun. I'll kill you myself, you stupid old man."

He rearranged himself, knowing they were closing in as he glided into the cab. He threw the machine in reverse and began raising the bucket for protection, only to discover the most agile of the remaining attackers was suddenly standing up in the vibrating bucket. He unloaded nine or ten shots in rapid order, hitting everything in the cab except the driver. The bullets were blowing out the windows, tearing up the seat while he blasted his whole load in just a few seconds. He was out of ammo now, searching his pockets for a clip, bobbing and weaving with an empty gun, when Van Vedic slid up in the seat, shot him twice, and destroyed the man's chest. It was as if he had dived out of the bucket backward—he threw his arms out to his sides, and crashed down on his back.

The captain was in reverse, somewhat under control, putting some distance between them all, and could see them running towards him and shooting long rifles.

Another sprinter came into view, waving two guns, trying not to fall and shooting erratically. The gunslinger blew his arm off at the elbow. That was where he died; he bled out in a few minutes.

Unfortunately for the backhoe, big and strong as it was, all the hydraulics had suddenly gone to shit after being severed during the attack. The back tires were screaming air out of the bullet holes. He ran off the road right in the middle of the arroyo, up and over a berm wall, in a cloud of dust only fifty yards from where it all began. The race was on again. Rowena never quit chasing. She had picked up Gabby's bloody gun, screaming the whole time and cautiously closing in on his right, closer and closer, with the men beginning their pursuits once again when they realized the engine had stopped.

All three had stood momentarily traumatized as they stared at their friends, human bodies that had been very much alive not long before. As she got close, Van Vedic made it to the ground and planned his defense. She suddenly crested the berm and fired two shots from fifteen feet. He blew her away with his left-hand cannon and spun her like a top only a few yards in front of her true lover. As the heavy-duty unit got close, he saw what was left of his future bride, literally the brains of the operation, and started shooting a long semi-automatic gun before he even pointed it on purpose. That's no way to play cowboy and assassins with mister Van Vedic. For his daring, the groom inherited two slugs at precisely the same time, which made a mess of that whole area. There was only one last aggressor out of the original six, but the captain had lost track of him.

The only thing he could do was start limping back to his house as best and fast as possible, reloading new full cylinders; while his cane carried almost all his weight, he searched for the enemy. His Spivey sense told him there were three left, not one, and those four sets of footprints he'd seen in the sand could not be ignored. He feared an ambush from up ahead and tried to hide behind cactus and sage, one big bush at a time, until he was on the far side of the arroyo—still a long way to go.

There's an old rule in gunfighting that demands the shooter not scream at the top of their lungs before they start shooting; no matter how exciting the moment might be, don't yell a warning. It never works, especially if one is about to shoot at the likes of Vincent Van Vedic, who always shoots back straight. His assailant was almost exhausted, needed water in the worst way, carried an AK47, and had snuck up on the captain's left side. It was almost like they surprised each other, sixty feet apart, when their eyes met and the shouting began.

As far as the shooting was concerned, there were only three bullets left in the 47, and a full tumbler in Van Vedic's right-hand 45 cannon that he half-emptied in his target. The first slug stood him straight up, the second knocked him back a few feet, and the third spun him in the air like a top, all three impacting within fractions of a second. His dead body pulled that automatic trigger, and the aim was a dead man's guess.

Just below the face of Jesus on the cane and slightly above the handgrip, the third bullet from the AK was buried half an inch into the dead center of the shaft. No further, no damage; the absolute perfect first-finger circle grip. The captain held the cane with his left hand, the pistol in his right when the party began, lasting five seconds at the most, with the rod protecting his throat from a death shot. In those next few seconds, his scorecard told him there were still two left, but he had no idea where they were —possibly drawn to the arroyo because of the noise and hiding along the ridgeline. They had to be close.

He would hold the cane with both hands, turning the head in a sweeping motion while resting in a sagebrush bush's dismal shade for ten minutes. His boot had filled up with blood. He was dehydrated, thirsty as all get-out, but was still about a mile from home, all uphill, and he was aware he was ninety years old.

He mapped his destination with a clear mind, bush to bush, standing up and leaning on the cane, making good progress, no noise, and all ears. He could still hear with the best of them, always had, and while most folks seem to lose their hearing as they age, his hearing was ten times as sharp as ever, all because of the cane. In his most recent battle, he had actually heard the shouter walking in the sand a moment or so before the idiot jumped into view and started shouting.

A long-eared jackrabbit came bounding through the cactus field alongside the road, running down and away from something that had scared it up on the ridge. They only run like that to get away from something, which confirmed what he knew. The remaining two were up in front somewhere, and now he was so thirsty, kind of dizzy, ancient and wounded, and working his way up a very long hill. Another thing that kept him in the game was his anger, waves of rage that held his attention, and just like back in the war, it wasn't over till all the enemies were dead. All of them. They had entered an arena where only the strong survive, where experience counts as much as anything and the body reacts instantly to the ever-changing environment. His cane carried all his weight from one big sage bush to the next, where he would pause and scour the hill up ahead, sucking on a small pebble that caused his mouth to get wet, but he knew he had to have water immediately, or he'd pass out from the heat.

In that instant, when the bullet finds the flesh, if it isn't fatal, our bodies almost instantly go into shock, allowing us to understand what's happened to some degree. Every bullet hole emits a different reaction and a different response time. In the captain's case, he had actually become somewhat delirious. He was literally walking upright and could see the garden hose when they shot him in the neck. The sniper squealed with delight when Van Vedic fell in a heap, and after he didn't move for a brief time, the spotter and the sniper ran up to his bloody body to reshoot him if necessary. They were the last of the gang still left alive and had seen their co-conspirators get blown to pieces right before their binoculars. What had started as eight to one, a failproof plan, was now over. The others were all dead, the old man had been killed, and instead of him being the only fatality, the two of them were all that was left.

Neither team member had a clue as to what they could have searched for. No one did, but they all believed there was something hidden in that home, something to make them wealthy, and they could find it if given enough time. These remaining two had virtually nothing to do with the planning itself and only knew their victim was old, lived alone in a mansion, and legend had it that he had a treasure of diamonds and gold. That was what they were there to find. In the rehearsal sessions, it appeared unlikely that the sniper team would even be needed, as the organizers seemed to think they could kill Van Vedic in private out where they pretended to be stuck. Just shoot him in the head from the back, quick and easy; after all, it was just one old man.

That was when they discovered the captain was basically faking, being their very last joint discovery. The sniper team got close enough to recognize the bloody pants and jacket and saw the body was face down, blood all over his collar and hair from their shot, not moving at all, which caused them to lose their edge. They relaxed, calmed down, when suddenly their trophy rolled over and roared. His assassins were standing together a few yards away, still shocked by it all in every way, not being used to seeing brains scattered all over everything, no matter how tough they sounded and looked. Both were proud of what they had done and told each other so, and were glad to be alive. And now Van Vedic suddenly rolled over, winked, and fired twice. He allowed their minds that microsecond to realize they were looking down a pistol barrel before they both lost consciousness.

It wasn't that long later that the captain reached the garden hose and let the water flow all over himself inside and out. The wound to his neck was excruciating and out of his vision, but he measured it with his fingers and decided it wasn't all that bad. But unfortunately, he was losing consciousness, falling asleep, and there didn't seem to be anything he could do about it. Finally, after a brief mental discussion and a few sips of water, he went to sleep at the bottom of his front porch steps. He would be in danger of bleeding out himself if he didn't get immediate help.

As fate would have it, three BLM surveyors were headed for a corner section at the end of the county road when they came upon the VW bus. That was a sight to behold, with three bodies that were badly torn up and partially dismembered lying in a row about fifteen feet apart. One body had lost its head, one lost an arm, and one was flat on his back with his chest an open subject. Not one of the surveyors had ever seen such a thing, and they didn't handle it all that well, not at the start; who would? Two of them vomited right at the beginning. They walked around from behind the Volkswagen, saw those bodies, and both instantly turned and went back out of view. All three staggered to their truck and sat there, stunned and wondering what to do next. They knew Van Vedic lived up that road, and they could see his backhoe over on the edge of the arroyo. There were also more bodies over there. It wasn't all that far away, and there was no doubt that there were at least three more.

"I think we should... I think I need to drive up to the captain's house. What do you guys think? Let's drive over to the backhoe."

Our driver, Chester T., was also the boss of the crew. Usually, a field survey crew boss can be very bossy, loud, and typically impatient. However, in this case, he became gentle with his team, had his feet on the ground reasonably quickly, and took control of his ship, a heavy-duty one-ton dually that he put in gear and drove on, staying out of the crime scene.

At the risk of getting stuck, he made a new set of tracks in the sand quite a ways out from the backhoe. Both the big rear tires were flat as could be, all the windows were blown out, same with the door, and there was no doubt those were bullet holes. The first body they came across had been shot quite a few times, was flat on his back, still holding his weapon, and dead as a doornail. Over on the far side, there were two bodies, and one was a woman. Both had been shot up bad, but none of the bodies was the captain. They continued up the hill, and no sooner had they entered the circular drive than they found a dead man and another one sitting in a pool of his own blood, but still alive. He raised a hand at the truck when it stopped.

He needed all sorts of medical attention, and when the boss man climbed out and was about to head that way, he could see Vincent lying in the shade by the steps to his front porch.

"Check this guy out and pick up their guns. That other guy is dead. I'm driving up to look at the captain. I'll call the sheriff from inside the house."

Both his passengers got out and approached the bleeding man. He was pretty close to being finished, but for now he would just sit there, gurgling, bleeding from the wound to his face, and would wait and see if he lived through it. A good percentage of his jaw was gone. If he made it, he would have a lot of trouble remembering what the man in his mirror used to look like.

The lead surveyor was a Ute Indian, an army guy from Vietnam, with a name tag of Chester T. Begay. He knew and respected Van Vedic. He stopped the truck, jumped out, raced up to the captain, took him by his shoulders to steady him, and asked where he was shot. He dropped his hand covering the hole in his neck, and circled a gash there on his pants on his thigh. Then, like a field medic, he grabbed the edges of the tear and ripped his pants so he could see the wound. Sure enough, it was long and deep and still bleeding, but not critical.

"How bad is the neck wound? Has it stopped bleeding? The phone is in the kitchen, and I hope it's working. You better go call somebody."

"Captain, I'm not a medic, but I'd say you were fortunate and they'll fix this."

The captain took the hose again, swallowed some water, and let it run on his neck wound, which stung like crazy to start with, but when that went away, it felt terrific. He did the same to his thigh, kicked off his boots, and a tsunami of blood and water flowed away and down the walkway. He gently washed the thigh wound as Chester ran up the steps and into his house. He changed position and thought about standing up when he went to sleep again and looked very much like he was dead.

Three sheriffs in their squad cars, along with two New Mexico State Police, started arriving within thirty minutes. Two ambulances from Durango came in, and they even sent a fire truck from Ignacio for who knew why.

The first police on the scene had both patients ready for when the ambulances arrived. The most extended crime scene in the history of both states started there in the arroyo and ended at the foot of the steps to the captain's porch. Things took a turn for the worse when both ambulances barely made it through the sand to the start of the big hill with police cars in hot pursuit, and they managed to get bogged down and buried. The lead officers realized what was happening and tried to stop others from following in their tracks, but it was almost hopeless. By the time the captain arrived at the Durango hospital, over a hundred different police and investigators were trampling all over everything from one corner of his homestead to the next.

A heavy-duty tow truck showed up to start winching some of the squad cars out of the predicaments they had driven into. While they were loading the wounded at the top of the hill, that was one thing, but when they headed back down that hill, they ran into the log jam in the arroyo. Most were stuck in the arroyo because they tried to avoid other cars already stuck, which made a big mess of things. Let it be known that just because a man is driving a wrecker truck doesn't mean he can't get stuck and make matters worse than all get-out. Finally, a Colorado road department grader showed up. This guy made a new route in less than an hour through the arroyo so that all the vehicles could go back and forth, especially the ambulances. While the captain rested in his chariot, the paramedics treated him as best they could and assured him that he would be okay, nothing life-threatening, to which the captain asked about the sniper he had shot.

"How's that fella doing I saw sitting in the driveway? I hope he makes it. He'll have quite a story to tell, and like I say, I hope he survives."

"He's not doing all that good. The bullet hit him in the jaw, and from what I could see, he will be lucky to live through all this. We should get to the hospital in fifteen minutes, and we'll know better then."

"He tried to kill me, shot me in the neck from behind the sagebrush like a coward, wanted to steal my money. I don't have any money here; I keep it in the bank. Everybody keeps their money in the bank. He must have twitched there at the end, and that's what saved him. Otherwise, he'd look like his spotter. I heard them talking when they ran up on me; they thought I was dead."

"Captain, from what I could see, the guy with the facial wound will have a hard time talking if he manages to live through all this. You carry a very high-powered weapon, and I think the rumor out in front of my bumper says there are seven dead and two criticals, with you being one of them. Once we get you to Mercy General, I think you'll be just fine."

Sure enough, and because of the delay in getting to the hospital, the captain received the very best care available in the Southern Rockies when he finally arrived. News went out in that social circle very quickly that there had been a mass shooting, that an eccentric elderly gentleman had been targeted by a gang of radical leftists. According to the confession of a badly wounded lone survivor of the group, it appeared their ambush site went bad from the start, and the next thing the sniper survivor knew was that he had been shot in the face by the man he thought he had killed.

In the hospital interview, he slobbered out a confession that took three hours. "Never kicked that tire like we should have. The body was covered with blood, and we assumed he was finished. He wasn't finished, not even close. Rowena wanted to have her way with the old man, there at his house, make him tell them where his gold was hidden or else. Her dagger was deadly and painful, or so she claimed. She became enraged while we were walking up the hill, said the three of us could hold him down and she'd make him talk. They were so close."

Both of the captain's wounds were patched up and bandaged in no time at all. The medication kept him sedated for twelve hours, but almost as if nothing were wrong, his order for breakfast the following day was just like any breakfast he would usually cook up. Having no trouble talking in the slightest, with minimal swelling where the wound was, he had his nurse sit down and take notes. They'd told him to order anything he liked for breakfast, not to worry about the expense, and that he would be released and sent home that afternoon. He chanted off a list that included two or three of the usuals, hopefully resembling Huevos Rancheros, and about four specifics concerning coffee and milk. He hoped she would keep an eye on him, and there was a distinct chance that he would duplicate the order if it was that good.

It turned out to be that good, and sure enough, all the paperwork was done, so they allowed him to be discharged. And wouldn't you know it, there in the lobby was his best friend Rahellio waiting to take him home. He planned to haul the hero back through Ignacio and all the way to Arboles and his ranch house. There would be two full-time nurses and a cooking lady waiting at his ranch to help him for the next month, and since he didn't have anything better to do, Rahellio volunteered to sit and stand and be nearby until Van Vedic had had enough.

Anytime the retired mortician visited the ranch, he had his own bedroom, bath, and porch that couldn't be beat, and that's where he was when the screaming started. He discovered the cook and cleaning lady had just found Captain Vincent Van Vedic dead in his bed, flat on his back, eyes closed and almost angelic looking. His beautiful hands were interlaced on his belly, and that's how he was when Rahellio entered the room. Basically, there was nothing to do other than check for a pulse. The time of death had been recorded as "3 a.m. MST October 16th, 1979. His ninety-first birthday. He'd died in his sleep, possibly due to complications after being shot twice, once in the neck and once in the thigh only a week before."

Rahellio touched the bandage on his captain's neck, and even though there was no pulse to be found, it was still somewhat warm in the area, so he knew an approximate time. His signature was all that was needed in the paperwork to end the story of Vincent Van Vedic. He'd willed *Vanessa* to his estate, a brilliant move that included his cane and his six guns, and that inspiration had come from his personal advisor, he always said, an entity that had never steered him wrong and that honored the fisherman's dream to have his fortune given away in the form of all good and worthy things.

Truth be known, that personal advisor who managed things was nicknamed Dizzy by the staff there in Aztec, and even though few people ever saw him, he came and went at the strangest of hours, signed documents at times, and was evidently staying at the ranch; no one knew for sure. Dizzy did, he always knew, and he was there up over Van Vedic's right shoulder at three that morning, daydreaming with the captain about sailing in calm waters and alongside peaceful shorelines. For the captain, it was time for his soul, his spirit, to leave his body, let the body go back to the earth, and not even Dizzy knew where that spirit went. Nevertheless, he convinced his captain that wherever that was, it would be exactly where a *Gold Book* spirit like his should spend eternity.

THE END

ABOUT THE AUTHOR

A STATEMENT FOR THE RECORD

SUMMARY

All storytellers get better with age, they say, and I'm old enough to know that any form of self-criticism is essential to the survival of the entertainer. Unless one does it for free, which seems to be the case because I'm producing a product that can't be remembered. It's almost like it came out of nowhere, this ghost, this guardian, a make-believe artist, this storyteller phase that has sat me down at my computer for years at a time. I have disappeared to a little corner in the den room, an open door onto a porch, and a view to die for. It's quiet and very friendly, and I love having it open to the deck and the rest of the world.

At some point in the distant past, in the early seventies, after the army, I was visiting relatives in Topeka, Kansas, staying in my grandfather's spare bedroom for a night or two and simply being his grandson. 727 Twiss Street, and I can see the porch, the very simple inside furnishings of a seventy-five-year-old man; I can see it really clear. While he and I were visiting (you should see this table where he drinks coffee and eats his simple meals), I looked at my grandfather, and a question came to mind.

"Grandpa, you were born in Russia? How did you get to Kansas?"

That question and the answer were stimulants that I constantly entertained for what appears to be the rest of my life, but in those days, the *Encyclopedia Britannica* and The UNM Library were about it when it came to historical discovery. At the time, he and I were left with 'word of mouth,' and that conversation fell on forgetful ears. Forty years later, the memories took form in words, fictional stories of our history, three books of which I'm very proud. I'm not sure of the count, but perhaps a thousand pages, and I never intended to hurt anyone.

I try to stay on the subject as best I can, and I know I create questions that I never answer, mention things that matter and never return to the topic. Sometimes I feel myself bouncing from the seventeen hundreds to yesterday, from happiness and prosperity to the most unimaginable horrors anyone could endure. My distant relatives experienced extremely difficult times to have enabled me to get to here. You almost have to write it down to appreciate its truth, so I did.

I think back to that time in my childhood when I first heard a few stories about the adventures of my great-grandfather, a man my grandfather called Dad, stories told by his own son once or twice, his grandchildren, those being my dad and the aunts and uncles, and absolutely no one was taking notes. All of the heroes in my family who were part of the greatest generation were born starting at the turn of the century, survived the First World War, the Spanish flu, the Roaring Twenties, and the Great Depression, all while living in and around Topeka, where they almost choked to death in the dust bowls of the thirties, living in the desert in Albuquerque during the Second World War, and forever after that for many of the families. I don't think they knew all that much about the details of Peter Aloysius's journey because they, sure enough, had been on a harrowing trip themselves. It's sometimes hard to appreciate what happened to Grandpa when you're totally occupied with surviving your own personal journey. It's that way for every generation, even today, just as hard as ever, or so they say. Besides all that, their educational resources were minimal, and they were still waiting for television to show up. Everyone, of course, agrees that it had to have been an incredibly challenging trip. (My grandpa) Aloysius John Domme was four when they arrived at Ellis Island in 1892, and the family lived those first ten or more years in that new village in the heart of Kansas. They had nothing when they arrived and lived in a relatively extensive mud-covered communal barn. I've seen pictures of my immediate relatives living like swine out on the Kansas prairie in the 1880s and '90s and the turn of the century. They were sinking their roots again, and it didn't look like fun. Other shelters sprang up, farmhouses and barns out there on the prairie, and that's when they eventually built their magnificent church. This time they built it out of rock.

Holy Cross Catholic Church, Pfeiffer, Kansas. It's still there to this very day, and when I walked through the front doors into the church, I was absolutely astounded. I don't say that lightly.

I've imagined the main street celebration parade through Pfeiffer, Kansas, on New Year's Eve 1900. After ten years, things were improving quickly, and there was plenty to celebrate. There never were any promises of fortune, and barely any talk of future prosperity, even if they made it because, as a matter of fact, they were simply escaping death at the time. This story recounts the details of the trip, where the villagers from one Pfeiffer went to another Pfeiffer as a last resort, and the rules said to take some of what you cherish, leave the rest, or die of thirst.

"THE WAGON TRAIN IS LEAVING ON TUESDAY!"

The written-down versions of the journey reside in a historical museum in Hays, the diaries of prominent families with lots of children who came from there to here in 1892. Why? As a young adult, I had no idea what the entire story was about with my limited amount of information and experience. Still, I understood enough to realize that I was sure glad I hadn't been born back then or there in my personal selfish way. It's taken my entire life to be able to look back on it all as best as possible and investigate those times as well as history will allow me to know and vaguely understand all that happened to those people, my people.

It usually takes a while for the Homo Sapiens to quit asking, "What about me?" We get in that groove pretty early in life, and it helps us survive because we all understand inherently at birth that we only get one chance at all of this. Even in the womb during an abortion, we fight the forceps once we know what's happening. Fight like our existence depends on it even though we have no fundamental understanding of what life really is. Our tiny bodies fight till we're dead, till we're torn apart and murdered. It's sometimes on film and proves our most basic instinct is to stay alive. So the best thing to do not long after we get in the race is to scream at the top of our lungs until things get right with us in this new world. "Where's my bottle?" It took a while for me, it probably took time for you, and that's how it works. Eventually, I realized that the place where Great Grandpa Peter ended up with his family, the second Pfeiffer, might have been close to the end of the road for him, but the story had just begun in the modern-day reality of facts for all of his descendants, and there are now thousands and thousands of his many, many great-great-great-grandchildren. The name and gene pool spread from Pfeiffer like seeds from a tall tree, and a sad note to his legacy is that many of those descendants have no idea whatsoever as to who he was, who his wife was, and what they had to go through to get to Kansas in 1892.

Unfortunately, it wasn't the great-grandpa who my cousins and I immortalized; it was his son, our ever-living Grandpa. I named my son after him, and he makes me very proud. For a hundred years and six months, Aloysius John Domme, 1888 to 1989, roamed around the western United States, worked for the Santa Fe Railroad, bowled until he was 90, and most important of all, he took care of my invalid grandma for ten years in the 50s until she died.

Elizabeth mothered nine children starting around 1910 and up through 1950; she was the glue that kept it all together when unfortunately, she had a full-blown brain-killing stroke and was alive in body only. I remember her through my childhood eyes, in her primitive wheelchair, not there at all the way she had once been, and Grandpa fed her like a baby and showed his grandchildren how to do something right. The man went to Mass almost every day of his life. Our grandpa and his exploits kept us plenty busy, with me wondering at times if his parents ever thought to themselves out on the desolate plains of Ukraine if they might have made a mistake while they were considering dying of thirst and being blown away in the dust storms. They were almost out of water, almost out of food, with five hundred miles behind them and at least five thousand up ahead. They didn't know it at the time, but what they were escaping would go down in history as one of the deadliest times ever in Russia.

There were more lethal times to come because... In February 1892, 14-year-old Joseph Stalin's school teachers took him and the other pupils to witness the public hanging of several peasant bandits; Stalin and his friends sympathized with the condemned. The event left a deep and lasting impression on him. Stalin would become the leader of Russia in thirty years, Lenin's successor. In the next thirty years, he would kill at least fifty million of his fellow citizens, his comrades, until he finally died in 1953.

Those were awfully deadly times, went on and on for what seemed like forever, and might still be going on for all I know. Bad as that was, it's been totally overshadowed by a worse time by godly standards when abortion became legal. It is, in fact, the worst mass murder ever on this planet, but the citizens who survived that dangerous time in their mother's womb, starting more or less in 1973, don't seem to get it or appreciate how lucky they are to be alive. A considerable percentage of the misdirected born after '73 were once abortable, and the simple fact that we end the life of a tiny baby human two and a half thousand times a day in this constitutional republic proves—make that a capital PROVES—we are a society of Stalin lookalikes. He killed his supposed enemies, but in the modern world of America, we kill our offspring and think nothing of it. Through my simple research, I'm told they believe we total out at no less than a million abortions per year. These past few lines are an eye-opener, and at an imaginary tribunal that judges societies, their verdict would be that we really have no right to exist.

As far as 1891 is concerned, had there not been the drought

and the threat of famine and/or dying of thirst, it's entirely possible that Peter Aloysius Domme might not have ever left Pfeiffer, Russia. Instead, all of his descendants would have ended up comrades in Joseph Stalin's world. Pfeiffer is approximately fifty miles north of Stalingrad, and the town was directly in the way of the early action of World War Two. During the Christmas holiday season of 1942, "The greatest battle in the history of mankind, the Battle of Stalingrad," would find the ruins of Pfeiffer on the Illava River and the remnants of Saint Francis of Assisi Catholic Church steps where Peter had his son Aloysius baptized in 1889. On their way through, headed for Stalingrad, the Germans bombed villages like Pfeiffer into oblivion, and then the Russians did the same thing to anything left as they retook the land and slaughtered the Germans everywhere they could. In those times, drought and famine happened all the time in Russia, and the peasant settlers of Pfeiffer, Kansas, would try to scrape out a living in the hostile plains, not the slightest bit easy, with no guarantees about anything. The 1930s proved to be the worst of times for farmers. However, there were two things in particular that those people had never experienced in Russia, with one being a hundred thousand gigantic buffalo walking through their pastures and gardens or category five tornados falling out of the thunderheads and wiping the surface clean.

Peter Aloysius and all the residents who felt up to it left Pfeiffer one day and made it to Hamburg, where they climbed aboard the *SS Foust Bismarck* Ocean Liner and came to America. A manifest tells all their names. They flowed through Ellis Island just like a peasant is supposed to. When it came to looking like peasants, Peter and all of his family and friends were a hard act to follow, so much so that they ended up gone before the week was over.

I've created a picture in my reminiscence of that dock area where a throng of dirty Russian peasants came onshore, one of whom is my great-grandfather when he was a young man, with a wife and two kids—a newborn infant and my four-year-old grandpa. The whole bunch just recently got off the boat, are exhausted, are so poor you wouldn't believe it, and haven't found all that many smiling faces so far. They are far from the first immigrants from over there to be passing through the gates of Ellis Island, and they surely won't be the last. They all have the same face, the same hat, and the same coats, and the women are all dressed by the same designer. There are slight variations in the crowd, but for the most part, these are peasants, and they've got nothing.

The sign said something about bringing the poor and the wretched, so Peter and his brothers and cousins and neighbors took Lady Liberty up on her offer and were now standing in a Philadelphia train station, waiting for their ride to Hays, Kansas. The huge maps on the walls showed where they were and what was out there, and luckily for the Pfeiffer folks, their route seemed to be a straight line due west for fifteen hundred miles.

Language issues prevailed, along with misinformation and all the rest of it, but eventually, all those people stayed together and ended up living in rolling box cars for who knows how long? That was the issue because, in 1892, as one might imagine, keeping the tracks worthy of heavy traffic was not the easiest thing to do, and there were times when the train would sit on the tracks and not move for a while. I would think it was slow going at times, but better than walking, boring and lonely, and frightening to be riding into the wild and uncharted western wilderness until they pulled into Hays. From there, they worked their way due south, maybe fifteen miles on a perfectly straight dirt road that the pioneers called Pfeiffer Boulevard. The land is as flat as back in Russia, full of nasty flying bugs that they learned to deal with, and then the road drops down off the plateau and into the beautiful little river valley where the original pilgrims established Pfeiffer, Kansas, where they put down their meager luggage and started life all over.

Getting to that new Pfeiffer from the original Pfeiffer must have been one epic journey. I know it's been said a million times that it was 'epic,' but there are epics, and then there are epics. People have done it repeatedly throughout history. They epic here, and they epic there, and some of the epics are really epic. Like Moses, Noah, the Vikings, Columbus, Apollo 13, or any of the great discovery giants from the past, you know who your favorites are. Sometimes you 'epic' yourself into the limelight, and people talk about it for a long time, if not forever. Sometimes, however, you 'epic' yourself and your family and everything you're all about, along with all of your extended family, your close friends, your entire fortune, all of your faith, hope, and charity, and you leave for a promised land on the other side of the world.

Here is a riddle for you, a dilemma, and I ask you to 'try and take this story personally.' Try to put yourself in the position of Mr. Peter Aloysius Domme, one of Johan Thomae's great-great-grandsons, a small-town guy, poor as a church mouse, who has a wife and two kids, lots of family and friends in Pfeiffer, but unfortunately, everyone is on the verge of dying—unless they pack up and leave. If they don't go, if they stay, death will come in the form of disease, of which there is a long list, while dying from starvation and thirst at the same time. Horrible beyond horrible. We must understand that these people were hard-core Catholics instead of Russian Orthodox, and still spoke a form of German in a rather large enclave all over the Fertile Volga Basin. Even after a hundred years, the signs were all in German, which angered the officials who tried to manage the people. When all of

Catherine's guarantees went away in 1870, that anger boiled over, and just about everything changed overnight. First came conscription into the army, then all sorts of new taxes, and out on the fringes of the Volga diocese community, their churches were attacked, and everyone was killed by hordes of Mongols and gypsies. It's a well-worn understanding that the government people did not care, couldn't be trusted, and were thieves! They were suffering like everyone else and were just as savage as the next thief.

Let me take you there. First, we must go to Russia, get down on the southern end of the western time zones in what most Russians call "the Fertile Volga Basin." The Volga is one of the world's greatest rivers, drains a great deal of central-western Russia, and dumps it into the Caspian Sea. From there, it eventually evaporates. The Volga waters never make it to an ocean. When one sees a river the size of the Volga down near Stalingrad, Volgograd, or by whatever name you might refer to it, and you understand that none of that water makes it to an ocean, it makes you wonder. Russia is so big that it's almost too big, ten or twelve time zones; however, the Volga Region has always been a great and fertile basin, dwarfing many other fruitful basins in the world in width, depth, length, and any dimension you might favor. That's one basin, but there's another, the Don Basin.

Twenty miles more or less west of the Volga riverbanks is a minor continental divide, where a crest line of minor mountains runs for a few hundred miles south to north, starting down near Stalingrad (Volgograd) and heading north. This long mountain range separates two great rivers from each other by as little as fifty miles. The Mighty Don drains a great deal of western Russia and is, in fact, Russia's gateway to the rest of the world, a route that takes large vessels through Rostov on Don, through the Sea of Azov, around the edge of Crimea, and into and across the

Black Sea, which puts said Russian vessel at the entrance to the Straits of Istanbul, then the Dardanelles, and into the Mediterranean Sea. Their destination might be to leave the Mediterranean by either exiting at the Rock of Gibraltar and into the Atlantic Ocean or taking the Suez Canal down into the southern side of Mother Earth. (It shouldn't take but a few months or a year.)

On the eastern side of that divide is the Volga. This long, elevated land bridge where the two rivers parallel each other only fifty miles apart for at least a hundred miles is why Pfeiffer, Russia was annihilated in 1942. Up near the top of that bridge lies Pfeiffer, and Stalingrad is down near the bottom. First, the Germans poured through on their way to Stalingrad, and then a million-man Russian winter army pounded their way south and trapped the Germans in Stalingrad. If you could draw a line depicting the perfect "front-line" of the Eastern Front in the Second World War on Thanksgiving Day 1942, that line would have gone right down the middle of main street Pfeiffer, so to speak. Fortunately, the one hundred percent Catholic community had been abandoned a long time before, a very long time, starting with the famine and drought in 1891. Later, Lenin made it against the law to believe in God, and they would kill you dead and burn down the church if they thought you weren't obeying their rules. That all started almost twenty years before the start of the greatest battle in the history of mankind. The Battle of Stalingrad, all during Christmas and New Year's, 1942.

The land was settled in the seventeen hundreds by swarms of Christians and Jews from the Rhineland, and peasants escaping medieval chaos in the center of Europe. They were offered free land, and lots of it, by Czarina Catherine the Great, queen of the largest country in the world. She baited her hooks with promises that couldn't be topped, but you would have had to have been there at the time to appreciate the offer. Freedom of religion and no military obligations for a hundred years, starting around 1770. No taxation and a few other stimulants got the peasantry all excited.

Take the village of Lohr Am Main, for example, just down the road from Bonn. It was full of Catholics for the most part because that was the only way for people to live out in the country of the Rhineland regions. People frequently fought to the death over who had the right religion—nasty stuff, killing everybody, burning down their houses, and raping the women. Medieval chaos at its most insane. The invitation from Catherine was read to the faithful from the pulpits, where the priests, ministers, and rabbis asked their congregation who wanted to give it a try. It would involve packing everything worth packing onto the wagons—the chickens, pigs, dogs and cats, the cows and horses, besides all the children—and then traveling east into the sunrise for two years, crossing through sometimes hostile regions, very slow with everything in tow. There were mountain ranges, river valleys, terrible roads and few bridges, deserts, and long stretches of little to no water or food. There would be Gypsy gangs and hostile armies all along the route, a trail at most, and for the most part not very well defined. The parish priest would stand at his pulpit, spread his arms to his sides, and ask who wanted to go.

Can you imagine for a moment a young gentleman named Johan Adam Thomae and his 1760 bride, five children already—and somehow or another, it sounded like a good thing to do? The Thomaes and their close families and friends answered that "yes," they did, packed all their belongings on their wagons, and headed for the promised land, two thousand miles east. No one knows what happened to the people who stayed behind, because Central Europe would be a battleground off and on for the next two hundred years. To the modern-day traveler, explorer, and adventurer, if any of those people were asked about the idea of walking from some small village near Bonn, Germany, to Volgograd, Russia, most would say that's not possible. But, believe it or not, that's precisely what tens of thousands, if not hundreds of thousands, of them actually did.

They stayed together somehow, as former communities from the Rhine Lands. Usually, they were all of the same religion, made promises to each other, and for that very reason, they survived for the most part. The exodus from those Germanic lands began in the 1770s and started off slow, but that changed as more and more people joined the parade. Scouts went out and came back, talked about a land that went on forever, and it was true what Catherine suggested. It went on for dozens of years, with different armies improving extended portions of the roadway. The later travelers had fewer problems, but it was hazardous and perilous. Johan Thomae and his family survived on the trail, and after two long years, they made it, found a spot, and created Pfeiffer, Russia, on the Illava River. That man is the patriarch of the Domme family and all of the off branches. He named his only son Domme instead of Thomae, and Johan's son Balthazar had eight or nine sons who eventually took over and spread the name further.

They are all listed in a well-researched genealogy format. It's astounding! Now I find myself a few months into my 74th year; my grandson Lincoln Edward Clarence Domme just celebrated his seventh birthday. I can only wish the best for him like I do for all the others. Their world will be a place I can't even imagine. It now appears that I am the oldest living male Domme on a rather extensive family branch of the Aloysius John Domme tree. Someone needs to wish me good luck.

There are many branches, and to the best of my knowledge,

there's no financial reward for attaining this vaulted position other than knowing that my grandson with my last name had his birthday in May. I have seven other grandchildren who seem to treasure me, and my incredible daughter Lauren is due in October with their second, a little girl to go along with an absolutely spectacular, beautiful two-year-old boy named Owen. Aubrey will be my ninth grandchild, and I could go on about the others and probably should and likely will. There's a fantastic and lovely young lady in Ft. Collins, Colorado, whom I adoringly call Hannah Banana, born in 2012, nine months after her grandma died. Considering the fact that Susie Lee never saw one of them, and this is just an old grandpa talking, they are the most beautiful creatures in the Universe.

Then, of course, there's the truism that I'm still here a dozen years later and stand as possibly the luckiest man ever. I truly am, and when it comes to being rich, even though I'm not, truth be known, I'm as rich as rich can be. Somehow, I managed to end up with all kinds of beating hearts who love me and have proven their love repeatedly. Unfortunately, many of my peers have nothing of the sort. My class is hooked together via the internet, 88 of us on an email list, and we can participate if we follow some basic rules, such as not going off on the liberals, and vice versa. All that aside, I am moderately aware of how lucky I've been compared to some of the people I grew up with and whom I've known since we were fifteen or so, and this is true; I have friends from when I was five and six, the first grade, to this very day. People don't contribute all that much, it seems, and at this age, it's a dying thing because I believe people are retiring from life. But because of that email thing, I know to a small degree what the situation is for many of my high school classmates, class of '66. Put a different way, if I'm still alive, I'll find out if one of them is not. Phyllis will send out an email.

They tore down my alma mater Saint Pius Xth High School, at the corner of Indian School Road and Louisiana in Albuquerque, and built a vast California-style shopping and entertainment complex on top of the dust and ashes. The memory of the place only exists in a rather select group of Catholic families starting in 1960. It closed in 1980 when the Diocese of Santa Fe moved Saint Pius High to the other side of the city, across the Rio Grande, to the abandoned University of Albuquerque site, the old Saint Joseph's College campus. It was officially labeled the most valuable corner property in New Mexico. But, because of the pedophilia problem with the priests, the Diocese was forced to sell the land to pay off the endless accusations, both real and traumatic, along with the frauds, creating huge liabilities, and all the result of men being sexually stupid. I know once again of what I speak. My tiny corner of the world, a small Catholic School on the edge of the mesa, was introduced to the Holy Sacrament of Penance at the age of seven, taught the Act of Contrition, which I still know to this very day, and confessed my sins every Friday as part of the curriculum. We were directed by the Sisters of Charity through my first eight years, kept in line, and taught everything they thought a child should learn, and I would never want to believe that they knew what was happening in the Sacristy of their beautiful chapel in the convent to the altar boys. They had a monster back there and didn't even know it.

Concerning me trying to measure things, I only know things about my high school senior class to a slight extent, and if anything, I have been taught through their stories that life can be wicked and brutal. I was witness to something that killed their children, or them, might have paralyzed them from the neck down, all sorts of nastiness in untimely ways. People born around 1948, the class of '66, and who are still alive today have seen all kinds of things, and now it seems we may see the death of our society that ate itself alive from within. I remember thinking as a younger man and trying to understand in my simple way what was going on in this world and being as aware as possible of where the God-blessed USA was in the whole scheme of things. I thought, "Boy, the world will surely be in a hot spot if the USA ever goes south, so to speak, and runs off the rails." So, I sit here at 2:00 a.m., alone, very much aware of all the insanity going on out there, and I deeply fear for the world. It seems we are toying with World War Three, and crazy people are running the world. We have been taught the meaning of pandemic, and the worst part about it is that the governments of the world have, for the most part, learned how to deal with us in the next one, and there probably with be another.

Concerning all that, I can't believe I've never gotten sick. It's true, and (knock on wood) I think everyone I know has gotten sick with the China Virus except for me. Seriously, I don't want it and can't explain it because I've given the virus every chance there is to get me and kill me, but it hasn't. For crying out loud, when I got admitted to the hospital with sepsis eating me alive, since they didn't know that and it was Christmas after all, they put me in the Covid ward of San Juan Regional for a couple of days, and then all hell broke loose. Truth be known, I missed most of it, stayed unconscious for the most part, and toyed with being dead for a couple of weeks, but damned if they didn't save me. In hindsight, I considered them all miracle workers. They all wore masks and gowns and gloves, kept me medicated, kept me fed, and saved my life. Those were extraordinary times to be in the hospital, and they didn't know me from Adam, but they did their jobs and helped me defeat sepsis in my body. I have had absolutely no repercussions from that near-death experience, and there again, yours truly is trying not to trivialize that time in my life. That three-month event, coupled with a two-stent heart attack the year before, along with a self-poisoning pukeathone ambulance ride the year before that, along with a total reconstruction of my neck, three through seven, in '03, all lead me to conclude there might be something still in store for me that I couldn't possibly imagine.

Then again, maybe it's time to sit back and watch Ancient Aliens on Mondays and Fridays. I'm fascinated by our ancient past. I believe that there were Atlantis-type civilizations in the far, far distant past that visitors from the Belt of Orion or the Pleiades Constellation and other systems used to visit Mother Earth and left behind literally billions of tons of evidence that they were here. Giants roamed the Earth at times. I believe in extraterrestrials, and I hope and pray they are watching over us out there tonight. I think we humans are making a mess of the Blue Planet. A nuclear war of only a hundred weapons would kill all sorts of people, but the Earth would also enter a nuclear winter which would end the extraterrestrials' experiment. I think they designed us, altered our DNA some forty thousand years ago, and let evolution take its course from there. This experiment has been going on for a long time, perhaps hundreds of thousands of years, and eventually, they ended up with half a dozen different varieties of homo erectus, got rid of all the failures, and kept beings like us instead of the Neanderthals and all the others. Here we are in '23, and on the verge of destroying everything it's taken all this time to build and evolve into our destiny. It's the great test that every sophisticated society must eventually deal with. Understanding the atom is probably just routine stuff in the universe of evolution, but it is essential. Then the evolving entity must survive the weaponization of it all.

If we fail and launch thermonuclear weapons at each other, more than likely, we as individuals won't even know it's happened. In most cases, we'll be incinerated, blinded for sure, and if one were to live through all that, they would probably end up wishing that they hadn't. Just me talking. Therefore, I vote that the ETs show themselves and put an end to the madness. Once we have proof that they exist, I believe we will come together and understand where we, as intelligent creatures, belong in the Universe. Assuming they are coming from a great distance with ease and are thousands of years more advanced than us, they may instead realize they have infested a rare blue water planet with a virus that's killing it. A virus species that kills its own young and fights never-ending wars and has now found itself on the verge of Armageddon.

This oldest living Domme male specimen understands and appreciates a whole slew of matters of fact, including that I was fortunate enough to have been born the first son of Ed and Peachy Domme. By age four, I lived at 1808 Indiana NE, Albuquerque, NM, on the very edge of the eastern desert, over three miles from the river and downtown Albuquerque. Phone number 64397 (the tattooed number on Jude's arm), and when they got rid of the party lines and the operators, they added AL to it, and we, as a society, were off to the races. Colored TV was just a few years away, and the evolution of a screen in front of our faces seems to be one of the outcomes of all this technology. Many of us look at screens all day long, whether a TV, a movie screen, our phones, computer monitors, patches, pads, tablets, or dashboards. I have to wonder if this world I basically know nothing about is sick or healthy, in danger or not, destined to fail or succeed. We've been at war with someone all throughout my life, and I'm beginning to think it's the nature of the beast.

Made in United States
Troutdale, OR
08/11/2023

11981638R00317